SoulShares

STONE COLD

Rory Ni Coileain

For more information contact:
Riverdale Avenue Books
5676 Riverdale Avenue
Riverdale, NY 10471.

www.riverdaleavebooks.com

Design by www.formatting4U.com
Cover by Scott Carpenter

Digital ISBN 978-1-62601-404-6
Print ISBN 978-1-62601-405-3

First Edition September 2017

Chapter One

November 14, 2013 (human reckoning)
The Realm

Slowly Maelduin gave ground, up the uneven terrain of the washed-out river bank. The high ground was his friend, and his opponent's enemy, provided he could stay on his feet. Blood dripped from his sword-arm, splashed on the toes of his boots, the stones and earth under his feet.

His opponent moved in, keeping a tempting but careful distance; Maelduin was certain that if he yielded to that temptation and lunged, he would come up an exact hair's-breadth short, overextended, and in danger of losing a limb, and then his life. He knew, because that was what would happen should his opponent do likewise.

It might have been a bad idea, letting that mage imbue it with the ability to kill me if it can.

Maelduin shook his head, sending sweat trickling into his eyes, blurring his vision. He would never have learned what he needed to know, never honed his skill to such a lethal edge, if his life had never been at risk.

His opponent smiled. A rarity—it, he, had never

spoken, and had seldom smiled, during all the years of their extended contest. Like Maelduin himself. Why waste time on pleasantries, when his opponent was all that stood between himself and the prize he sought? Smiles would not make him the greatest blade-dancer in the history of the Fae race.

His opponent circled below him. Seeking another way to come up the bluff, most likely. And he would surely find one, because Maelduin had.

He stepped back onto flat ground and continued to pace backward, following the line of the bluff to keep his opponent on uneven ground, and to give himself time to catch his breath, to let the burning pain in his sword-arm subside. The wicked slice had been meant solely to distract, of course—Fae healed too rapidly from any wound not lethal for his opponent to have had any other intention.

His opponent followed, inexorable. Watching him flow up the bluff was like watching a parasol-seed caught in a breeze, beautiful and iridescent and weightless.

Only this seed would be his death, if it reached him—

His opponent blurred into motion, leaping to the high ground, his sword raised despite his own evident exhaustion. Not to parry or defend, but to attack. And even at the limit of exhaustion, after a day and a night and a dawn of fighting for his life, Maelduin was breathless, in awe of the beauty of the other male's lethal purpose.

His own purpose. His own face, his own form.

His opponent was a mage's creation, a *comhrac-scátha*—a magickal ghost, a living mirror, with all

Maelduin's skill with a blade, all his grace, both natural and learned, as well as the wiles and unpredictability of living magick. And all the hatred in the Fae's heart, his single-minded need to become the best *scian-damhsa*, blade-dancer, the Fae race had ever known, to allow him to kill the one whose death was the true focus of his life.

The *comhrac-scátha* was contained in a crystal; normally when he fought it, he carried the crystal in a pouch attached to his belt by a thin cord, easily broken, so he could cast the thing away and end the combat. Yesterday, though, in preparing for this combat, he had laced the crystal into his boot, where there could be no retrieving it in the heat of the fight. It was time to discover whether his decades of training had prepared him to fulfill his vow. The only end to this combat would be death.

And not his own.

Maelduin charged at the same instant his opponent did, sword raised to guard position. Swords rang against each other, louder and more musical than the birds in the dawn light. Gazes locked, two pairs of faceted blue topaz eyes promising pain and death. If there had ever been any strangeness to looking into his own eyes with such hatred, he had accustomed himself to it long ago.

He could feel his opponent's exhaustion, even desperation, where they strove together. It was time to end this trial. He twisted back and away, opening up enough space to size up the other. Grappling was useless—neither of them had the advantage of physical strength. Just a moment's opening was all he needed—

His magickal twin slashed down through the

space between them. A line burned down Maelduin's forehead, his cheek, his chest. Blood spilled hot, blinding him in one eye, soaking his blouse.

Distraction. Only a distraction.

Maelduin stepped back. His opponent, still engaged, followed him, off balance. Maelduin spun on the ball of one foot, stomped with the heel of the other on the back of his opponent's knee, staggering him. And in the instant his twin's gaze dropped, Maelduin's sword slashed down, slicing through long blond hair and spine and softer things.

He barely had time to yank his sword free before the mutilated corpse, the image of his own, vanished. The crystal in his boot burned cold with the return of magick to its source.

Slowly, slowly, Maelduin straightened, hardly noticing the crawling burn as flesh knit to flesh or the tightness of drying blood on his skin.

The test was over.

* * *

Maelduin glared at the iridescent dragonfly hovering inches from his face. The dragonfly, unimpressed, glared back, its eyes tiny opals afire with the rays of the setting sun and a spark glinting between its open jaws. The crystal gazebo he had channeled for his garden was a delight to the eyes, but given his lack of knowledge of appropriate warding channelings, he was required to share it with the local microfauna. Which cared nothing for whether or not a Fae might have things to be about, other than staring crossed-eyed at bronze-scaled wings and a minute barbed tail.

Grumbling, Maelduin bent again to his work, smoothing his open right hand over the soft vellum spread out on the table before him, clearing away its fine sprinkling of metallic scales. He raised his head again, sharply, at the smell of scorched hair. A few strands of his pale blond hair fell to make elegant patterns on the vellum before him, their tips charred black.

I swear it's laughing at me. Dragonfly fire smelled like burning *uiscebai.*

Enough. Maelduin cupped a hand around the tiny creature and urged it on its way, then bent again to regard the document he was writing. Was trying to write. The first few words he had written still gleamed wet and black on the fine sheepskin, sprinkled with tiny bronze shards.

Eithne, mo colcathrair le cúrtés...

Even Maelduin wasn't certain whether he spared Eithne, by naming her as "cousin by courtesy," or insulted her. She was, in fact, a near-cousin by Fae standards, her grandmother having been the half-sister of Maelduin's grandsire. Fae, even bound as they were beyond all reason by love of kin, were loath to be recognized as sharing his tainted bloodline. Distancing the fair Eithne from the Cursed House was, perhaps, an act of kindness. But, then, Eithne and her entire line had rejected him from birth onward, because of that taint. So why concern himself with whether or not he spared her anything?

Probably because considering such matters allowed him to put off what he had to do. What it was, at last, time to do. Taking a deep breath, he picked up the quill once again.

By my own hand and will, I do resign to you all rights and titles and magicks falling to me as Head of House...

The ancient words were pretty, but carried little true meaning, at least the part about the magicks of a Head of House. Some of the Great Houses, the lap dogs of the Royals, invested their Lords and Ladies with unique magicks. His own House had been poor even before its fall, and now possessed little more than its pride, which had been destroyed, utterly, before Maelduin had been born.

Now he would reclaim it.

No Fae would ever know that the honor of his House had been restored, of course. Not even the new Head of that House. Maelduin supposed that was a pity. He couldn't be sure, though, as he'd never had any use for pity, and knew himself unlikely to recognize it in whatever guise it presented itself.

But he, himself, would know. That would more than suffice.

Single-minded Fae were rare. No one discipline could hold the attention of most Fae for longer than a double hand of years or so, before the Fae grew bored. To the extent, that is, that any Fae other than a mage would bend to something called a 'discipline' at all. But Maelduin's entire life, over a century and a half of it, had been devoted to a single purpose. A purpose he had at last achieved.

The cost had been high, as other Fae might reckon it. The last of his House's wealth, save only what was needed for the crafting of his blade, had gone to an ancient mage, years ago, for the creation of his *comhrac-scátha*.

The crystal that had housed the *comhrac-scátha* sat on the edge of the table, now, glowing a faint, dull violet. A good keepsake, perhaps the only one that interested him. He palmed it, and tucked it safely away.

Fae had no patience for signs or portents. Yet his victory had been one such, he knew. The time for training was over. It was time, now, to pay the final cost, half his soul. Time to take up the weapon he had become, and kill the male who had been the best *scian-damhsa* before him. The male who had murdered his father and disgraced his House, and left behind a child to be suckled on scorn, never to so much as imagine the cherishing every other Fae child knew.

Maelduin stared at the sheet of vellum, pondering. He had nothing more to say. His journey lay before him, the journey from which no Fae ever returned. It was time to lay down the pen, and take up his sword, the oath-blade with truesilver beaten into the steel of it, the blade that would not taste blood until it drew the blood of his father's killer, or else it would turn on him and take his own life for his oath-breaking.

One last task for the pen, though. He dipped the quill, and waited for his hand to steady. And signed away his old life, to make room for the new.

D'rér mo lámh—
Maelduin Guaire.

* * *

You should be away, sister.

The word forming out of the silver-blue lines under Aine's feet was not 'sister' in any language remembered by post-Sundering Fae; it had nothing to do with the blood kinship so prized by the Fae, and everything to do with the ties of magick, the web of the Loremasters.

"I know," Aine murmured. Her official task was complete; she had added to the Pattern the channeling she had discovered in the Loremasters' ancient library, to give those who passed through an Air Fae's gift of understanding all languages borne on the air. Time was too short on the other side to risk any misunderstanding.

But she made no move to rise; her lilac skirts still pooled where she knelt, gathered close in places where she had had to move it to read the *d'aos'Faein* script used by the Loremasters still within the Pattern. "I must go. Yet I do not wish it."

She tilted her head back and looked up, at the sliver of the full moon visible at the edge of the round window. She shivered slightly, wrapping her arms around herself. Of all the strange news from the human world, Cuinn's tale of binding the moon and its magick—no, *her* magick—was the most unsettling. Cuinn had bound one of the Mothers of the *Gille Dubh*, and forced her magick to serve the Pattern.

The Dancer must pass through.

"He is death itself, dancing the blades. And he is sworn to kill the guardian of the nexus. How can this bode well?"

Lines could not shrug, but these lines tried. *We have not Foreseen everything. But we know he must be allowed to pass.*

Aine closed her eyes with a sigh. She participated in the group Foreseeing, as best she could; she knew the truth of the vision as well as her voluntarily imprisoned peers. And if her unofficial task bore the fruit she hoped it would, perhaps the worst possible consequences could still be avoided. Her fingertips brushed the little parchment scroll tucked under the hem of her skirt; she dared not be too specific in her warnings, but surely even a vague oracle was better than the silence upon which the other Loremasters insisted. And might distract the Dancer from his purpose. "Let us hope, then—"

And froze, like a dart-wing in amber, in the throes of a lesser Foreseeing. The dark-haired human, Kevin. Tiernan's SoulShare. His body wracked with sobs, shuddering, unable to draw breath. Alone.

She would have collapsed as the vision released her, had she not already been kneeling. Not trusting herself to stand, or even to speak, she extinguished the magick of the wall-mounted torches with a whispered word, and Faded.

But only to a copse of trees, a stone's throw from the tower. She was, after all, the closest thing the Pattern had, or needed, to a guardian.

And when the moon rose, and with it the wind, and the screams, she was the closest thing to a witness.

Chapter Two

Washington, D.C.

"This floor is going to be fucking amazing."

Terry couldn't help laughing at Garrett's enthusiasm. The blond pole dancer was bouncing up and down on the balls of his feet on a six-foot-by-six-foot section of ash sprung flooring, with a grin on his face that could have lit up any of the monuments on the Mall. "It is. Talk Tiernan into installing it downstairs on the pole stage, too."

"Hells to the yes."

The square of flooring Garrett was checking out was a sample—one of several supplied by various dance floor manufacturers eager to get the business of a brand-new state-of-the-art dance and fitness studio, and in Terry's opinion far and away the best of the lot. And it looked as if his business partner agreed with him. Or would, once he stopped bouncing.

"You look ready to get back on the pole."

"Once again I say, hells to the yes." Garrett jumped down, circling his shoulders and pulling his elbows across his body to stretch out his triceps as he wandered around the shell of what would eventually become one of the three planned studios—one ballet, one pole and aerial, and one that would be used mostly for fitness classes, but could be tricked out as a small performance space for special occasions. Even a shell was better than what they'd had a month ago, and it would be even better soon, once some of the workers who were busy with sheet rock, flooring, and ceilings in Purgatory proper were freed up to start on the studios.

Not that anything about Purgatory was, or had ever been, proper. Terry missed the hell out of the place, and he knew that whatever he was feeling wasn't even close to what Garrett was going through. Terry had only been forced to put off his studio dreams for a few months when Purgatory imploded after the gas leak—dreams he had only let himself start to have a month or so prior to the collapse. But the club—more importantly, the dancing in it—had been Garrett's whole life for more than ten years.

Except for the part of his life that involved Lochlann, of course. By now, the twinge of jealousy that plucked at Terry every time he was reminded of a friend's partnered bliss was such an old familiar companion, he barely noticed it. Except, of course, when he was reminded of Josh and Conall, given that Josh was the proverbial One Who Got Away. Or maybe the proverbial One He'd Been Dumb Enough to Leave for a Rich Asshole. Who had then dumped him for a supermodel, or close enough to one.

Garrett paused next to a pile of construction debris and nudged it with a toe, simultaneously nudging Terry out of his swiftly-deepening funk. "What's this all doing in here?"

Terry frowned. Paint trays and rollers, a couple of tarps that had seen better days, a flat-bladed concrete rake, a stack of ceramic tiles and lengths of pipe, and what he thought was a urinal, albeit one designed by someone with Tiernan Guaire's sense of humor. "Looks like we're the dumping ground for all the miscellaneous stuff from downstairs."

Garrett shook his head. "I suppose they're running out of room outside."

True enough—the trailer the general contractor had been using as an office had been hauled out three days ago, once enough of the electrical had gone in downstairs to let them set up in a corner of the once and future club, because the walls of the new building were crowding the trailer out. "And most of this can't go in the dumpster in the alley."

"It's ruining the aesthetic." Garrett pouted.

"Soon, Little Grasshopper." Impossible to stay in a funk when Garrett was trying to make him laugh. "Let's worry about getting the floor in and the walls up before we worry about the aesthetic."

"Says the man who spent 14 hours last week looking at paneling samples."

Terry laughed. He couldn't help it. "Guilty."

Garrett glanced at his watch. "Damn. I have to run, or I'm going to be late for dinner. You want me to talk to Mac about getting this shit out of here?"

Mac had been acting as Tiernan's liaison with the general contractor since construction had started, with occasional help from his husband Lucien, and their partner Rhoann, when a construction worker needed a talking-to. Lucien wasn't big on the talking part, but a bouncer who was nearly as broad as he was tall and furry from neck to toes could be amazingly persuasive without saying a word. And Rhoann... well, 6'5" of spectacularly well-muscled blond could get more or less whatever he wanted out of more or less anyone.

"Nah, don't make yourself any later than you already are. I'll take care of it."

"If you're sure..."

"Shoo." Terry waved a hand toward the door. "I'm going to be around for a few more hours anyway." Truth—he had a client booked at Raging Art-On in half an hour, to add some color to a lion he'd outlined for the guy last week, so he'd still be around if Mac showed up.

"Okay." Garrett glanced around one more time before grabbing the hoodie he'd left draped over a saw-horse—D.C.'s November was doing its usual November thing, balmy one day and raw the next. "See you tomorrow."

"Sure thing."

The door clicked shut behind the departing pole dancer, the sound satisfyingly solid. It was nice to be able to close off the studio space. Made him feel like they were making some real progress.

Terry huffed out a breath through his nose, and wandered off into the next studio. The front studio, the space where its large window was going to be currently occupied by reinforced plywood, was going to be used mainly for pole and aerial work—the sight of Garrett and the other Purgatory dancers doing their thing would bring people into the new studio in droves, and both of the proprietors knew it. There would eventually be a short hallway leading back from that studio, with a door on one side giving onto a changing room with showers, and another door opposite opening onto the fitness studio-*cum*-performance space. Right now, all there was was a row of support beams, but Terry's imagination could fill in the rest, no problem.

And then, tucked into the back, would be Terry's own pride and joy.

Even when he'd lived in New York City, even when Bryce Newhouse, cursed be he, had been bankrolling his trockadero dance company, he'd never had his own custom-designed studio and rehearsal space. He'd never even let himself dream about it. He'd begged space, and borrowed it, and pledged too much of the box office from every performance for it.

No more.

Terry hugged himself against the chill of the evening air, turning around and around in the starkly-lit space, his imagination filling in walls and floors and brilliant lights. And a room full of dancers, shaping Tchaikovsky and Minkus and Ravel and Stravinsky with their bodies. Making magic, like in the old days.

The best old days had been the days with Josh, before Bryce had entered the picture. Terry knew that, now that it was years too late to do anything about it. Working shoulder-to-shoulder with Josh in their hole-in-the-wall tattoo parlor, running out for midday classes and rehearsals. Performances, a season of three performances here, four there, and the chaotic Nutcracker season when the company earned most of its working budget for the rest of the year.

And coming home to Josh every night, or in the chill clear hour before dawn, when even New York City held its breath. Giddy with the joy of another performance, and Josh grinning with delight at Terry's happiness.

Yeah, well, I took care of that, didn't I?

The light clipped to a wall stud in the ballet studio space was humming loudly; Terry wandered over to check it out, his footsteps echoing in the open space. Not that he'd know an electrical problem if one leaped up and bit him in the ass, but if felt better to think that he was doing something.

Things with Bryce hadn't actually been a total shit-fest at first. Not that it had ever been good enough to make up for the way he'd hurt Josh, letting himself be lured away by the investment banker with the fancy suits and the fat wallet. But it had seemed like Bryce had cared, for a while. He really had seemed to enjoy playing Santa Claus to Terry, and to Trock Bottom. Terry had realized the enormity of his mistake fairly early on, though. Bryce had wanted to take him away from Josh, period. And once he'd managed that... well, for Terry, there had been no way to go back.

Terry changed the angle of the clip-on light to keep the built-in fan from vibrating against the metal stud or column or whatever the hell it was it was clipped to. The humming stopped.

What do you know?

He shrugged. Dance was his first love. Always had been, ever since he could walk. And that love made him stupid, made him make bad choices, especially when it came to the other kind of love, the kind of love that involved another man and a life together and being in love. *Maybe you only get one kind or the other.*

Maybe he was cursed.

Terry rolled his eyes. When he started dwelling on what he no longer trusted himself to look for and was never going to have, it was a sure sign it was time to get back to work on what he *did* have. He walked down the hallway leading from the back studio to the reception area, though there wasn't any need to use the hallway given that neither hallway nor studio nor reception area actually existed yet. They would soon. That was enough.

He laughed softly at sight of the piece of sample flooring. Apparently readjusting the angle of the light had done something he hadn't expected, because it almost looked as if the thick square of sprung floor was glowing, or spotlit. Like the omen he wasn't looking for, because he didn't believe in omens.

Like magic.

Magic. Ha.

Terry slipped out the door, locking it behind him as he went. He was only going to be across the little courtyard the reconstruction had added to separate the storefronts—the new studio, Big Boy Massage, Raging Art-On, and the spot where Purgatory's above-ground entrance would soon stand—but better safe than sorry.

All the magic in the world wasn't going to keep his dream safe. Because there was no such thing. Any idiot knew that.

Chapter Three

Breathe. Just breathe.

Considering that Maelduin had been unable to do just that, only moments before, breathing felt like an unspeakable luxury. He lay motionless, curled in on himself, his left hand still on the hilt of his oath-blade. Still shivering in the aftermath of what he had just endured.

If it worked, it was worth the pain. It will be worth any pain imaginable.

But for now, breathing was enough.

Maelduin sensed light through his closed eyelids, light that was neither moonlight nor the silver-blue flare of magick—the last thing he had seen as the chaotic wind had forced him through the sieve of blades that was the Pattern.

Maybe I'm safe.

He managed a little laugh as he opened his eyes. 'Safe' was, he suspected, going to be a highly relative term for a while, at least until he had adapted to his new world. But anything was safer than the crystal floor falling away beneath him to show him the stars through a net of knives, the whirlwind hammering him through it. And the moon gazing coolly down on it all through a tiny round window.

There was no moon where he was now. A yellowish light coming from somewhere behind him showed him what looked like a mostly-unfinished hall, a maze of slender pillars of wood and metal and a floor of flat gray stone. He wasn't sure, but it seemed as if he lay on a dais of some sort. And the wood beneath him glowed faintly, in the unmistakable hue and patterning of living magick. Which seemed wrong, somehow, though he could not recall why.

But he had other hawks to train to fist at the moment. Steeling himself against the pain, he pushed himself up on an elbow. Higher, relieved as the pain proved to be more a memory than a present truth.

Something beneath him rustled.

Maelduin frowned. He wore only leather and linen, and the fastenings of his sword-belt were bronze and copper. He had carried nothing with him from the Realm, or at least nothing that would make such a sound.

The corner of a piece of parchment poked out from under his loose linen blouse.

Reaching under himself, Maelduin pulled out a small scroll, once probably rolled, now flattened. He pushed himself up to a sitting position, more slowly than he would have liked, and unrolled the scroll.

Maelduin, late Lord Guaire, salutation and warning. If you have survived to read this, it is well, I suppose.

Maelduin blinked, wondering how much gratitude it was appropriate to feel for his unknown correspondent's lukewarm concern for his welfare.

Yet you are still in danger. There is a flaw in the Pattern, and that flaw has surely maimed you. In soul, or in body, or in some other way only the Pattern knows.

Heart racing, Maelduin touched his face, his ears; flexed fingers, toes; shifted his weight enough to feel the pressure of fabric against his cock. Nothing was missing. Nothing physical.

Your only care now must be finding your human SoulShare, and regaining what you have lost. You can imagine no task more important than this.

Maelduin snorted. He had heard the stories, of course—children's cautionary tales, mostly, warning of the loss of part of one's soul to pay the passage between worlds. He could imagine several things more important than regaining something he would not have missed had he not been told he had lost it.

More cautiously than was his wont—in case the pain returned—he gathered his feet under himself and stood.

He stepped on the scabbard of his sword. He staggered, thrown off balance, and fell off the low dais. Or whatever it was.

The sudden sharp pain of his ankle twisting sent Maelduin stumbling to one side. Catching himself, he stepped on the blade of what he had a split second to identify as probably some sort of gardening instrument before the long handle arced up and struck him squarely in the nose.

Tears of pain—and humiliation—burned in Maelduin's bright blue eyes. Blood poured from his nose and splashed on the floor and the dais. He could feel his ankle swelling in the confines of his boot.

There is a flaw in the Pattern, and that flaw has surely maimed you...

By rendering him unable to avoid maiming himself?

Maybe regaining what he had lost was going to be more important than he had thought.

* * *

"You don't have to stick around if you don't want to, Terry." Josh looked up from where he was bent over the light table next to the register. "I doubt we'll be getting any walk-in business tonight."

If Terry craned his neck, he knew he'd be able to see the design Josh was working on. Something fabulous, he was sure. Terry's own designs were good, but he was nowhere near being in his former lover's league, and he knew it. And as grateful as he was to Josh for taking him in as a business partner after Bryce had ditched him—and no matter how many times Josh told him it had been the best business decision he'd ever made—he was going to be glad to get the studio off the ground and be back on his own two feet for good.

Still, he owed Josh. And despite everything, the easygoing brunet was a good friend. "You're sure? You aren't looking for an excuse to get home early?" Terry's appointment had cancelled on him, a good ten minutes past the scheduled time. Terry would be within his rights to charge a cancellation fee, but he usually only did that if the client was being a straight-up asshole, and that hadn't been the case tonight.

"Are you kidding?" Josh grinned. "Someone bought Conall a complete set of *Keeping Up Appearances* on DVD, and he's binge-watching. I'm not going home till I get the all-clear."

The red-haired twink's fascination with TV and

movie kitsch contrasted strangely with the brutally elegant bondage demos he and Josh had enjoyed doing at the old Purgatory. Tiernan had promised them a proper dungeon once the club was rebuilt, too. If Tiernan built in a plasma screen TV with a DVR, Conall would be the happiest man in Washington, D.C.

Eyes front, Terrence. "Hyacinth Bucket is enough to make any man's blood run cold. I'll see you tomorrow afternoon, then."

He was halfway down the block to the Metro station before he remembered his jacket, left back in the studio. He debated leaving it for the next day, but a chill damp gust of wind changed his mind. *Good thing I don't live someplace that has proper winters, I'd be dead of pneumonia.*

Idly wondering why catching pneumonia, breaking his neck, and putting his eye out were the consequences for every imaginable kind of misbehavior—at least according to his mother—he fished the studio key out of his pocket and turned it in the lock.

A man dressed like a Musketeer looked up from the square of sprung-floor sample, most of his face covered by his bloody hands, his body hunched protectively over what looked like a sword lying across his thighs. A beautiful sword, going by the gold-chased hilt and the gorgeous tooled leather scabbard.

For some reason, Terry instantly flashed on Duke Albrecht, from the ballet *Giselle*. A nobleman masqueraded as a peasant to steal the heart of the simple village girl Giselle; Albrecht's deception was revealed by the quality of his weapon, and the sudden appearance of his inconvenient fiancée the Princess Bathilde; Giselle went memorably mad, and died of a broken heart. *Gotta love Romantic ballet plots.*

It was, of course, pure coincidence that *Giselle* was the last ballet he had staged, and Giselle the last role he had danced, with Trock Bottom before Bryce had given him the boot.

And the fact that the bloody-handed intruder staring up at him with impossibly blue eyes made him think of *Giselle*, rather than about calling 911, was proof positive that he, Terrence Miller, was too easily distracted to be allowed out without adult supervision.

"Who the hell—who are you? And how did you get in here through a locked door?"

* * *

The human who stood before Maelduin, hands on hips, looked nothing like any Fae he had ever seen. Maybe there was a slight resemblance to the *adhmacomh*, the bark-hued descendants of trees who were possibly the only Fae who came anywhere near being despised as much as the last true scion of the Cursed House... but surely none of the dark Fae were as pleasing to the eye as the male who glared at him. Dusky skin, hair a few shades darker falling in loose corkscrew curls around the male's face... and if the rest of the human's body matched the outlines revealed by tight-fitting singlet and trousers, that, too, was more than a match for most Fae.

The male's eyes would probably be beautiful, too, if they weren't narrowed in evident anger. Maelduin wondered if he would lose any tactical advantage if he were to lower his hands so he could see better.

The human spoke.

"Who the hell—who are you? And how did you get in here through a locked door?"

Maelduin blinked, puzzled. *I must be able to speak human. Either that, or humans speak* Faen. *Which I doubt.*

He let his hands fall—from the feel of things, his broken nose had healed itself with normal Fae speed.

"t'Mé Maelduin." He did *not* speak human, apparently. "And who are you?" Well, perhaps a *little* human. But only words he had already heard.

Anger turned to a puzzled frown. "I'm Terry Miller. And you're trespassing, Maelduin. I'll ask you again, how did you get in here?"

'Trespassing.' With the word came all its meanings, all its implications. The human—Terry—owned this unfinished place. Maelduin had no idea what rights this might give a human, but it was probably safe to assume that Terry thought he was entitled to evict him. And the prospect of venturing out into the wider human world alone, while helpless under some bizarre curse of clumsiness, was frightening in a way Maelduin was unaccustomed to being frightened.

But how to make Terry understand the urgency of his need? When their current shared vocabulary was some 25 words, none of which conveyed any meaning close to 'I need sanctuary?'

The answer, of course, was obvious. Or it would have been, to any Fae before the Sundering, and instincts were eternal. Some of them, anyhow.

"Cadagh dom a tacht ar'shúl ó anseo le you.*" Allow me to come away from here with you.* Carefully,

Maelduin got to his feet. Not carefully enough to avoid the mysterious curse, though; his ankle betrayed him, and he staggered.

Terry's arm shot out. Hands clasped forearms and Maelduin's breath caught in his throat. Terry's touch called to something in him, some power. The power surged, rose like a wave—but broke, before it reached the human.

What is this?

"What… did you say?" Terry frowned, blinked.

Whatever the energy was, Maelduin could not let it stop him. Humans were prey, so the old stories had it. Often delightful prey, but prey nonetheless. Letting the hint of a smile shadow his eyes, he channeled magick, the oldest channeling known to Fae, common to all Demesnes, all Houses.

"*Ta'bhar mé fhéin le* you," he murmured, watching the human's eyes unfocus. *Take me with you.*

And once he had been taken… he would do what needed to be done, to ensure his safety until his curse was lifted and his oath was kept.

Chapter Four

Kevin eased his Mercedes into the gap between buildings that was eventually going to be the new Purgatory's valet parking area. Letting the steering wheel glide back to center under his palms, he was happy to see that his hands had finally stopped shaking.

Fuck premonitions.

Switching off the headlights, he eased out of the car, quietly closing the door and locking it behind himself. Conall's ward masked sound at least as well as it did sight, but it was a bare-bones, low-wattage affair, and Kevin didn't trust it entirely. And some of the subcontractors occasionally had people on the site at night, to whom it would be awkward to explain the invisible back door into Purgatory.

The little rectangle of truesilver set into the stone door warmed quickly under his thumb; with a click more felt than heard, the door swung open, then closed behind Kevin. Truesilver was a damned handy thing to have, Fae-forged metal that knew its own purpose. It was a shame they had so little of it—Conall, Lasair, and Tiernan had arrived from the Realm in chains, and with Conall's help, or Cuinn's, the links could be reforged and repurposed. Into, say, a magickal lock for a magickal door.

The lawyer's footsteps echoed as he descended the tight spiral staircase leading down into the underground sanctuary. Normally he enjoyed the sensation of the stone under his feet—because it was elemental Stone, created and sculpted by his husband while in the throes of multiple orgasms he himself had been more than pleased to engineer.

Tonight wasn't normal, though. Kevin's hands might be steady, but his chest still felt tight. The premonition that had seized him as he was shutting down his computer for the night still had its claws in him.

The light at the bottom of the stairs, bright but flickering, beckoned, and he hurried. Rian, the Prince Royal, had channeled his Fire magick into torches set at intervals around the new nexus chamber, torches that dimmed when they were told to but never burned out. Fire magick—elemental magick in general—was safe to use around the wellspring that shared the chamber with the nexus, or so Conall said. When it came to the nexus and the wellspring, Kevin was just happy someone seemed to have some idea what was going on.

Kevin came out into the light with a sigh of relief. The torchlight seemed brighter than it really was; the elemental Stone his husband had used to sculpt and reinforce the walls looked like the cracked concrete and gouged earth that had been there originally, but the raw materials had been infused with a crystal so clear and beautiful it put Waterford to shame. Even the battered black leather chaise positioned over the nexus—near-miraculous survivor of the collapse of the original Purgatory, thanks to Conall's emergency ward over the nexus itself—took on a sort of beauty, in that light.

But there was a shadow in the room. A shadow that existed only in Kevin's head, he was sure. But that didn't make it any less real—his first struggles with the *Marfach* had been solely in his mind, after the monster sent him on his first visit to Purgatory, and that fight had been entirely too damned real.

And now...

Kevin sat down on the chaise. Slowly, as if his knees bothered him the way they sometimes used to before he started getting regular therapeutic massages from a Fae healer. As if he'd seen a future hiding around some unseen corner, waiting to jump out and... and what?

He leaned forward with a weary sigh, resting his elbows on his knees and grinding the heels of his hands into his eyes. He'd been shutting down his computer for the night, waiting for the ancient software to do its thing so he could go home. And then he'd jerked in his chair, nearly tipped over backwards, with a sensation like falling-asleep vertigo as a flood of images hit him like a tsunami.

He'd seen this room. A sword. His husband, whose skill with a blade had been legendary in his old world and took Kevin's breath away in this one. And he hadn't seen, but he'd felt, a lust for blood, hanging in the air like a thick mist, clogging his lungs and making his skin crawl.

Then?

Nothing. Emptiness. No way out of this room, not for him. No future, no life.

Then he'd been staring at his computer screen, which had still been stubbornly telling him that he had to shut down the timesheet software he'd already shut down twice if he wanted to log out.

What he really wanted was to feel his husband's arms around him until he forgot what it felt like to imagine losing half his soul. But a little bit of exorcism first couldn't hurt.

It helped to look around the nexus chamber, to remember how many times pure evil had tried to destroy him, and Tiernan, and all of them. Hell, the *Marfach* tried to pull the club down around them and bury them all in the rubble. It hadn't worked. It wasn't going to work. The walls rising around him, the club being rebuilt over his head, they were proof.

The *Marfach* was only part of the story, of course. And probably not even the source of Kevin's premonition—if that's what it had been, rather than just plain old dread. Janek O'Halloran's undying and undead hatred for Tiernan Guaire was no secret—and it, too, had been born in this room. Kevin was pretty sure he could identify the exact spot on the floor where he'd lain with the former bouncer's knee in the small of his back and his head hauled up, waiting for his throat to be cut, when Tiernan had shot a rod of living Stone out of his hand and drilled it through the bastard's eye. It should have killed him. Would have, if the *Marfach* hadn't been lurking in the ley lines under their feet, and hadn't seized its first chance at escape in over two thousand years.

So now the gargantuan Polish/Irish bouncer was discovering that the Walking Dead were living the life of Riley compared to him. And the rest of the community of Purgatory had a zombie on their hands, a zombie with a passenger bent on destroying two worlds. Which zombie and passenger had probably escaped the prison Conall had crafted for them, right around the time of Mac and Lucien and Rhoann's wedding and SoulSharing.

Which, in turn, was more than enough reason for anxiety masquerading as premonitions. Maybe exorcism wasn't going to work after all—

A brittle, musical chime filled the air, an instant before three figures appeared, water cascading off them as they sat in the middle of a spreading puddle in the heart of the wellspring: a Fae with a crest of blond hair dripping water into his aquamarine eyes, a man with a military buzz-cut maybe a shade longer than regulation and an artificial leg, and another man who resembled, as Kevin had often thought, the improbable love child of a bulldog and that bulldog's favorite fire hydrant.

"That wasn't so—oh, hell, Kevin!"

As deep a funk as he'd been in moments before, Kevin still had a hard time keeping himself from bursting out laughing at the look on Mac's face. Rhoann had something of an aversion to clothes, and was getting his human partners accustomed to going without in private. And they'd all apparently come from their home away from home at the bottom of the Pool in Central Park, where clothing was less than optional—it was pointless.

"I'm not looking." Not strictly true, but close enough for jazz.

"I call bullshit." Lucien's gravelly voice sounded as if the bouncer, too, was trying hard not to laugh. "If you don't want to look at my husbands, you and I are going to have to have words, Counselor. And I'll win. Even if you *did* wrestle in college."

Rhoann blushed—Kevin suspected the blond-crested Fae might be the only representative of his race capable of doing so. "*Laród-ar*-Fuzz…"

Hearing Lucien called "Fuzzball" in English was generally enough to set Kevin grinning; the *Faen* equivalent, "ball-of-Fuzz," was too adorable for words. And just like that, something unclenched, deep inside Kevin. The triad—Mac had vetoed 'throuple' right off the bat, said it sounded like a childhood illness—was exactly the medicine he needed right now. It was a pure delight to watch the three of them falling in the kind of love Mac and Lucien had fallen in over 30 years ago, before either of them had realized they were meant to be part of something larger.

He even had good news for them, news that had almost been pushed right out of his head by his case of the vapors. "Mac, you're just the man I was hoping to see."

"Maybe. But you probably weren't expecting to see quite this *much* of me," the gray-haired Marine dead-panned, before bending to check the waterproof seal on his C-leg.

"I can deal if you can. And I have some good news for you."

"Fire away." Mac relaxed into Rhoann, holding Lucien's hand. SoulShares craved touch, and the new triad was apparently no exception to this general rule.

Yeah, this was definitely what I needed. "We took on a new associate a couple of weeks ago. Her name's Katy Lorimar, and she's involved with a *pro bono* project I thought might interest you."

"For good project?" Rhoann frowned. The channeling Aine had worked for him before he came through the Pattern let him understand any language spoken to him, but it didn't differentiate between, say, English and Latin. Every language was 'human' to him. And Rhoann was strikingly literal-minded to start with.

"It's a legal term." Simply explaining what a lawyer was had been an interesting exercise, and Kevin still wasn't entirely sure he'd gotten through to the Fae. "It describes a project a lawyer takes on without being compensated. Something for the public benefit, a way of giving back to the community. And Katy's affiliated with a local group called Conduct Becoming—she describes herself as an Army brat, and she found out about it through her dad."

That got Mac's attention, as Kevin had known it would. Mac had received an other-than-honorable discharge from the Marines, seven years after coming home from Vietnam minus a leg, for what was euphemistically referred to as "conduct unbecoming"— meaning that someone had evidence of Mac and Lucien's relationship, and had taken that evidence to Mac's commanding officer, a galloping homophobe even in an era when homophobia had been nothing remarkable.

"What do they do?" Mac shifted uncomfortably on the concrete and Stone floor.

"They work with veterans in your situation— discharged solely on the basis of sexual orientation— and walk them through proceedings to review their discharges and have them upgraded. The process takes a while, but they've been able to get all the way through it with maybe a half dozen people so far. Mostly Army, but I think they've helped at least one Marine."

Rhoann finally broke the silence. "I am… confused."

Lucien chuckled. "Anyone surprised?" There was nothing but love in his crooked smile.

A smile that Rhoann returned in kind. "The two of you have explained most of what I need to know, I think. Your military is not unlike the Royal Defense in the Realm. And I would be pleased to put an end to the officer who thought to steal my *scair-anam*'s honor."

Kevin blinked. *Maybe he's not quite as different from the other Fae as I'd thought.*

Rhoann didn't seem to have noticed Kevin's momentary disconnect. "But this 'upgrade'… why does it matter, after so long?"

Mac cleared his throat. "Well, an honorable discharge—or even a general under honorable conditions —would give me access to Veterans Administration benefits. Health benefits. Hospitalization. I could have taken care of Lucien, if I…"

Lucien leaned in and kissed Mac soundly. "Fuck the 'if only.' It's all good."

"Health benefits?" Rhoann didn't sound any less confused. "I am a healer. Lochlann is a healer. We would both be pleased to benefit you."

Kevin had to work harder not to laugh out loud. "If Mac can get his record cleared, there's a chance he might be able to get his hands on 30 years or so of back pension benefits. Which would amount to a nice chunk of change."

"You are not helping," Rhoann informed him.

"I could have told you that," Lucien added helpfully. Then, sobering, he laced his fingers with Mac's and looked Mac square in the eyes. "The most important thing about getting your discharge fixed is that you damned well deserve the *maudite* respect of the *maudite* United States Marine Corps."

"*That* I understand," Rhoann pronounced with evident satisfaction.

Kevin thought he saw tears in the corners of Mac's eyes, and was fairly sure he wasn't supposed to have seen them. So he cleared his throat and looked away. "I can send you Katy's contact information in the morning, if you want."

"Morning would be good." The catch in Mac's voice made Kevin pretty sure about the tears. "Still have things to do tonight."

Now it was Kevin's turn to blush. 'I'm interrupting something, aren't I?"

"Well... not exactly." Lucien's smile was one Kevin might have expected from a cat caught wet-whiskered in fresh cream. "Not yet, anyhow."

"Let me guess. You decided it was time to try out the chaise for yourselves." Kevin patted the leather next to him.

"Famed in song and story." Lucien laughed softly.

Rhoann perked up. "There are songs?"

"Not yet. But if you want some, Lasair might be willing to oblige." The Master of the Fade-hounds—Fade-hound, now—had picked up a vintage Stratocaster at a pawn shop a few blocks from Purgatory, and was trying to figure out in his spare time how to replicate Prince's 2007 Super Bowl halftime rendering of "Purple Rain."

"Maybe some other time." Mac reached around and ruffled Rhoann's still-damp crest of blond hair. "We'll make our own music tonight."

The SoulShare bond was an amazing thing. Granted, it manifested differently in every couple— *every bond*, Kevin corrected himself, watching Mac and Lucien and Rhoann size up the storied chaise and one another. His own husband had vehemently resisted Sharing at first, courtesy of a vow he'd taken in the Realm, never to love. And Bryce, literally soulless for so long, had apparently put up a fight as well—though he didn't talk much about it. Or about much of anything, really. Yet Bryce loved his *scair-anam*, and was loved, as deeply as any of them.

All it took was the slightest spark of hope. The belief that love might exist. SoulSharing could fan that into a flame. And when you started with more than that…

… you ended up with what Kevin was looking at.

"Have fun, you three." Kevin stood. "I promise you, it's going to be one hell of a ride."

"That's what we hear." Mac grinned, as he waited for Lucien and Rhoann to get to their feet and help him to his.

Between the well-muscled, gray-haired Vietnam vet, the stocky, broad, and extremely furry former bouncer, and six-foot-five of blond Fae perfection, all sans clothing, there was a great deal of male flesh on sudden display in the wellspring. Maybe the *daragin* were watching, or at least listening. Kevin hoped they were. There was a truce of sorts in the hostilities between the Fae and the *Gille Dubh* and their *daragin*, and it rested in large part on what the *daragin* had overheard through the wellsprings in Lucien's room at the rehab center, and at the bottom of the Pool in Central Park. Namely, Fae, and humans with Fae souls, who understood love and compassion and empathy. Fae who were different from the ones who had executed all the folk of the wood, 2,300 years ago. Fae the *Gille Dubh* and the *daragin* might, just might, be willing to forgive.

"Anything we need to worry about?" Lucien, ever practical, ever protective of his partners. Turned out Lucien's uncanny knack for spotting cops and other forms of bad news trying to get into Purgatory had been a SoulShare gift all along, his way of making sure nothing bad happened to the man he loved.

"I don't think so. The nexus may put on a light show for you—it does that around elemental magick, but there shouldn't be any harm in it now that you're Shared. But let Conall know if you notice anything unusual from the wellspring. Not that there's likely to be anything." Unlike the nexus, which consisted of ley energy—the raw stuff from which living magick was made—the wellsprings were pure living magick. They seemed to be appearing where magick was channeled strongly, and lately they were behaving rather ominously when more living magick was channeled around them. Which was why Conall's outer wards around the construction site were bare-bones minimum—no sense waking up a problem none of them could figure out how to put back to sleep.

And which was also why nobody used living magick to Fade directly into the nexus chamber any more. The network inhabited and maintained by the *daragin* was still useable, but Mac and Lucien and Rhoann were the only ones who were completely comfortable using it, probably because of the way Lucien's healing had been brought about. Travel through the wellsprings might now be as safe as Coinneach and his *darag* had promised, but... well, Tiernan was fond of saying that there were few words *as'Faein* for trust, but a great many words for its opposite. And Fae were not anxious to put themselves totally at the mercy—another un-Fae concept—of a race they had once destroyed.

But the triad didn't need to worry about any of that. Not tonight.

"I kind of envy you." Kevin started for the opening into the stairwell—stopped and regarded the three trying to arrange themselves on a chaise built for two, and grinned as they looked back at him with poorly disguised impatience. "The first time at the nexus is fucking amazing—no other word for it. Enjoy it." *Enjoy each other.*

And without waiting for a response—expecting none—he started up the stairs. It was past time to get home to his husband. To the magick that was waiting for him.

Chapter Five

"We're almost to our stop, Maelduin. Hang in there."

Hanging would be kinder than... this. Maelduin clung to the pole set into the metal floor, almost as tightly as he gripped his oathblade, and did his best not to look past the crowd of humans gathering around him at the lights whipping past the reinforced windows of the room into which he had stupidly let Terry lead him. A moving room. Under the ground. *I was insane. I am insane. Or I soon will be.*

At least he was overhearing many useful words from the curious humans. He hoped he would remember some of them for later use.

"Sure looks like a panic attack to me." A curvaceous female, one whom Maelduin would probably have found delightful had he not been quite so preoccupied with not screaming, looked from him to Terry as if uncertain as to whom to address her concerns. "Is he going to be okay?"

"I'm sure he's going to be fine."

Maelduin appreciated Terry's confidence. At least, he thought he did.

I might survive this. None of the humans seem to think our demise is imminent.

That argument might have been more persuasive had Maelduin ever trusted anyone's judgment other than his own.

"Maelduin?"

The Fae wished he could enjoy the sensation of Terry's body supporting his own. He would. Soon. If he survived this piece of idiocy. "What?" The trickle of cold perspiration down his face was unpleasant.

Terry drew back, and Maelduin instantly regretted his tone. "I'm sorry. I don't know what's going on with you, but I didn't mean to freak you out."

Freak me out. What a perfect phrase. "You... did not do this. My panic attack. Not yours."

"I wish you'd told me this was going to happen. We could have taken a taxi."

Maelduin had not thought the iron-taloned owl in his stomach could grip his intestines any more tightly than it had been until his new language gift showed him what a taxi was. "This is better."

"That's one hell of a phobia."

So that was the human word for stark unreasoning terror. Good to know. Why it should so offend his sense of everything that was right with any world, to walk into a small room, have the doors close behind him, and then see those same doors open onto a different place entirely, he was not certain.

But rooms were not supposed to move. Of that he *was* certain.

The floor shook. Gravity changed. Maelduin had learned that this meant the subway-room was slowing. He closed his eyes. Perhaps if he did not see the doors open this time, it would not be so bad.

"Jesus, Maelduin. I'm sorry."

Maelduin could not help opening his eyes. Terry was looking up at him with what seemed to be genuine chagrin, dark eyes framed by a tumble of light brown curls. And Maelduin's eyes were focusing properly again.

He feels sympathy. For me. Even without my channeling.

For a moment, Maelduin simply looked at the beautiful human.

The room stopped, and the doors slid open.

"Our stop." Terry seemed to have trouble speaking.

Together.

Maelduin wiped the sweat from his hand and offered it to Terry. His own clumsiness was lessened when he touched the human. And hopefully, contact—and soft-hearted sympathy—would make possible what he had to do.

* * *

By the time Terry let go Maelduin's hand to turn the keys in the locks on the door of his dwelling, Maelduin felt almost himself again. He would be happier if cold sweat didn't break out all over him every time he remembered the changing gravity, and the sight of the subway-room's doors showing him new sights each time they opened, but he was well enough. And he would now have a refuge, a place to wait until his curse was lifted. Confronting the Realm's second-best swordsman in his present condition would be suicide.

"Sorry about the mess." It was dark within, or at least Maelduin supposed it would seem so to human

39

eyes; then Terry touched a spot on the wall, and light sprang up, revealing…

A 'mess,' apparently. Clothing was strewn over the main room's furnishings and floor, sacks made of paper and small white boxes were piled on a small low table, and dishes were piled in a basin in a separate tiled area to one side that he thought might be a kitchen even though it lacked anything resembling a fireplace.

But Maelduin scarcely noticed the 'mess,' because the walls were breathtaking. Terry's walls were covered with images of human males, and Maelduin felt an actual physical ache in his chest at their beauty. Males in clothing as tight as a second skin, captured at the height of prodigious leaps, or in balances so exquisite as to be impossible without magickal aid, or so he would have thought. Poetry, given human form.

And several of the images were Terry. A younger version of Terry in chalk-white makeup and some sort of military-looking uniform with a red blazon on its breast, caught at the top of the arc of an amazing leap. Another, draped in white and his thicket of curls cut short, on one knee and playing some sort of musical instrument. And today's Terry, in an elegant doublet that would have allowed him to blend in anywhere in the Realm, wearing tights leaving almost nothing to the imagination, cradling a rose in one hand and looking up at what appeared to be a balcony.

Maelduin rested a hand on the frame encasing the image. *I want to be on that balcony, looking down.*

Where had *that* thought come from?

"You like Romeo?" Terry turned from where he was hanging his jacket in a garderobe. His smile was sweet, even shy. "I loved that role, so much—that picture's from when I was dancing with the Brooklyn Ballet. Before I started Trock Bottom."

The human had spoken of 'Trock Bottom' before, trying to put Maelduin at ease. Maelduin suspected the name was supposed to be a play on words, Unfortunately, his new language gift was no help at all with puns, so he would ignore them and get on with the work he was here to do. The work of self-preservation. Although it was something of a shame that he had no real use for the human's sweet shyness.

"I like Romeo. Very much." Maelduin smiled as Terry came up beside him. But Maelduin had never been shy—never known a Fae who was—and his smile had a purpose. His hand brushed Terry's arm, and magick arced from Fae to human, a subtle pattern of light, flaring where it touched. "He is you."

"I'm... just a dancer." Terry stared at the place where Maelduin had touched him, almost as if he could see the magick. His breathing was uneven, and he caught his lower lip between his teeth in a way Maelduin found quite fetching. "Not Romeo."

Maelduin's gift showed him a little of what the name meant. He had heard no human word, during his hell-ride, expressing the sense of the *Faen* word *tragód'mhan,* a dramatic form dealing with the unfortunate complications arising from the improper expression of desire. But he would make do with the words he had.

"If you were Romeo, I would let you love me."

"Oh, God..."

Terry's whisper was like a flame to tinder; there was no seducing another without opening up oneself to the same magick. Slowly, holding the human's gaze, Maelduin worked his fingers into Terry's curls, brushed his thumb along one sharp cheekbone, bent his head until he breathed in Terry's every panting breath. "Please…" It was a word that mattered to humans, he had learned that much from his unwitting tutors. Perhaps a magick word, if humans still believed in magick.

And whether humans believed or not, there was magick here, seething below the skin of human and Fae. Maelduin would wonder about it. Later. After he had done what was necessary.

Again Terry bit his lip, and this time Maelduin decided to resist temptation no longer. He bent his head and kissed the human, slipping his tongue into his mouth and teasing out the soft full lip to take it between his own teeth.

He felt a shiver run through Terry's body, where it was suddenly pressed against his own, felt hardness nudging insistently against the inside of his thigh. He could almost taste Terry's faint moan, and answered it with one of his own.

Time to decide. The living magick he had channeled and released would capture him in a net of pleasure, just as it captured his chosen human. He had a choice, to be bound or not.

He laughed, softly, into the kiss, light musical Fae laughter, so unlike the laughter he had heard on the subway. No binding of body or heart could hold one of the Cursed House. Terry would be bound—would give him shelter, refuge, whatever he might ask. But he himself would slip the bonds of magick and go free when his purpose was accomplished. Blood would tell, and the blood of House Guaire was impervious to anything that might be mistaken for love or desire.

However, he might wish it to be otherwise, even if just for a moment.

Maelduin inhaled deeply, taking Terry's scent into himself. Fae senses were keener than human, so the stories said, and Maelduin scented sweat and nervousness and fear and arousal.

Soon he would scent and taste surrender.

"What the fuck?" Terry whispered. "I don't do this."

"Maybe not. But *we* do." Maelduin reached down, working a hand between their bodies, gently cupping Terry's hardness. And then not so gently, as Terry thrust into his hand—a short, jerky movement, as if the human tried to control himself and failed.

Yes. You will fail. And it will be glorious, I promise you.

* * *

Maelduin stroked Terry's hardening cock firmly, and Terry's knees threatened to buckle; Maelduin caught him with a hand against his lower back, but overbalanced himself and nearly toppled, sending them both staggering into the arm of the sofa. "Here," he murmured. "I want you here."

I don't do this. Not true, not exactly. He hadn't objected to the occasional one-or-two-night stand, not after being so ignominiously dumped by Bryce. A guy needed some warmth, some pleasure. Some fun, damn it. But it was always his choice, when it happened. And even though the two of them were presently in his apartment, at his invitation, Terry wasn't sure this tryst had been his idea.

"Yeah." Terry clenched his teeth against a groan as Maelduin's hand slid down the back of his jeans, as strong fingers sank slowly and deliberately into his ass cheek. Damn, that hand felt good. And he had to admit, he loved the shivery feeling he got when the blond touched him like he meant it. "Here is good."

Maelduin's smile brought Terry's Steadfast Tin Soldier the rest of the way to attention in a heartbeat— he'd seen the other man eyeing that photo, along with his Romeo. And then the blond's hot plundering kiss came closer than anything had in a decade to making Terry forget all about ballet.

Terry tried to sit down on the arm of the sofa, but Maelduin leaned into him and sent them both tumbling back onto yesterday's laundry and what sounded like a couple of empty take-out bags. *Oh, well.* His legs tangled with Maelduin's—and with something long and slender and hard. Maelduin's sword.

What the hell was Maelduin doing with a sword?

Maelduin caught Terry's lower lip between his teeth and worried it with a soft growl, sending that breathless sensation shimmering down his spine and all the way to his toes. And the sword didn't matter anymore, except as he tried to figure out what to do with it once he'd managed to get the other man's peculiar belt unfastened.

Maelduin laughed softly and tongued Terry's earlobe into his mouth. "You *sol'fiáin* me." Hot breath in his ear, a hot hardness thrust at his groin in a way that was both playful and deadly serious at the same time.

"What does that mean? '*Solfyayn*?'" Terry was pretty sure he'd botched the beautiful sounds. One more thing not to care about, not when his hands were busy discovering that his gorgeous blond was commando.

"I don't have the words. Yet." The tip of Maelduin's tongue traced around the curves of Terry's ear. He'd always been self-conscious about his ears, the way they stuck out. But when Maelduin did that, they were just right.

Careful, Terry. Don't get carried away. Remember, this doesn't mean a damned thing.

Just for a second, the sweet spell Maelduin was weaving around the two of them dissolved, and Terry was tangled up, somehow mostly naked, with a near-total stranger on top of the laundry he'd forgotten to put away last night. Not that this wasn't a good place to be, or that he didn't want to be here. He just wished he had a better idea how it had happened.

A hard smooth heat that had to be the head of Maelduin's cock nudged playfully at Terry's sac before gliding up alongside Terry's own eager erection, making Terry gasp. Which in turn made Maelduin grin, and it was the wickedest and hottest grin Terry had ever seen.

"You want this. Yes?" A thrust of Maelduin's hips left no doubt as to what 'this' referred to.

He didn't mean for that to be a question. Terry clenched his teeth against a groan, but the sound escaped despite him. *Because he already knows the answer.* "Hell yes."

To his astonishment, the kiss that followed was slow, thorough, almost sweet. And he was so caught up in it, the head of Maelduin's cock had breached his entrance before he had time to react.

"Wait!" He pulled back, breathless. "Condom!" *Smooth, Miller, really smooth…* well, he'd been startled.

"Condom?"

"Yeah, you don't know me, I don't know you, we need to use…" It took a second for it to dawn on Terry that Maelduin was regarding him with utter incomprehension. "Please don't tell me you don't know what a condom is."

For another second, maybe two, Terry was sure he'd been right, that Maelduin was really that clueless. Then the blond smiled again, running a thumb along Terry's cheekbone. "I know. And there is no need."

"Like hell." Terry shook his head. "Sorry, no bareback on a first date. I don't care if you have a certificate of celibacy signed by the Pope."

The pure mirth of Maelduin's laughter aroused Terry all over again. "Not likely. Sorry." Another slow, scorching kiss. "So, we will not…"

Terry's throat felt tight as Maelduin's voice trailed off. "We will. But you're going to have to get off me. Just for a minute." Condoms and lube were in the drawer of his bedside table, and as soon as he was free to move he rolled off the sofa and made a beeline for the bedroom.

As he slid the drawer open, there was a crash from the living room. "*Fola'magairl!*"

Whatever that word meant, it was definitely a curse. Terry snatched up a condom and a half-full pump bottle of Slipnslide and stuck his head back out into the living room.

Maelduin was bent over next to the coffee table, stark naked and nursing his shin, still cursing under his breath. Terry bit his lip hard to keep from laughing. *The most gorgeous man I've ever seen in my life, but I swear to God he could break his leg tripping over a stain on the carpet.*

"Are you okay?" he ventured at last, unsure whether it was safe to re-enter the living room.

Maelduin straightened, wincing only a little. "I am."

"Maybe... you should join me. In here." Terry didn't want to deal with the possibility that his new lover might fall off the sofa while in the throes of passion.

Maelduin edged around the low table. "I will try."

Terry laughed. Maelduin didn't.

Terry switched on the light, then took Maelduin by the hand and led him into the bedroom. Which was at least as much of a mess as the living room, even after he kicked shut the gaping drawers under his platform bed, but Terry didn't care.

Neither did Maelduin, apparently, going by the firm possessiveness of his grip on Terry's ass cheek, and the way he used that grip to draw Terry tight against him. "Are we ready now?" Maelduin nuzzled his way through the fall of loose curls around Terry's ear and nipped at the curve.

"Condom?" Terry shook the little foil packet, not quite stifling a giggle. "You're easily distracted."

A finger and thumb took gentle hold of Terry's chin, tipping his face up. All thought of giggling faded away, as he looked up into impossibly, almost hypnotically blue eyes, framed by pale blond hair. Yet, somehow, his delight was all still there, making him almost giddy.

Easy, boy. Don't get carried away.

Maelduin kissed him, just a brush of the lips. And those incredible eyes never closed.

Something about his eyes…

"Show me." He could feel Maelduin's lips moving against his own. "This condom. Show me."

He's kidding, right? But the last thing he was going to do was say that out loud, because as strange as Maelduin's request was, it was also arousing as hell. "You want me to do it? All right… kneel on the bed and I'll put it on you."

Obediently—but with a backward come-hither glance over his shoulder and a subtle flexing of his ass muscles that nearly set Terry off on the spot—the blond climbed up onto the bed, fortunately without tangling himself in anything. Terry clambered up after him, motioning him to kneel and sit back on his heels. "Okay, first we need to get you—um, I guess that isn't an issue…"

Maelduin stroked his glorious cock, pausing only to play with the taut foreskin; Terry watched, fascinated, as bead after clear bead welled up from the slit at the tip. Almost like liquid glass.

"Get me hard?" Maelduin leaned forward and stole another kiss, leaving Terry feeling dizzy and breathless. "I have no problem with that. Not with you."

"I… um, I can see that." Terry couldn't help himself; he bent and took the huge brick-red head of Maelduin's cock into his mouth and swirled his tongue over it. And groaned as the other man's hips jerked and the hint of a sweet and musky taste filled his mouth.

"You should hurry." Maelduin's voice trembled; he buried his fingers in Terry's curls, and Terry could feel the unsteadiness of his grip. Along with more of that strange, shivering energy. "If this condom is supposed to go on before I…"

Terry's own hands shook as he opened the foil packet. "Right." Checking the direction of the roll, he pinched the tip and fitted the circle over the head of Maelduin's cock, holding his breath until he was sure it was going to fit. Starting quickly, but lingering over the soft skin and hard heat under his hands, pulsing in time with the rapid beat of Maelduin's heart, he rolled it down.

Maelduin sucked in his breath between his teeth, and let it out in a faint keening. "Yes… touch me…" He leaned back, taking his weight on his arms, thrusting gently up into Terry's hand, his abs hard and defined as marble, his eyes unfocused.

When was the last time someone loved my touch like that?

When Terry had unrolled the condom as far down Maelduin's cock as it would go, he slid a hand around and cupped the other man's sac, rolling one ball and then the other between his fingers, biting his lip as sweat started to gleam on those perfect abs and pecs. "You ready?" Christ, his voice was cracking.

Instead of answering, Maelduin closed his eyes, his hips undulating in an almost imperceptible—and totally fucking sensual—rhythm. The oldest dance known to man. Or men.

The samba was a mating dance. Terry had always known this. But he had never seen the truth of it on such subtle but blatant display.

What will he do, if I… Holding his breath, Terry stroked with a fingertip between the base of Maelduin's cock and his entrance, teased at the tight puckered hole.

Maelduin surged up from the bed, caught Terry by the arm, and pulled him into a kiss hot enough to scorch. At the same time, he leaned forward and bore Terry down to the mattress, planting his hands to either side of Terry's head and nudging his legs apart with what turned out to be an amazingly hard-muscled thigh. And heat like a coal burned at Terry's entrance, while his own cock dripped sticky fluid to glisten on his happy trail.

"Lube!" Terry squeaked, not caring that he squeaked, needing to get Maelduin's attention any way he could. He was good at stretching to fit, but he had limits.

There was another one of those pauses, the ones that made Terry wonder every so often if Maelduin had any idea what he, Terry, was talking about. But as long as Maelduin kept kissing him, Terry could wait. Not patiently, but he could wait.

"Yes." Maelduin nibbled along the line of Terry's jaw until Terry thought he just might go crazy. "But I have none."

"Oh, for the love of…" Terry fumbled for the pump bottle he had dropped, nudged it into Maelduin's hand. "There's plenty. Waste not, want not."

Maelduin blinked solemnly—as if neither one of them was half crazed with need at the moment. "That makes no sense."

This is weird as fuck. He'd met Maelduin 45 minutes ago at most. The majority of those 45 minutes had been spent watching the blond have a prolonged panic attack, and most of the rest had been spent getting naked. Yet the way the two of them slipped back and forth between lust and laughter, the comfortableness of their embrace... something in the ease of it felt like he'd known this utter stranger his entire life.

Yeah, right. Fairy tales can come true. It can happen to you—

Terry gasped and arched, as lube-coated fingers slid into him, found his sweet spot after a few seconds' delicious searching, and started playing him like Heifetz played violin. Over and over, stretching him, each repetition sending him deeper and deeper into a blissful place he'd never touched before even in the throes of orgasm, boneless and yet quivering like a bowstring. "Holy shit..."

"This is good?" Maelduin leaned over him again, the ends of his hair falling free of his shoulders and stroking Terry's face, shoulders, pecs; the blond was watching him with an intensity that suggested he would like nothing better than to find his way inside Terry's skin.

All that came out when Terry tried to answer was a long, low groan. *This can't be happening.* Wave after wave, slow, his whole body caught up, transformed, lost.

Maelduin raised one of Terry's legs and draped it over his shoulder. Blue eyes blazed down at Terry over a smile that should have set the bedding on fire. "Are you ready?"

Terry managed a nod, mesmerized by the music of Maelduin's voice—then cried out as Maelduin's whole lubed-up length sank slowly and smoothly into him, finding that spot, barely pausing before sinking deeper.

The waves were more intense. Terry couldn't breathe, but that was all right, because he was pretty sure he no longer needed to. He was pleasure, nothing more. Every time Maelduin hit his spot, his body jerked. Maelduin was laughing, too, a fey sound laced with groans.

Maelduin reached for Terry's stiff and aching cock, closed his hand around it. And the whole world went brilliant blue-white as Terry shot, thick white jets that did nothing to ease the sweet painful pressure in his cock and balls.

Maelduin slammed into him, circled, pressed deeper. Impossibly deep. Terry tried to work the length buried in him, had no clue if he was succeeding. And then Maelduin cried out—his cry sounded as if it started right there, where he was balls-deep inside Terry. The blond was frozen, like the most fucking erotic statue ever carved, head thrown back, eyes closed, barely breathing. Totally focused.

Focused on the pleasure—his own, and Terry's, *sweet Jesus* that hand never stopped. And neither did Terry's orgasm. Not for a hella long time.

When it finally ended, it was like someone cut the strings on a marionette. Two marionettes, actually, though Terry didn't have anywhere to fall. *Never having to move again would be great.*

Maelduin made a soft, indistinct sound into the pillow next to Terry's head. For some reason, the sound made Terry giggle. And the sound made Maelduin raise his head, and the blond's bemused expression turned Terry's giggles into delighted laughter.

"I am funny?"

"No, I am happy." The truth of his own statement startled Terry a little. It had been a long time since he'd laughed out of pure happiness.

"Then I am happy."

Amazing how good four words could make him feel.

"Should I be doing something with this… condom?" Thick blond lashes fluttered innocently. Well, not innocently.

"You don't know… here, let me. Though you're going to have to move if you want me to help."

"Life is full of hard choices."

Comfortable. There was that word, that thought, again. Terry carefully didn't grimace—he didn't want Maelduin to think there was anything actually wrong. He knew better than to wreck something this perfect by getting his hopes up.

Though would another night be asking so much? Or even just breakfast in the morning?

With elevenses to follow, no doubt. And second breakfast. *Listen to me. I never learn.*

Terry looked down as he slid the condom off Maelduin's half-erect cock and knotted it, and then busied himself looking around for the wastebasket.

He gasped, softly, and nearly missed the basket as a gentle hand stroked his ass. "Lube is messy." Lips caressed the back of his neck. "I would like to clean you."

Would you quit being so damned perfect? "I'd like that. Thanks." He twisted around and kissed Maelduin's cheek, then nodded toward the open bathroom door, just the other side of the bedroom door. "Washcloths are in the cabinet right over the sink."

The bed gave behind Terry as Maelduin rolled out of it, and he was treated to the lovely sight of the most perfect ass he could ever remember seeing, even in a lifetime of dancing and dressing rooms. And when Maelduin paused in the bathroom doorway and looked back at him, and the light caught those incredible blue eyes... *Guess he's not going to quit being perfect. Shit.*

There was a soft click as the cabinet door opened. Then silence.

"Oh—I almost forgot—the bathroom taps are backwards. Hot water on the right, cold on the left. I keep asking the landlord to fix them, he keeps telling me it'll be a cold day in hell."

Another silence, then water running, then silence again. And then a loud thunk. "*Fola'magairl!*"

Terry took one look at Maelduin, emerging from the bathroom clutching a wet washcloth in one hand and rubbing his head with the other, and immediately rolled over, presenting his ass for Maelduin's ministrations and conveniently burying his face in the pillow to smother another gale of giggles. He felt weight on the backs of his knees and his thighs— Maelduin straddling him—and then the warm caress of a washcloth.

Wouldn't mind getting used to this.

As if.

The washcloth thwacked wetly on the floor. And then Terry caught himself holding his breath, as Maelduin turned him onto his side and made him the inside spoon of a pair.

"You, uh, want to go to sleep?" The bedside light gleamed on the dusting of golden hairs on Maelduin's forearm, where it was wrapped around Terry. Terry watched the play of light, fascinated; he still didn't want to move, but he managed to raise a hand enough to trace the tip of a finger through the gold.

He thought he felt lips curving into a smile against the back of his neck. "Yes. Please."

For a second, he debated getting out of bed to turn off the light at the wall switch, or asking Maelduin to do it. But in the end, he just stretched as far as he could, and switched off the lamp, then settled back in against Maelduin.

I'll have the morning, at least. That's something.

Maelduin's palm opened against Terry's chest, over his heart. And he could feel Maelduin's heart, too, beating against his back. Or he thought he could.

Love had felt like this, once, or so he'd thought. Wonderful. Warm. Magical.

It was kind of a shame he didn't believe in love any more.

Or in magic, for that matter.

Chapter Six

Do you have even the faintest notion what time it is?

"It can't quite have been three hours since we got in, since the sun's not yet up." Rian's smile wasn't quite angelic—at least, Cuinn couldn't imagine an angel with his bondmate's quarter-to-orgasm gleam in his eyes. Which was just too fucking bad for all the poor angels, and all the better for Cuinn an Dearmad.

At least I'm not hung over yet, there hasn't been time. It was very hard for Cuinn to sound as if he were actually grumbling, given the way the Prince Royal was mouthing his way down his abs, leaving a faint trail of fire in his wake. But he felt honor bound to try. *Didn't you get enough in the alley behind Maelstrom, for pity's sake?*

"What is this 'enough' of which you speak?" Rian's Belfast accent only caught for the barest instant on the word 'speak,' which Cuinn counted as an improvement over the last few months. Since Coinneach's *darag* had stolen Cuinn's voice, his Fire elemental lover had been in something of a state. But at least he hadn't followed through on his original threats to burn the only other known magickal races in the human world down to their shared roots. Yet. "Is that but another word for the brick rash on my knees?"

That healed as fast as I could give it to you, and you know it—Cuinn's mental speech dissolved into an incoherent cry as the first few inches of his cock disappeared into Rian's mouth and Rian cranked up the heat a few degrees.

He felt the other Fae—his Irish almost-human Fae changeling, his Prince, his beloved—chuckle. *Still think we've had enough of one another?* Rian could communicate mind-to-mind as well as Cuinn himself could, courtesy of their *ceangail* bond, but usually didn't do so unless his mouth was otherwise occupied.

Did I say that? I never said that. I would never say that.

"And you call *me* a horndog. Don't you two know what time it is?"

Cuinn had been both a voyeur and an exhibitionist since before either word existed in any form currently used by humans. But he preferred to choose the time and the place for both. *You're incredibly fucking lucky I'm feeling mellow, Twinklebritches.*

Conall was shaking his head before Rian had half finished translating Cuinn's thoughts into speech. "I'm trembling, had you noticed?"

The red-haired Fae mage was leaning against the doorjamb, and while he wasn't exactly staring, he wasn't averting his eyes, either. And something about the way his lips were twitching in an almost-smile told Cuinn he didn't mind the 'Twinklebritches.' Much. Conall had spent months, after Coinneach's *darag*—on behalf of all the *daragin,* and all the Gille Dubh—had stolen his, Cuinn's, voice, insisting that he didn't fucking want to hear Cuinn's irritating-as-all-fuck nickname for him coming out of any mouth other than

Cuinn's own. But Cuinn had suspected the mage didn't mean it, and sure enough, he'd finally caved.

Rian cleared his throat. "Not that you're ever unwelcome here, *draoi ríoga*—"

Cuinn sent his Prince the mental equivalent of a sprained-eyeball eyeroll. *Since when did you become a diplomat?* Of course, the word *as'Faein* for 'diplomat' derived from the ancient word for the individual in any room least likely to leave a trail of bodies in his wake.

Rian carefully ignored him. "But it would do my heart good to think you had some reason for interrupting me and my consort in the middle of sweet playtime."

The responsive smirk Cuinn was expecting from the mage never materialized, which fact alone was enough to make Cuinn sit up and take notice. Or at least prop himself up on his elbows and take notice. A Fae had his limits.

"I do, actually." Conall raked a hand through his hair, and the streetlights from below—which would have left the little third-floor apartment in near-darkness to human eyes, but were enough and to spare for a Fae—showed Cuinn a decidedly unhappy *draoi ríoga,* court mage. "Josh and I were having some sweet playtime of our own when I felt a shift in the nexus energy. I think conditions are going to be right for getting a message through to the Realm, for maybe the next half hour. So I need help."

"There's a message wants getting through?" To Cuinn's great disappointment, Rian swung a leg over and sat himself down cross-legged on the California king that took up most of the royal apartment, all business. Or as close to all business as his bondmate ever got.

Conall sighed. "I really think it's time to let the Loremasters know about the situation with the wellsprings. I don't know if there's anything they can do about it from their end, but we could sure as hell use some help."

No shit. New wellsprings were popping up on an almost daily basis, whether in proximity to channelings or under pressure from the generation of new living magick in the Realm or just out of living magick's desire to fuck with the *Tirr Brai*, and they all had to be warded, just in case the motherhumping *Marfach* was really loose and somehow figured out how to get looser. Which meant trusting the network of *daragin* to handle transport duties, because the Fae who were capable of putting up the warding couldn't do it without their human SoulShares, who couldn't Fade or be Faded.

Still… *You couldn't have called first?*

The ginger Fae's eyes narrowed as Rian spoke for Cuinn. "Did it ever occur to you that I have good reason to hate phones?"

Frankly, no. I've always assumed you were just the king of the absent-minded wizards.

Well, shit, now even Rian was giving Cuinn a warning look.

"What do you see when you look at your phone?"

My home screen. Which, at the moment, was a close-up of his bondmate's Prince Albert. But Conall didn't need to know that.

"And your reflection."

I ignore that.

"I can't. Not after being Faded and trapped in a mirror while the *Marfach* and its decaying minion stomped on it. And me. And oh, yeah, being pretty damned sure my *scair-anam* didn't know I was gone and wasn't coming after me."

For once, Cuinn couldn't think of anything to say, and at the same time managed not to say anything.

"He apologizes."

Cuinn turned a startled gaze on his bondmate, who returned it with a neatly arched brow, the one with the stainless steel pin through it. *I what?*

You apologize. You call me your conscience, so every once in a while I decide to act like one. The pure innocence of Rian's half-grin somehow made it unspeakably wicked. *Mayhap with a bit of practice, you'll start getting the hang of it your ownself.*

The expression on Conall's face was one Cuinn imagined he'd see if he ever happened to witness someone whacking the mage upside the head with a rubber chicken. "Apology incredulously accepted. Now, would you mind coming back to the nexus chamber with me, before the nexus decides to stop being cooperative?"

* * *

Josh lounged against the Stone-and-earthen wall, thumbs hooked in the front pockets of his jeans. While he glanced every now and then at the doorway to the nexus chamber, most of his attention was reserved for the twin whorls of energy on and in the floor in front of him.

The artist in him wanted to make something of the two figures, something he might someday ink onto flesh. Galaxies, maybe, orbiting their own centers and each other, each sending out tendrils toward the other, but not quite touching.

He shook his head. Trying to define magickal shapes, the way he'd once tried to sketch Conall's Pattern-mark, was a good way for a human to get a headache. The image of galaxies got the shapes right, or almost right, but not what filled them. The great nexus looked kind of like a galaxy, he supposed, a swirl of restless foam shot through with a white energy so pure it made Josh's eyes hurt, and occasional ghosts of the colors of elemental magick. This was, so far as anyone had been able to tell, the only place on earth where four ley lines carrying all four forms of elemental energy as well as ley energy intersected. Which made it a natural point of connection with the Pattern, on the Realm side.

But the interior of the wellspring occupying most of the other half of the chamber looked nothing like a galaxy. Like the Pattern-marks most of the Fae sported, the living magick making up the wellsprings sometimes looked like intricate Celtic knotwork, and sometimes like something closer to a tribal design. But unlike the Pattern-marks, which waited until the person looking at them looked away to start looking like something else, the wellsprings were in a state of constant flux. Though Josh had never actually been able to see the design changing—he always had the nagging feeling that he'd just missed it. And lately, he'd started to notice... well, ripples. As if something was coming up from underneath the shining blue-silver, the way Rhoann's back occasionally broke the surface of the water when he was in his salmon form.

Josh was pretty sure he didn't want to see what might break the surface of living magick from beneath.

Of course, his ability to see any of this was a pure fluke. Or it would be, if there were any such thing as random chance where the Pattern was concerned. None of the other human SoulShares could see magick the way he could — he could only see it because he'd gotten so much of Conall's innate magickal talent when Conall had come through the Pattern. Even the Fae with Noble or Royal blood — Tiernan, Rian, and Rhoann — had trouble seeing ley energy or living magick, unless the nexus or a wellspring was being particularly fractious.

And speaking of fractious... *Come on,* d'orant. *It's getting late.* Or early. Interrupted in the middle of knotting Conall into the most elaborate *hishi-kikkou* he'd yet attempted by his lover's abrupt announcement that they had to hurry if they were going to take advantage of a rare opportunity to communicate with the Realm, Josh had forgotten to don his watch before coming down to the nexus chamber, but the sun had to be near to rising. And from what Conall had told him before hurriedly Fading to fetch Cuinn and Rian, they didn't have long to do what Conall thought needed doing—

"... Sorry to drag you out of bed, Highness." Conall's voice, coming from the top of the stairs, made Josh smile. As it always had.

"No trouble," came Rian's thickly-accented reply. Followed almost immediately by "You have no regrets as far as I'm concerned, I see," in the same voice but Cuinn's unmistakable tone.

"If I apologized to you, you'd hold me down and take my temperature the hard way." Conall grinned in response to the sound of Josh's laughter as he emerged from the narrow stairwell. "Not to mention that apologizing to you after you apologized to me would be setting a terrible precedent."

Oh, I can't wait to hear about that one. Josh crossed the room and took his partner's eagerly outstretched hands. "Do we still have time for what you need to do?"

"I think so. Provided you and I make a proper start of things." Conall slid a hand up Josh's arm. "Stupid clothes."

Josh agreed whole-heartedly. He had no objection at all to being on display for his *scair-anam*; however, given the tendency of some of his tattoos to come alive under the right circumstances, which circumstances included exposure to a powerful channeling such as the one Conall was about to create, it was prudent to keep his ink covered, at least around the nexus.

Josh knew how much Conall hated to be prudent. He wasn't crazy about it himself, especially when it meant he had to keep his clothes on around his partner, a Fae who craved physical contact the way other men craved air. But *Árean*, the black-headed hawk on his chest, couldn't resist Cuinn's hair when he was free-flying, and as for *Scathacrú*, well, one miniature gold fire-breathing dragon winging around while Conall was trying to channel was one miniature gold fire-breathing dragon too many. A long-sleeved shirt made sure they both stayed asleep.

Conall brushed the backs of his fingers along the line of Josh's jaw, and Josh spent a second getting lost in faceted peridot eyes. A second that was about an hour long, long enough to let Josh read Conall's memory of every minute of three hundred years he'd been forced to live without a single loving touch. And then the centuries-old red-haired twink pulled Josh down into a kiss that made the rest of the nexus chamber go away without the need for any magick at all.

Josh slid his arms around Conall's waist and drew him in close. Fae magick needed the channeler's arousal in order to be at its strongest, and he was always glad to oblige the greatest mage the Fae race had known since the time of the Loremasters. But there was no separating arousal from love, not when the one in your arms and in your body was your SoulShare.

Dimly, Josh heard a scraping sound that he guessed was Cuinn and Rian moving the battered black leather chaise away from the center of the nexus. He ignored the sound, because Conall needed him.

Conall nipped lightly at Josh's lower lip. "When we're done here, can we go back to our shibari session?" The question was punctuated with a swaying of the Fae's lower body that wasn't quite a thrust of the hips.

"Of course we can—"

"I thought you said we were on the clock, Twinklebritches."

Josh grimaced at the sound of Rian's voice and Cuinn's chiding.

But Conall shook his head, almost imperceptibly, and pulled back from Josh. "We are. These calm periods usually don't last long." His smile was all for Josh, pure innocent wickedness. "Ready to finish me off?"

"You're impossible to finish. You just pause to

catch your breath, and sometimes you fall asleep."
Josh grinned. "Need to come inside for this one?"

"Yes, please."

"Horndog," someone muttered.

"Don't make me channel a gag for my Prince,
Cuinn, it's not respectful." Conall tiptoed and nipped
Josh's chin, then quickly Faded and was lost to view.

Josh knew, though, that his *scair-anam* wasn't
going anywhere—other than for a very short Fadewalk. He pushed up the sleeve covering his inked
truesilver bracelet, then stood perfectly still until he
felt the cool touch of metal encircling his wrist,
binding Conall within him.

I'm in. Conall's voice, in his head, was just added
confirmation of what Josh already knew. *You may fire
when ready.*

Give me a second. Yes, they were in a hurry. But
there was time for this. Josh closed his eyes, wrapped
his arms around his torso, and released a long, slow
breath, letting himself feel Conall inside him. The first
time they'd done this, it had been an act of
desperation, the only way to get the disembodied Fae
back to the great nexus to get his body back. And then
they'd discovered that the mage could only work his
greatest channelings when he had the added support of
his human SoulShare. But it also hadn't taken them
long to acquire a taste for the extreme intimacy of this
contact—*the ultimate penetration,* Josh had called it
once. Too intense to endure for long... yet they kept
coming back to it. Loving it. Loving each other.

Do me a favor? Conall's inner voice was almost
wistful. *Imagine us in the shower. Like the first time.*

Conall's favorite. And Josh's, too, frankly.

Keeping his eyes closed—he knew Cuinn and Rian were out there, but he didn't care, because where it mattered, he was entirely alone with his lover—he set the scene, with loving attention to detail. Bryce and Terry's shower, it had been then, tiny worn white tiles scattered with black and a frosted glass door set in stainless steel tracks. It would have been sterile, if not for Conall slowly going to his knees at Josh's feet, red hair turned auburn by the water and plastered to his head, apple-green eyes fixed on Josh. Wanting to know if he was doing it right.

Was I? Doing it right? Even after all this time, Conall still wondered.

Instead of answering, Josh let Conall see and feel and hear his memories. Let himself feel a mouth even hotter than the water sealing itself around his rising cock, taking him deep. Gorgeous green eyes. Soft throaty moans—even when Conall hadn't dared to let himself feel physical arousal, for fear of the damage his unleashed magick might do, he'd wanted Josh, and he'd left Josh no room to doubt it.

He could hear and feel Conall moaning now, too, with his own arousal and with Josh's. One more thing they shared, when they loved this way. It was strange, but a strangeness Josh was used to by now, looking down in his imagination to see Conall stroking his cock base-to-tip with a flat tongue, and at the same time feeling Conall inside his body, sensing everything along with him, his own erection sheathed inside Josh's and straining upward.

You're too damned good at this. Conall wasn't complaining, not really, and Josh knew it. *You make me want to stand here like this until the sun comes up.*

You need me to back off a little? If Conall came before he channeled, everything would have to wait until he was ready again—so far as anyone knew, Rhoann was the only Fae whose magick was more potent in the afterglow.

No. Conall's inner voice was breathless, as impossible—or at least unnecessary—as that was. *Keep me right here. Right on the edge.*

You don't ask much. Keeping Conall on the edge of orgasm meant doing the same for himself. And living with a Fae was gradually removing concepts like delayed gratification from Josh's sexual vocabulary. *The things I do for love.*

Conall's faint, wild laughter nearly pitched Josh headlong over the edge he was trying so hard to balance on. Then he felt the surge of living magick rising in Conall, and braced himself, opening his eyes to help orient his partner.

Reach out, dar'cion—*just one hand.*

Obediently, Josh extended a hand toward the center of the nexus. Cuinn knelt next to the center, with Rian beside him. They didn't need to be making out—Cuinn's role in what was about to happen didn't require much in the way of magick, as far as Josh knew—but they were still holding hands, and the young Prince was leaning on his consort's shoulder. Craving one another's touch.

Josh knew just how they felt.

* * *

Kneeling in the ley energy was more than a little unnerving. And Cuinn really didn't need to be unnerved more than he was—the restless wellspring, and the very real possibility they were being eavesdropped on through it, were already giving him a serious case of the *inní-cnotálte.*

What's chafing you, then? Rian's gaze never left Josh, but his hand tightened around Cuinn's.

There were disadvantages to having a bondmate who could literally read his mind if he didn't take care to keep his thoughts to himself. Especially when his bondmate was a Fire elemental who had already expressed a heartfelt wish to burn down the entities who were responsible for his knitted guts. Entities who were the only beings capable of giving him back his voice, and who were unlikely to do so if turned to ashes by a volatile Fire Royal.

Best to stick to the ley energy as an excuse. Honesty was the order of the day, at least if they didn't want the *daragin* frying Fiachra's brain from the inside, but Cuinn was willing to bet there were still some things it was better not to be brutally honest about. *I'm not sure how Conall got the idea the nexus is calmer than usual tonight. It feels loaded for bear to me.*

He could feel Rian nodding against his shoulder. *Maybe that's why the center's calmer—when the energy's moving faster round the outside it stays clear of the—oh, he's starting.*

'He,' of course, was Twinklebritches. Or Josh, *in loco scintillans braccis,* with what looked like the rolled socks of an entire basketball team pushing out the fly of his jeans and his hand stretched out toward the center of the nexus. His usually-but-not-always tattooed truesilver bracelet gleamed in the torchlight, and a stream of carefully crafted magick issued from his fingertips, arcing toward the center.

The magick found its target just a few inches from Cuinn's knees, spilling into the foam of ley energy. And somehow stilling it, turning the foam to glass, in a circle that started out as wide as Cuinn's palm, then slowly expanded to the size of a Frisbee, or maybe a record album. Cuinn doubted a kid Rian's age even had any clue what a record album was.

"You can start any time."

Cuinn found Josh's voice fascinating, when he was speaking with Conall inside him. He could hear both of them, somehow, tenor and baritone. Oil and vinegar. Peanut butter and chocolate.

Rian nudged him in the ribs with an elbow.

Ow. Ask them what I'm supposed to be writing, will you?

Rian obliged, and Josh frowned, no doubt reflecting Twinklebritches' ruminations.

"Tell them... living magick is breaking out into the human world faster than we can ward it. And that the *daragin* are awakening, and we can't ward the wellsprings without their help. And that a better solution would be to stop the magick from breaking through in the first place. Ask them if they can do anything to help us. Because otherwise the *Marfach* is going to find an unwarded wellspring, sooner or later, probably sooner."

Cuinn thought about it, trying very hard to forget that he'd ever considered it a pain in the ass to communicate with the Loremasters in the Pattern by writing in a notebook or on an iPad, from the comfort of his bed or his sofa or the john or wherever the hell he happened to be. *I'd just like to remind you that there's no shorthand form of* d'aos'Faein.

Josh put up an eyebrow as Rian translated for Cuinn. "I wouldn't mind having crises that could be expressed in 144 characters or less, myself, but the hostage doesn't get to choose the grace-blade he falls on."

Cuinn snickered at the expression on Josh's face at Conall's use of the common *Faen* proverb, then bent to his work as Josh returned to the task of keeping the mage aroused. Whatever Cuinn wrote here with a fingertip, in the ancient nonlinear *d'aos'Faein* script, would be invisible here, but would be traced out in silver in the center of the Pattern on the other side of things. Hopefully it would stay there until someone had a chance to read it; they had no way of knowing for certain.

Cuinn really, really needed someone on the other side to read it, and to have a bright idea or two. There were an extra couple of reasons for urgency, neither of which it was advisable for him to remind Conall of out loud within earshot of a wellspring. The truce with the *daragin* depended on the tree folk never overhearing a Fae lying. And he strongly suspected any chance he had of getting his voice back hinged on the *daragin* and the *Gille Dubh* becoming convinced the Fae as a race had mended their ruthlessly self-centered ways— the ways he himself had so admirably demonstrated when he stole the Moon's magick and killed off the mutually symbiotic races of *daragin* and *Gille Dubh*.

And Cuinn wasn't sure how long they could keep the *daragin* from overhearing something that would totally fuck up either chance.

He wrote quickly, and as carefully as he could, given that he couldn't see the tracings his fingertip was leaving behind. *I hope I'm not inviting all the Loremasters to fornicate with basilisks next Midsummer's Eve. There isn't all that much difference in the* d'aos'Faein *script, and I don't think any of them would find the request unusual, coming from me.*

I think I'll keep that bit to myself. The snicker Rian didn't let out permeated his inner voice. *I suspect my court mage is a bit on edge as it is.*

"Are you almost done?" Cuinn couldn't tell whether the strain in the voice was coming from Conall or Josh. Might have been both. All that arousal was undoubtedly a strain on both of them, a strain Cuinn considered poetic justice.

Keep your britches on. Cuinn grinned as Rian elbowed him again. *Almost done.* One last whorl, a quick slash, and the message was finished. *All right, Josh, you can let him—*

Silver etched itself against the glassy surface, and Cuinn held up a hand before Rian had finished. *Wait. There's an answer.*

A few curves of *d'aos'Faein* script, a hurried note.

GUARD THE GUARDIAN.

Conall's magickal barrier, holding back the ley energy, burst, spilling the foaming energy over the glyph, erasing it.

"Guard the guardian?" Rian repeated. "What kind of a feckin' answer is that?"

That was Aine's writing. And maybe it wasn't an answer.

"Tiernan's the guardian of the nexus." Conall's voice, unmixed with Josh's; Cuinn looked up to see, not an aroused twink, but a frowning mage. "We may not be the only ones having problems."

Chapter Seven

The design in the floor is so beautiful, so hypnotic, that for a second even a male as driven as Maelduin is capable of forgetting what he's come here to do, content simply to stare. The fine lines of bluish silver set into the black glass of the floor could be lace, or fine knotwork. But on the edge of vision, they move and change; they cast their own light, vying with the moonlight.

Maelduin shifted uneasily in his sleep. Beauty had lied.

Moonlight. He looks up, at the face of the moon, visible through the chamber's sole window, an odd round hole seeming only slightly larger than the moon itself. The orb nearly fills the window. For some reason, the Fae thinks of the ancient children's story of the Mother in the Moon, brushing out her long hair in front of her glass, her skirts spread around her. He had never known his own mother, but sometimes he had wondered if the one in the moon might be his. Now he wonders if she might be looking at him, whoever she is.

An arm came around Maelduin, hard-muscled, soothing. A soft murmur, felt but unheard, erased the line from between his brows.

He blinks, brushing a hand across his face as a breeze stirs his long blond hair. The breeze grows stronger, sending a leaf or some small thing skittering across the beautiful floor. The sound makes him look down, and a fine sweat breaks out all over his body; his breath catches, and he feels his heart kicking like a barrel-drum in his chest. The lines are moving, vibrating with an energy he can almost hear. And in the spaces between the lines, where there is glass no longer, he can see the stars of another sky. A sky, far below him.

He tries not to fall.

The wind howls to life and hits him like a smith's hammer—

Maelduin's whole body jerked as he woke, the sweat of his dream slicking his naked body. He fervently hoped the echoes of the cry he heard were only in his imagination.

"You okay?" Terry's voice in his ear was blurry and indistinct, as if the human were not yet fully awake.

Maelduin frowned, looking down at the arm wrapped around his waist, in the sunlight slanting in through the sheer-draped window. He had never awakened in the embrace of another before—no Fae had ever been tempted to spend a night in his bed, not with the reputation of his House and his line, and frankly he had never been tempted to ask any of them to stay.

Yet he liked this sensation. Or at least he thought he did, having so little with which to compare it.

Carefully, he sorted through his available vocabulary. The human language was oddly structured, but between the comments of the bystanders in the underground moving room and his limited conversation with Terry the night before, he hoped he had the words he would need for the task ahead. "I'm okay, yes. Just… hungry." Hopefully that would explain any untoward sounds he might have made in his sleep.

He definitely liked the way Terry's laugh felt, where the human was spooned against his back, the opposite of the way they had fallen asleep. The sensation drove away the last clinging tendrils of his nightmare. "Worked up an appetite, did you?"

"I would have to say yes." Maelduin was surprised to catch himself running his fingertips over the fine hairs on Terry's forearm. And enjoying doing so.

I am not supposed to be able to enjoy this.

Maybe I don't care.

"Well, I'm not in any mood to get up just yet." A line of gentle nips and nibbles ran down the back of Maelduin's shoulder. "But if you want to get up and make us both some breakfast, I think I might regain enough of my strength for another round."

The thought warmed Maelduin, and he grinned— even though his back was to Terry, and there was no way the human could see him. Another thing Fae were not known for. "I can do that."

I hope. His initial optimism was somewhat frayed by the time he made his way back to what he thought was the kitchen. There was still no fire in sight, and no place to make one, unless the metal basin was some kind of fire pit. He suspected not, since the fittings over the basin resembled those in the bathroom, which had yielded water. *Unless they're meant to put out the fire…*

Fae were not given to headaches, but Maelduin thought he felt one coming on. Everything around him was strange beyond belief and wanted figuring out, he himself was hopelessly clumsy… and emotions were stirring in him unlike any he had ever known, or was supposed to be able to know. The combination left him feeling naked, in ways much less pleasant than his present nudity.

"Know what I'm in the mood for?" Terry's voice wafted in from the bedchamber.

"Sex?"

Spluttering laughter left Maelduin feeling as if something inside him glowed, a banked fire ready to spread and catch alight.

"Of course. But you're feeding me first, or did you forget that part?"

Maelduin could imagine Terry, sprawled out on his back, his hard abs rising and falling with his laughter. If all humans were as perfectly toned as Terry, life in the human world was going to be distracting…

… assuming he ever wanted to look at anyone else.

Wait. What?

"What do you want to eat?"

"I was trying to tell you." There was still laughter in Terry's voice. "There's a good-sized chunk of roast beef in the fridge, I didn't feel like cooking for one night before last. And there should be a couple of bagels in there, too. And horseradish mustard. We can pretend roast beef sandwiches are breakfast—I have to get my strength back up."

The flood of images accompanying Terry's instructions left Maelduin feeling dizzy. But at least now he knew what the tall white box against the wall was. *Fridge.* He tugged on the box's metal handle, and cold air spilled out. On one shelf was a thin film wrapped loosely around two small round loaves of bread pierced through the center. *Bagels.* On another was a platter, with a slab of cooked meat tented with more of the clinging film. *Roast beef.* Maelduin touched the film; it dented under his finger, then sprang back. He could not imagine what it was. At least he recognized the beef. He knew cattle, from the Realm, though they were more often raided than eaten.

He wondered what a "horse-radish" looked like. That image had not been forthcoming, or else he had missed it in the flood of others.

Enough.

Maelduin nearly dropped both bagels and platter in the course of removing them from the fridge. His clumsiness was frustrating—agonizing, even, for one as accustomed to grace in all things as he was. But he could imagine Terry's smile when he returned in triumph, carefully bearing sandwiches, and the promise of that reward was reason enough to endure the aggravation.

The film around the bagels made a sack; he shook the loaves out, surprised at the heavy sound they made as they hit the cutting surface. *They want cutting, I suppose. He can hardly mean for me to pile one of them on top of the other.* A block of wood stood on the cutting-table, handles of some featureless black substance protruding from it and the blades of knives barely visible. Good enough.

He pulled a knife from the block, and was pleased to note its serrated edge. Perfect for the cutting of bread. He rested one hand on top of one of the bagels, and cut into the heavy bread.

The knife skidded off the smooth surface; the serrated edge tore into his hand, leaving a flap of skin hanging and spilling blood all over bread and blade and cutting surface.

Maelduin was too appalled to cry out. He stared at the jagged wound until it started to heal over, the way all Fae wounds not mortal did.

The blade had turned in his hand. A simple bread knife.

Without willing it, he looked through the doorway into the room he and Terry had first entered. Everything was as they had left it in their haste, clothing strewn about and Maelduin's sword, scabbard and belt draped over the back of a divan.

His oath-blade. He had sworn one of the most solemn oaths known to the Fae, a vow sealed in blood, that the first blood that blade would taste would be the blood of his father's murderer. If his curse of clumsiness turned *that* blade in his hand...

If it did, he would be forsworn. And his own blade would kill him.

I have to break this curse.

Maelduin grimaced, his gaze going from his sword to the pictures he had so admired the night before. Terry was the epitome of strength, of grace— everything Maelduin himself had once been, before coming through the Pattern.

What had the note said, the one that had come through the Pattern with him? It was tucked into a belt-pouch, but he had no need to fetch it to recall its warning.

There is a flaw in the Pattern, and that flaw has surely maimed you. In soul, or in body, or in some other way only the Pattern knows.

Maelduin stared unseeing at the bloodstained bread under his hand.

Your only care now must be finding your human SoulShare, and regaining what you have lost.

Lost? He had been robbed. The Pattern had stolen everything he had spent a lifetime acquiring, the skills he would need to defeat a Fae who had been a legend.

And if 'soul-share,' *scair-anam*, was more than just pretty Fae poetry, if he shared a soul with the human male who awaited him in the bedchamber, he suspected he knew where his gifts had gone.

He needed more than shelter from Terry, and more than time to collect himself. He needed the missing half of his soul, and everything that had left him along with it.

A muffled roar from the street below interrupted Maelduin's thoughts, along with the faintest whiff of oily smoke. A 'truck,' no doubt. 'Cars' made less noise, and the predatory 'taxis' announced their presence with blaring klaxons. Or at least, the one that had nearly run him down last night upon his emergence from the underground labyrinth had done so, too late to do anything other than taunt him. Augmented Fae senses were a decidedly mixed blessing in the human world.

He shook his head, and raised his hand to inspect his nearly-healed wound. Not for the first time, he wished the ancient tales had been less cryptic about what awaited Fae who made the ill-starred crossing between the worlds. Specifically, it would be helpful to know how he was supposed to reacquire what had been taken from him.

When one Fae took something from another Fae, the death of the thief was the usual solution.

If Terry shares my soul, I think killing him would be a bad idea. Maelduin closed his eyes, remembering the human's shivering moans, the sweetness of his surrender. The gentle warmth of the embrace in which he had awakened from nightmare. *And I have no wish to kill him.*

If his salvation lay in some kind of rejoining, his answer surely lay in the bed he had just left. By any measure, though, last night should have accomplished his purpose—and it had not, the pink new skin on his hand spoke that truth eloquently enough. *Maybe I need to take him more than once. Or differently.*

One thing was certain, though. He could allow himself no more distractions. He could not afford to indulge laughter, or delight, or any of his other strange new-budded emotions. If the opportunity to kill found him before he regained his skill with a blade, he would die. As his father had, and by the same hand. Or his own.

At least he knew he could safely disregard the stirrings he had felt—no, had only thought he felt— toward the human. They could mean nothing. The Fae of House Guaire were incapable of love, after all.

Though… I wonder. He stifled a sigh. *I wish…*

"I'm *staaaaarving* to death in here. Wasting away."

Maelduin's wishes were worthless. Especially wishes that went against the truth of his blood and his line, and distracted him from his purpose.

Shrugging, he tossed the bloodstained bread into a nearby waste receptacle—twice, as he missed the first time—and swept the cutting surface with a roll of soft paper apparently left there for that purpose. Terry's requested 'sandwiches' were not so different from a hunter's day-meal in the Realm; he channeled two of those, shaping the bread as close to a bagel as he could manage with the undamaged one as a guide, and crafting the roast *martola* he remembered from the Realm, spiced and delectable. Fae food would not satisfy a human for long, of course, not if the old stories were true. But it would cease to be an issue before it became a problem.

As a Noble Fae, Maelduin's command of living magick—commoners' magick, the sort of magick that created food from nothing—was sorely limited. But this most basic channeling was well within his capabilities.

It might also solve all his problems.

According to the tales, once a human ate Fae food, that human was marked, fated to belong to the Realm. To a Fae.

"I'm coming, *lán'ghrásta.*"

Yes, Terry was the graceful one. But not for long.

* * *

Starving. Damned right.

Terry made a face, then grabbed a pillow and covered his head with it, just in case Maelduin picked that moment to bring him breakfast. He had to keep things light; now was definitely not the time to start waxing philosophical. He'd been given a gift, one

80

night of amazing sex and cuddling, and the possibility of a little more—he had to accept that, and then let it go.

Which was a problem, since he sucked at both, accepting and letting go.

Fake it till you make it, Miller. He could pretend not to care about anything but the sex for a few more hours. Forget how he'd totally surrendered to a total stranger. And say 'so long, and thanks for all the fish' with a smile on his face. How hard could it be?

"How are you going to eat with that on your face?"

For a second, even lying flat on his back, Terry felt dizzy, as if the bed had opened up and dropped him into a bottomless pit. Maelduin's words were ordinary, but there was nothing ordinary about the way he said them—the other man's voice was suddenly smoking hot baritone sex.

Terry's hand was shaking as he took the pillow off his head. He hoped Maelduin didn't notice. *I really, really need to get hold of myself.* The tall, lean blond was just another one-night stand.

Maybe two, his traitor mind whispered.

Maybe two. But no more than that. He'd done that before. After all, if he'd ever believed in love, that phase of his life was long over; he had a baccalaureate in Too Stupid To Know A Good Thing When I Had One, signed off on by Josh LaFontaine, and a graduate degree in Love Is For Morons, courtesy of Bryce Newhouse. One-nighters—*or two*—were exactly his speed.

Except when he forgot, and started hoping for more. He wasn't going to forget this time.

Pasting a grin on his face, he rolled to face Maelduin.

He was *not* in love. He wasn't. But that didn't mean his new favorite way to wake up couldn't be to the sight of a stunning naked man, blue eyes so bright they almost seemed to have light of their own, smiling a smile that whispered 'I can't wait to be balls deep in you' directly into his ear and sealed the words with the figurative tip of a tongue, and bearing a roast beef bagel sandwich in each hand.

A guy would have to be an idiot not to appreciate that. An even bigger idiot than Terry Miller.

Maelduin's bare toes caught in the fringe on the edge of the carpet; he stumbled, but managed to catch himself before he went sprawling. And somehow the man had wrapped one end of a roll of paper towels around his ankle and dragged the whole roll all the way back from the kitchen.

Terry fell back onto the pillow, biting a finger to keep from bursting out in another fit of giggles. *God, I haven't felt like laughing like this in... how long?* Just one more thing to lo—

Cut it the fuck out, you idiot.

"I am funny?"

Maelduin had asked that once before, but the words hadn't smoldered the way they did now. Or at least, Terry imagined they smoldered. It had to be his imagination.

"You're, um, dragging a roll of paper towels." Terry pointed, and just barely managed not to laugh.

Maelduin glanced down at his foot, then looked back at Terry, and something in those blue-blue eyes melted him. "Does that make you smile?"

What's the right answer?

Why do I think it matters so much? "Yeah. It does." He cleared his throat. "Someone as perfect as you, being such a klutz? It's adorable."

"Adorable?" Maelduin looked as if he were tasting the word, the way a cat tasted cream. Slowly he smiled. "Yes. For you, I will be adorable."

"Only for me? I'd say you're adorable to anyone with eyes. Or ears. Or…" Hell, he was blushing. He could tell by the way his face suddenly felt sunburned. *It matters so much because I used to laugh like this with Josh. Never with Bryce. And never with a one-night stand. Or even two.*

"If you say I am adorable, that is enough." Maelduin eased himself onto the edge of the bed and held out one of the bagel sandwiches, tempting Terry, apparently not noticing how flustered he was.

Breakfast in bed. Tempting. Adorable. Domestic.

Fuck it, the next thing you know I'm going to be inviting him to move in. Buying 'His' and 'His' bath towels. Learning to like Nepalese cuisine, or monster truck rallies, or Tuvan throat singing. And then kicking him to the curb. Or being kicked there myself, again.

I don't do domestic any more. Tears stung Terry's eyes. *And I almost forgot.*

"You know, I don't think I'm all that hungry right now, after all."

"What?"

Terry flinched—and only then realized Maelduin hadn't sounded angry. Startled, maybe even alarmed, somehow, but not angry. And now he was looking at Terry like…

Terry recognized the look. He'd been, oh, four or five years old, out shopping for back-to-school clothes with his mom. And he'd followed her up two escalators before he'd realized he'd somehow started following the wrong flowered sundress. Too scared to cry, he'd bolted and run off, looking for his mom. And right before she'd come racing down the aisle looking for him, he'd caught a glimpse of himself in one of the standing mirrors they put out in the clothing sections.

And he'd seen the same wide-eyed world-is-ending look Maelduin was now giving him.

I am most definitely cursed.

* * *

"I… thought you were hungry." *This has to work.* And he had to calm himself. He knew better than to give away his vulnerabilities. One never ceded the high ground to an adversary.

Or even to a *scair-anam*.

Terry half-smiled. "Maybe not for food." He looked at the sandwich Maelduin held out to him, and shook his head. "Not right now, anyway."

He knows what I plan. Impossible, of course. But a blade-dancer survived on instinct as much as on cold calculation, and his instinct told him the human was resisting him.

What had that woman in the moving-room, the subway, called Terry's attempt to devise an alternate plan for bringing the two of them home, when he, Maelduin, had started to breathe so fast white spots had danced in front of his eyes? Looking for a Plan B?

Yes. It is time for Plan B.

Humans, he had observed, made a shrug say a great many things. So he shrugged, as best he could while still ridiculously leaning on one elbow and holding out a sandwich. "What should I do with these?"

Terry rested a hand on Maelduin's forearm. "Just put 'em in the fridge. For later." The sparkle in his eyes left Maelduin no doubt as to what Terry hoped would fill the time before 'later.'

"Later."

With a smile to match the human's tone, if not his own mind, Maelduin slid back out of the bed and returned to the kitchen. He doubted channeled food would last long in the fridge. By the time it became an issue, though, Terry would no longer care.

The subtlety of Fae food had been a bad idea from the outset. This time, Maelduin would do what was necessary to make certain Terry was his.

Whatever that was.

How had matters spun so far out of his control, in less than a day? A lifetime's work and self-discipline, consummated at last, would have been wasted and worthless, had he not come through the Pattern… but the act of coming through the Pattern had robbed him of every fruit of that discipline, left him cursed and clumsy and helpless.

Helplessness was not a state any Fae could bear. One of the darkest of the many words *as'Faein* for torture, *danamhris*, meant, literally, nothing more than 'to be done unto.' Maelduin could not endure it. Would not.

Humans, on the other hand, so far as Maelduin had ever heard, had always been largely oblivious to

Fae manipulations, going wherever they were led, succumbing gladly to whatever channeling was put on them. So much so that some of the ancient Fae had ceased even to consider toying with humans proper sport.

But *this* human did not appear to be oblivious.

And Maelduin was not toying. He could afford neither to toy, nor to indulge emotions he could not possibly be experiencing in the first place. After all, his only hope of regaining his skills, of keeping the vow that had kept him alive since he had been old enough to take up a sword, lay in seducing a human.

Why does this thought disturb me? Maelduin opened the door to the fridge and set the sandwiches on a shelf, taking care not to lean so far into the cold-box that he risked cracking his head on the smaller box on top of it when he straightened. *Humans like to be 'done unto.' And I will do him no harm—I will give him pleasure for what he will give me. As soon as I can summon the proper magick to make him give it to me.*

The fact that he was worried about causing a human harm was mildly alarming. The reasons for his solicitude—emotions that were an impossibility to anyone of his cursed lineage—were even more so.

And his target's possible imperviousness to Fae magick?

I will pet that cockatrice when I wake up next to it.

When Maelduin returned to the bedchamber, Terry had swept away the bed-coverings and lay watching the door, with his head pillowed on one arm and his other hand playing slowly over his own body. Displaying.

Maelduin would have commented, but he was fairly sure 'displaying' was a human word he did not yet know. Instead, he gathered himself for a dive, intending to scoop up the compact package of human delectation and roll the dancer over until he was breathless and off his guard—

"Maelduin, don't!" Terry's eyes were wide, and he reached out a hand toward the door as if he could stop Maelduin in his tracks.

"Why not?" Maelduin tried not to pout.

And Terry, apparently, tried not to giggle. "I just don't want you to hurt yourself."

"I... thank you. For your concern."

A smile, and a slow approach, suited Maelduin's purposes better, in any event. By the time he joined Terry in the bed, the human's eyes were wide, his attention captivated and his arousal apparent.

Maelduin drew Terry into a full-body embrace, tangling his long pale legs with Terry's tanned ones; he thrust his hips gently but insistently against the growing heat at the human's groin, and worked his fingers into Terry's brown curls.

Terry's breath caught hard, and Maelduin smiled. A few strokes of the hand, breathless kisses traded, perhaps another condom if Terry insisted, and Maelduin would be clumsy no more and helpless no longer.

Something was pushing on his chest. Terry's hand. Not hard, not insistently... but pushing.

I do not understand.

"Can I just... look at you?" Terry's smile was almost shy. "For a minute? I didn't get to do that much last night."

Startled, and trying not to show it, Maelduin nodded. *Perhaps humans need to take things more slowly.*

Being looked at, watched, was a strange experience. It made Maelduin feel more naked from one moment to the next. Not that any Fae of his acquaintance had ever objected to feeling, or being, naked, under the present circumstances.

Besides, it afforded him an excellent opportunity to look back. He cupped Terry's jaw in his hand and ran his thumb over the soft stubble on the human's cheek, smiling at the dimple that appeared in response. Terry's eyes were large, darker than almost any Fae's. And strange—where Fae irises were subtly faceted, human eyes were all smooth curves, like cabochons. One could almost believe one could see into a human, through windows such as those. The effect was disconcerting, especially seen in dark *sule-ainmi*, animal-eyes... but Maelduin liked it.

What I 'like' is unimportant, compared to what I must do. He ran his thumb over the bow of Terry's upper lip, a touch imbued with the living magick that had been rising in him since he woke with Terry's arm around him; he leaned in and kissed where he had stroked. "Have you stopped wanting me?"

"Do I look dead?" Terry put up one eyebrow, then turned his head and kissed the pad of Maelduin's thumb. "I just want more than..."

Terry's voice trailed off, and his gaze drifted from Maelduin's. Then, suddenly, Terry's hand wrapped around Maelduin's mostly-erect shaft; and when Maelduin could see his eyes again, they were windows no longer. "You're right. I want you."

The magick lingering on Terry's skin where Maelduin touched him went colorless and dissipated.

…I am not supposed to be the confused one here…

What Maelduin was seeing, sensing, was not possible. Another Fae, fully aware of the existence and potential of magick, might turn aside a concerted attempt at magickal seduction, but not extinguish it altogether. There was no chance a human might do either, none whatsoever.

Terry groaned softly, turning his head from side to side so Maelduin's fingers tugged at his hair.

What was the human doing, in order to accomplish this impossibility? Arousal was supposed to be fuel for Fae magick, a match set to oil-saturated tinder, and Terry was seeking out sex—Maelduin was already finding it unexpectedly difficult to think, with Terry stroking his erection. Yet Maelduin could not deny what he sensed; Terry's desire for sex was somehow blocking the magick Maelduin directed at him.

"Did you change your mind?" Terry's touch was more insistent by the moment, but Maelduin's magick—unlike his cock—refused to respond. Even the human's gentle nip in the hollow of Maelduin's throat, a pleasure it had not taken Terry long to discover how to administer to Maelduin's exact specifications and perfect delight, brought the Fae achingly erect, but left his magick slumbering.

Terry wanted sex.

Terry wanted *nothing more than* sex.

Perhaps sharing a soul, the *scair-anam* bond, was something more than sex, something more than seduction. Something more, perhaps, than any Fae of the Cursed House was in a position to give or receive.

I am in deep, deep trouble.

"I have not changed my mind. Not at all." *But I have to change my methods, if I can.* The alternative was a lifetime of clumsiness—a short life, ended by a broken oath and a turned sword.

But what was he supposed to do?

Share…

Yes. If he wanted Terry to be open, to receive him, to want more from him than the touching of bodies, he had to open himself. Of course, one might as well try to shoe a flying horse in mid-air… and the effort was bound to come to naught in the end. Even if he could afford to be diverted from his lethal purpose, no male would want a true union with a Fae incapable of what limited love a Fae could know. But before the end, surely the trying would be enough for Maelduin's purposes; it would have to be.

Maelduin was almost relieved. Everything finally made sense. He knew at last what he had to make himself do, make himself feel, make Terry feel. It could not be real, it would not be forever, but at least it would be simple.

Maelduin opened his palm along Terry's beard-roughened cheek, circled it gently, and shivered at the pleasure of the soft abrasion against his skin. "That feels… wonderful."

"Huh?" Terry blinked. "I mean, thanks, but—"

A gasp cut off whatever Terry had meant to say, as Maelduin browsed kisses over the new growth. He had wondered how the stubble would feel against his lips, and saw no reason not to find out, not when the discovery was so sweet for them both. At the same time, he rolled to pin the lithe human to the bed with his weight, lying in the cradle formed by hard-muscled legs.

"Mmm..." Terry arched up into Maelduin, stroking his back with a touch as gentle as a butterfly's wings, eyes half-closed as if the lids were weighted. Or as if he were being careful not to have to look Maelduin in the eyes.

Humans are stubborn, but no matter.

He made his kiss as gentle as a Fae might, the slightest brush of the lips, the touch of a tongue asking for entrance, or for capture. Terry chose capture, claiming his mouth briefly as he gripped Maelduin's ass and drew him closer.

"What do you like, *lán'ghrásta?*" he whispered against Terry's mouth, smiling as Terry nipped at lips already pleasantly abraded.

"I'd like to know what that means." Terry's fingers dug into Maelduin's cheeks, kneading.

Maelduin swore to himself, even as his hips jerked in response. "If I had the words, I would tell you." He frowned, sorting through the list of human words he knew. "A dancer who touches the ground only when he wants to. Who sings with his body." This was only a fraction of the poetry that was *lán'ghrásta*, but it would have to do for now.

Terry's face flushed, and for an instant his guarded gaze gave way to the shyness Maelduin had found so endearing. "Thank you."

Kissing shyness was even better than kissing boldness, Maelduin decided. Terry's mouth was soft, and his eyelashes fluttered against Maelduin's cheek like captive grace-wings before his eyes closed.

"Tell me. Please." He nibbled the softness of those lips, breathed in Terry's gasps, laid a hand over Terry's ribs to feel them rise and fall with those gasps. "What you like."

"You cannot possibly be real." Terry swallowed hard.

"Pretend I am. And tell me."

Once again Terry's eyes were windows, beautiful eyes that gave away secrets instead of keeping them. Or they would, perhaps, if Maelduin knew how to read a human's strange eyes.

"Your mouth… on my cock." Even Maelduin, with a Fae's enhanced hearing, had to strain to hear. "I dreamed, last night…"

"Then I will give you your dream."

Why did that bring the shadows back to Terry's eyes?

Maelduin's shrug was an inward thing, this time. Surely giving Terry his dream was the way to open him. And he himself would open as well, in the only way a Fae could. The Pattern could ask no more of any Fae—certainly not a Fae of House Guaire—not and expect to receive what it asked.

And why am I worrying about such things, when I have a delectable male in my arms begging me to sate myself on his cock? And the end of a curse, waiting at the end of it all?

Maelduin thoroughly enjoyed the way Terry undulated beneath him, trying to present as much of himself as he could to Maelduin's mouth as he licked and kissed his way downward. And when he ran his teeth lightly along the male's *trora*, the hard ridges of muscle over his hips, he had to grip the base of Terry's

92

already weeping cock and squeeze tightly to keep him from finishing before Maelduin got so much as a taste.

"Oh, fuck." Terry already sounded exhausted, in the best way imaginable. "I'm not sure I'm going to— oh, Jesus, *now* what?"

Maelduin laughed, as innocently as he could manage, as he stroked between Terry's sac and his entrance, again and again, with a single fingertip, flirting around the puckered hole. "If I could choose a pillow-name, I do not think it would be Jesus. But as you will."

The little explosions of laughter issuing from Terry as he tried in vain to contain his reaction to Maelduin's words were delightful and strangely erotic at the same time. "Would you mind keeping your mind in the gutter? Just for a little while?"

I made him do that. Maelduin smiled as his lips browsed Terry's sac. *He lost control because of me. And I like to hear him laugh. No, I love to hear him laugh.* "As long as yours is there, so mine will not be lonely."

There were other sounds, too, he had heard the human make before, delicious sounds. He wanted to hear those, too. His hand still encircling the base of Terry's cock, tightly enough that he could feel the human's pulse, he sealed his lips around the almost arrow-shaped head and slowly worked the rest of Terry's slick length into his mouth. He tasted salt, faintly, and an earthy musk unlike that of any Fae he had ever known well enough to know his or her intimate tastes.

"Fuck…"

Maelduin glanced up, pleased to notice the sweat coming out on Terry's forehead. But he had no way to comment on it at the moment, so he contented himself with sucking harder, and slipping his first finger into Terry, almost all the way up to the palm. Terry's back arched, twisted; releasing his cock, Maelduin licked firmly from Terry's entrance to the base of his sac, toying with the wiry hair before licking again.

He, too, was caught up in the sounds, the scents, the taste of Terry's pleasure. He thrust roughly down into the rumpled sheets, keening in the back of his throat. And Terry's hands were fisted in his hair, holding tight, urging his mouth back where it had been. And once Maelduin had obeyed, and his moans vibrated against Terry's erection, Terry's whole body trembled, twitched, arched.

"Oh, God... oh, God... oh, *fuck*..."

Maelduin's magick heard Terry's pleading, and it responded. He felt it more than he saw it—Nobles could see living magick if they concentrated hard enough, but Maelduin was concentrating on other things—welling up in him, spilling out onto his skin, a myriad swirling miniatures of the Pattern, waiting for the right moment to fill the human, find the other half of Maelduin's soul, end Maelduin's curse.

The right moment. Surely it would happen when release heightened Maelduin's magick and lowered Terry's defenses. Any moment now.

"So fucking close..."

Maelduin tasted Terry in the back of his throat. Delicious.

I should end this. Give him what I promised, and take what I came here to find.

Humans had *átenna milis*, buried in their holds, just as Fae did; Maelduin had discovered this last night. He reached deep with one finger, then two, and knew he had found the *át* when Terry swore and let go his hair to grip the sheets. Again, and again, finding the rhythm Terry had loved so well the first time. Every thrust of Maelduin's fingers brought a sharp gasp, and every gasp drove Maelduin closer to an untouched release.

And Terry's every soft cry threatened to wake... what?

A longing for more. More that could never be, because wishing for love of any kind, or the joy that might come with it, was the act of a child, or a fool.

Now. Before I forget myself. Maelduin drilled deep, sucked hard, tasted salt and musk and groaned with the pleasure Terry needed to feel and hear.

Terry's cry was raw and cracked in the middle, as his heat spilled down Maelduin's throat. And the cry, the heat broke something open inside Maelduin; pleasure wracked his body as liquid like molten glass pulsed from him to pool like molten glass in the sheets, the seed of an Earth Fae.

And Maelduin channeled, as he thrust moaning into the bed-clothes, as best he could without knowing what it was he was trying to do. He called up his magick, the living magick that was every Fae's birthright, and hurled it at the writhing human, to feed his pleasure and by it to bind him. Maelduin hoped.

Magick flared up around them in a halo of brilliant blue-white.

Magick faded, charred to black, and fell away.

Terry collapsed to the bed with a breathless whimper, a faint shiver. Maelduin himself lacked even the breath to curse—it was all he could do to crawl up the bed and fall face-first into the pillows beside Terry.

He ought to be angry, disappointed—but he was not. Instead of anger, there was thunder in his ears, from the pounding of his heart, and at the same time he was wrapped in silence, and an odd sense of anticipation. The combination was pleasant, and even peaceful. Maybe it was a human thing, part of the human world—he had certainly never known any feeling like it in the Realm.

I wish this could last. The thought startled him, coming out of nowhere, as did the sharp pang that accompanied it. It was not a Fae thought, or a Fae wish. And even if it were, it was a wish that would always be beyond the reach or the grasp of a Guaire.

Neither this moment nor its emotions could last. He had no time to linger in an irrelevant peace or long for the impossible. He had to start over. And once he had what he needed—once he had worked out how to overcome Terry's resistance—the hunt he had barely begun would resume. The hunt that had become his reason for living.

Still…

Is it wrong of me, to be glad I have another chance to try to make the Sharing work?

Terry was still sprawled on his back, arms flung out, trying to catch his breath. Maelduin rested a hand on his arm. "Was it as good as your dream?"

He felt Terry tense, startled, then relax. "Better than any dream." Gathering himself with an obvious effort, he rolled just enough to reach over and run a thumb along Maelduin's cheek. "You missed a little. But it's sexy as hell." Something unknotted in Maelduin as the human smiled.

Then it all knotted again, as Terry sat up. "Shit, it's late, I'm supposed to open the shop this morning."

"I... what?" Maelduin would have panicked, were he not far too physically relaxed for his body to do anything of the sort. He was not sure what Terry was talking about, but the human obviously had some sudden urgent purpose, and it was unlikely that such purpose involved Maelduin.

"I'm supposed to be at work in 20 minutes and there's no way I'm going to make it." Terry slid out of bed, padded around to Maelduin's side. "Where did I leave my jeans?"

"In the other room, by the sofa." Maelduin hoped he was remembering the word correctly.

"Oh. Right."

Terry disappeared through the doorway, reappearing moments later with his trousers in one hand and his shoes in the other. Maelduin watched appreciatively as the human worked his way into the close-fitting trousers, then gave way to give him room to sit while he put on his shoes.

When Terry had finished with the laces of his shoes, he stilled, staring at the floor between his feet.

Sweat prickled on Maelduin's forehead. *If my magick had no effect at all...*

"Do you... oh, hell... I don't know what you were doing inside the studio last night, when I found you." Terry turned, not his head, only his eyes, to look at Maelduin. "And you don't have to tell me. But if you need a place to stay, for tonight..."

"I do." Terry seemed to be waiting for him to speak, and when he did it was as if a weight was lifted from his back.

Terry's gaze dropped again. "Please don't get any ideas, but I'm not going to throw you out."

There was something Maelduin was supposed to say. He was certain of it. He tried to remember them, as Terry opened a chest of drawers, took out and donned a shirt, slipped a small leather package into a back pocket and clipped a ring of keys to his belt. But perhaps the words he sought were words he did not yet have.

"Help yourself to whatever's in the fridge. I ought to be home around eight, I have a client till seven."

Terry paused in the doorway, turning back. Maelduin had not moved; he had simply watched, enjoying the human's grace and beauty. The grace was borrowed, true—not stolen, that had been the Pattern's act, not the human's—but the beauty was all Terry's.

"See you tonight, Maelduin."

Terry disappeared; a moment later, the door opened, closed. Keys turned in the lock.

Too late, he remembered the words.

Thank you.

Chapter Eight

Terry spun the last handle, clamping down the autoclave lid. Out of habit, he tested the seal before flipping the switch to set the machine heating. It had been a good session—Ngai was happy with his lion, and the whole thing had only taken a half-hour longer than he'd planned.

Still… his mind had been somewhere else, for quite a bit more than that half-hour, and as soon as the autoclave started hissing, Terry went out into the lobby, where Josh was hunched over the light table they both used for design work.

"Are you going to be here a while yet?" Terry hated to impose—he always did, not that he did it all that often given that it left him feeling like a schmuck—but something about the idea of Maelduin spending the day all alone in his apartment didn't sit right with him.

Josh nodded, flashing him a grin before looking back down at his work. The man was so good-natured, it ought to be illegal.

And I walked away from him.

"Yeah, this sketch is being difficult." Josh tilted his head, regarding whatever it was he was working on from a different angle. "I gave up on it last night, and the night before, but I'm going to be stubborn tonight."

Terry tried not to wince. It sucked when the guy you dumped what, seven years ago, kept acting like he could read your thoughts. "Would you mind keeping an eye on the autoclave, then? I just loaded it, and I'd love to be able to get home—I have a house-guest."

Well, shit. It also sucked when you couldn't stop letting the guy you walked away from know how completely over him you were, when the guy you walked away from was the one who'd gotten screwed, and had less than no reason to give a damn about you being over him.

And it did nothing to reduce the suckage quotient when Josh gave him one of Josh's trademark in-love-with-the-world grins, pure joy in a dark-haired dark-eyed gorgeously-inked happily-partnered package. "Good for you!—yeah, sure, get your bad self home, I'll take care of unloading Bertha when she's done steaming."

Josh was obviously happy, genuinely happy, that Terry had someone waiting for him at home. Terry wasn't sure if that made him feel better about the whole situation, or worse. "Thanks, I owe you."

He was glad Josh didn't respond with *No, I owe you*, the way he sometimes did. Josh was convinced that Terry showing up when he had, after Bryce threw him out, had been a lucky break for Raging Art-On. Or he'd spent the last six months trying to convince Terry it had been, anyway.

Once out the door, Terry turned right, toward the Metro station… stopped, recognizing the sensation of his subconscious making a decision without him.

Nodding, he turned and headed left instead. It was just a few blocks to the bus stop, and he could go down to Sunan's Sea Palace, at 6th and C Street, just the other side of the Mall, get the best Thai take-out in D.C., and surprise Maelduin with it.

He suspected nothing he could buy would be as good as the bagel he'd turned down this morning. He couldn't have accepted, though. Bringing home take-out was nice, but it was impersonal. Eating breakfast made for you by the guy you just woke up next to…

Woke up. That was it. He'd been caught up in the fairy tale last night, a dream of a chance encounter with a handsome—and endearingly klutzy—prince, and mind-boggling sex, and falling asleep wrapped in strong arms and feeling warm breath on the back of his neck and hair tickling his shoulder.

And then… he woke up. A little surprised to find the prince was still there, and even more surprised to realize how good it had felt to be the outside spoon, to wake up holding someone who wanted to be held. But the spell had been broken. Mostly. Sure, the sex had been amazing, but not quite as—well, primal—as last night's.

Because last night had been different, from start to finish. He'd managed to forget he didn't believe in fairy tales, at least for a while. Which wasn't quite the same thing as believing in fairy tales. But he suspected it had made a difference.

The bus was mostly empty, and Terry dropped into a window seat as it pulled away from the curb, watching but not really seeing the storefronts, restaurants, parking lots glide past and fade away into the darkness. It was as if they only came into being as he approached them, and stopped being when he couldn't see them anymore.

Kind of like Maelduin.

Oh, Jesus, listen to me. Terry caught a glimpse of the face he was making, reflected in the bus window, which of course only made the face worse. Maelduin had come from somewhere, which meant he had somewhere to go. He must. A guy didn't just appear out of nowhere, perfectly turned out and gorgeous enough to stop a heart.

Or wake one up.

* * *

"Hey. You okay?"

The words washed over Terry without registering. Nothing was registering, really. He wasn't sure how he'd gotten to the sidewalk outside the Duplex, or why he'd come there in the first place. He sat on his hard-shell suitcase, the only one he'd felt like taking the time to pack—maybe Bryce would send the rest of his stuff along to wherever he found to crash, maybe not. He wasn't even sure what was in the suitcase.

He hadn't needed a suitcase to pack Bryce's parting shots, though. He'd be carrying those around with him the rest of his life.

I need this place more than you do. And... I need you not to be here.

He'd never heard Bryce sound like that before. His boyfriend could be cold, cutting—on second thought, there wasn't any 'could be' involved. But he'd never sounded... lifeless. As if words that should have been angry, or cold enough to smoke, were just dead.

I wonder how long he was that sick of me.

People had been walking past him for a good half-hour, he guessed. Everyone going someplace, because everyone had someplace to go. Everyone but him.

A hand waved in front of his face. "Are you okay? It's Terry, right?"

Terry made his eyes focus. He recognized the face of the man bending to try to look him in the eyes, though he wasn't sure from where. Running a dance company, even a pocket-sized one, you met a lot of people. The whole dance company thing was also over, probably, because how was he going to run a ballet company out of a suitcase, with no computer, no records, no receipts?

"What happened to you?"

"Sorry, sorry." Now Terry recognized him, though he couldn't put a name to the face—the guy had been a bartender, at a piano bar he and Josh had enjoyed hanging out at, years ago. Rose's Turn. What were the odds? "Boyfriend threw me out, I guess I'm still kind of shell-shocked."

"Josh did that?" Shock was plain on the bartender's face, and even plainer in his voice.

Terry winced. "No. The guy after Josh." Now he was even more embarrassed about his bad memory, though he supposed bartenders had to have a better memory for faces and names than he himself would ever have. "Life happens, right?"

"It does. It would be nice if every once in a while it happened fairly."

Terry was proud of how easily he pulled off a noncommittal shrug. "You play the hand you're dealt."

The bartender—*Kyle*, he finally remembered—didn't look as if he was buying Terry's nonchalance. "Your dealer was a cheat."

"Even so…" There wasn't much to say after that, so Terry shut up.

Kyle looked past him to the door of the Duplex, where a cluster of people stood waiting to get in, then back at him, with a quick tight nod. "Look, I have a voice student who's singing here in 20 minutes, and I promised her I'd catch her show. But if you can hang around till she's done, I have a couch you can crash on, for a few days at least. I have a studio up in Hell's Kitchen—it isn't big, but you don't look like you take up much space."

Terry was stunned. His ears were ringing, and he had a feeling that if he tried to stand up his knees would have their own opinion about it and it wouldn't necessarily agree with his. "I don't. Thanks—"

* * *

The squeal of the bus brakes brought Terry back into the present moment. No, he couldn't throw Maelduin out. Not yet, anyway.

* * *

"Here you are, sir."

Bryce hardly noticed the cab driver, as he took the offered handle of his rolling carry-on bag. "Yeah, thanks." He was already craning his neck, looking up and down Constitution Avenue. *Why did he want to meet up here, instead of at the hotel?*

By the time he thought to turn back to the driver, driver and cab were both gone; Bryce thought he recognized the cab merging into the flow of traffic. He shrugged. *At least I remembered to say thank you this time.*

Bryce Newhouse was living proof that just having a soul, after three decades without one, didn't guarantee civilized behavior or even the ability to live up to what a man might want to be.

A high-pitched yelping bark came from somewhere in the trees on the far side of the sidewalk, out on the edge of the Mall proper, and Bryce forgot all about being civilized. Grinning, he took off at a brisk walk, following his ears, ignoring the walkways, and cutting through the line of trees, coming out into a large open space with a walking path around it, and benches along the path. And next to one of the benches, a blond-haired man stood, holding on to a short leash, speaking sternly to a leaping dog.

Like that's going to do any good. Bryce broke into a run, picking up the carry-on bag so it wouldn't jounce across the grass.

Setanta leaped toward him, yelping in frustration as his harness brought him up short. The pup hadn't yet forgiven them, or Conall, for figuring out how to incorporate truesilver into a dog harness. But they really hadn't had any choice—a blind dog needed a harness if he ever expected to go walking in Manhattan, or anywhere else. And Bryce and Lasair were both sure Lasair would have the Fade-hound pup trained to voice eventually, but until then they really needed a way to keep him from Fading off after one of the other of his masters any time he felt like it.

Dumping the carry-on, Bryce dropped to his knees in the grass and let Setanta climb up onto him. Swarm all over him, more like. Funny how nothing made him feel more like a normal human than the unconditional over-the-top love of a dog.

Almost nothing. He looked up, and closed his eyes as Lasair bent to kiss him.

"*Sumiúl*. We missed you."

"It's only been what, four hours?" The time it took for Bryce to catch a flight from New York to D.C., while his *scair-anam* and their Fade-hound puppy took a shortcut only Fae could take. Yet Bryce smiled. He couldn't help it, especially not with Setanta crawling all over him, flopping on his back across Bryce's thighs, and generally being a wriggling ball of adoration.

"Four hours is a long time." Lasair dropped to sit in the grass beside Bryce, and immediately came in for the same full-body love-up treatment from the puppy. Not surprising, since the Fae had been Setanta's master first, before the two of them had left the Realm.

Bryce couldn't help laughing at the way the blind Fade-hound puppy—which looked a lot like an Irish wolfhound, but which had the genetic capacity to grow to the size of a stag and have six-inch fangs, which was going to be interesting to explain to Animal Control in Manhattan someday—couldn't just wag his tail, but had to involve everything south of the ribcage. "Somebody sure thinks so."

Lasair turned his turquoise gaze on Bryce, and all of a sudden everything else around the three of them went away. "We both did."

Bryce did what he usually did when Lasair said

inexplicable things like that; he took a nice, long slow breath in through his nose, and worked hard on not letting his expression say *you're shitting me*. Because he knew his partner meant what he'd said—if the Fae race had ever produced anything close to a straight shooter, Lasair Faol would be that Fae. He, Bryce, was the one who couldn't wrap his head around talk like that. People never missed him. Usually just the opposite, in fact; people tended to be disappointed when he *didn't* go away.

Of course, 'people' weren't his SoulShare. And if only one person in the whole world grokked him, well, that was one more person than there had been before Lasair came along.

Setanta flopped his head into Bryce's lap, his dull-marble eyes not quite focused on Bryce's face, his tongue lolling out the side of his mouth.

The dog probably grokked him, too. Or at least made him want to be the kind of human worth a Fadehound's lavish adoration.

"I missed you, too," he mumbled. "Both of you." The weird thing was, it was true. One of the few things he remembered from his time as the *Marfach*'s slave was a desperate desire to be alone. A desire he could never realize, not with a piece of the monster literally buried in him and the rest of it keeping Janek's eye on him whenever it could. Since he'd been free… well, he'd missed having Terry around, but that was one of those things he was never going to be able to fix. And finally being alone, genuinely alone, had felt like a little slice of heaven.

Only it wasn't any such thing. Not any more.

Lasair unwound a bit of Setanta's leash from

around his hand, and grinned as the puppy tried to burrow into Bryce's lap.

"Why did you want to meet up all the way on this end of the Mall?" Bryce started to brush dog hair off his trousers, but remembered the futility of such an action before he'd properly started; Setanta rewarded him by slobbering all over his hand, which he managed to find quite nicely without being able to see it. "It's a hella long walk back to the hotel from here." True enough — the Hotel Mandarin Oriental was at the other end of the Mall from the corner on which Bryce had gotten out of the taxi, and on the far side of it into the bargain.

Lasair laughed, ruffling Setanta's soft-wiry fur. "This vicious beast"—he paused to let the puppy thump his tail against Bryce's leg in ecstatic acknowledgment—"is going to need some exercise before we go to bed. You know how he gets, his first night in a new place." The Fae's smile combined all the best features of naughty and nice. "Assuming you want to go for more than a few minutes at a time without him Fading into bed with us."

"Point taken."

Lasair's fingers laced through his, and for a while Bryce was happy to enjoy Setanta's antics and have some quiet time with his Fae. Genuinely quiet time—this wasn't something they could do regularly in Manhattan. Rhoann was pretty cool about them spending time in the sheltered area around the Pool in Central Park, but he made Rhoann's husbands Mac and Lucien uncomfortable, if they were around, which they usually were whenever Rhoann was in residence. He could see where he might unsettle the bartender and the bouncer, after the little incident when the motherfucking *Marfach* had forced him to try to blow up Purgatory.

As usual, thoughts of the monster caused a sharp unsympathetic pain in Bryce's gut. Also as usual, Lasair noticed, and squeezed Bryce's hand tighter.

"Why do you feel you have to do this?" The Fae's voice was soft, but found its way into Bryce's ears with unerring accuracy. "No one asked you."

"No one would." Bryce shrugged. "They say they don't want to put me at risk. Maybe they mean it. But I'm the only early warning system we've got. And if the *Marfach* is really loose… I'm at risk whether I'm in New York, or D.C., or on the moon."

"Maybe not on the moon." Lasair leaned into Bryce, and Setanta took the opportunity to wriggle across two laps at once. The puppy was growing at a phenomenal rate, at least to Bryce.

"Yeah, but the moon would just present a whole new set of problems." Not the least of which was the possibility that it—she—might be as pissed off at the Fae as her children the *daragin* and the Gille Dubh were.

He could feel Lasair's chuckle where they touched. "We could have stayed someplace where you could be protected, though. Conall has wards around the Colchester."

Yeah, they could have gotten a room in the pocket hotel where Lochlann and Garrett lived, courtesy at least in part of Bryce's management of the money Lochlann had amassed during his two-thousand-plus years in the human world. No Fae who still had his magick ever lacked for money, but

Lochlann had lost his magick sometime during the Black Death.

"I can't stay anywhere there's a wellspring." Bryce grimaced.

"Why not?" A thumb stroked the back of Bryce's hand; Setanta squirmed around to rest his head in Bryce's lap.

Bryce loved Lasair. He truly did. He'd finally stopped arguing with himself, on that one subject at least. But there were times when his belovéd didn't get him, and this was one of them. "The same reason I won't travel by the good graces of the *daragin*. They're listening to us through the wellsprings. Maybe even reading our thoughts. They're trying to decide if their truce with the Fae is a good idea. And if any of us are caught in a lie—in anything less than what the *daragin* and the Gille Dubh consider to be 'good behavior'—the treaty's in the trash, and quite possibly Fiachra's head blows up." Which was another good reason for him to avoid the Pool, since there was a wellspring lurking at the bottom of it.

"But you are not a liar."

Lasair's evident confusion warmed Bryce's heart. Yet it hurt, at the same time, because naturally Bryce had to try to clear things up for the male he loved. "I have been. Most of my life." A lot worse than a liar, actually—the Fae and humans of the Demesne of Purgatory, along with more or less everyone who had ever encountered him, saw him for what he had been, the consummate cold-hearted bastard. Maybe it hadn't all been his fault—the Pattern's machinations had left him without a soul from birth, until Lasair came through the Pattern and late delivery was made of that ethereal commodity—but even if it wasn't his fault, it was still his responsibility. And how the hell did he make good a whole lifetime's worth of thoughtless cruelty?

Well, by not waiting to be asked before putting his life on the line by being a living *Marfach* detector, for starters. Before the monster had managed to incarnate, through some bizarre fusion of Janek O'Halloran's physical substance and the magick Lochlann had been forced to pump into it, only humans had been able to see it at all, like the kind of hallucinations a person carried with him from sleeping to waking. Any Fae that tried to look at it was guaranteed to go rat-fucking insane. Now the Fae could see it—but only Bryce, who had carried a piece of it around in his gut for over a year, and had been permanently altered by the experience, could sense it from a distance.

He had also demonstrated that he could use that altered part of himself to suck magickal energy out of the *Marfach*, but his lover had threatened to break both of his legs and chain him to the nearest concrete pillar with truesilver if he ever tried that again. *"Lochlann will heal you afterward."* Lasair had smiled. Kind of. Bryce wasn't keen on testing that particular limit.

But here and now, Lasair was regarding him with the kind of anxiety one didn't see in Fae all that often, and nodding. "Setanta and I will not Fade into or out of our hotel room, then. I promise."

Because there's no telling how much magick it takes, these days, to call a wellspring. Bryce wasn't exactly sure what was going on with the magick escaping from the Realm—no one was going to sit down with him one on one and explain matters to him, so all he knew was what everyone was told, and everyone else talked about, on those occasions when the Fae and humans of Purgatory all got together. He gathered that feeding ley energy back into the Realm, to replenish its depleted stores of living magick, had been a decent enough idea—saved the Realm—but things hadn't worked that way before the Sundering, and the new arrangement was causing problems no one had anticipated. Apparently shooting raw ley energy into the Realm with God's own fire hose was causing the Realm to spring leaks. Wellsprings. Any one of which the *Marfach*, cursed be it, could probably surf back to the Realm. And the one in the old nexus chamber was starting to break down.

Bryce almost didn't notice Lasair drawing his head down to rest on his shoulder, pillowed on all kinds of flowing blond hair. He noticed lips brushing his temple, though. Fae kisses were hard to miss. So was Fade-hound slobber soaking into one's pants leg.

"You fret too much, *sumiúl,* over things you cannot help."

"Only because you gave me the soul that makes me give a damn." Bryce's eyes abruptly watered, stung. There had been a time, not all that long ago, when the death of a world he'd never seen, and never would, would have been Someone Else's Goddamned Problem.

Not anymore. Because that was Lasair's world, and fuck if he was going to let anything happen to it. Or to Lasair.

"Does our soul cause you pain, lover?" There was a line between Lasair's brows that hadn't been there a few seconds before. "Would you give it back to me, if you could?"

The question was like cold water flung over him; Bryce couldn't breathe with the shock of it. He'd been stupid enough to try to reject Lasair's gift, over and over again; he still wanted to curl up and die with the shame of it, when he remembered how one of his rejections had driven his Fae lover to try to flee back to the Realm. There was nothing inevitable about a SoulShare joining, and he'd damn near thrown the other half of his soul away.

"Please, *m'anam-sciar*. Please don't cry."

* * *

Terry muttered to himself as he rounded the curve onto the north edge of the walkway around the National Mall. *Cazzo* road construction, *maledette* unmarked bus detours, *mamma cazzo* expired *cavolo* transfers. Somehow his Nonna Maddalena's old-country curses made him feel better in a way nothing else ever did.

Thankfully, his unexpected detour—courtesy of two blocks of torn-up sidewalks and re-routed city buses, with public notice of the same apparently disseminated via Ouija board—was almost over. Once he hit the northern edge of the Mall, behind the Vietnam Veterans' Memorial, he could cross over to 21st Street and catch a train home, hopefully before the crispy beef and the pork Masaman curry and the prik khing curried scallops with green beans got cold.

Would you look at me, for the love of God? Actually, Terry was starting to get a little tired of that phrase, given the way it had been on an endless loop in his head since he'd realized he was going to have a half-hour wait for take-out at Sunan's. Yeah, he was being domestic. Exactly what he'd been trying to avoid becoming, last night and again this morning. Because there was no point to being domestic, centering your life around someone else who was just going to leave, or show you the door.

Terry heard the rhythmic clanking of a bike chain behind him just in time to step out of the way as a lithe young man in tight bicycle shorts sped past. *Bet he's cold.*

The guy was almost out of sight before Terry realized what he'd done. An incredibly aesthetically pleasing ass had just floated past him, clad in skin-tight spandex, and all he, Terry, had been able to think was *bet he's cold.* Because he had an even more aesthetically pleasing ass waiting for him at home, and didn't feel right about speculating about other asses under those circumstances.

Would you look at me?

Jesus. I'm pitiful.

Terry tucked his head down and kept walking. Concentrating on putting one foot in front of the other, and occasionally glancing up to make sure he was still going the right way and hadn't wandered off down a side path, helped to keep his thoughts off his own dismal track record in relationships and why it was such a bad idea for him to even entertain the possibility of considering another one.

I'm being ridiculous anyway. This is literally some homeless guy who was planning to crash in my dance studio until I caught him. Sure, he'd been an ass for bringing Maelduin home with him, but he supposed a guy was entitled to be an ass for a night or two. Especially with a man as gorgeous as Maelduin, and with appropriate precautions being taken. It was the daydreaming about more that was ridiculous. He knew better.

"If you were Romeo, I would let you love me..."
Goddamnit.

A dog's barking and whining dragged Terry out of yet another round of self-chastisement. Just past where the row of park benches along the walkway ended, two men sat on the grass, with a dog trying to wedge its way in between them, whining, tail wagging. One of the men had his head on the other's shoulder. It looked as if he were being comforted by both the other man—a guy with long blond hair and the kind of wedge-shaped torso that belonged in fashion magazines—and the dog.

That was something real. Not the kind of 'relationship' he was trying to conjure out of thin air.

Terry couldn't even make himself feel jealous, not really. Yeah, he wanted what he saw—someone to care about him that much. More than that, someone he could care about that much. But he'd already dumped someone he'd cared for—and who had cared back—in favor of an unmitigated cold-hearted son of a—

Holy fuck.

The blond was kissing the other man's forehead, palming away his tears. And Terry recognized him, not to know his name, but he'd seen him a few times at Purgatory. The other man wasn't looking at Terry—his eyes were all for his studly blond boyfriend—but Terry would know Bryce Newhouse anywhere, in profile or otherwise, in broad daylight or under the streetlights of the National Mall, flickering on in the gathering dusk.

Even unmitigated cold-hearted sons of bitches had better luck with men than he did.

Maybe the blond was more lovable than Terry was. Or maybe all it took to turn Bryce human was the right guy, who obviously wasn't Terry.

Terry clutched the handles of the take-out bags, his knuckles as white as the bones under the skin. Neither man looked up as he strode past. Which was just as well—he had a farewell dinner to serve at home, and didn't have time for any interruption.

Chapter Nine

The apartment seemed very quiet when Maelduin pushed the button and silenced the spirits. He wondered where they went, when darkness fell over their prison, the trapped spirits with the strange names—HBO, Food Network, Animal Planet, SSTARMAX, National Geographic. Perhaps they appreciated not being forced to entertain any longer at the whim of the one who held the flat black rectangular key to their prison—or sat on it, as he had done initially. It puzzled him that none of them attempted to escape—none of them listened to his exhortations, although he supposed he understood, as whatever channeling kept them imprisoned kept them from hearing or seeing him—but surely they wanted their freedom? Yet instead of attempting to flee, or planning escape, they persisted in creating food out of ingredients even a Fae found peculiar, engaging in palace intrigues and debaucheries that were nearly Fae in their complexity and the rhythm of their speech, whispering to cats possessed by demons, and attempting to sell him Medicare supplement plans, whatever those were.

At least the spirit named Gordon Ramsay had

taught Maelduin the proper use of a stove, assuming it would ever be safe for him to be around open flame again. And thanks to the talkative spirits, when Terry returned, Maelduin was fairly sure he would be able to say whatever he wished.

What did he wish to say, though?

Maelduin lay back on the sofa with a sigh, dropping the key on the floor. The spirits had offered a great deal of advice—most of it on subjects in which he had no interest other than the acquisition of vocabulary. Not one of them had had anything useful to say on the subject of the seduction of an outwardly enthusiastic but inwardly reluctant human male. Well, one had offered some insights into changing the human mind, but Maelduin had no can of whoop-ass to hand to implement any of that spirit's suggestions.

And, unsurprisingly, none of them had been able to help him know his own mind.

Have I lost my purpose? Forgotten my task? Maelduin shook his head, mildly irritated with himself for asking the question. He could no more forget his reason for coming to the human world than he could forget to be a Fae.

Remembering his purpose and being physically capable of carrying it out, however, were cockatrices so different it was impossible to believe them hatched from the same clutch.

I have to join with Terry, to have any hope of regaining my skill with a blade. Or even being safe to walk across a room without causing some kind of catastrophe. Yet physical joining moves him not at all. This morning's sex certainly had done nothing to help Maelduin's cause, in any event—all he had to do was close his eyes, to see again the total failure of his channeling, magick itself shriveling and crumbling away, failing to find anything to hold onto.

He had not thought to look last night, to see if the same thing had happened then. But he had not regained what he had lost—obviously—so his efforts had likely fallen short then as well.

Did seduction require something more?

Maelduin shook his head. *This should be simple.* Humans were prey, had always been so. Though an individual Fae might once have treated an ensnared human well, if the mood struck him or her, there had never been anything complicated about the glamouring.

Yet I do not wish to glamour him.

This was, possibly, why the matter was not simple. Maelduin remembered the human's laughter. Remembered his small gestures of thoughtfulness, and the unexpected joy of waking from nightmare to the strength and shelter of a freely offered arm. Such things, he suspected, would be lost if he blatantly seduced Terry—and they were things Maelduin wished to have, with the single-mindedness of any Fae.

But did he want those things more than he wanted the rejoining of his soul? More than he wanted release from the stumbling prison of his own clumsiness? The death of his father's murderer?

Impossible.

If he cared, he might have such desires. If he loved. But Fae did not love. Especially not the Fae of the Cursed House, House Guaire—

A key turned in the lock; the door swung open, and Terry was preceded into the apartment by the scent of food, savory enough to tempt even the most jaded Fae palate.

And another scent. Tears.

By the time Terry was turning the locks on the apartment door, juggling the sacks from which the wonderful smells were emerging, Maelduin was on his feet. Resigned to barking his shin on the small table in front of the sofa, he refused to wince as the table legs screeched across the wooden floor and his shin reminded him that even his *comhrac-scátha* had done it less damage overall.

Terry winced enough for both of them. "Still having one of those days?" He shook his head when Maelduin extended a hand, offering to help with the bags. "That's okay, I've got it."

Maelduin followed Terry into the kitchen, his frown deepening with every step. Tears, yes, definitely, there was no mistaking the scent even mingled with meat and fish and spices. He wondered if Terry—if any human—would expect him to notice such a thing. "Terry, are you—"

"Could you reach us down some plates?" Terry pointed with one hand toward a cupboard. "Carefully?" The human's voice caught, edged with an odd harshness.

Maelduin arched a brow, opened his mouth to reply, to defend his ability to remove plates form a shelf without inviting disaster… but something caught his attention. Pain. Sorrow. Instead of snapping out a retort, he turned to look at Terry. And saw red eyes, the tracks of tears incompletely scrubbed away.

Fae did not love.

Perhaps, then, his desire to put an end to Terry's

pain was something other than love. It had to be. Because it was something he wanted, and a Fae would not want love.

But he was a Fae, which meant he would have what he wanted, whatever that was.

Instead of doing as Terry asked, Maelduin rested a hand on Terry's arm, slowly turned him away from the bags on the counter, looked into his eyes. "What has made you sad?"

"I'm not—"

"You are." *And I want it to stop.* "What happened?"

Terry's mouth opened, closed. His gaze slanted away, then back again, then down. "It's nothing. Really. I just… ran into an old boyfriend. With his new boyfriend."

Maelduin frowned. Jealousy was something any Fae could understand, and jealousy was surely called for in the circumstance Terry described, though he was not certain of Terry's feelings. "Do you want someone hurt? I could do that." *Assuming I can walk down the street toward the one who wanted hurting, without being hit by an out-of-control truck.*

Terry made a sound in response; Maelduin had no idea whether it was laughter, a groan, or something else altogether. "I kind of believe you."

"You should believe me." Such a statement, from one Fae to another, would be cause for peals of musical laughter. In this instance, though—just this once—Maelduin meant every word.

Terry shook his head and looked away, leaning against the counter and staring at the gray stone between the heels of his hands. "Would you quit being so fucking perfect?"

Maelduin had hoped for something that would make him feel less confused, rather than more. "If I am perfect, why would you want me to be less so?"

Terry had beautiful eyes, even when he was regarding Maelduin with an easy-to-read *you make as much sense as an inebriated Sibyl* expression. "Because then your leaving wouldn't suck quite so badly."

Maelduin's stomach felt as if someone had dropped a stone into it. Or perhaps a block of ice. He could not leave. Not now, not yet. Not without the half of his soul incarnate in the human.

Not without seeing Terry smile.

"I am not going anywhere. Not yet." Hesitantly, he rested a hand over Terry's.

I am too tentative. During his long training, this sort of indecisiveness would have resulted in his death on the blade of his *comhrac-scátha*. But perhaps this, too, was his curse at work.

Terry was staring at Maelduin's hand. "No. Not yet. *I'm* not the type to put someone out on the street before dinner." The human's smile seemed forced, his gaze hooded. "Sorry, I'm being a bitch."

The human probably thought his voice gave nothing away. To Fae ears, though, it trembled, carrying the weight of some deep human emotion barely kept in check.

Any such emotion stood between Maelduin and what he needed. That was why he had to draw Terry out. The only reason a Fae would ever do so. Of course.

And what would the whoop-ass healer spirit say? "Talk to me, Terry. Tell me what's wrong."

Terry laughed, a harsh grating sound. "Please don't pretend you give a damn. That only makes it worse."

"Why?" Maelduin caught Terry's hand as Terry tried to pull away. "Why does it make it worse?" Fae relationships, such as they were, layered pretense on top of artifice, as any Fae would expect of that most capricious of art forms. *Humans must be very, very different.*

Terry huffed out a sharp sigh, but the slight catch at the end of it betrayed something more than mere exasperation. "Look, we both know you and I were a hook-up. A mind-blowing hook-up, granted, but still..." Terry pulled his hands away, opened the paper sack, and lifted out one container after another. "You're breaking the rules. You do know the rules, right? Pretending to give a shit about your bedwarmer is gauche. You just say 'thanks for the great sex,' and in this case you say 'hey wow, thanks for the amazing dinner,' and then you move on."

The smells coming from the containers made Maelduin's stomach rumble. He ignored both smells and hunger, and caught Terry gently by the wrists. "If you think I care about rules, you know nothing of me." He smiled as Terry's eyes went wide—though the redness of those eyes caused a muscle to jump in his jaw. "And this knowing nothing of me wants fixing."

"I suppose I should have guessed you don't give a damn about rules. After all, we met while you were breaking and entering."

"Breaking, yes." Maelduin could not help wincing at the memory of the long-handled implement, and the crunch as it had impacted his nose.

And the blood. Noses always bled copiously, so he had learned. "The entering came later."

Terry's laugh sounded reluctant, but genuine enough. He turned his hands under Maelduin's, and took Maelduin's hands in his own. And Maelduin wondered at the racing of his heart.

Something is happening. Something I cannot allow.

Yet Fae cared nothing for rules, for what was allowed.

"I'm sorry. I don't mean to be a bitch. But I told you, I ran into an old boyfriend on my way home. And his new boyfriend. And they were both getting on perfectly well without me. You know what I mean?"

It was as he had suspected. "You are jealous. This is normal," he added reassuringly; stating the obvious seemed a safe enough gambit to comfort the distraught male. And it was as if a weight slid from his shoulders—at least now he understood *some*thing.

"*Jealous?*"

The crack in Terry's voice, and the way he snatched his hands away and balled them into fists at his sides, made it clear as living Stone that Maelduin understood much less than he thought he did.

"… not jealous?"

"No." Terry's voice was as dull as lead. "There's nothing there to be jealous of. I was an idiot, I dumped a good man for Bryce. And then Bryce and I… well, we didn't work out." Terry slumped against the counter, and now Maelduin could see that his face matched his voice. "I have epically lousy taste in men. No offense, I'm sure you're an accident."

Maelduin felt his face grow hot. "No offense taken."

Terry said nothing. And, having never experienced

an awkward silence before, it took Maelduin a moment to recognize what was happening. "I said something wrong. What can I say to make it right?"

"There you go, being perfect again." Terry glanced up, driving home the difference in their heights, then down again. "It's like you studied to know exactly what to say."

What would you say, I wonder, if I told you you were more right than not? "If I were saying the right things, this would be much less uncomfortable than it actually is. Because you would be letting me help."

Terry stared, tears welling in his eyes once more. "I doubt it. I'm not only an idiot when it comes to men, I'm stubborn as a mule, my grandma always said. *Testardo come un mulo.*"

Terry tried to laugh. The sound was painful to hear.

Painful. *I am feeling pain, simply because a human feels it.*

And, as Maelduin watched, a single tear contradicted Terry's laughter. Terry ignored it, but Maelduin could not look away.

I think... this is no longer a pretense of caring. Though what it is I am actually doing, if not pretending, is still a mystery.

"Look, as long as I'm quoting wise Italian women, I might as well say there's no sense in letting good food go to waste." Terry turned away from Maelduin and peered into the bag, as if concerned some morsel had escaped his notice. "We can talk after dinner, okay?"

Humans had nothing whatsoever to teach Fae about the art of deflection. And Terry had no idea, yet, how tenacious Maelduin was.

Chapter Ten

Tiernan settled back into the hot tub with a blissful sigh, the ends of his unbound hair trailing in the scented water. All Fae were born sensualists, but most kicked that tendency up several notches into hedonism. And Tiernan was in a class by himself, at least in his own opinion.

A simple channeling was enough to lower the lights; if Kevin were with him, he would have lit the scattered candles, too, but under the circumstances—

"Mind some company?"

Kevin's voice drifted in from the bedroom an instant before the male himself appeared in the doorway of the master bath. Tiernan had had an enthusiastic appreciation for suit porn long before he met his husband, but the sight of Kevin in charcoal gray Armani and a full day's growth of dark stubble was enough by itself to bring the head of Tiernan's cock out of the water, as if to find out for itself what all the excitement was about.

"If I ever answer that particular question 'no,' do me a favor and put me out of my misery permanently."

"Not funny." Kevin stepped back into the bedroom, and from the sound of things was quickly stripping out of his office attire.

The foggy mirror on the bathroom ceiling gave Tiernan back a blurred version of his frown. "Why not? It usually is."

One of Tiernan's favorite sights was Kevin, naked, demonstrating by his mere presence why his past girlfriends had universally dubbed him 'Elephant Dick.' This sighting did not disappoint... yet something about Kevin's face, his demeanor, as he climbed into the water left Tiernan unsettled. He slid over, making room for Kevin on the underwater seat, and rested a hand on his husband's thigh.

Husband. What an un-Fae thought. And yet it was second nature by now. As was not understanding what went on behind his husband's deep brown eyes. There was a time he could have found out, of course— humans were simple to manipulate—but manipulation stopped being an option once a Fae Shared. Human morality was contagious, apparently.

And even if it wasn't, there were the *daragin*, and their dead-Fae's-switch buried in Fiachra's brain. Manipulating humans was undoubtedly somewhere on the list of Fae behaviors that would earn Fiachra a one-way trip to the madhouse, and totally fuck up the Fae-*daragin-Gille Dubh* truce.

Kevin slowly let out his breath in a deep sigh; Tiernan could feel taut muscles relax under his hand. "Sorry." His head fell back against the hot tub's padded headrest, his eyes closed.

Tiernan leaned over and kissed his way up the side of Kevin's throat, until he was in range to nip his earlobe. Which he did, as gently as he could stand to. "So what's eating you? Besides me." A moment's concentration dimmed the lights even more and lit the candles, lavender-scented like the water. An aphrodisiac for Fae males as well as human, not that either of them usually needed the help.

Kevin shook his head, almost imperceptibly. "Nothing. Just some… bad dreams, I guess."

"You guess?" Tiernan nipped harder, then licked where he'd bitten.

"I don't want to call them premonitions. That's giving them more weight than they're worth." Kevin's fingers threaded through Tiernan's under the water. "I think it's just nerves. Not knowing what the hell is going on with the *Marfach*, or what our next move is. Knowing we live on top of a wellspring and might be eavesdropped on. I know we're probably too far above it for the *daragin* to bother, but…"

Tiernan didn't want to let go of Kevin's hand, not as long as it seemed Kevin wanted him to be holding it. So he stroked his husband's broad shoulder with his other hand, and busied himself tracing the curves of Kevin's ear with the tip of his tongue. Less blatant seduction techniques were sometimes even more enjoyable than more direct options—and to a Fae, seduction tended to be the answer no matter what the question was.

Kevin shuddered slightly, his lips parted in a silent sigh. Tiernan smiled, and leaned even closer to let his human hear the hoarseness of his own breathing, the catches in it. Soon he'd ease Kevin onto his lap, slip a couple of fingers into him, make him ready—

"Were we fated to meet?"

"Hm?" Tiernan blinked, startled, as Kevin turned to face him.

"Our SoulShare bond. Was there something there before we had sex? Something that drew us together?"

Maybe this is what's been bothering him. Empathy didn't come naturally to a Fae, or at least to any Fae without Water blood, but Tiernan was learning. Slowly. "No one's sure exactly how the bond works. Cuinn wasn't in on the crafting of it, he was busy with other parts of the plan for the Sundering. And we don't really have a large statistical sample—"

"Oh, fuck statistics." Kevin was smiling, a little. "What did it feel like to you?"

"Interesting question." Tiernan didn't feel much like thinking at the moment, but he loved his husband, so he tried. "I knew I had to have you, the moment I saw you. But that by itself doesn't mean all that much, when you're talking about an unShared Fae."

Tiernan loved Kevin's deep chuckle. "So I've noticed."

"An observant lad, you are." Kevin's soft mouth begged for a kiss, and Tiernan had never been able to deny that particular request. After a necessary moment to clear his head, he went on, "I knew I was going to take you somewhere and get you to drop those incredibly well-tailored trousers. But when I touched you…"

He fell silent. The memory of that first touch always took him out of the present, and he was glad to let it. In the Realm, love had ruined him, the only kind of love a Fae was supposed to be able to know. His love for his sister had driven him to murder the brother who had raped her… and the forbidden killing had stolen his sister's vengeance, and for *that* his sister had Oathbound herself to see him exiled to the human world for his crimes. Her act of spite had left him fucking determined to live the rest of his life without love of any kind, without intimacy.

Until chance—which didn't exist—had brought him and Kevin to Purgatory on the same night. And he'd come up behind the young lawyer, rested a hand on his shoulder…

And the shiver of magick racing from his hand, up his arm to his heart, his mind, his soul, had told him that he was never going to be alone again. No matter how much he'd wanted to be at the time.

Kevin returned Tiernan's kiss, with interest. "The touch woke up our bond."

"Yes. I think so. And a few other things." The memory of Kevin's expression, when he'd first whispered in his ear, taking his conquest of a new human for granted, was another one of those things that never failed to make Tiernan instantly hard. Or harder.

Kevin noticed, and let go of Tiernan's hand to stroke the proud curve of Tiernan's cock. "But we weren't fully SoulShared then."

"Right. One of the few things we know for sure about SoulSharing is that the bond only fully asserts itself once the Shared couple—or threesome, or for all any of us know moresome—share pleasure the same way." Tiernan slid his hand up Kevin's thigh. "Giving and receiving."

"So sharing souls is really just about sex?" Kevin's grip on Tiernan tightened; he swept his thumb over the head of Tiernan's cock, tickled the nerve bundle under the head, and smiled at Tiernan's involuntary grunt. "Just about pleasure? Seems kind of shallow…"

"I wish you'd quit asking questions that require me to think at the same time you're making my brain switch-off." Tiernan couldn't help a grin of his own, as he settled deeper into the water.

"Want me to stop?" Kevin let go of Tiernan's cock, crossed his arms behind his head, and stretched luxuriously, his toes poking out of the water on the far side of the tub and the broad dark head of his erection poking out considerably nearer.

"Bite your tongue. Or mine, I'm good either way."

"Later."

One of the many things Tiernan generally loved about his *scair-anam* was the way his relentless intelligence never entirely deserted him, even during sex. It made him the perfect magickal partner. Unfortunately, it also made him nearly impossible to distract. "Fucking tease. What were we talking about?"

"Sex and SoulSharing." Tiernan caught a brief glimpse of a wicked grin, before Kevin ducked his head and took the first few inches of Tiernan's cock into his mouth, swirling his tongue around the head until Tiernan's hips jerked involuntarily.

"Shit." Tiernan worked the fingers of his crystal hand into Kevin's dark hair, drawing his husband's head to rest on his shoulder. "Stay up here, at least your mouth isn't distracting me this way."

"Optimist, aren't you?" Kevin nipped at Tiernan's throat.

"*Scilim g'fua lom tú.*"

"I hate you too, just as much."

Reluctantly, Tiernan forced his thoughts back to his *lanan*'s question. "The SoulShare bond is about a lot more than sex. Trouble is, we're not sure what, exactly. Aine might have been able to tell us something, if anyone had thought to ask her before communication with the Realm became so difficult. It's quick. Usually. Which I suppose makes it seem strange to most humans—Fae don't really have anything to compare it to, so unless we fight the bond, the speed of it doesn't seem odd to us. But it's definitely more than just falling for a piece of ourselves. Self-love. Even humans have stories about soul-mates, one soul in two bodies."

"I'd wondered about that, from time to time." Kevin wrapped his arm around Tiernan, snuggling in close. Another one of Tiernan's favorite sensations.

And wonder of wonders, tenderness only heightened his arousal. Never in a hundred lifetimes would such a thing have happened before his SoulSharing.

"Carrot and stick," he murmured.

"I beg your pardon?" Kevin's large hand cupped Tiernan's balls, rolled them gently.

"Talk now, beg later. Sex and SoulSharing, carrot and stick. Or at least carrot. I'm not sure it would be possible to get an unShared Fae interested in love. The only Fae who love are the ones who have already Shared. No unShared Fae is ever going to care about someone else, unless that someone else has something he needs."

"I've heard that story before." Kevin's breath was warm against Tiernan's neck and shoulder. "From Conall, and Cuinn, and probably a few other Fae. And I think it's high time someone called that theory out for the bullshit that it is."

With some difficulty, Tiernan turned his head, the better to look into his husband's eyes. "It's not bullshit. It's the way Fae are."

"The way you think you are." Gently, Kevin gathered up a lock of Tiernan's golden-blond hair, and just as gently kissed it. "The way you've told yourselves you are, for whatever reason. Told yourselves for so long that you believe it."

"And you know better?" Tiernan couldn't help arching a brow.

"Maybe looking in from the outside lets us humans see something you don't." Kevin ran his fingertips lightly along Tiernan's collarbone. "I've been watching you, and the other Fae, for a couple of years now. And it's perfectly obvious from your actions, toward your humans, and even toward one another, that you know how to love. Hell, half a Fae soul was enough to give Bryce Newhouse the ability to love, starting from a stone cold heart."

Tiernan curled his fingers of warm living Stone around his husband's wandering hand. "Assuming you're right…" Not an assumption Tiernan was prepared to make immediately, or necessarily at all. "Then what do you think SoulSharing is for?" He'd always suspected it was tied up with love—specifically, he'd deduced, or thought he'd deduced, that Sharing was what gave a Fae the ability to love in the first place. But he was no Brathnach the Wise, no Sherlock Holmes; he had, on exceedingly rare occasions, been known to be wrong. Most of which occasions tended to involve underestimating the male in his arms.

Kevin laughed softly, thoughtfully. "I think that was kind of what I started out asking you."

The human was silent for the space of a few breaths, the pounding of his heart perfectly audible to the acute senses of a Fae. *This* does *have something to do with what's bothering him.*

"Maybe SoulSharing is a wake-up call for the Fae, reminding them of something they've thrown away. Something they need. But…"

The hammering was louder, more urgent. "But what, *lanan*?"

Kevin worried his lower lip between his teeth, making Tiernan want to kiss the breath out of him. But no, not yet. Not until his husband finally made plain what he himself was too dense to see.

"None of that tells me what SoulSharing is to a human. To me." Kevin's gaze dropped. "Whatever you brought to our bond completed me." A tremor ran through his body, and Tiernan held him closer. "What if I have to do without it someday?"

Shit. "You never will, *m'lanan*." He pulled Kevin onto his lap—roughly, needing to show the male he loved that he was strong, that he could keep a vow—and settled him astride his thighs. "*Lasr, s'oc as fola.*" Flame, frost, and blood. "I swear, you never will."

Chapter Eleven

This feels fucking amazing.

Terry sat back against the back of the sofa, pleasantly full, watching as Maelduin licked the last of the curry sauce off his fingers. Almost the last, he corrected himself—the golden-brown splotch on Maelduin's linen shirt was probably technically the last of it. Anyone else would have looked like a slob. Maelduin looked adorable.

This is fucking agony.

Terry tipped his head back, closed his eyes, and hoped he didn't look anything like he felt. Which was… what? Confused. Frustrated. Sad. Turned on.

Spin the wheel and win a prize, every slot's a winner.

"What are you thinking, *lán'ghrásta*?"

Terry didn't open his eyes. The last thing he needed to see was more gorgeous. More of what was just going to pass him by, walk off into the night. "I'm thinking I'd love to know what language that is. Is it Gaelic? It sounds like it."

He thought he heard a sigh. "I suppose Gaelic is close enough."

There was a tightness to Maelduin's voice.

Maybe it was irritation. That would make total sense. The stunning blond had spent most of dinner finding new ways to be impossibly perfect while making awkward small talk over curried scallops. Small talk which was going to get Maelduin nowhere, in the end, because Terry's mind was made up. Period.

Yes, he was attracted to Maelduin. He'd have to be dead not to be—for one thing, if Terry crossed his eyes just a little, Maelduin looked a whole lot like Tiernan Guaire, the landlord of Raging Art-On and Terry's new dance studio, and one of the most stunning men Terry had ever met. But really, the simple fact of his attraction to Maelduin alone was more than enough reason for Terry to show him the door. Because Terry had the world's worst taste in, and luck with, men. If he, Terry, felt anything for a guy, that feeling was surely fucked up, and enough reason by itself to call for the hook.

And attraction was all it was. Chemistry. He'd known that since he first saw Maelduin, sitting on the edge of the sample of sprung flooring Garrett had been so crazy about, stopping a nosebleed. Something had happened, deep down in Terry's gut. And other places. He knew better than to pay attention to that sort of reaction—if he let himself give in, that would mean he hadn't learned anything at all from losing Josh, or from the clusterfuck that had been Bryce.

If he hadn't learned anything, what had the point of it all been?

A hand rested lightly on his. More perfection, more of what he would be happy to acknowledge as something-more-than-just-fucking-chemistry if that weren't even crazier than the one-night stand had been.

He opened his eyes—reluctantly, because he knew what was going to happen. Sure enough, Maelduin was leaning in, no doubt to make sure everything was all right with him, and Terry felt his heart bang on his chest wall like it wanted out. Maelduin had eyes as gorgeous as the rest of him, eyes that made Terry want to do clichéd and anatomically impossible things like fall into them and drown.

Yeah. There was something in him that wanted to do that. Take a chance, throw the dice, every idiotic cliché in the book, and maybe a few he'd come up with on the spot, special for the occasion.

I can't let myself do this. Not again. Not when I know better.

"You don't want me to stay, do you?"

The question, circling back to fragments spoken and then silenced during dinner, was almost casual, yet there was sadness, almost despair, under the surface of it that left Terry short of breath. And the hand resting on Terry's was shaking.

Fuck. I don't want to be the bad guy again. It had been bad enough to do that to Josh.

But he was short on choices. No matter what some secret corner of his psyche wanted, he knew that in the real world, it came down to one of two things: he could either be the bad guy now, or the fall guy down the road.

Yet he couldn't agree with Maelduin. He couldn't make himself say the words. "How is it you don't see how totally bizarre this is? Me picking up a homeless guy and bringing him home for a night of incredibly hot sex—"

"And a morning."

Incredibly, Terry had to fight not to snicker. Maelduin did that to him, way too easily, made him smile, made him laugh. "And a morning. But... that isn't normal. Not for me. And it's not something I can let go on."

"Why not?"

Because for some reason I don't understand, probably sheer loneliness, I want to be falling in love with you. And I can't. Yeah, that would work just great. "Because—"

"You are able to fly." Maelduin gestured toward the wall of photographs, Terry's dance roles, the chronicle of his former life. "Why are you afraid to fly now?"

Terry sat, stunned, as Maelduin's words settled into him. *He sees right through me.* "I'm not afraid," he finally managed.

"Then why will you not let me stay?"

Terry shook his head, hard, feeling as if he were trying to break a spell. "Christ, it's like trying to talk with someone from another planet."

The pause that followed was long, and awkward. "Well... not exactly."

* * *

Not exactly...

Possibly the stupidest thing he had ever said. But it was the only thing he could have said.

Terry was staring, eyes wide and startled. He reminded Maelduin of a yearling fawn. No doubt he would be as graceful as one, should he choose to bolt now.

138

Should he choose? Maelduin dared not let him choose, not with so much at stake. His vengeance, his oath, his life. He had far too much to lose to pay any attention to feelings no Fae could possibly understand, much less experience.

Surely he only imagined those feelings, himself.

Yet, feelings or not, real or not, he had to convince Terry to join with him, whatever form that joining took. Their charmingly disjointed dinner conversation had, in the end, amounted to nothing more than an unsuccessful attempt on Maelduin's part to assay the *rinc-daonna*, the ancient name *as'Faein* for the dance of seduction, when it was performed by Fae and human. Useless to get Maelduin any closer to what he needed. And he would stand precious little chance of any kind of joining, ever, if Terry put him out on the paved lanes that were home to cars and trucks and buses and taxis and any number of other wheeled private hell-realms.

"I'm kind of afraid to ask you what you mean by 'not exactly,'" Terry murmured at last, his eyes slowly narrowing.

Sex had failed. Seduction had failed. What was left, other than honesty? *Macánta*, the word *as'Faein* for honesty, came from the same root as *machtar*, desperation. Fitting. "Not exactly another planet. Another..." Frantically, he searched the vocabulary the imprisoned spirits had given him. "Reality. Next to this one."

He was surprised to find himself holding his breath, waiting for Terry to speak. *If he rejects me now...*

"I think I ought to be more freaked out by that

than I am." One side of Terry's mouth turned up in what Maelduin hoped was a smile. "I brought home a *crazy* homeless guy. But at least you're the harmless kind of crazy. Right?"

Now it was Maelduin's turn to stare. "I am not crazy. And even if I were, I am as far from harmless as you can imagine." His gaze flickered to his oath-blade, on the floor beside the small table covered with take-out food cartons. "Or I was, before I came here."

"I was going to say, right now I don't think you're a threat to anything but the carpet, which you just might beat to death with your nose."

Maelduin felt the blood rushing to his face and stinging his cheeks. Yet... *as long as you allow me to stay here long enough to deliver the beating and then to join with you, it will be enough.* "It seems you don't think I'm serious."

Terry shrugged, even that simple movement graceful enough to make Maelduin's breath catch. "Of course I don't. I'd have to be even crazier than I am, to believe fairy tales."

Magick itself shrivels and dies when it touches his disbelief. Why should something which is nothing more than a story of another world reach him?

His bloodsworn blade gleamed in the human-made light. He reached for it, hefted the comfortable and comforting weight of it.

"Before you put me out... come with me, *lán'ghrásta.* Back to where you found me. I need to show you something."

* * *

"Here." Terry linked arms with Maelduin; it was awkward, because of the difference in their heights. But there was no denying the stairs were easier thus.

"Thank you." Maelduin's cheeks burned as his own helplessness was driven home to him once again; he managed a quick smile at Terry, then turned his gaze upward, to the top of the stairs and escape from the subway station. He suspected contact with Terry let him touch, temporarily, what he had lost coming through the Pattern.

I need to regain it permanently. Whatever 'it' was. His grace, his skills, his kinetic sense. Everything he needed to keep his vow, fulfill his purpose, save his life.

Holding fast to that vision had helped him survive another imprisonment in the moving room—somehow, knowing that humans called it a "subway," and barely remarked on traveling thereby unless something went wrong and delayed matters, did nothing to make the experience more palatable to a Fae.

Terry squeezed his hand; Maelduin squeezed back, but knew better than to look down at him. He had always been a quick study, and the art of seducing Terry Miller was proving to be different from what little a modern Fae knew of seducing humans in general. Let Terry's own thoughts, his natural curiosity bring him closer to the enigmatic stranger.

Maelduin hoped he could remain enigmatic for another few minutes. It was difficult to remain mysterious while tripping over one's own sword. Although he might have been somewhat less likely to trip over it had he not channeled enough magick to conceal it from sight.

Or perhaps not. Whatever had happened to him in

his transit between the worlds seemed determined to keep him from accomplishing what he had sworn to accomplish.

Terry held the door at the top of the stairs, and the two of them emerged into the crisp night.

"Which way?"

Terry tugged gently at his arm and led him to the left, sidestepping people determined to descend into the subway's depths. "You really didn't notice which way we went last time?"

"I was… preoccupied." Almost exactly as he was now, in fact; absorbed in the task of trying to make his limbs follow instructions, as his thoughts insisted on wandering to the male beside him. The warm fingers laced with his own, the strong arm trying to brace him against his own clumsiness.

I shouldn't care about warmth or strength. As long as I get what I need, the rest is irrelevant.

But it was not irrelevant.

Terry dug in his pocket and withdrew a ring of keys; sorting through them one-handed, still holding Maelduin's hand, he fitted a key into the lock and the door swung open. "Mind your step—sorry."

"No problem." That seemed to be the correct answer, given that the long-handled implement missed his nose this time when he stumbled onto it, and simply clattered off into a corner.

Even before the lights came to life, Maelduin could see the faint glow he remembered. And now he remembered why it had seemed wrong to see it there; the glow was living magick, what little a Noble could see of it, where legend said no magick could possibly be. All the tales of the Sundering were clear; the entire

142

point of the Sundering, the last desperate battle with the monster the ancient Fae had called the *Marfach,* had been to withdraw all living magick from the human world and create a barrier to isolate the monster from its food source.

Yet magick was here. And if his luck had not entirely deserted him, somewhere between the worlds, magick would help convince the beautiful human he was already beginning to think of as his, to be his in truth.

* * *

"So what did you want me to see?" Terry craned his neck to look around the unfinished space. *What am I supposed to see that wasn't here last night?* The wood and metal supports marking the lines where the walls would go... the lights clipped to them, and to the tracks where the ceiling tiles would soon go... the pile of construction debris from downstairs... the concrete rake that had tried to wreak havoc on Maelduin's face... the six-by-six square of sprung flooring...

Maelduin frowned. Even his frown was gorgeous. "Let me start with this."

Before Terry could open his mouth to ask what 'this' was, Maelduin made a pass in the air with his fingers. And suddenly there was a sword hanging from his belt, in a fabulous tooled-leather scabbard.

Now it was Terry's turn to frown. "You've had that since I found you. And I keep forgetting you have it. Or not noticing it. Even though there's no reason in the world for you—or anyone—to be carrying a sword around Washington, D.C."

Maelduin's hand rested on the hilt of the sword, as if it had always hung at his side, as if it were part of him. "No reason in your world, *lán'ghrásta.* But in mine, it is the *comart'*, the symbol, of my life. My oath."

Terry had spent most of the subway ride sheltering Maelduin from the view out the train windows and trying to figure out whether he was irritated with, fascinated by, or afraid of Maelduin's strangeness. He still hadn't quite worked it out, but at the moment he was feeling somewhat put out. "Why do I keep forgetting about it, then?"

"Most of the time, I have kept it hidden. For safekeeping."

"Hidden? How? It was right there all along."

"I know a few small, useful channelings." Maelduin caressed the sword-hilt, not seeming to notice that he did so. "This concealment is one of them."

Yeah, put out was winning. "This is your proof you're from another world? Hiding things from me?"

Maelduin blinked. "It would never have occurred to me to prove anything to you that way. Concealment… is simply what Fae do."

As soon as he had spoken, he turned an interesting shade of red. Like he'd give anything to have back the words he'd just spoken.

"Fae."

The word hung in the air between them, almost visible.

"Yes. Fae."

Lovely. I really, truly did bring a crazy man home with me. Terry wished the thought felt a little more

144

vehement. Especially since Maelduin had just basically admitted to hiding things from him. Lying. *Did I learn fucking nothing from all those years with Bryce?*

Yet Maelduin didn't look like a liar. He'd drawn himself up to full height, squared his shoulders... looking down into Terry's eyes like he was waiting for a verdict. Or maybe a firing squad. And damn, it just made him even more beautiful. Ethereal, almost.

For some reason, Terry found himself staring at Maelduin's hand, the one resting on the hilt of his sword. *That hand is real.* No doubt about that. And he could almost believe it was magical, after everything it had done to him and for him over the last 24 hours. He was jealous of a damned sword hilt, sitting there under that hand, warming to that touch.

He could almost believe. But 'almost' was a big word. Too big.

"So you're magical. But there's no such thing as magic."

Maelduin stiffened. "There is, I assure you."

Terry fought down an urge to laugh. "It's probably all tied up with love, isn't it? You'll cast a spell on me, and I'll fall madly in love with you, unable to resist your fairy wiles."

"Fae. And we call it channeling magick. Not casting spells." Maelduin's voice was almost too soft to hear. "If I knew that channeling, and if I thought it would work on you, yes, I would use it. But you resist what little magick I possess."

"Oh, for the good God's sake." Terry's eyes rolled so hard he wondered if he'd strained something.

"Maybe you should have found a more credulous mark."

A sudden wave of bitterness surprised Terry. He'd actually let himself think—last night, and again this morning—that something special was happening with the tall, hard-bodied blond. Not something he'd be able to hold on to, of course, but something it would have been sweet to remember. Now he wasn't even going to be able to deal with the memories, not without remembering what an idiot he'd let himself be. Again.

"Terry…" Maelduin laid a gentle hand on Terry's arm.

For a second, Terry imagined he felt a tingle racing up his arm, and down into his hand. "What?" *Lame.*

"Did you feel nothing last night?"

"What do you mean, nothing? You gave me an orgasm like nothing I'd ever felt before in my life." He paused, swallowed hard. *And laughter. You gave me laughter. You took care of me.* He remembered giggling into his pillow, the gentle softness of a warm wet cloth, a kiss on the back of his neck. Tenderness. "Are you going to tell me that was magic?"

"It might have been. I'm not sure."

Not sure. "If you don't know, how do you expect me to believe you?"

"It's complicated."

Terry couldn't quite keep back a snort. "No shit, Sherlock."

Maelduin seemed genuinely startled. "I forgot. This might be as hard for you as it is for me."

Every time I think I get what's going on here, I have to start over. "Hard for you? All you have to do

146

is talk me into letting you stick around for a few more days." The irritation Terry had felt only moments before was elusive now, hard to retrieve.

"And you have made it very clear that that will not be easy." A slight smile touched Maelduin's lips, but was quickly gone. "But I have more to do than that. I have to make you believe in magick."

"Good luck with that." The expression on Maelduin's face made Terry wish he'd been a little less flip. Terry's belief, or lack of it, really mattered to the guy.

To the Fae.

Right.

"Will you try something for me?"

Jesus. When Maelduin talked like that, Terry was willing to do just about anything. Except believe in magic. Or believe in magick—you could hear the 'k' in Maelduin's voice. Or believe in love. "Within reason, sure."

"Reason has little to do with our situation. But there is magick here. This is where I came into your world, and the magick lingers. If you cannot feel my slight gift, perhaps you can feel this." He gestured...

...toward the slab of sprung flooring, where Terry could still see the scuff marks from Garrett's sneakers. And what looked like bloodstains, near where Maelduin had been sitting when Terry first saw him.

And... something else? A faint glow?

I can't give in. I can't believe him. If I cave now, I'm just as stupid as I was with Josh, and with Bryce.

Maelduin's thumb stroked the back of Terry's hand, a caress somehow as intimate as a kiss. "Please. Come stand in the circle. Feel the magick, if you can."

147

Chapter Twelve

Janek O'Halloran figured he'd lost the capacity for gratitude... oh, probably the third or fourth time the parasite riding in his head had fucked him over in his quest to swing Tiernan Guaire's head around by its blood-soaked hair. But if he could have been grateful for anything anymore, he figured he'd probably be grateful the bitch couldn't feel the cold. She was in control now; the body the four of them shared perched on a frozen chunk sticking out of the giant berg, as frigid as the fucking ice, blood-red skirt swirled around her pale bare feet. She stared out over more ice—solid looking, partly covered with grayish wet snow, with a clinging fringe of a crumpled-looking kind of ice with a lot of green and blue in it. Ice that might have struck Janek as pretty if everything in his life didn't suck frozen donkey balls right now. And if the pretty shit hadn't nearly killed all of them, crumbling away under them when they were trying to claw their way up out of the freezing water.

The water. At the bottom of an ice cliff they'd clawed their way up by the bitch's pointed fingernails, surrounded by the chaos of giant blocks grinding against one another, falling into the water and coming back up like fucking breaching whales, making choking snow clouds and cracking treacherous chunks of ice off to slide back down into slushy frozen hell. Way too much fucking water.

What's so important about the ocean? The male wasn't as full of piss as he usually was, probably because he *did* feel the cold, and hadn't liked the way his balls tried to shrink up and hide behind his kidneys the last time the female had gotten tired of his bitching and forced him to be their body for a while. He was sick of not being able to jack off, too, and made fucking sure they all knew it. But he hated the water. They all did. Janek could feel it in their bones. His bones.

"If we cannot conquer our terror of it—if we cannot find some way across it—we are trapped here as securely as we were trapped in the wretched mage's toy." The female got to talk, since she was the one who controlled the vocal cords.

The male didn't seem to have an answer for that. He never did. And Janek sure as hell wouldn't have offered one even if he'd had one. He'd been laying as low as he could ever since they'd all come up hissing and roaring from the underside of the ice—he didn't want any of them getting the bright idea of forcing him out to face the Antarctic air.

Of course, if they did that, they were all going to be dead. Janek hoped that would occur to them before they decided to do anything fuckheaded.

Then we need to do something. Not just sit around till your dripping quim's frozen and stuck to an ice floe.

The female sniffed. But she also shifted where she sat. Making damn sure she *wasn't* stuck.

Even if we could get off this fucking forsaken berg, where would we go? Janek was pretty sure the male wanted to spit. Which didn't sound like a bad idea, come to think of it. Except that even if he had any spit, it would freeze before it could hit the ground. He was pretty sure it was supposed to be warmer in Antarctica when the sun was out all the time. But the weather was as fucked up as everything else.

The Antarctic coast was behind them, on the far side of a ridge of ice; every once in a while, the bitch wandered over to have a look at the land behind them. It had receded behind them for a few days, right after the ice shelf trapping all of them had broken up, and Janek for one had been fucking glad to see it go—the only nightmare worse than the one he'd been living ever since Guaire almost killed him had been the nightmare of all of his passengers fighting for control of their body and clawing their way up through grinding, tumbling ice, trying to put as much distance as they could between themselves and the liquid ice that had almost drowned them all.

They hadn't moved all that far from shore at first—back when he'd been alive, Janek might have been willing to swim for it, then, at least if his share of the body wasn't wearing iron-soled boots that were functioning mostly to hold his feet on. But then there had been a jam-up, not far from shore, and now nobody was going anywhere. Except when one berg came unstuck from another, and everything jerked and tipped and threatened to dump them all back in the fucking ocean again. Welcome to hell.

Damn, he couldn't think straight. Couldn't focus. Until the image of a headless Tiernan Guaire dropped back into what passed for his consciousness. *That* was enough to perk him right up. *Gonna hold on. However long it takes. They owe me.*

The female's head jerked up. She wasn't staring at the water any more. "We can find out."

How?

The bitch was smiling. And not the cold smile that would make a corpse deader than Janek piss himself and whimper. She was really happy about something. "We will need to spill untouched magick out onto the ice, and make it our own, and channel it back into our body. And when we regain it, it will know the way to safety. It will draw us."

Everything was quiet. Janek thought he felt the abomination stirring. *Shit.*

Once we taint it, we'll have to consume it, you know. The male was talking fast, and loud, like he'd sensed the monster himself and was trying to make sure it couldn't get a fucking word in edgewise. *It won't be good for anything else. Like keeping us alive.*

"We would have had to do that in any event. Sooner or later." The smile was getting colder. Janek was glad he hadn't needed to piss for a long time. "It will sustain us for a while. And we will know where we need to go."

DO NOT WASTE OUR ESSENCE.

Janek's balls tucked themselves up into their favorite refuge, right behind his kidneys, as the abomination weighed in.

"It will not be a waste. We will understand, at last, where we must go. And once we know that, we can begin to plan."

151

Janek had to admire the bitch, at least a little, standing up to the monster that way. He could feel her heart pounding, the sweat on her palms. What was left of his brain wasn't too rotted to let him appreciate the way two-thirds of the monster was scared to the point of runny shits by its own third part.

The gag would have been even funnier if he wasn't fucking terrified of the monster himself. He'd only caught a few glimpses of it inside the mirrored ball they'd all been trapped in, under the ice, but those were more than enough to make him wish he was blind in his remaining eye.

Long pause. ***VERY WELL.***

The male, the female, and Janek all heaved huge sighs of relief. Which beat just plain heaving, which Janek thought he might have at least tried to do if he'd had to listen for the scorpion-thing's bone-grating-on-bone voice any longer.

Then they all got still again, as the female braced her feet, shoulders'-width apart, held her hands out in front of her, palms up, and closed her eyes. "Let go of your magick," she whispered. "It must come from all of us."

Janek didn't have a fucking clue how to let go of the force that was keeping him what passed for alive. And he wasn't going to.

He wasn't given a choice. He could feel a trickle of life running out of him, being pulled out, joining thin, grudging streams from the others and pouring into the bitch's cupped hands. *At least it isn't running down my leg.* That would have been too much like what his life had been like right before his bodily systems started shutting down for good.

Red-nailed hands spread apart, and something Janek couldn't see—but even though he couldn't see it, it was beautiful, like nothing he'd seen since his zombie life began, even though it had just come out of three monsters and whatever he was—spilled out of them to splash on the ice and spread in a puddle of... well, nothing, except that he couldn't see the ice under it, so he could tell there was something there. He'd probably be able to see it for real, if one of the others was riding his senses, the way the male had done when they were all trying to break into the tattoo parlor next door to Purgatory. He could still remember the feeling like a dagger in his one remaining eyeball, when he'd let that happen. Fuck that noise.

Another few seconds, and he started wishing he couldn't see as much as he *did* see. The place where he couldn't see the ice... crawled. Oozed. Probably smelled, too, not that he could tell any more.

Then the female started talking to it, in the language the Three Faces of Evil used sometimes when they were talking to each other, and Janek went from being glad he couldn't see what was really happening to being glad he couldn't puke any more. He'd never seen snow and ice rot before, but they were doing it now. Everywhere the invisible slick spread, the snow sagged under it and went a putrid purplish-black.

And then the circle started to drop away. Like a fucking elevator. Down toward where the water waited.

Call it back! the male shouted, so loud his voice cracked.

Janek could feel the abomination digging clawed

talons into the ice. Didn't matter that it didn't have control of their body.

The female shrieked out another couple of words and dropped to her knees, reaching out toward the hole. Reaching down the hole. Which meant Janek could see into the hole. Twenty, 30 feet deep, easy. He wondered how much farther the rot had to go before it hit bottom, and whether it would let the water in when it got there.

Another shriek. This one sounded like the female *and* the male. And—*oh shit*—the monster, and Janek's throat burned with their grinding shout.

The unseen rot paused. The hole went no deeper.

Something started rising up the tunnel into the ice. Whatever it was the bitch had poured out of her hands. But it wasn't beautiful any more. Janek still couldn't see it, but he was fucking certain he didn't want it touching him.

Once again, he wasn't given a choice. The magick they'd sent out was coming home to roost, and he was nothing more than part of the perch.

And the other three sucked down the filth like an alcoholic sucking down a stolen fifth of Jim Beam. They were getting off on it. He could feel it.

Janek wanted almost nothing more than he wanted to stop feeling.

Just give me Guaire, and I'll send us all to hell along with him.

Hell was going to be a picnic.

It's working.

The male's voice in their head was thick and clotted, like the spoiled yogurt Janek had once loved to make his passengers endure. *Karma's a stone bitch sometimes.*

"Yes. Yes." The female started turning in a slow circle, one hand stretched out in front of her like she was feeling for something in a dark room. Then she stopped and stepped forward. Another step. Another. Janek thought he felt something—a string, a fishing line, wrapped around his guts and being gently tugged. He wondered what would happen if he tried to step back.

Probably something like Bryce felt when the piece of the *Marfach* in his guts had been ripped out. Karma could go fuck herself.

"This way."

Great. Now all we have to do is figure out how to walk across a thousand miles or so of ocean—

Janek's gut wrenched. The female stumbled and turned. The pull was a hell of a lot stronger now. And it was urging him—urging all of them—back toward the hole to hell.

Fuck, they're going to walk right into it. And there was no way that was going to end well.

He wasn't sure whether his will was responsible, or someone else's, but their shared body lurched and dropped to its knees, right at the smooth circular edge of the hole, staring down into it.

What the particular fuck?

The female was the first to start laughing. Then the male. The monster's laughter made Janek want to rip off his one remaining ear.

Have a look, Meat.

One of them must have loaned Janek its senses, because what had been a crawling mist at the bottom of the hole now shrouded a glowing blue-silver design, in a perfect circle at the bottom of the hole. It made

Janek think of frost, or crystal. A doily, like his Irish grandma's lace, but made of ice.

He recognized it. He'd seen that design surrounding Josh LaFontaine's tattoo parlor. And he'd caught glimpses of it since then, usually when he was being goaded through a ward. Or forced to do something else that he knew was going to hurt like a motherfucker.

"The Fae call them wellsprings." The bitch ran the tip of her tongue over her fangs. "The way to our true home is closer than we thought."

Chapter Thirteen

An outsider would have heard nothing but the whispering of leaf on leaf in a breeze, though no breeze blew; a scattering of rain on leaves, though the sky was clear. Would have seen nothing but moonlight on leaves, in a patterned circle on the leaf-covered forest floor, though the moon was a sliver past new. All this was the language of *Gille Dubh* and *darag*.

Then, perhaps, a patient watcher would have seen the figure under the tree, seated on a root, leaning against the bark, unmoving save for breathing, and the movement of his green-flecked brown eyes.

LONELY, YOU ARE.

Coinneach sighed at the gentle whisper from his *darag*, stirred the fallen leaves among its roots with his toe. *There is no use in loneliness, and the wood is different now.* Only a few of the *daragin* had awakened, when wellsprings opened at their roots, so there were few of his own kind to talk to. Humans avoided this part of what had been Alba but was now Scotland, finding it inhospitable. Even his Cradle-mother the Moon looked away, her gentle but adamant magick turned to a purpose that had nothing to do with the human world, or with her children there.

The creaking of the ancient tree was like a hand on his shoulder. *Daragin* had never understood the enjoyment the *Gille Dubh* took in the company of humans—the trees had difficulty with the concept of more than two beings, those two being any *darag* and its companion *Gille Dubh*. But, then, Coinneach had never understood how the great Grove of the *daragin* thought of itself as a single being, either.

It was a good thing indeed, that nothing depended on Coinneach's understanding for its existence.

MEMORIES ARE WITHIN, AND ARE HELD THAT THEY MAY BE LIVED.

A corner of Coinneach's mouth quirked up at his *darag*'s reminder. The Dark Men gave over most of the memories they made in the world outside their trees to the keeping of their *daragin*. And the trees, with their lack of concern for which particular moment constituted the 'present,' were fond of taking treasured moments out of their stores of memory and reliving them while their *Gille Dubh* indwelt, sharing them as vividly as if the events were happening again. Coinneach could have again and again every lover he had ever known, down to the last shudder and sigh and caress and delight.

Faintly, far off in no direction his eyes could look, Coinneach heard water splashing. And laughter. He recognized the voices by now, two human males and a water-loving *slaidar*. A magick-thief. A Fae.

He was coming to understand why the *daragin* preferred the company of their *Gille Dubh*, and their memory-hoards, to anything the outside world might offer. What had their beloved human world given them, when he and his *darag* were scarcely emerged from the all-but-death to which Cuinn an Dearmad had consigned them? *Slaidarin*. More of the magick-thieves than Coinneach had ever wanted to deal with, and certainly more than he had ever wanted to spend his nights and days listening to.

The *darag*'s laughter was a faint whisper, the brush of falling leaves against Coinneach's dark skin. **DISTANCE MAKES TOLERABLE EVEN A *SLAIDAR*?**

Let us hope the Mothers throw no more of them at our roots. One had been bad enough, and in his heart Coinneach hoped Mother Sun and Mother Moon had had nothing at all to do with their cousin Fiachra Dubhdara's appearance.

Strangely, the *darag*'s laughter stilled.

Coinneach looked up into the oak's branches, curious. *Were you... happy... to see the thief arrive?*

THIEF, YES, BUT COUSIN. KIN. A RARE THING.

True enough. Fiachra Dubhdara—Darkwood, among the humans—was dark-skinned, dark-haired, dark-eyed, at least for a *slaidar*. And his blood had confirmed what his skin suggested; before the sundering of the Fae Realm from the human world, perhaps thousands of years before, some *slaidar* female had enticed a *Gille Dubh*, and the blood from that mating had followed a capricious path, creating a line of dark Fae. *Kin, but we share nothing but a few drops of blood.*

The *darag* was silent.

Do you regret what we did to him?

REGRET? EXPLAIN.

Coinneach frowned in thought. *Do you wish that you had acted differently?*

More silence. Coinneach sighed. For the *daragin*, the past was a real thing, as real as the present. He had spent many pleasant hours, in their old life, trying to explain to the sentient oak the concept of 'might-have-been,' a past that was not the actual past. In this instance, a past in which they had not sent the newly-arrived and disoriented *slaidar* half a world away and 17 years into the past, simply to be rid of him.

WISH? The leaves overhead rustled. **WHAT IS, IS.** More leaves brushed Coinneach's skin, as the *darag* struggled to express concepts foreign to its being. **A DIFFERENT PAST ACTION TOWARD THE *SLAIDAR* WOULD CREATE A DIFFERENT PATH, TO A DIFFERENT THIS-MOMENT.** Coinneach sensed the *darag*'s satisfaction at grasping the concept of 'difference,' of alternate possibilities. **AND THIS-MOMENT, THE *SLAIDARIN* LEARN HONESTY. TRUTH.**

Only because they know the blood price they will pay, should they return to their old ways. Dubhdara had given the *darag* his blood, willingly, thinking it was only asked of him to allow the oak to determine whether the dark Fae, called *adhmacomh* by others of their own kind, were kin to the *Gille Dubh*; now, though, having taken that willingly-given blood into themselves, Coinneach and his *darag* could enter into the *slaidar*'s mind, and do there as they willed. Could, and would, if any of the *slaidarin* showed any signs of considering a betrayal like the one that had condemned *Gille Dubh* and *daragin* to thousands of years of what might as well have been death. *Can we ever trust them?*

ASK NOT FOR THE TRUTH OF A MOMENT NOT YET KNOWN BY TRUNK AND

SAP AND LEAF. The crown of the tree tossed gently in an unfelt breeze. **THE FATE OF THE** *SLAIDARIN* **IS THEIRS TO DETERMINE.**

As ours never was, Coinneach grumbled.

Another voice drifted to Coinneach's inner senses. More laughter, followed by a voice that made his *darag*'s roots curl and blacken at their most tender tips.

"The Fae call them wellsprings. The way to our true home is closer than we thought."

The *darag* whispered, a rustle of dead leaves and heart-rot and the terrible moments when Mother Moon turned away and hid the face of Mother Sun, plunging the world into a darkness that was as much despair as the absence of light. The tree folk had never given a name to the creature the Fae called *Marfach*, but they knew it for what it was, a slow and twisted death that had never paid them any attention.

Until now. Until it stood over a wellspring of the magick that gave life to the whole symbiotic race of *Gille Dubh* and *daragin*, and contemplated poisoning the well.

Quickly. The seeds of a mutual defense plan existed, among the other tree folk who had awakened. But bringing those seeds to growth would require the cooperation of all the *daragin*, all the *Gille Dubh*. And the *daragin*, at least, did nothing in haste. *Quickly!*

YES. QUICKLY.

Chapter Fourteen

I'm as crazy as he is. Terry shook his head as he stepped up onto the square of sample flooring, marked with Garrett's sneaker prints and what was probably Maelduin's blood.

But he wasn't crazy. Probably. He was just humoring a crazy person. And just because there wasn't any reason to, other than the way the fine hairs on the back of his hand still stood on end, and the way the gorgeous smile Maelduin was giving him was making him feel, didn't make him crazy.

Well, maybe the way that smile was making him feel wasn't quite sane. He was being manipulated, Maelduin had as much as admitted it. And he was letting himself get excited at the prospect.

Although… Maelduin was scared green of the Metro. That couldn't possibly have been an act. And yet he'd ridden the train to bring Terry here for this. Whatever 'this' was. *There were probably a million better ways to manipulate me. Most of which would have involved sex.*

"Do you feel it?"

For a second, Terry wasn't sure what Maelduin was talking about. He was too captivated by

Maelduin's clear blue gaze, the way his beautiful smile had faded to something more thoughtful, intent.

Jesus. I have issues.

So what?

Then he followed Maelduin's pointing finger, down toward his feet. Light pooled there, the way so many spotlights had surrounded him in the past.

Only… there were no spotlights here in this half-built shell of a dance studio.

And this light was coming from underneath the floor.

Terry's feet tingled.

"What the hell?"

* * *

All we have to do is fall forward. The male didn't seem fazed by the prospect of a 20-foot drop onto solid ice. ***We'll never even hit the bottom. We'll just fall into the wellspring and come out in the Realm.***

Where his parasite would gorge its three-headed self on all the magick the Fae Realm had to offer. And where he, Janek O'Halloran, would be of no use whatsoever and would be quickly dead. Without ever having had the satisfaction of putting a bloody end to the fucking Fae who had sent him to hell.

"Yes. It is time, and past time."

Janek could feel the other three crouching, getting ready to jump.

Fuck no.

He thought he'd figured out how much control he had over their shared body. It was time to find out if he was right.

163

Gritting what few teeth he had left, he imagined their body stepping back from the drop. **This wasn't part of our deal, asshole. Assholes.**

* * *

THIS-MOMENT. THIS-NOW.

Coinneach, incorporeal within his *darag*, had no need to cover his ears against the ancient tree's shout. Yet he did. And still he felt the echoes of that cry to the bones that only existed in his *darag*'s memory.

What he did not feel was the great shift, powered by the magick of all the *daragin, Gille Dubh*, and Mother Sun, placing the network of the wellsprings out of the monster's reach for as long as they could hold it there.

He could not feel the shift because he, like the *daragin* and the other *Gille Dubh*, were caught within it. At least, he hoped that was why he felt nothing. The other option, the possibility that the untried plan had not worked, did not bear contemplating.

* * *

The female lurched backward and fell hard on her ass on the ice.

Janek couldn't tell who was more freaked out, him or his parasite. But the bitch's steam-whistle shriek of rage gave him a pretty good idea.

The male was a lot calmer. Outwardly, anyway. *Not sure where you got the idea it was smart to dick with us, Meat.* Christ, his voice was almost as cold as the monster's.

It was a lot fucking harder to stand his ground than he'd thought it was going to be, when he didn't have control of what his body—their shared body, the only body they had now that they were out of Dary's prison—was doing, and the male's voice was enough to make his nonexistent balls shrivel to the size of raisins. But if he didn't stand up to it, them, right fucking now, he was going to lose the only thing he'd been living for, these last couple of years.

You made me a promise. Back when I was all you had. Janek didn't have a lot left to be proud of, but he was proud his voice didn't shake or catch. **Guaire's head, to pay for what he did to me. And as long as you still need my body, that deal's still on. When you don't need it any more...** He shrugged. **I don't give a shit.**

Which was a pure fucking lie. The only death he wanted almost as much as he wanted Tiernan Guaire's was his parasite's. But even a mostly brain-dead zombie was smart enough to keep that to himself.

You putrefying piece of—

"Wait."

Janek couldn't remember the last time he'd been glad to hear the bitch's voice. Probably because he never had before.

"Even before the Fae divulged the true function of the wellsprings in front of the toad-human, we knew that we could draw living magick through them." The bitch smiled. The smile felt oily. "We can restore ourself to full strength... and then, perhaps, we will be able to find a solution that will let us keep our promise to our meat wagon before we go home."

Janek knew better than to let himself hope the

bitch meant what she said. But if she could hold off the male, and the monster, for a while, he might have a chance.

The male's laugh reminded Janek of slime. ***Never thought of you as the sentimental sort. But sure, we can give that a try.*** Janek felt the male's gap-toothed grin. ***Thing is, either way, we have to touch the wellspring.***

Fuck me bloody.

Gonna trust us, Meat?

He wasn't given a choice. Their body toppled forward—

And bounced. Hard. On the suddenly glowing air, a few feet under the edge of the hole, and a good couple of stories over the pretty magick.

* * *

Maelduin dared not look anxious, or at least not as anxious as he felt. Too much depended on Terry's acceptance of what was happening to him. "Magick. The proof you wanted."

Terry was silent, watching the play of eldritch light around his feet. At least, Maelduin thought he was watching. He had no way of knowing what a human could or could not see of magick.

He waited as long as he could stand to. "What are you seeing, *lán'ghrásta?*"

Terry looked up, and his intense expression, his slight frown left Maelduin flushed and short of breath.

"Do you see the magick?"

"I'm not sure." Terry's gaze went back to the floor around his feet. "I shouldn't. I shouldn't believe

166

a word you're saying. Every time I listen to sweet talk from a guy who's too good to be true, I fuck up my entire life."

There was pain shadowing Terry's voice. Maelduin wanted to put a stop to that pain, with an intensity that surprised him. "This is not 'talk.' Sweet or otherwise." His heart pounded like a Midsummer bonfire drum. "This is magick."

"So you say." Terry leaned on the last word, drawing it out. "And you ask me to believe you."

Human. Stubborn blind beautiful human. "I ask you to believe nothing but your own eyes."

Terry looked down again. Maelduin held his breath, and was angry with himself for holding it. *Have all humans stopped believing in magick? Or only the one I need to convince of the truth of it?*

Terry traced out a slow arc on the floor with his toe. And when he looked up again, something was different. Something that made Maelduin remember how it had felt to hold this male, after sex, to feel him relax into the warmth of an embrace Maelduin had never offered to another. Something that made the Fae forget to breathe.

Maelduin wanted to be different from the others. The ones who had been too good to be true, who had made Terry wary. He wanted to deserve Terry's belief, to deserve his trust.

Would a human call this strange stirring love?

A human, perhaps, but never a Fae. And surely not a Guaire.

Was it need, then? Impossible. He needed what Terry had in his temporary custody, yes. But needing Terry, himself… no. Fae needed humans for nothing.

Even the SoulShare bond suggested in the note tucked into his boot was only a legend, and the suggestion itself might have been nothing more than a step in someone else's dance.

Fae could want, though. Any Fae could want. Even a Fae of the Cursed House.

Yes. That had to be it. His heart *wanted* Terry, in the heedless way of his entire race. Perhaps he wanted something new and unique from Terry, but that was all. No Fae was capable of more.

Terry glanced back at the floor, then met Maelduin's gaze squarely. His hesitant smile made Maelduin's heart race. And in that instant, Maelduin realized that everything he had ever believed about Fae, about his line and House, about needing, about wanting, was wrong.

Terry took a step forward. "I want to—"

Between one word and the next, Terry disappeared.

Chapter Fifteen

"What the hell?"

The floor tilted and swooped under Terry. Except that it did no such thing—his inner ear assured him he was on solid ground. The rest of his body, though, totally ignored his inner ear, because it was convinced he was on a tumbling satellite being piloted by a drunk. He dropped to his knees, bent forward until his forehead touched the floor, covered his head with his forearms, scrunched his eyes closed. Anything not to fall off the floor; anything not to have to look at the distorted nothingness that had surrounded him in the instant before he shut it out.

I've been here before. Done this before. Which was the most insane thought he'd ever had, because if he'd ever been surrounded by reality turning itself inside out in ways that made his stomach try to do the same thing, he was sure he'd have noticed. But yeah, he was having deja vu. On steroids.

"*Maelduin!*"

He was screaming into the floor, and into his knees. Nobody was going to hear him that way. Well, he'd just have to scream louder, then. Fine with him. "Maelduin! Make it fucking stop!"

* * *

"No, seriously." Josh tilted his head to one side, just enough to let Conall lean forward and read the computer monitor over his shoulder. "It's an ancient Roman recipe for tattoo ink."

Conall frowned. An Air Fae's natural gift, understanding every language carried by the air, didn't extend to written languages, and while Josh was well aware the ginger mage was a quick study, his written vocabulary was nowhere near as extensive as his verbal one. "What's vitriol?"

"Iron sulphate, I think."

"You're not seriously thinking of trying this."

Josh, grinning, decided to say nothing, and Conall shook his head. "Egyptian pine bark, well, I suppose I can see that… what's gall?"

Somehow, Josh managed a perfectly straight face. "Insect egg deposits."

"Humans are strange—"

Conall's head jerked up, his peridot eyes wide with alarm.

Josh suddenly had trouble breathing. "What is it? The nexus?"

"No. Next door, the dance studio. Someone's shouting. Yelling for Terry."

Josh had no reason to doubt his partner's acute Fae senses. He bolted for the door, upending his chair and sending it skidding across the floor of the little alcove in the lobby of Raging Art-On he used as a design studio, Conall practically stepping on his heels. He slammed through the door—the sound of it crashing against the outside wall was still echoing when he burst into the dance studio next door.

Now he could hear the voice Conall had heard from next door. "Terry! *Lán'ghrásta!*"

A man with long blond hair and what looked like a sword belted at his waist stood toward the rear of the unfinished front studio, his back to the door, silhouetted by a glowing column of translucent air traced through with feathery patterns of what could only be magick—though it didn't look like any magick Josh had ever seen, whether with Conall inside him and using his senses or any other way.

Conall pushed past Josh, but stopped short of the figure on the far side of the room. "Tiernan?" The question skidded off the upper end of Conall's vocal register, uncertain.

The man spun around, and for a second Josh thought Conall had called it. The hair was nearly right for Tiernan, maybe a shade too pale, and the light caught faceted blue topaz eyes that could only be Fae, in a face that could almost be the Noble Fae's. And the way the man's hand went to the hilt of his sword as if the blade were a part of himself, *that* was all Tiernan.

But there all resemblance to Tiernan Guaire ended. The man—the male, the Fae—glared at Conall, his eyes like chips of glacier ice. And the hand gripping the gorgeously-worked silver hilt of the sword, white-knuckled, was obviously flesh, bone, and blood, not living Stone.

"I am here to wipe that name out of memory." The voice wasn't Tiernan's, either; the accent was different, the pitch a little lower. "Let it be as forgotten as the name of my father."

* * *

171

Maelduin's instincts were at war with themselves. Unknown enemies were before him, one of them a Fae bearing a striking resemblance to descriptions of a Fae mage whose disappearance over a year ago had startled a Realm unaccustomed to that sort of startlement.

Behind him, Terry was... gone. Though Maelduin thought he could sense the male, behind the wall of light that had sprung up between them. He hoped. He would have 'prayed,' as he had seen some of the trapped spirits in the box do, if Fae had any more of gods than the memory of the ones worshipped by humans in the time before the Sundering.

As it was, Maelduin and his sword were all Terry had. But what were they—what was he—supposed to do for his human, when faced with foes friendly with the very male he was sworn to kill? A male with whom he dared not risk any contact at all, until he had back from Terry what the Pattern had stolen from him? Too late to try to Fade to Terry's aid; he dared not leave himself vulnerable even for an instant, much less the time it would take to Fade to the other side of the strange wall. If such were even possible.

"Who are you?" This was the dark-haired human, who seemed to be trying to look at Maelduin and the mage and the wellspring all at once. "What are you doing here? And where the hell is Terry?"

The high ground was his friend, and his opponent's enemy. "I could as well ask you the same, as you are the intruders here. And how is the human your concern?" A safe enough question, surely, for a human who consorted with a Fae.

Unless the human had no idea what his

172

companion was. Maelduin was suddenly dewed with cold sweat. *I cannot afford carelessness.*

The sharpness of the gaze the human brought to bear on him did nothing to make Maelduin any more comfortable. "Josh LaFontaine. And my partner, Conall Dary."

Yes. The most powerful Fae mage since the Sundering. *I may have a whole new problem.*

Josh didn't seem to notice Maelduin's sudden unease. "And Terry Miller is quite possibly my oldest friend, and my business partner. I know Fae well enough to know that you—"

Conall was making a violent shushing gesture at the human. "I think this—" His head tilted toward the column of light serving as Terry's prison. "There's a wellspring in there, Josh. There has to be."

Josh turned pale beneath his scruff of beard. "I know you... have a good reason for wanting him back."

"That is not what you meant to say." Maelduin's grip tightened on the hilt of his oath-blade.

"That's *exactly* what he meant to say." The mage suddenly seemed several inches taller, his stony expression a solemn promise of dire consequences for wrong speaking. "And it would be a very good idea for you to tell us what that reason is."

Maelduin thought about scoffing at the notion that he should reveal anything to friends of his foe. However, the expressions of the mage and the mage's consort—surely that was what Josh was, one only had to look at them to see it—made it clear that the near environs of a wellspring were a bad place for him to indulge such an impulse.

Waste no step. Yet be wary of the ground; it may shift under your feet. The only thing constant is a Dancer's heart.

He could not remember where that wise counsel had come from. Some scroll, some tome on the art of the *scian-damhsa*, the blade-dancer. But he knew it for truth. His heart was his constant, his truth. His heart had been trained on one thing, since he had been old enough to know one end of a blade from the other. His heart demanded vengeance, for the mother he had never known, for the father who had been no more to him than a tale no one would tell, for the curse his father's murderer had laid on them all.

Yet...

His heart now quietly, insistently, impossibly, demanded something else. Someone else.

Waste no step.

Be wary of the ground.

Josh and Conall were both waiting for him to speak, and there was little of patience about the way they eyed him. There could be no trusting a Fae—that, at least, went without saying. Especially not a legendary mage who had mistaken him for his father's killer, and who apparently thought of that male as a friend, or at least an ally. It could be no safer to trust a human in thrall to that Fae. He would be worse than a fool to tell either of them the truth, whether it was his revenge he sought, or aid in recovering Terry.

But while Maelduin stood here parsing the problem, the male he had been so sure only moments before he neither needed nor loved was sealed away from him, somewhere on the far side of a wall of magick. And he had no hope of regaining him without help, and the only help to be had was the help of the friends of his enemy.

An'Faei a ngaill, ta'Fhaei an tráll. The Fae who needs is a slave. No matter what was needed, and no matter the reason for the needing.

Shall I be a slave to my enemy's friends, for the sake of the beautiful dancer?

If it meant seeing Terry's smile again? And learning whether this strange yearning might be enough to bring down the wall the human had built to lock magick away?

"There is a thing in Terry's keeping that belongs to me. And... I want him back." He cleared his throat, his gaze retuning yet again to the glowing wall, behind which a figure might be moving.

Or perhaps he only saw what he wished to see, needed to see, in the play of the magickal light.

Chapter Sixteen

Terry's stomach offered the cautious opinion that it might actually be safe to look up. He gave it the space of a few ragged breaths, just in case, then lifted his forearms off the back of his head and slowly sat back on his heels.

The rocking in three dimensions had indeed stopped. If it had ever been happening to begin with. And reality had stopped trying to turn itself inside out.

Though what it had decided to do instead was a mystery. Standing in a little island of what passed for normalcy, except for the silver-blue light playing around his feet, he was surrounded by... well. If he were in a YouTube video, he'd say someone had applied a blur effect to everything outside the circle of light he'd stepped into. And somehow put up a wall between him and the blur. He wasn't quite sure why he thought there was a wall, but he was as sure as he could be.

Looking at the blur—at anything outside the circle of light centered on the flooring sample he stood on—made Terry feel dizzy. Plain old dizzy, thank God, not what he'd just been through, but it still wasn't a feeling he was used to, not after years of pirouettes and grands jetés, and it was definitely one he didn't like. *I'm not going to look any more. There's no point.*

Until he found himself looking again, trying to make sense of the weird chaotic blur all around him, where a few minutes ago there had been the shell of his studio. And a gorgeous Fae.

Fae. No doubting that now. Unless he wanted to assume he, himself, had suddenly had a psychotic break, and was imagining all the whirling insanity outside the calm eye in which he sat.

He had to get out, though. Which meant he was going to have to try to penetrate the not-quite-there barrier between his new little island of almost-normal and whatever was still out there. Slowly, carefully, he got to his feet, bracing himself, his feet shoulders'-width apart, his knees slightly bent.

Almost exactly the way Maelduin had been standing on the subway. As if he expected the whole world to go insane, around and under him.

Nothing went any crazier than it had been a few seconds ago, though, so it was time for the next step. Terry made himself look, one more time, trying to figure out where to make his attempt; he knew there was a light clipped to a drywall stud not far from the flooring sample, but every time he thought one spot of the wavering translucence was brighter than another, the brightness moved. Same for the faint shadows that might be Maelduin—except that no matter how those moved around, there always seemed to be two of them.

What. The. Fuck. Terry reached out a hand.

Something pushed it back. Hard. And it was numb, dead like a novocained jaw at the dentist.

He took a couple of quick steps back from the barrier. Too far. His back hit something, and the something hit back. He fell to his knees, hard.

Not going anywhere. Not yet.

"Maelduin, damn it, where the *fuck* are you?"

Yelling didn't change anything. The sound fell completely flat. And besides, whatever the wall was made of, it was completely soundproof. It had to be. Either that or Maelduin had been able to hear Terry from the start, shouting his name, screaming, and just wasn't answering. Wasn't coming in after him.

Had, maybe, intended this all along. Had brought him here so this could happen, whatever this was.

That particular thought grabbed Terry by the throat. And the balls. And was a whole lot worse than the world going away. He didn't believe it, didn't want to be thinking it, but that didn't stop the idea from making a horrible sort of sense.

"Tell me you didn't do this on purpose. Maelduin, please."

Terry was appalled at the way his voice shook, even when he was just talking to himself. He clenched his jaw tightly, as if to guarantee he wouldn't sound that pathetic again. Ever.

He wouldn't do this on purpose. He wouldn't.

There was no reason for that to be true, of course. People did shit to one another all the time. He'd dumped Josh for a fast talker with a practiced smile, a platinum AmEx, and the social skills of a Tasmanian devil with mange. And Bryce had, in turn, put him out on the street with nothing but a suitcase. The last seven or eight years of Terry's life had been a case study in the care and feeding of bad decisions.

178

No reason to believe in a man he'd just met, just brought home with him. Except... he could still see Maelduin's smile, feel the gentle touch on the back of his hand. And he'd just been about to entertain the possibility that there was something more than a one-night stand going on between the two of them. Had just been about to tell Maelduin that he wanted to try, wanted to believe him.

Fucking lousy timing. And fucking stupidity. The thought felt like having a wound ripped open.

He'd deal with that later, though. Dancers were good at ignoring injuries until a more convenient time. He'd danced on a broken foot, more than once. This was worse, but he'd cope.

Slowly, he eased himself out of a kneeling position and sat cross-legged on the floor, in a pool of light that maybe was there and maybe wasn't. He could feel his ass tingling. *Right. Sure it is.* The sensation was all in his head. Probably.

Merde.

The all-purpose ballet dancer's curse made him feel a little better. So did sitting. At least, sitting helped him feel more stable, which was good. But it also meant that unless he wanted to spend all his time staring at the floor, he had to look up in order to see the chaos around him. Which *wasn't* good. It made him feel like a kid again, a feeling he subconsciously associated with getting knocked down and stomped on.

I should be getting out of here. Making plans, at least. Figuring this shit out. But how do you make plans when nothing makes sense? Resting his elbows on his knees, Terry closed his eyes and ground the

179

heels of his hands into them. Nothing outside him made sense, nothing inside him made sense.

Wind. He heard wind. Leaves rustling, branches creaking. There was light against his closed eyelids, the unmistakable hue of moonlight.

Impossible.

The wind became more insistent. Except there wasn't any wind. There couldn't be any wind, not closed off inside the dance studio, where the only window was boarded over with half-inch plywood. And definitely not walled off the way he was.

Terry opened his eyes. He was staring at the floor in front of him. And at two bare, dark-skinned feet.

The wind slacked off, and Terry looked up. The feet belonged to a tall, lean, long-haired, naked... well, 'man' would have been his first guess, until he saw gorgeous deep brown eyes scattered with flecks of a green so bright it seemed to cast its own light, peering out from the thatch of black hair. So, not a man.

"Are you a Fae?"

The wind that wasn't a wind whipped into a gale, and brown-green eyes narrowed in a fury needing no words to be perfectly obvious. The clenched fists were another good sign Terry had said something very wrong.

"Okay. *Not* a Fae."

The being glared down at Terry for another few seconds, before his attention was caught by something else, and rage yielded to something that might have been satisfaction. Terry turned to see what the handsome male was looking at—Maelduin's blood, staining the ash wood floor.

This isn't going to end well.

The male knelt beside the bloodstain, covering it with the palm of his hand. And when he raised his hand, the blood was gone.

The wind rose again, with an edge, a bite. And there were words in it, or nearly so.

... understand me?

Terry blinked. *Did I really hear that?*

... not... habit... talking... myself...

"You *heard* me?"

The male winced. *Think... please...*

You can hear me that way? Because I can barely hear you.

One dark, delicate brow arched. But then the handsome not-a-Fae frowned. *Blood... not yours?*

No. Terry was determined to say nothing more; if the being despised Fae as much as it seemed he did, he wasn't likely to react well should Terry tell him he'd just consumed Fae blood.

... slaidar!

Terry heard the strange word, and 'thief,' at the same time, somehow. And damn, this time the wind was actually strong enough for him to feel against his skin. Apparently he needed to learn how to keep his thoughts to himself. In a hurry. Like, right now.

If you aren't a Fae... who are you? He'd almost thought 'what,' but that seemed a rude way to address a male as gorgeous as the one who had just magically appeared in front of him. Even if he *had* just managed to piss said gorgeous male off. Again.

... Gille Dubh... Coinneach... The male shook his head. *Your blood... not slaidar's... conversation...*

You need my blood so we can talk? Being able to talk clearly with a being who had managed to magically materialize inside his prison struck Terry as, just maybe, a very good thing. But anyone who had ever read a fairy tale—and that sure as hell seemed to be what he'd landed in the middle of—knew that giving your blood to a fairy creature was almost never a wise choice.

Honestly, though, could things get any worse for him right now?

Terry was very careful to put up every mental fence he could imagine around that thought. Tall fences built from stone and topped with barbed wire. No sense giving Gille Dubh, or Coinneach, whichever his name was, ideas.

The dark male nodded.

How are we talking now?

The warning frown started to come back—then vanished so utterly Terry wasn't sure he'd seen it to begin with... *slaidar has...* Wind and moonlight, in Terry's mind, beautiful and dangerous... *yours... connection...*

Terry shook his head. *I don't understand.*

... you must... The being held out his hand. And as Terry watched, one of his fingers changed, became a slender dark wooden blade... *help you...*

Terry swallowed hard. Given everything he'd seen lately, a being that looked like a man turning to wood wasn't all that startling. But he had other things to worry about. Other people's blood mostly didn't bother him—there had been a time when it had, but years of working as a tattoo and piercing artist had helped him get over it. His own blood, on the other hand, had a way of causing him problems.

But there was no way he was going to look away

from this. He extended his hand to the mesmerizing being and held his breath.

The cut was swift, and not too deep; Terry snatched back his hand and stuck his finger in his mouth, sucking away the sting as his blood was absorbed into the wood, and the wooden finger became flesh once again.

Better. The being's smile was very white in his dark face. *I am Coinneach. And a* slaidar*'s blood was a path to your mind because you share a soul with a* slaidar.

A magick-thief. Terry fully understood the word now.

You may be in danger. And I would save you, if I can.

Chapter Seventeen

"You *want* Terry?" The expression on the dark-haired human's face was unreadable, as was the look he directed at the slender Fae mage.

This puzzled Maelduin. He would surely have recognized hostility. And while the human—Josh—was obviously protective of Terry, he seemed as curious as he was angry.

"He's a Fae, *dar'cion.*" Maelduin was at a loss as to why anyone would call the human 'brightly-colored,' but Fae were known for their inventiveness with pillow-names. Conall was smiling, but his faceted peridot eyes were cool, intense, and noticing. "Most of us are very good at wanting. And very bad at not getting."

Maelduin felt himself reddening, stinging as if slapped. The implications of the other Fae's words were all too clear. "Terry is neither *selbh* nor *bragan.*" *Neither possession nor plaything.* Maelduin was certain of that much, at least.

Human and Fae turned to him, heads cocked to one side at an almost identical angle. "I'd ask you what exactly he *is* to you, but I think we have a problem that needs to be dealt with first." Josh's voice was soft, the kind of softness that in Maelduin's experience generally overlaid tempered steel, and betokened someone not to be taken lightly. "Namely, finding out what happened to him."

"And whether you had anything to do with his disappearance," the mage added with a false brightness that probably wasn't intended to fool anyone. Certainly not another Fae, for no Fae would take anything another Fae said at face value. "I'm not a great believer in coincidence, not where the Pattern's concerned."

"The curse of an accursed line be on the Pattern," Maelduin snarled. The flaw in the Pattern had maimed him—the note tucked in his boot was a constant reminder of something he was in no danger of forgetting. The Pattern had snatched away the vengeance for which he had lived since his earliest memories, and now, if Conall was right, it had played a part in taking from him the male who might yet make him forget that his race and his line were incapable of love. "If I could get him back—"

The mage and his human stared at Maelduin, but it was not their stares that cut off his reply. It was a memory, where none had been a moment earlier. A memory of Terry, screaming his name.

"Maelduin! Maelduin, make it fucking stop!"

Conall, suddenly pale, was the first to find his voice. "Tell me you didn't just curse the—"

He had heard the screams just before Josh had burst in, he remembered. But that was impossible, he had heard nothing, because he himself had been reacting to the appearance of the translucent wall, shouting Terry's name at the top of his own lungs.

185

And it was even more impossible that he had heard those screams and done nothing.

Yet he had heard them, because he remembered them.

"I heard him." Was that movement, behind the wall? Surely a Fae's keen senses should be able to pierce such an insubstantial barrier… yet he could see nothing. Or too much. Shadows moved, but were they part of the wall, or hints at what lay behind it?

I heard him. I must have heard him. And I did nothing.

"You heard Terry?" Josh took a few steps closer to the magickal wall, then stopped, squinting into the light, a hand shading his eyes. Maelduin glimpsed a gleaming silver chain around the human's wrist, where he would have sworn there was nothing a few seconds ago. "Just now?"

"No. Yes. I'm not sure." Maelduin's hands clenched into white-knuckled fists at his sides. "I just remembered hearing him. But what I remember is that I heard him before you came in here."

"*Maelduin, damn it, where the fuck are you?*"

Terry had shouted this just as Josh and Conall had burst through the door. Maelduin had not heard the cry then. Yet he now remembered hearing it, as clearly as he remembered the sound of the door crashing open.

"That makes no sense—"

"It might." The mage held up a hand, cutting the human off, and moving to put himself between the much larger male and the wall of magick. Protecting him? Conall's brilliant green eyes seemed to glow in the reflected light from the barrier. "It makes perfect sense if this is what I think it is."

186

"What is it?" Maelduin had no time, and less patience, for cryptic mages. "And how do you know?"

The unsettling gaze turned to him. "Why don't you convince me I owe you any kind of explanation of anything? Especially given that little bombshell you dropped a few minutes ago."

Maelduin closed his eyes and drew in a long, slow, deep breath, centering himself. *No Fae has the right to deny me what I want. Not justice for my father... and especially not my human.*

Yet... I need.

I will show them as little as possible. But I will show them what I must.

He opened his eyes. The mage looked no less suspicious, but Maelduin no longer cared. "My name is Maelduin Guaire. I came through the Pattern seeking my father's murderer. And I have reason to believe that Terry holds half of my soul."

Total silence fell.

"Oh, shit," Josh whispered.

"Tell me you didn't do this on purpose. Maelduin, please."

* * *

Fae were naturally immune to human diseases, but it hadn't taken Conall long, after his arrival in the human world, to learn that he was as prone as any human to tension headaches. And he could feel a dandy coming on. Yet another wellspring had emerged within shouting distance of the great nexus. His partner's ex-boyfriend was trapped in it, and Conall would eat someone else's shorts, since he never wore any himself, if the trap had been laid by anyone other than the incredibly touchy *daragin* and *Gille Dubh*. Whose magick he, Conall, supposedly the greatest Fae mage since the Sundering, could do precisely nothing about. And then there was the problem of Tiernan Guaire's newly-arrived long-lost nephew, who claimed a SoulShare bond with said ex, not to mention the right to blood vengeance for the crime that had originally gotten Tiernan thrown out of the Realm. All of which was sorely tempting Conall to use the kind of language it was an extremely bad idea for a Fae to use anywhere within earshot of a wellspring, where a *darag* or a *Gille Dubh* might overhear. Assuming it was still possible to hear through whatever it was the tree folk had done to the wellspring.

At least there's nothing left to go wrong.

Maelduin went pale as birch-bark. "He thinks I did this to him."

Fuck. Me.

"And did you?" Josh's voice was smooth, smoother than Conall thought he could have managed on his own. Hopefully whatever happened next wasn't going to require him to Fadewalk into Josh's body to channel magick in order to avoid a shit-storm — staying incorporeal long enough to share bodies with his *scair-anam* required a level of calm and focus he wasn't capable of at the moment, not to mention the fact that Fadewalking — or Fading, or any use of living magick whatsoever, was no longer a good idea anywhere near a wellspring.

The pain that flashed across Maelduin's perfect features was brief, and quickly gave way to a cold, considered anger. "If I were not crippled, and my blade bloodsworn, I would teach you—"

"Conall?"

Rhoann's voice interrupted Conall's instinctive channeling; Rhoann's form appeared in the corner opposite the trap holding Terry, its colors and textures and solidness filling in. *Maelduin Guaire, you are the luckiest Fae since the lightning missed the Sea Queen's lover.* "Rhoann. Over here. Stay away from the light, it's caught Terry."

"Have no fear of that." The half-Royal shapeshifter edged around the column of magickal light, hardly sparing a glance for Maelduin as he passed. Maelduin, for his part, did a decent job of not losing his composure at the sudden appearance of 6'5" of blond-crested naked dripping wet Fae. But, then, Maelduin was still preoccupied, looking cool murder at Josh. Which he, Conall, was going to have to put a stop to right fucking now.

The gift of the Demesne of Stone, House Guaire's Demesne, was invulnerability to harm from magick, and not even a mage of Conall's power could prevail against that gift. But power channeled, a whispered "*tátha,*" and a flickering gesture wrapped an unbreakable cord around the Fae swordsman, binding his arms to his sides; "*dalle*" brought sudden darkness to the clear blue eyes.

"*Magairl snáthith ar'srang!*" Maelduin took a step forward, shaking his head violently, lurched, tried to catch himself, tripped over a concrete rake, and toppled like a felled tree. The sound his head when it hit the concrete floor made Conall wince despite himself. He made himself watch, as blood pooled under the fallen Fae, until the gash in the pale forehead started to close.

Once he had proof he hadn't just inadvertently killed Tiernan's nephew, Conall checked him off his list of immediate concerns and turned back to Rhoann. The half-Royal was probably the least social of the Fae of Purgatory—which was quite an accomplishment, all things considered—which meant he undoubtedly had a very good reason for leaving his husbands behind and Fading to the neighborhood of the great nexus. "What's happened?"

Rhoann seemed fascinated by the groaning Fae on the floor—well, the Water Fae *was* a healer, albeit a specialist in magickal injury rather than physical. Conall supposed the professional interest was hard to quell; all the same, he needed a bit more of Rhoann's attention than he had at the moment, and cleared his throat.

Rhoann arched a brow. "My apologies, *draoi ríoga*. I was nearly caught, just now, in a trap like this one, around the wellspring at the bottom of the Pool."

There's more than one. Conall's breath caught hard in his chest—right about where his heart was trying to kick its way out. *If there's one at the wellspring in the nexus chamber… mac'fracun fola'the*, the magick of the *daragin* and the *Gille Dubh* and maybe even divine magick next to the great nexus…

No. There might well be a wall around the chamber's wellspring. But if its magick was as incompatible with the ley energy of the nexus as the living magick of the wellspring itself was, none of them would be standing here right now wondering about it, and neither would anyone within a couple of city blocks.

Conall hoped, anyway. Because if things were otherwise, there wasn't a whole hell of a lot he could do about it at the moment, unless he could figure out how to be in two or more places at once.

Rhoann cleared his throat, sounding uncannily like Conall.

Conall fought the urge to facepalm. He was all too aware that he looked like a human or Fae teenager—he, like all Fae, had stopped aging when he came into his birthright of magick, and the more powerful a Fae's innate magick was, the younger that Fae came into it—which meant he had to work harder than most mages to maintain an appropriate level of gravitas. "Sorry, I was distracted. Details, please. And sometime before I have to deal with our guest would be good."

"Our guest—"

"Later. Please."

Rhoann arched a brow. "As you wish. I was caught shortly after Mac and Lucien and I finished lovemaking. I used the post-coital magickal surge to shapeshift—I was in my seal form. Mac and Lucien surfaced, and I dove; I was swimming near the bottom of the Pool, when a column of light—magickal light exactly like the light behind us—appeared around the wellspring. And I was stuck, half within the column and half outside it."

"Magairl snáthith ar'srang." Conall had to admit, 'balls threaded on a wire' was an apt multi-purpose curse. So many things he needed to know, and even asking questions wasted time he couldn't be completely sure they had.

Have to start somewhere, though. "How did you

get out?" What had worked for Rhoann might, just might, work for Terry. Which would solve one problem and let him focus on the others.

Rhoann shook his head, as if he were following Conall's thoughts. "I was only able to escape with help from Mac and Lucien. I changed forms so they could take my hands and pull. But they could find no purchase, no way to brace themselves—except against the wall, and neither of them wanted to try that—and it took much longer to free me than any of us would have liked." Rhoann looked as if the memory of what had happened to him was making him uncomfortable. "And... there are no words to explain this, but... I could not see the part of my body that was trapped, but when I changed back to my Fae form, I am as sure as I may be that the part of me on the other side of the magick did *not* change."

Conall blinked rapidly. "You were half Fae, half... seal?"

"It was unpleasant."

"I'll bet."

"Though that condition did not last." As if the thought had just occurred to him, Rhoann channeled a towel and wrapped it around his waist. No doubt the thought *had* just occurred to him—Rhoann was a nudist at heart. "It took my *scair-anaim* several minutes to pull me out, and I believe the part of me within the trap changed to match the rest of me before Mac and Lucien were able to pull me all the way out. And everything of me we could see was Fae as I emerged."

Trap, yes. A trap laid by the *daragin* and the *Gille Dubh*. But why? To catch what? The tree folk had no quarrel with humans—yet Terry, the human, was unable to free himself, while Rhoann, the Fae, had managed to do so, with help. And then there was Rhoann's peculiar delay in changing forms. And trying to fit all the pieces together would probably be easier if he weren't still bristling over the threat to Josh from—

"I heard wind."

Speak of the devil.

Maelduin wasn't moving—he looked almost as if he would hug the concrete, if only his hands were free, as insurance against it somehow rising up and smacking him in the head again. "I remember hearing wind. Leaves whispering. And there was moonlight, I think."

Conall was grateful for the arm Josh slid around his shoulders. "Fasten your seatbelts," he murmured. "It's going to be a bumpy night."

"Don't you mean 'ride'?" Josh placed a light kiss on the top of Conall's head.

"If the *Gille Dubh* and the *daragin* are directly involved in this mess now, we're in enough trouble. I'm not going to misquote Bette Davis on top of it all."

Chapter Eighteen

Save me? From what? Terry blinked up at the being in front of him, trying to keep most of his thoughts to himself. Especially the probably unpopular ones about sharing a soul with Maelduin. *From this trap?*

The dark male shook his head, sending tangled hair tumbling over his shoulders. *We are caught together, for now. But we are safe here.*

The language the being used was fascinating. Terry felt as if he were standing under a tree, and was somehow able to make sense of the way the leaves whispered against each other in the wind, and the way the moonlight shone through them. Under other circumstances, he'd probably be happy to just sit, watch, listen.

Not now, though. *We're safe in a trap?* Terry was reasonably sure he sounded like an idiot. But realistically speaking—if 'realistic' was even a word that applied to anything in his life any more—he had more than enough good reasons to be confused.

This is not a trap, not exactly. The dark male looked almost as perplexed as Terry felt, which Terry found comforting, in an odd way. *More like a shield. But when one cannot come out from behind a shield, I suppose it is something like a trap.*

194

This isn't helping. Terry was getting tired of looking up at the being, so he stood, careful not to touch the wall enclosing them. *There's nothing out there I need to be shielded from.*

And even more important, there was something out there—someone—Terry had to get back to, someone he wasn't sure it was even safe to think about around his strange companion. He'd obviously been wrong about the magick. Maybe he'd been wrong about other things.

Or maybe—more likely—he hadn't. Either way, he had to get out. He had to learn the truth.

There is a... thing... against which all the wellsprings must be warded. Strange, it looked as if the being's eyes were brighter, glowing green. *We have guarded them the only way we can.*

We? I only see one of you.

The being smiled faintly. *The other* Gille Dubh. *And the* daragin, *the trees with which we share our essence.*

At least now Terry knew the being wasn't named Gille Dubh. And as for the bit about the trees, and sharing an essence... he'd decided Maelduin was crazy for a lot less, but that had been before everything went insane. Everything, including him, or so it seemed. He wasn't sure what his total capacity was for handling the bizarre, but apparently he hadn't reached it yet, so it was probably best to go with the flow, for now.

The flow, though, wasn't taking him where he needed to be. *Every answer you give me just leads to more questions. And I'm not interested in a Q-and-A— I just want to know how to get out of here. How to get through this wall.*

Dark eyebrows disappeared into tangled bangs. *There is no wall, human. And there is no getting through it.*

Terry bit back several of the choicer words his Nonna had always saved for special occasions. *No wall?* He pointed at the translucent, numbing barrier. *Even Maelduin didn't tell me to ignore what I could see with my own eyes.*

Coinneach smiled, but his expression sent a chill through Terry. *Oh, shit.*

If the *Gille Dubh* heard that thought, he didn't let on. Probably because he didn't need to. *What you call a 'wall' is simply a discontinuity between what was, and what is. You see it, you see the magick that keeps the past from the present, only because you share a* slaidar's *soul.*

If it keeps me in, and everything else out, it's a wall. Terry shrugged. *You can call it what you want to. I just want to know how to get out of here.*

It is not 'here' that you seek to escape, human. It is 'now.'

* * *

The human's blank stare pleased Coinneach. In his experience, it was always easier to get information from a confused human than from one who thought he understood what was happening to him. Other *Gille Dubh* had valued humans chiefly as lovers and companions, in the time before *Slada'mhor*, the Great Theft; Coinneach had enjoyed human males from time to time, to be sure, but his own gift, his own responsibility, had always been the protection of the twinned races, *Gille Dubh* and *darag*. A responsibility he had failed at once, and would not fail at again,

What's that supposed to mean? Terry's gaze flickered to the barrier, and back again. *Escaping now?*

Humans were not equipped to understand a *darag*'s view of time. Still, Coinneach supposed he owed Terry at least an attempt at an explanation. Humans were not *slaidarin*, after all. *The network of wellsprings has been timeslipped.*

Another one of those answers that just generates more questions. The human's chin came up, his eyes narrowed.

Terry's show of spirit was an inconvenience... yet Coinneach had to admire it. *Perhaps my* darag *could explain everything to you at once, but I cannot. Yet I will try.*

Please.

The human did not appear to be pleading. Coinneach found himself rather liking him. *My kind and I experience time much as you do. But time is a very different thing for our* daragin. *To them, time is a collection of moments, to be stored, and savored, in whatever order pleases them. 'Now' is whatever moment they choose to inhabit.*

Terry glanced around. *I don't see any* darag *here.*

The human's doubt was palpable. And remarkable, considering everything he had seen, and his close association with a *slaidar*. Perhaps there was good reason for him to doubt the Fae—and if there was, Coinneach intended to uncover that reason and bring it to light. *Patience. First root, then branch, then leaf.*

Being patient isn't high on my list of things to do right now.

Coinneach smiled. *And my* darag *calls me hasty.* He shook his head, shedding moonlight laughter. *The* daragin *have always been able to share their choice of 'now' with their indwelling* Gille Dubh. *It is a pleasant way to pass the daylight hours, when we are otherwise trapped in our trees. But now... with the help and the power of our Mother Sun, we have bound the magick of the* daragin *to the whole network of the wellsprings—the channels through which magick flows from the Realm of the* slaidar—*those wellsprings which feed* daragin *and* Gille Dubh *and those which do not.*

Terry reached out a hand toward the barrier, but pulled it back before it could make contact. *Bound it how? With these walls?*

In a way. Coinneach held back a sigh. A *darag's* lack of time-binding made speech, bound into the whisper of leaves and the gleam of moonlight and dependent on concepts such as 'past' and 'present,' awkward at times, but the ancient trees excelled at conveying complex concepts in a single whispered thought. *All the wellsprings, and all within them, exist in a different 'now' from the rest of your world.*

Terry went pale. *How different?*

Coinneach shrugged—a human mannerism, but a useful one, worth borrowing. *I am unsure—I am no* darag, *but measuring time is still foreign to my kind. But at a guess, perhaps five minutes, or a little longer. We have been moved into the past of your world.*

How do we get out? White showed all around the brown irises of Terry's eyes, eyes like a *slaidar's* save for the jewel-like faceting of a magic-thief's eyes.

Terry was handling his situation remarkably well,

all things considered. The humans of Coinneach's past experience had not been nearly as resilient. *We do not, until the* daragin *release the magick once and for all, or until it falls of its own accord. And we dare not allow that to happen.*

The chaos of the human's poorly-guarded thoughts sounded like fitful gusts of wind, the kind heralding a change in the weather. Coinneach could not make out individual thoughts, only fragments tossed on that unpredictable wind. Terry thought of traps, of fear, of wonder, of loneliness. The strangeness of the being he found himself trapped with. A driving urgency, and his *slaidar*. And doubt.

Doubt, yes. Coinneach could use doubt. *You have not told me how you came to be here.* Surely the tale had to do with the magick-thief... and surely there was something in that story he could use.

What do you care? You and I are just... I don't know, castaways. Together. Terry paced the bounds of their shared prison, breathtaking grace edged with fear.

Coinneach liked the word 'castaways.' Terry's mind showed him a sunlit isle, strange trees with feathers at their crowns, deep warm sand. *I told you I want to help you. You have fallen in with bad company, I fear, in the form of the* slaidar *who brought you here.*

Terry stopped, as if rooted, his expression still and closed. *If you think Maelduin is a bigger problem than being out of sync with the rest of the world and having no way back, I'd really love to know why.*

Coinneach carefully kept the smile in his heart from reaching his eyes or his lips. The human did not leap to the *slaidar*'s defense, but rather asked for an explanation.

The truce among the *Gille Dubh*, the daragin, and the Fae was not to Coinneach's liking. His memories of Cuinn an Dearmad's duplicity, and his own death, were too fresh for him to want or trust any kind of alliance with those who had stolen his life.

But his *darag* had promised, had bound *Gille Dubh* and *daragin*. So an end to the alliance would require evidence that the Fae had already broken the terms of the truce.

Terry could give him that evidence, and with it Coinneach could free the folk of wood and earth and root from bondage to the faithless ones, forever.

And once the comely human's eyes were opened to the *slaidar*'s enchantment and deceit, something might be done about the danger his *darag* suspected the human and the Fae posed to the barrier against the *Marfach*.

Once, long ago, yet only yesterday, the slaidar-*kin broke faith with us. They told us a convenient truth, and then took from us what they needed and left us to die. Have they done the same to you?*

Chapter Nineteen

The view from the far side of the cylinder of magickal light didn't tell Conall anything he hadn't already figured out. It did, however, let him be alone with his thoughts for a few seconds. Not that his thoughts were great company at the moment. What had happened to Terry was bad enough, thank you very much. The more-than-implicit threat to Josh had brought him closer to his own personal edge than he liked to be. And now the possibility that the *Gille Dubh* had gotten themselves directly involved with their trap, and the human caught in it? Well, that had just added several old tires to the dumpster fire that was his night.

Fuck me 'til my knees buckle.

Footsteps grated in the construction grit covering the floor, and Conall looked up. It was Josh, of course. "Sorry, *dar'cion*, just trying to work things out in my head."

"You have nothing to be sorry for, *d'orant*." Josh came around behind Conall, slipped his arms around his waist, and rested his chin on Conall's head. One of Conall's favorite ways to be held—it reminded him of being incorporeal inside Josh, which was his favorite place in two worlds to be, for all that the experience was too intense to bear for anywhere near as long as either of them might wish. "Relax, let me take care of you for a minute."

"My favorite words."

"I know."

Soft laughter, followed by a light nibble on Conall's ear, made it clear what sort of 'taking care of' Josh intended; the surge of living magick in Conall's body was almost as sweet as the arousal taking his mind off their immediate problems. He groaned—as quietly as he could—as the soft sounds made by the tip of Josh's tongue probing his ear mimicked an even more intimate penetration.

Josh's arms tightened around Conall. "Sorry there's no time for rope," he whispered. His warm breath felt almost as good as his tongue.

"That makes two of us." Conall stifled a sigh. Nothing calmed him like being bound as only his *scair-anam* was able to bind him. He had spent centuries, in the Realm, avoiding the touch of any other Fae, in constant fear of the magickal onslaught even his accidental arousal might unleash; the first time he had submitted to Josh's binding, though, the fear had vanished. Utterly. When Josh bound him, he was safe, and so was everyone and everything around him. His unFae trust in his *scair-anam* was so profound, even the living magick within him submitted to it; Josh could undo any binding Conall could channel.

"Tell me when to stop." Josh tongued Conall's earlobe into his mouth and sucked gently.

"How about never?" But even as Conall spoke, he shook his head. *No rest for the wicked.* He gestured, channeling just enough magick to create a sound-screen around the two of them. "We're on the clock. In addition to figuring out how to get Terry back, and finding out what the *Gille Dubh* and the *daragin* are playing at, we're going to have to do something about our interloper." He rested his hands on Josh's strong forearms, squeezing just hard enough to be sure *Scathacrú* was still asleep under Josh's shirt-sleeve. "If he's half the blade-dancer Tiernan is, I'd rather try to outrun a pack of Fade-hounds naked and slathered with barbecue sauce than tangle with him. And even if I were prepared to forget the way he was looking at you before I stepped in—which, I assure you, I am not, and never will be—he's sworn to kill Tiernan."

Josh stiffened. "You sure about that?"

"When a Fae says he wants to wipe someone's name out of memory, believe him. And, as a general rule, don't get between him and his target unless you're very tired of living yourself." Conall worked his shoulders, burrowing deeper into Josh's arms. "I'm guessing this is what Aine was warning us about, in the message that came back through the Pattern."

"'Guard the Guardian,' you mean."

Conall nodded. It would have been nice if the ancient Loremaster could have been a bit more forthcoming, but no use trying to put the lightning back in the cloud. "She must have known our new friend was coming through. And if she saw fit to warn us, one way or another he's definitely going to be a thorn-ball under Tiernan's scrotum."

Josh ran his hands, open-palmed, up and down Conall's arms. "Something's not right about that. About Maelduin's vendetta, I mean."

"There are a lot of things not right about it. Especially the part where he could conceivably kill the guardian of the great nexus." Conall really, really wished all their problems would go away, at least long enough for him to properly surrender to his partner's embrace.

"That wasn't quite what I meant." Conall felt a kiss stir his hair. "You've always told me the only love Fae know, Fae who aren't SoulShared, is love of family—and that familial love, to a Fae, is something most humans can't even imagine. And Maelduin is—"

"Tiernan's nephew. I know." Conall nodded, slowly, so as not to dislodge Josh's chin from the top of his head. "But the Guaires are different. Ever since I can remember, House Guaire has been known as the Cursed House, both because of what Tiernan did and what drove him to it." No need to repeat the whole sordid story, not when they both knew it. Tiernan's crime, kinslaying, was unthinkable to any Fae, but so was the crime he was avenging when he did it, his brother raping his sister. And instead of being grateful, Tiernan's sister had been the one to have him banished for what he'd done. It was obvious to any Fae that love of kin was missing from the Guaire genetic makeup.

"Do you think Maelduin knows the whole story?"

Conall blinked. "You know, he might not. Cuinn said his mother died in childbirth... so he probably wasn't raised by close kin. And whoever raised him might have decided to spare him at least some shame."

Josh's sigh sounded and felt more like a groan. "Someone's going to have to tell Tiernan what's going on."

"That would be me. Though I wish there were three of me right now."

"I'd be in heaven. But I'd never get any sleep."

"And you call me impossible." Conall smiled, surprised he didn't have to force it. But he probably shouldn't have been surprised; his *scair-anam* always knew exactly what he needed. "I hate leaving without finding a way to get Terry out of the wellspring and away from the *Gille Dubh*. And I hate leaving you and Rhoann alone with our guest, though he's not going to be going anywhere until I get back to let him out of his bindings. But I don't have any choice if I'm going to go break the news to Tiernan. *And* I can't go anywhere until I at least take a look at the nexus chamber and reassure myself that everything there isn't about to go boom."

Josh made a soft shushing noise. "Breathe, *d'orant*."

"I know," Conall grumbled. But it was hard to grumble when his partner was turning him around and trying, with a fair amount of success, to form a human cocoon around him. A cocoon he was going to have to exit much sooner than he wanted to. "Do me a favor?"

"Anything. Name it."

You would *do anything, wouldn't you?* Sometimes Conall wondered how he had endured more than three centuries without the male holding him. "Just tell me everything isn't about to hit the fan."

"I would if I could."

"Damn."

"I could, you know, kiss you again."

"That'll do."

205

* * *

The door clicked shut behind Conall, and Josh shook himself, realizing he'd been staring. No Fae Faded into or out of the nexus chamber any more, not if he had any other choice, with the wellspring there as unstable as it was, and Conall had decided he needed to satisfy himself as to how things stood there before going off to let Tiernan know about the state of affairs in Terry's studio.

Josh had felt the tension in his lover, the product of too many worries and too little he could do about any of them. And Conall wasn't the only one on edge. Terry, trapped behind a wall even Conall couldn't figure out, much less do anything about, wasn't just Maelduin Guaire's SoulShare, he was—despite Bryce, despite everything—one of Josh's oldest friends.

Not being able to do anything didn't sit well with Josh, either.

I have to do something.

And chances were, his best shot at doing something was lying on the floor on the other side of a column of subtly shifting light. Maelduin was their best chance to get Terry back. Josh was sure of it. His own link with Conall had led Conall out of a mirror-trap and back to corporeality, even before they'd completed their Sharing. If Maelduin and Terry really were SoulShares, something like that was possible. It had to be.

Josh was sure the two were *scair-anaim*. He'd seen SoulShare jealousy often enough to recognize what had happened when he suggested Maelduin might have harmed Terry. Maelduin probably hadn't been able to help his reaction, any more than Conall had been able to help his.

Yeah, it's probably not a good idea to forget that a blade-dancer wants to kill me.

Wait. Wait a minute. What exactly had Maelduin said?

"Were I not crippled, and my blade bloodsworn..."

Josh shucked off his shirt and tossed it behind a pile of stacked pieces of drywall. *Scathacrú* stirred on his wrist, *Árean* on his chest.

Maybe the lethal Fae wouldn't try to kill him—maybe he couldn't—but it wouldn't hurt to even the odds a little.

Chapter Twenty

Kevin's breath caught hard in his throat as Tiernan's hooked crystal finger loosened his heavy silk tie.

Tiernan's chuckle would have been too soft to hear, if his lips hadn't already been so close to Kevin's ear the breath of his laughter tickled the shell of it. "You need to keep breathing while you still can, *Ianan*. Else what's the point?"

"Fuck." It came out sounding more like a prayer, but that was all right. Tiernan had taught Kevin to love breath play, early on in their relationship, and by now his response when Tiernan slipped his tie up over the collar of his dress shirt and started tugging to tighten it again around his throat was pure reflex: rapid heartbeat, shallow panting breaths, and a hard-on that could have used its own zip code.

"Maybe you should lie down." Tiernan started slowly backing them up toward their bed, still tightening the improvised noose around Kevin's neck and working his body against Kevin's in a way that made Kevin pretty sure he wasn't going to make it to blackout before he came like a—

"Oh, sorry, bad time?"

Kevin didn't understand the *Faen* obscenity his

208

husband whispered. He didn't need to, though. "Yes, Conall. A very bad time." He laid a finger over Tiernan's lips; he didn't have to turn to identify the speaker, and it required no crystal ball for him to know what his husband's reaction to the mage's intrusion was likely to be. "What couldn't wait?"

"Karma. Which was not one of the human race's better inventions, can I just say."

"I don't think you can put that one on us." Kevin hoped neither of the Fae in the room noticed the chill sweeping through him at Conall's words. He didn't want to have to explain his premonition—not to a Fae mage who didn't believe in coincidence, and most definitely not to his own husband and the star of said premonition.

Tiernan's low growl was, under most circumstances, sexy enough all by itself to steal Kevin's breath. "*Draoi-ríoga*, can I interest you in a small wager? We'll see if you can bind me before I can manifest a knife and pin you to that wall behind you by your balls."

Caught between a pissed-off blade-dancer and a master mage. I'm not even going to have a chance to duck.

"Not a good idea. You're going to want to hear what I have to say, and I'm hard to understand when I'm screaming. Or so I'm told."

"Could you move your thigh?" Kevin whispered.

"What?" Tiernan tilted his head slightly to one side, eyeing Kevin with the every-time-I-think-I-understand-humans-something-like-this-happens expression Kevin knew only too well.

"I can't zip my trousers unless you move."

Kevin tried to hide his sigh of relief as Tiernan shifted his weight, but he was pretty sure his husband heard it just the same.

"I'm not really going to hurt him," Tiernan muttered.

Kevin kissed Tiernan's cheek. "See? You're growing a conscience."

"Don't push me."

Banter was better than premonitions, and probably better than whatever Conall's news was. But the red-haired mage's patience was finite. "So what is it, Conall?" Kevin's belt buckle jingled softly as he turned to stand beside his husband, facing their unexpected guest.

Conall didn't even seem to notice the dangling belt. *Houston, we have a problem.*

In fact, the mage didn't even seem to notice Kevin at all. He was staring at Tiernan, who was starting to look uncomfortable under the scrutiny.

"You have a visitor, Lord Guaire. From the Realm." Conall actually appeared to be just as uncomfortable as Tiernan.

"Bullshit. Or gryphon shit, since we're talking about the Realm." The words, the attitude, the stance were cocky as hell... yet a muscle jumped in Kevin's jaw as Tiernan's arm slid around his waist, seeking comfort. "I haven't been Lord Guaire for a century and a half. And I was exiled. No one wanted me, and no one's going to come looking for me."

Conall sighed. "No one except your nephew. Maelduin Guaire."

Only once before had Kevin seen his husband so pale—when Janek O'Halloran, as yet unburdened with his terrifying passenger, had been about to cut Kevin's throat, on the concrete floor of the storeroom of the old Purgatory. Not a moment Kevin cared to bring to the forefront of his memory.

"Maelduin... followed me here? Now?"

Conall nodded. "Apparently I don't have to tell you why."

"No. Not necessary."

Kevin looked from Tiernan to Conall, and back again. "Anyone want to take pity on the human, and tell *me* why?" *And while you're at it, explain to me why I'm asking to have my heart ripped out and handed to me?*

It was Conall who spoke, finally. "Tiernan killed Maelduin's father. And he's here to take payment for his father's life."

The arm around Kevin's waist tightened. "Which, under Fae law, he's totally entitled to seek."

"Seek?" Kevin croaked. "Not entitled to take?" The fear he had experienced in his premonition flooded him again, the paralysis, the certainty that if anything touched him, he would shatter. *I can't go on without you. Don't make me.*

Is this the SoulShare talking?

Or is it just love?

"He can try, *m'anam*." Soft lips touched Kevin's rough cheek. "But I don't have to let him succeed."

Chapter Twenty-One

Footsteps, one set, approached, where two sets had previously disappeared into a silence so perfect that it had to have been magickal. The tread was too heavy to be that of the slender mage, and the tall Fae, Rhoann, the one with a Royal's stars drawn on his skin, had not moved—soft breathing and the occasional drip of water onto concrete let Maelduin keep track of him easily enough, even over the persistent memory of leaf-rustle in a restless wind, seeming to carry words just below the level of his understanding.

A door had opened and closed, though; no doubt the mage had gone to warn Tiernan of Maelduin's presence, and Maelduin's oath. Which meant that if Maelduin failed to persuade Josh, or Rhoann, to release him in short order, he was going to be dead as soon as his uncle found him, even before he had a chance to attempt to raise his sword. 'Mercy' was a concept Fae had had to borrow from humans, after all.

But leaving the task of freeing Terry to strangers was worse than the prospect of dying without fulfilling his oath. And losing his chance to discover whether his strange new emotions were things Terry might want, welcome, let down his walls to receive… that was an even deeper wound.

Never again to wake with an arm around him, a body curved around his...

Enough. Maelduin had not become a *sciandamhsa* by surrendering. Now was not the time to begin.

"Josh."

The footsteps stopped. "Yes?"

Rhoann moved closer, bare feet whispering against concrete.

Blind, bound, and flanked by probable enemies. Maelduin allowed himself an inward shrug, nothing the others could see. He had faced worse odds, with far less at stake.

"Bind me or blind me, but you hardly need both. I'm in no position to do you harm." One step at a time. And let them think he was only pretending to be helpless as a ruse. Maybe they would fail to notice that he was telling the truth.

"True. But you've threatened quite a bit more than harm to someone we can't let you touch. Not to mention the bloody-minded murder you were looking at me a few minutes ago."

Damn. "I am no basilisk, to kill with my eyes alone."

No answer, except a gust of wind in Maelduin's memory. The sound made his heart race and his breathing quicken, with a fear not his own.

Except that it *was* his own. A human was frightened, and he shared the fear.

We are bound. Even if he somehow refused my magick. Something else binds us.

"Please." The word should have caught in Maelduin's throat—would have, if he were asking on his own behalf—but it came almost easily. "I am of no use to Terry this way."

This silence was different, somehow. "Do you think you're Terry's SoulShare?" Josh asked at last.

Admitting ignorance let one's opponent know he held an advantage—the equivalent of ceding the high ground. However, the high ground was something Maelduin had left behind some time ago. Right around the time his head hit the floor. And every bit of knowledge gained was progress toward freeing Terry, even if it was impossible for a member of the Cursed House to be a proper *scair-anam*. "You may know more of SoulSharing than I do. I know only ancient legends, and a hint that came through the Pattern with me."

"What kind of hint?"

"A note. Telling me I had to find my human SoulShare, and regain what I had lost. What the Pattern took from me."

"Hm. Aine must have tried to warn you, I can't think of any of the other Loremasters who would have." Josh shifted his weight. "What *did* the Pattern take from you?"

"Josh." An odd urgency shadowed Rhoann's soft voice.

"Don't worry, Rhoann, it's all right—"

The flutter of wings, both feathered and not, cut Josh off—followed by a hiss and the unmistakable, if faint, scent of dragonfire.

Maelduin held his breath so as not to sneeze. "Your definition of 'all right' is one with which I am unfamiliar."

Josh laughed. Maelduin liked the sound, large and

warm; it revealed the one who laughed, instead of masking him as Fae laughter would. And then fingertips brushed Maelduin's temple, and he could see.

The first thing he saw was a miniature golden dragon, diving straight for his face. He cursed and rolled away, waiting for another hiss and the scent of burned hair, or worse.

"*Scathacrú!*" Josh spoke sharply. "High perch. Now."

Maelduin dared a quick look back over his shoulder; the dragon was in the process of wrapping its tail around one of the slender metal supports standing in ranks around the room. Once it was settled to its liking, it glared down at Maelduin, opened its jaws wide, and emitted a tiny flame. Purely to establish that it could, Maelduin was certain.

Josh shook his head. "I swear the attitude wasn't part of the inking."

"I have no idea what you are talking about." Admitting ignorance was going to become a habit, at this rate. As was not registering astonishment; Josh had been wearing a shirt when Maelduin lost his sight, but had shed it at some point, revealing a chest and arms covered with brilliantly-colored designs. *Dar'cion* indeed.

"I think an explanation would take longer than we have—*Árean*, dammit!" Josh ducked—and now Maelduin was beginning to doubt his sanity, because a *savac-duí*, a black-headed hawk, had just narrowly missed tangling its talons in Josh's hair and was now bating to land on Rhoann's shoulder and glare down as if he, Maelduin, were a lure and it was trying to decide if he was small enough to carry off or needed to be eaten on the spot.

Rhoann flexed his shoulder, wincing, until the bird calmed. "Are you sure it was wise to take off your shirt?"

"It seemed like a good idea at the time." Josh shrugged.

Keeping the bird, the dragon, the Fae and the human all in view was challenging, but Maelduin could just manage it if he laid flat on his back. "Are you sure there is no time for an explanation? Because I would very much like to know how a bird native to the Realm, and for that matter a dragonet, came to a world that knows nothing of magick." And, perhaps, what either creature had to do with Josh's shirt.

Josh tilted his head, looking rather like a hunting bird himself. "You really remind me of your uncle."

Maelduin's cheeks stung, burned. "Not a welcome comparison."

"Sorry." The human, too, flushed. "But he's the only other blade-dancer I know. And I've seen him when his SoulShare's in danger—it doesn't matter what the odds are, how great the danger is, nothing gets to him. He watches, he waits, he studies, and when he moves, nothing stops him."

"His SoulShare?" Maelduin tried not to gape. "Impossible."

Dark brows drew together. "A friendly suggestion—don't say that within earshot of Tiernan. I'm still working on understanding Fae humor, but I do know that's not the kind of joke he finds funny."

"I am not joking." Tiernan Guaire was a kinslayer, the source of the curse on the Cursed

House—which was itself not so much a curse as a simple recognition of the grim truth carried by Guaire blood, the inability to love. If *scair-anaim* loved, as it surely seemed they did, no Guaire could be a *scair-anam*. Simple logic.

Impossible.

And yet I want Terry to let me in… I need…

If his line could love…

"You really believe you can't love. That you can't be a SoulShare. That you can't be *Terry's* SoulShare."

The only truthful and complete answer stuck in Maelduin's throat and refused to come out. "Do you understand what it means to a Fae, to be a kinslayer?"

"As much as a human can. It's a taboo. Tiernan was exiled for breaking it."

Maelduin couldn't resist arching a brow. "I suppose you might call it a taboo. Most Fae would call it impossible, the murder of blood kin."

"Yet you're sworn to do the same thing. Aren't you?"

The corner of Maelduin's mouth twitched, all the outward sign of annoyance he would allow himself. "I am of his House and line, and under the same curse."

Josh's expression was much like that of a large and interested cat crouched in front of a mouse-hole. "But if Tiernan can love—which he does—then he's *not* cursed." The human crossed his arms, one beautifully patterned, the other not, setting a chain of what looked like truesilver jingling on his wrist. "And if you're cursed through him, then you're not cursed either."

Maelduin's mouth opened. Nothing came out.

Josh seemed not to notice. "You owe it to Terry to at least consider the possibility that you might be *scair-anaim*. Even an incomplete SoulShare bond ought to be enough for you to connect with him, help get him back—it was enough for me and Conall, before we had a chance to finish Sharing."

Reality was beginning to bear a striking resemblance to some of Maelduin's more chaotic dreams. "You think our bond is incomplete?"

"Just guessing, but yes. You said you 'thought' you and Terry might share a soul. If you were fully Shared, believe me, you'd know."

The truth of Josh's words echoed in an abruptly hollow place in Maelduin's chest, He didn't need to close his eyes to summon up the memory of his failure; in a way, he had never stopped seeing his magick withering, blackening, falling away from Terry's refusal to accept it.

He had thought it was a failure of his magick.

Maybe it had been a failure of love.

He would not fail twice.

No doubt he looked like a netted fish as he rolled and lurched to his knees; his flailing startled the hawk into flight and earned another hiss from the insolent dragonet. No matter. "I can do nothing for Terry like this. You broke the channeling that blinded me. Can you release me?"

The only sound in the empty, skeletal space was the faint hiss of the dragonet's regenerating fire. No one else could hear the whisper of the wind, the creaking of branches in Maelduin's memory.

Josh sighed. "Conall is probably going to kick my ass for this."

"I will help," Rhoann put in.

"Who? Me, or him?"

Not waiting for an answer, Josh rested his hand briefly on Maelduin's shoulder, until the magickal constriction gave way, then extended this hand to Maelduin, palm up.

Why does he feel the need to tell me he is unarmed? Maelduin covered his momentary confusion by flexing his arms, testing the movement in his fingers.

"Need a hand up?"

Oh. He wants to help me. "Brace yourself. I am… clumsier than I am used to being."

Getting to his feet actually went better than Maelduin had any right to hope—neither he nor the human ended up back on the floor, and the sword hanging from his belt tangled in no legs and tripped no one. Still, he staggered, and it took him a moment to steady himself and shake off vertigo.

"Josh. Maelduin."

Rhoann inclined his head toward the far corner of the unfinished space, as far from the column of light as it was possible to get. Two figures were taking form, color and solidity filling into ghostly images; one slight and red-haired, the other tall, with long blond hair.

Maelduin's sword, though undrawn, was like a living thing in his hand, an extension of himself. Even with his grace in Terry's keeping, it could not be otherwise.

I cannot die. Not yet.

Chapter Twenty-Two

There was no sense in pacing, Terry decided, not when confined in a six-by-six space with a handsome naked man—or close enough—and surrounded by a barrier it seemed like a very good idea not to touch. Which was unfortunate, because as much as he normally loved to be on stage, at the moment Terry wanted nothing so much as to be alone with his thoughts, or at least not to feel quite so stared at.

I don't know what you're talking about, he offered at last. *Maelduin hasn't taken anything from me. Hell, he didn't even ask me for a bed for the night.*

Did he not? One straight black brow quirked up. *That would be most unusual behavior, for a* slaidar *confronted with a handsome human male.*

No, he… Terry frowned. Now that he thought about it, he couldn't remember exactly what Maelduin had said to him in the beginning. *I don't know what he said. I couldn't understand him.*

There is a Fae magick that lets them understand those words that are spoken in their presence, and use them again. Coinneach shrugged. *He did not need to speak. If a Fae wants something from you, he will have it, words or no.*

Terry's nails dug into his palms as his fists clenched. He didn't believe what the *Gille Dubh* was hinting. Or didn't want to believe him. He just wasn't sure why. And until he *was* sure, he needed to watch his thoughts. Coinneach had probably never heard of *Miranda* warnings, and it was a cinch he wasn't going to give Terry any. So, find something else to 'talk' about. *Is that how you're understanding me? And I'm understanding you?*

Slaidar *magick?* The *Gille Dubh* laughed, moonlight and a chill wind. *No. Your blood, shared with me, lets us understand one another.*

But I could understand you before you took my blood. A little, anyway.

Coinneach's eyes half-closed; Terry could almost feel his narrowed gaze on his skin, like a physical touch. *Yes. Your* slaidar *left his blood on this piece of wood, and that was enough.*

His blood let you read my thoughts? Terry hoped he didn't sound as confused as he felt.

The wind went still; when it resumed, it was the faintest of breezes, barely enough to stir the leaves Terry couldn't see. *He has not yet told you what you are to one another. Even that, he has kept from you.*

Damn, it would be wonderful if I could just stop thinking. Terry ground the heels of his hands against his closed eyelids, until the darkness started to sparkle. *Look, is there some way you can give me a little privacy, at least in my own head?*

It took a few seconds for the *Gille Dubh* to reply. *It is not as simple a thing to do as you might think. But I will try to ignore anything you do not direct at me.* The green of Coinneach's eyes was suddenly more intense. *You will need to trust me. More than you trust your* slaidar.

My Fae. The *Gille Dubh*'s insistence on what it obviously considered an insult was beginning to grate on Terry. Still, under the circumstances, keeping his temper was probably a good idea; instead of turning away, he closed his eyes.

He thinks—he assumes—I don't trust Maelduin. The temptation to crack open an eyelid, see if Coinneach was reacting to his thoughts, was almost too much. But if he gave in to that temptation, he had a feeling the *Gille Dubh* would consider his point proven.

And that would be bad. Terry wasn't sure why, but he knew. He had to keep Coinneach from concluding that he didn't trust Maelduin.

Unless he ultimately decided he didn't. But fuck if he was going to let anyone push him to a conclusion he wasn't ready to come to on his own.

Terry cleared his throat. *What did you mean, when you said Maelduin hadn't told me what we are to one another?*

If he had told you, you would not need to be asking me that question.

Obviously. He shrugged. *But if you can't answer it, just say so.*

Terry thought the sigh he heard was an actual sigh, not the wind-language. *A* slaidar *pays a price to cross from their Realm to yours. Half his soul is torn from him, and reborn in a human. In order to regain what he lost, he has to find the human who received it.*

The temptation to shut down—just for a minute, just to process—was strong. Terry resisted. *And you think I'm his human.*

222

They call their humans SoulShares. Yes.
You think I have half his soul.
Yes.
And you think he's lying to me.
A nod. *Yes.*

Being—or even seeming—rude to a supernatural being with whom one was trapped in a space that was feeling smaller by the second was probably not a good idea. However, Terry really needed space at the moment. *Excuse me.*

The best he could do was turn around, which left him staring at the shifting, whirling, glowing distortion that was apparently the border between now and five minutes ago. Not exactly calming, but it would do. It had to.

I only found Maelduin yesterday. Hard to believe—not so much that he'd brought an attractive man home with him, but that he'd felt a connection, right off the bat. He'd rejected it, of course, but—

Wait a minute. Why 'of course'?

Because Bryce. Because Josh. Because he made bad choices. Because he sucked at love.

Last night, he'd fallen asleep with a stranger's arm snugged up around him, a stranger's body spooning his. A stranger's lips brushing the back of his neck. He'd fallen asleep smiling.

He'd awakened wrapped around that same stranger.

And yet tonight he'd resolved to put that stranger... his maybe soulmate... out on the street.

Am I really going to let Bryce Newhouse, and the ghost of a dead relationship with Josh, order me around? Tell me I can't even try with Maelduin?

223

It wasn't just Bryce and Josh who were trying to weigh in, either. Terry could practically feel Coinneach's uncanny gaze boring into the back of his head, turning him against his Fae SoulShare. Or trying to. Reminding him of every bad choice he'd ever made, and telling him that Maelduin was nothing more than the latest entry in his personal hit parade.

Coinneach might be right. He certainly had the numbers on his side.

But… last night. If only Terry could let himself believe—for once—in the warmth of those arms. If he could somehow imagine himself in a relationship that had a fucking chance.

Jesus. When was the last time I really listened to the way I talk to myself?

The story he told himself, about himself, hurt. Soul-deep. But it was at least familiar. It made sense.

I'd rather be right than take a chance on being happy.

When had he decided to live like that?

He hadn't. He'd never made that decision. He'd simply let one acceptance of 'the way things were,' one way of coping with a hurt, slide into another, until the acceptance had become his reality.

Maelduin offered him magick, maybe more.

If he could take the chance. If it wasn't already too late. If Coinneach was wrong.

Terry turned on his heel to face Coinneach. *Why should I believe you, more than I believe Maelduin?*

Terry could hear Coinneach's breath catch. *Because… I have known* slaidarin *for thousands of your years. You have not.*

Something wasn't making sense. Actually,

nothing was making sense, but one inconsistency was jumping up and down and begging for Terry's attention at the moment. *You think I have half Maelduin's soul, you just told me that we're already connected somehow right down to our blood, but you're also trying to convince me he brought me here to betray me and cut us off from one another.*

We… The wind died to nothing; Coinneach stared at the floor, arms crossed.

Why do you want me to tell you Maelduin's lying to me?

An actual wind blew up from the floor, a wind carrying words. Words not directed at Terry.

RELENT. THE *SLAIDARIN* ARE NOT WHAT THEY WERE. THE TRUCE HOLDS. AND WE NEED THE HUMAN'S WILLING AID.

* * *

So what do we do next?

Nobody answered the male, which was okay with Janek. His ear was still ringing from the bitch's shrieking after they'd all hit the whatever the fuck it was, so he had problems hearing her speak when she tried, and nobody with half a brain—or, like him, a little less—wanted to hear anything the abomination had to say. He was sure no one was expecting *him* to answer, and even if someone was, he knew better than to open his mouth when the male was in the kind of mood he was in. Especially when Janek was the one who had put him there.

Janek could still think, though, in his own way. And he was thinking harder and faster than he'd thought since… probably since some time before he'd thought it was a good idea to try to shake down Kevin Almstead at knifepoint in front of his Fae fuckbuddy.

Whatever had been pulling their shared body toward the bottom of the pit had stopped pulling as soon as the shield went up. Like someone had been playing their body the way a fisherman played one of those big-ass tuna. Or a shark. Janek preferred the shark. And then someone else had cut the line.

Janek could still feel the first connection the bitch had made, though. It felt different—he wasn't sure how he knew, but he could tell that the other end of that connection was one hell of a long way away. Probably in D.C., though they had enough of a connection with New York or Cape Fear to make them possible, too.

None of which did any of them the slightest fucking good, sitting here freezing their shared ass to an iceberg in Antarctica.

"If you are interested in an actual conversation, instead of a shouting match, I might have an idea." The female's voice was even colder than the ice, which was pretty fucking funny considering she'd been the one doing most of the screaming.

Oh, by all means, do share. The male's voice was as sour as old vomit. Janek was pretty sure he could still remember what old vomit had tasted like.

"We have to—"

The female shrieked as the iceberg rocked under them. It had done that a couple of times since the rotten magick tunneled a hole into the ice. It freaked the female out every time it happened, but Janek thought she was screaming less. Lucky for her—he'd been ready to try to rip her throat out and fuck the consequences.

We have to grow a pair. Janek could feel the male urging the bitch's hand down, to scratch balls she didn't have. *Keep talking.*

"Vile." Their body shuddered, and the female kept her arms wrapped even more tightly around herself.

This was new. The shuddering was new. However much the three-faced parasite had bitched before, it had been obvious as hell that they got off on one another's disgusting quirks. Janek tried not to seem too interested in the change. But hell, yes, he was interested—if the monster riding him was starting to come apart at the seams, that could be very good for him. Or very bad, depending on when everything fell apart.

"We have to Fade."

Fuck no! Janek blurted.

Bad idea. He could feel all three of the monster's faces turning to look at him.

Seems like a decent idea to me, Meat. The only thing guaranteed to shrivel Janek's balls more than the male being pissed was the male being too fucking reasonable. *We have to get off this chunk of ice before it dumps us into the ocean*—Janek could feel the male choke at the thought of all that water, but it didn't slow him down much—*and I don't notice a whole lot of raw material around here to build a raft with*.

Raw material. Right. Janek would have nodded, but the bitch was keeping tight control of their body. *I'm your raw material. Your meat.* He was proud of not gagging on the word. *Your meat is human. Fading me again will kill me, you said so yourself the last time*

227

you did it to me. And if you kill me, you kill all of us. Which wouldn't be a bad endgame, actually, except for the detail of him not getting to off Guaire if shit went down that way, which was all he'd been staying alive for, the last couple of years.

"Perhaps. And perhaps not. But your delay cost us the only other choice we had." The female was back to smug. Shit.

Whatever this is, it's magick, right? Maybe you can eat it. He sure as hell didn't want the monster any stronger than it was, but if it could get rid of the weird glowing cap over the hole in the ice, then Janek could get back to the happy place where the only thing he had to worry about was whether it would keep its promise to do nothing but feed from the fucking wellspring.

Don't be even more of an—

"Wait." The bitch raised a red-nailed hand. "Meat may be right."

Brain death would seem to be contagious. Janek could feel the male trying to sneer. ***This isn't any kind of magick we've ever seen before***.

"Then how do you know it cannot sustain us?" The female's lips curled back from her teeth. "Are you so eager to risk our life?"

You call this—
ENOUGH.

Everyone, Janek included, stopped moving, stopped breathing, stopped thinking, when the abomination uncurled from whatever part of their shared brain it was curled up in. For Janek at least, the not thinking part wasn't hard.

WE WILL ATTEMPT TO USE THE NEW MAGICK.

The sound of the scorpion-thing's bone-grating voice made Janek want to clamp his hands over his ears. Ear. Or hit himself in the head till he passed out.

AND IF WE CANNOT USE IT, WE WILL TAKE OUR CHANCES WITH THE MEAT.

Shit.

The female knelt beside the hole in the ice. The cap was a few inches below the level of the ice. Janek didn't want to look at the magick—their body's eyes were the female's, but he was seeing with his own senses, somehow, the way he always did. And either there was something seriously fucked up about his eyesight, or humans weren't supposed to be able to see whatever this was, and he'd just been sharing head space for so long with a monster that his brain didn't realize it and kept trying to fill in the blanks. Either way, it made his eye hurt.

Janek didn't think the bitch really wanted to touch the stuff, even though she'd been the first to agree with him. But she reached out and rested a palm on the shiny surface. He could feel the skin prickling. She started talking to it, in their foul language, the way she had before they'd sucked down the tainted magick that had gotten them into this mess. Janek could hear the male's voice, too, and even the monster's.

Fuck, I'm going to hurl—

Blinding light exploded inside their head as they were hurled back from the edge of the hole.

Janek had time for one thought before the light went out.

If I'm not the first one to wake up, I'm never going to wake up again.

* * *

What do you need my help for? And what truce? And—who are you? Terry glared at the floor.

Coinneach's toes rooted briefly in the magick-imbued wood on which he stood. He drew scant comfort from the contact, but it was better than nothing. *The voice is that of my* darag. *My tree.*

Your tree talks. The human did not seem skeptical, merely resigned to one more strangeness in what undoubtedly seemed like a never-ending list of strangenesses.

ONLY WHEN NECESSARY. The *darag* seemed amused, in its slow way, if only for a moment. **MY INDWELLER MUST PUT SUSPICIONS ASIDE. WE FACE A DANGER GREATER THAN THE *SLAIDARIN*.**

Suspicions? Terry arched a brow at him.

Coinneach stifled a groan. *Daragin* had a tendency to assume that other beings sorted reality the way they themselves did, setting aside the dull and unimportant to deal with the most vivid and urgent matters. Humans, in Coinneach's experience, did no such thing. And a human with a Fae soul was likely to be stubborn and contrary enough to refuse to move on until he had the answers to which he felt entitled. *Was* entitled, he admitted grudgingly.

Merely because the human deserved an explanation, though, did not mean there was time for a lengthy one. Especially not if his *darag* thought there was a danger urgent enough to interrupt. *The* slaidarin *deceived the* daragin *and the* Gille Dubh—*they stole the magick that kept us alive. Now the magick is returning, and the* slaidarin *have come to us for help against a common enemy. We are aiding them, but on condition that they prove to us that we need not fear being deceived again.*

The human's face was as unreadable as bark. *There are more like Maelduin, then. And you suspect they're lying to you.*

Lying is as natural to them as—

You want me to tell you that Maelduin—my soulmate, my SoulShare—is a liar. Magick-light reflected and flared in Terry's eyes.

I wanted, yes. Coinneach could feel roots straining to escape his toes again, to become one with the small square of wood on which he stood. It would be even better, more calming, to feel the wood of his *darag* closing around him, but that comfort was not to be his, not yet. *To protect my kind from—*

THIS MOMENT IS NOT FOR FEAR OF THE *SLAIDARIN*.

Coinneach's mouth dropped open. His *darag* had never been so sharp with him before, not in all the centuries of their shared existence. But, then, he had never opposed it in anything, would never have considered it possible to do so. And opposition to his *darag* left him feeling hollow, as if he had damaged a part of himself. *I am… sorry.*

The air was filled with the sound of a great tree bending, or bowing. The sense of hollowness eased, leaving behind only a memory of itself. And a human who looked as if he were trying very hard not to say, or think, something.

THIS MOMENT IS FOR DECIDING, AND FOR ACTION, LEST THE TIMESLIP FAIL AND

THE ENEMY TAKE THE WELLSPRING IT CREATED.

Terry frowned. *The enemy? What is this shield of yours protecting us from?*

Coinneach winced. If whatever urgent thing had just happened left no time to indulge the ancient enmity between the Fae and the folk of the wood, surely there was no time to explain the *Marfach* and the threat it posed to two worlds.

SEE. UNDERSTAND.

A familiar vertigo swept through Coinneach, token of his *darag*'s sharing of a past-moment; when the disorientation passed, the sharing opened into a shady, sheltered horror, a pitched battle between a great many *slaidarin*, humans, and the roaring half-faced monstrosity that was the mostly-human guise of the *Marfach*. Coinneach thought he recognized the human Bryce, lying in a pool of blood, pale and unmoving, save for one hand which gripped the *Marfach*'s foot like white-knuckled death, drawing foul and tainted magick from it—living magick, tortured and defiled.

I did not see this when it happened. The Dark Men were no strangers to death—Coinneach himself had witnessed hunting accidents, murders, even a sacrifice or two—but the scene before him left him shaken.

I CHOSE NOT TO SHOW YOU. THOSE MOMENTS, AND OTHERS.

"Jesus fucking Christ, make it *stop!*"

The sharing dissipated, allowing Coinneach to see Terry, on his knees, doubled over, his arms crossed over his midsection. Coinneach knelt beside him, hesitantly wrapping an arm around his shoulders. *Shhh... it has ended. You are safe.* The blood-gift translated the spoken word less readily than pure thought, but it took no gift to let him understand the human's distress. The *darag*, too, understood, and was whispering, wordlessly soothing.

Terry did not seem to hear either of them. *What was... Jesus, that was Bryce. And his boyfriend. Lasair. And Josh, fuck, what was he doing? And Garrett...* Perhaps the silence of thought-speech was a comfort, after the creature's feral bellowing in shared memory.

Coinneach was unaccustomed to being gentle, but he tried. *I suspect you already know most of the* slaidarin *of Purgatory, and their humans.*

Terry's head came up at this. *Everyone I saw was either a Fae or one of their...?*

All but the creature they fought. The Marfach *is the special enemy of the* slaidarin.

IT HATES, DEVOURS, ALL THAT IS GOOD. The *darag*'s voice was the creaking and straining of wood near breaking. **ALL THAT IS LIGHT, AS WELL AS THE PEACE, THE SHELTER OF THE DARKNESS.**

Coinneach's chest hurt. He remembered the last days before the Sundering, and his *darag*'s calm insistence that the evil embodied in the *Marfach* could never touch the folk of the wood. It had been wrong. The monster defiled everything it touched. His *darag* would carry the wounds of the horror he had just witnessed—and more, it had said so—for the rest of their unending shared life.

And Cuinn had tried to warn them. Cuinn the *slaidar-mhor*, the great thief, had tried to spare them.

They had refused to listen.

Even at the end, he had given them one last chance, at a time when chances must have been few and desperate.

What's happened? Terry stared at the floor, as if he could see the *darag* through the silver-blue spark-dancing web of the wellspring.

IT HAS TRIED THE BARRIER. OUR MAGICK HOLDS. FOR THIS MOMENT.

Chapter Twenty-Three

Kevin stared grimly at the road, not really seeing it. No more than he was seeing the bone-whiteness of his knuckles where he gripped the steering wheel, anyway. All he could see was the scene he was trying not to play out in his head, the one where his husband Faded calmly into a room with a swordsman as good as he was himself, sworn to kill him.

A light turned red in front of him; Kevin slammed on his brakes and pounded the steering wheel with a closed fist. *Fuck. You promised you'd give me time to get there.* He'd left Conall and Tiernan behind; both Fae had turned green at the thought of accompanying him in the Mercedes, but had agreed to give Kevin a head start before Fading to confront Tiernan's nephew. Enough time to let Kevin try to stop the waking nightmare he still hadn't told anyone about.

Kevin was as sure as he could be that Tiernan wasn't going to be able to wait that long.

* * *

That thing is going to get through if this wall comes down? Terry sat back on his heels; he couldn't stop shivering, not after what he'd just seen, even hugging himself didn't help. But he looked Coinneach straight in his uncanny eyes—the *Gille Dubh* wasn't the one speaking, but he had to look somewhere, and the floor wasn't going to look back at him. *It's going to get into the wellsprings?*

YES.

Will it? Come down, I mean? He almost asked if the monster he'd seen could move from one wellspring to another. But asking questions he didn't want the answers to was a habit he'd broken a long time ago.

IT... MAY. Terry had a feeling the *darag* was uncomfortable with words of uncertainty. Maybe even with the whole concept—he could see how a tree might have problems with things that weren't solid or definite. **SOME CHOICES BRANCH INTO THAT MOMENT. SOME DO NOT.**

Coinneach looked down at his feet; Terry followed the direction of his gaze, and was startled to see the *Gille Dubh*'s toes rooted in the wood of the floor. He was mildly surprised that anything still startled him.

What has happened to the timeslip, m'darag? Coinneach's voice was softer than the *darag*'s, and quicker; moonlight glinted through the leaf-whisper and scattered.

IT FORMED WITH A FLAW. THE WATER FAE, RHOANN, WAS CAUGHT IN THE SLIP, HALF WITHIN, HALF WITHOUT.

Coinneach's reply didn't quite translate—it sounded like a rotten branch breaking. His expression, though, didn't need translating. The shit was deep, and getting deeper.

Is Rhoann all right? Terry didn't know Rhoann well, but he'd met him with his husbands a few times. Mac and Lucien. Rhoann was another Fae. Which meant Mac and Lucien were his SoulShares.

RHOANN IS WELL. HIS *SCAIR-ANAIM* **WERE ABLE TO FREE HIM.**

Ill fortune, though. Coinneach glanced around, as if he half expected to see cracks in the wall around them. *The only possible way for a flaw to have formed was for something magickal to have been both within and without the timeslip at the moment it was created.*

Murphy's Law of magick.

Coinneach's expression was perfectly blank, and something about the faintness of the breeze coming up through the floor told Terry the *darag*'s was, too. Even for a tree. *Never mind.*

M'darag, *what does the flaw portend?*

Terry thought the tree sighed. **WE KNEW ONE BREACH OF THE TIMESLIP WOULD WEAKEN IT EVERYWHERE, EVERYWHEN. BUT IT IS WORSE THAN WE THOUGHT. ANOTHER BREACH WILL COLLAPSE THE TIMESLIP.**

Terry couldn't stop seeing the monster, the blood. Couldn't stop hearing the screams, the forlorn crying of a puppy. *But it can't be breached again, right? If no one else was stuck part inside and part outside...*

Coinneach looked at Terry in silence. Terry counted a dozen of his own hammering heartbeats.

Someone else was. A soul was.

* * *

Bryce could get used to Lasair's gentle touch, the hand draped with a cool cloth stroking his temples and wiping the sick sweat from his face and neck. He could have done without the pocket nuke that had gone off in his gut, though. Maybe sometime he'd talk with his *scair-anam* about getting the one without having to go through the other.

Setanta was trying to get in on the act, too, of course. Right now, about the only thing available for him to lick was Bryce's nose, and the pup really didn't seem to care whether he licked the outside of it or the inside.

"Off," he grumbled. Neither the Fae nor the Fade-hound paid him the slightest bit of attention.

"What happened, *sumiúl?*" Well, maybe Lasair was paying attention. Lips brushed Bryce's forehead, and the burning where the piece of the *Marfach* had been ebbed.

"Damned if I know." Slowly, Bryce raised his head; Lasair cupped the back and held it up off the floor, enough for Bryce to be able to get a look around. He lay where he'd fallen, on the floor next to the bed; with Lasair propping up his head, he could just see the glow at the bottom of the corner window that told him where the Jefferson Memorial stood, several stories below and across the water. Other than the great view, he hadn't had much of a chance to take in the luxury of the Oriental suite before his early warning system went off. "About the only good thing I have to say about it is that whatever it was, it's a safe bet our favorite monster got a hell of a lot more of it than I did."

Setanta bared his puppy fangs at the mention of the *Marfach* and growled. Bryce wasn't sure, but he

238

thought those fangs had gotten longer since the last time he'd seen them.

"Should we warn the others?" Lasair rubbed behind Setanta's ears to calm the pup; Bryce could imagine him doing the same thing to the adult Fade-hounds he'd been in charge of, back in the Realm. Only then he would have had to reach up to do it.

"Probably." Anything affecting the monster enough for Bryce to feel it was Big News. And not news anyone was going to be happy to get, unless it meant the unkillable horror was actually dead. And Bryce didn't have that kind of luck. "I wonder if it would do any good to call Conall." The mage hated cell phones for some reason, and managed to 'forget' his most of the time—and he was the one who needed to know most of all.

Lasair shook his head. "I doubt it. Best if we went to his home. Do you need my help to a taxi?"

"Give me a minute. And…"

"And?"

"Hold my hand? It helps."

Chapter Twenty-Four

Amazing, how knowing one was Fading into the presence of one's mortal enemy focused one. It was also amazing how a few years of marriage to a lawyer fucked with one's vocabulary.

Even before he was fully formed Tiernan reached out with his magickal sense. Nobles were more sensitive to elemental magick than to the living sort, but the magickal wall Conall had warned him about would have been obvious as fuck to an eyeless *trych*. Rhoann, too, stood out from the background noise in the unfinished studio, a cool glow of Water magick. Josh wasn't visible yet, though *Árean* and *Scathacrú* were.

And...

Tiernan curled the fingers of his crystal hand around the grip of his sword; the sensation was his first upon becoming physical, and purely reassuring. No amount of reassurance, though, could have prepared him for the face and form before him. Fae genetics were often thought of as an elaborate joke played by magick on their race, and Maelduin Guaire was living proof that magick loved irony.

It wasn't quite like looking in a mirror—if anything, the intact left hand gripping Maelduin's sword hilt would have been enough to dispel that notion. But Maelduin looked more like Tiernan's brother than his nephew—more like Tiernan's brother than his own brother ever had. In fact, Maelduin looked a few years older than Tiernan did; Fae stopped aging when they came into their birthright of magick, and Tiernan had come into his early for a Noble. His hair was a shade or two blonder than Tiernan's, his face slightly leaner, his nose sharper.

One similarity, though, was more important than any of the others. Maelduin Guaire's training as a *scian-damhsa* was sure to have been at least as exacting as Tiernan's own. And Maelduin had had a very specific goal in mind during his 150 or so years of blade-dancing. A goal presently sitting squarely between Tiernan's shoulders.

What is it about my head, that so many people besides me want it?

Maelduin, too, was staring, which was unsurprising. "How can this be?" he murmured.

Fortunately, he didn't also have Tiernan's voice. Tiernan wasn't sure where his own personal 'freak the fuck out' line was, but he suspected it was somewhere short of that.

And at least Maelduin hadn't opened their dialogue with the recitation of his oath and the ritual challenge that went with it. Which was peculiar, all things considered. As was Tiernan's contentment to have it be so. Surely a male who had murdered his own brother should have no qualms about dispatching his nephew, especially when his nephew was undoubtedly waiting for just the right moment to continue the family tradition.

Hells yes, he had qualms.

"The resemblance isn't so strange, considering you're both *thair-mhac* and *fiur-mhac* to me." *Faen* drew careful distinctions between blood relationships—*brother's son* was different from *sister's son*. Usually. And commenting on such was safer than bringing up the ties of vengeance.

All the color drained from Maelduin's face.

Fuck me comatose. "No one ever told you."

* * *

Oh, Jesus. Terry blanched. He was the danger. Him and Maelduin. One soul in two bodies, caught on opposite sides of the wall keeping the monster out.

Coinneach nodded slowly. *This was the other reason I had hoped you might reject your* slaidar. *I have some small hope that if you do, the flaw might mend.*

I... can you give me a minute?

Just a day ago, it would never even have occurred to Terry to wonder what it would feel like, not to have something as simple as the privacy of his own thoughts. And he couldn't think of a time when he might have needed that privacy anywhere near as badly as he did right now. All he could do was turn his back on Coinneach, again, and hope the *darag* understood what he meant by doing so.

Assuming he now had privacy, though... what was he going to do with it?

The carnage the *darag* had showed him had to have been real—there was no way in hell his imagination could have come up with anything like that. And anything that kept the monster he'd seen away from here, away from what looked like a network of... something... that linked up places all over the world, and maybe even the other world Maelduin had come from, had to be a good thing.

And all he had to do to make that happen was reject Maelduin. The man—the Fae—he'd been planning to show the door anyway, since anyone who wanted to hook up with Terry Miller was bad news by definition. By association.

I fucking deserve better than that.

The thought surprised him. But maybe it shouldn't have. It felt like a thought that had endured through years of bad choices, buried under the weight of years of loneliness and self-abuse, waiting for the moment when he was finally ready to listen to it.

I wouldn't let someone else tell me I'm poison. Who I am and am not allowed to be with—to try with, at least. No one else gets to tell me that. Coinneach and the darag *don't get to tell me that. My own past, my own history doesn't get to tell me I can't try.*

All he had to do was close his eyes, to bring back how it had felt last night, going to sleep wrapped in the arms and the body of a Fae who had just blown his mind and tended gently to his body. He wasn't in love, not yet, anyway. But for the first time since Bryce, he wanted to try to be.

There was just one small problem with his maybe-happily-ever-after.

Opening his eyes, he turned back to Coinneach. *I could tell you that I reject Maelduin. But I don't think it would do what you need it to. Because I'd only be saying it to try to keep him safe—to keep everyone safe. My heart knows it isn't true, and I think that's what matters. Because whatever it is that links us doesn't have anything to do with my words. It's in my soul. Isn't it?*

He hated the way the *Gille Dubh* seemed to slump in on himself. *It is.*

A wind whispered around Coinneach, and Terry got the impression it was the *darag*'s side of a conversation he wasn't part of. Whether or not it was directed at him, though, it seemed to help; Coinneach's shoulders straightened, and he nodded.

My darag thinks there is another way. If we separate you physically, the danger your bond poses to the timeslip will lessen. And doing so will gain us time to devise a better solution. one that does not wall the wellsprings off from the rest of the world.

Separation was pretty much the last thing Terry wanted. But if the nightmare got through, got into the wellsprings, came after all of them, he would never get the chance he should have taken last night. This morning. Any time before the damned wall went up.

What do I have to do?

* * *

Maelduin was having trouble catching his breath. "Is that… why you killed my father?" The words seemed to be coming from somewhere else, not from him. "Because he was…"

He couldn't finish. But neither did Tiernan seem capable of speech.

No one had told him.

Neither of his parents had ever had the

opportunity to do so—fair enough. But surely the distant kin who raised him must have known. And no one had ever said a word, had ever so much as hinted. Wanting to spare him, perhaps, or hiding shame.

Neither made any particular sense. None of his distant kin had ever cared enough about him to be other than indifferent to his feelings. And as for shame... while the act by which he had been brought into being was taboo, forbidding a Fae to do something was like forbidding the stars to fall on a summer night. And it was definitely not unheard of in Fae history and legend for *fiur* and *thair* to conceive a child together. Doing so, though, had never been an excuse for the ultimate prohibited act of kin-murder.

"There is more to this story. More that has been kept from me. Else you are the cold-blooded kinslayer I have always believed you to be, and if you were that I would be fighting for my life."

This time, Maelduin's own words rendered him speechless. ... *if you were that*... Something deep within him had already decided he had given his life, his vow, his honor to a lie.

And why was Tiernan regarding him with what could only be pity?

"I *am* a cold-blooded kinslayer, that was your mother's verdict and the reason I was exiled." Tiernan's near-monotone spoke of pain in a way no theatrics could. "But even one as heartless as she supposed me to be would not tell you the whole truth." His gaze slanted to the others present, Conall and Josh and Rhoann; blue topaz eyes narrowed.

He warns them not to speak. "You have told those who are not our kin. Tell me."

Tiernan stiffened. "As you wish. I killed your father, my brother, in the act of rape. For love of your mother, my sister, I did justice, not murder."

Justice. And for that I am sworn to kill you, or die trying.

It took Maelduin a moment to recognize the howling in his mind as the memory of wind. Then a scream rose through the gale.

"Jesus fucking Christ, make it stop*!"*

Terry.

Terry needed him. Now.

But he was bound by his oath, as surely as if the mage's ward were still wrapped around him. His death, or his satisfaction of a now-empty oath, was watching him, waiting with the studied patience of a *scian-damhsa*.

Not only was his oath hollow, he could not fulfill it, not without the grace and skill in Terry's keeping. *Gafa id'r cú-cémne a's tine*—caught between Fade-hound and fire, and as likely to be devoured by either.

Slowly, gracelessly, Maelduin knelt. Bowing his head, he swept his hair aside from his neck, leaving it bare to a blade.

"I yield to you. Accept, and I shall be forsworn, my life forfeit. I ask only that you allow me to try to save my *scair-anam*, before you kill me."

* * *

The wind howled like a gutted crack-head and cut like broken glass. Which was okay with Janek—he didn't give a fuck about the noise, and he hadn't actually felt anything since his parasite had taken over their shared body. So being able to feel the cold was a step up. And being able to feel meant he was the first one awake.

Yeah, things are fucking great.

He'd fallen on his back, and on a tilted slab of ice, so he could see most of his own body. A few rags of his clothes were still with him, and his shitkickers—not enough to do anything useful about the cold, but at least his dick probably wouldn't freeze off in the next few minutes. Not that it had done anything useful lately either, and it wasn't like he hadn't lost a few other parts here and there, but even a zombie had limits.

And he still had his knife. His Fae-killing knife, tucked in the top of his right boot.

For the first time, or at least the first time he could remember, Janek acknowledged a thought that had been lurking in the back of his mind ever since he and his passenger had lurched and clawed their way up out of the water and slush and ice.

I might not live long enough to use that knife.

Janek's fists clenched until he felt the tight skin splitting over his knuckles. Two years of torture he'd lived through, slowly rotting, healed only to rot again, thanks to the abomination living in his head. Two years, and forever, waiting for his chance at the fucking Fae. He hadn't even known the word 'abomination' before he'd picked up his parasite—the monster loved the word.

And as soon as it woke up, the abomination was going to escape. Even if it killed him. Killed all of them.

No. No, it wasn't.

If anything killed the *Marfach*, it was going to be Janek.

* * *

The whisper of wind rose from the floor again, and moonlight glimmered in Terry's mind, as if seen through the leaves of a wind-tossed tree. Terry fought the urge to fidget—now that he'd made up his mind to do something, he needed to, well, *do* something.

The darag's *plan is not free of danger. We can send you anywhere in the web of the wellsprings, but you should go where the barrier is strongest.*

Makes sense—

The barrier is strongest where the Marfach *is.*

Oh, shit.

Coinneach nodded. *Mother Sun's magick is strongest there, and She loans it to us. Enough power resides there that we felt nothing when the* Marfach *tried the barrier; there should be more than enough to keep you safe until we work out another way to guard the wellsprings.*

Should be.

Coinneach's gaze went to the floor. *Nothing is certain.*

Except the flaw that's already there. Already here. Terry took a deep breath, the way he did before going on stage, to center himself. And he wondered when a world so strange, so completely off-center, had become normal. *I'll go.*

For the first time, Coinneach smiled. He was almost as beautiful as Maelduin, for all that the two were nearly total opposites in so many ways. *Then we have a chance. But you should go now, before the barrier weakens any further.*

Terry nodded, narrowing his eyes at the eerie

shifting opacity surrounding them. *I wish I could talk to him before I go. Tell him what's happening.*

Coinneach arched a brow. *If you speak aloud, he should be able to hear you, though he will remember your words as something he heard in the past.*

Has he been able to hear us all along? Can he understand us? Jesus, what had they said? Trust, betrayal, monsters... *You said it was Maelduin's blood that let me understand you, at first.*

Coinneach considered. *Your bond might let him hear you, but I doubt he can understand you when you speak this way. The speech of* darag *and* Gille Dubh *includes light, and light cannot pass the barrier. Without it, our speech is no more than wind.*

Terry's knees felt a little weak. *But he'll hear me if I speak now.*

Yes.

SPEAK QUICKLY. The gust from the floor startled Terry—and Coinneach, too, apparently. Terry guessed the tree wasn't in a hurry too often.

Terry nodded, swallowing hard.

"Maelduin..." *Fuck, what if he's not out there anymore? What if he gave up?* "If you can hear me... I was wrong. We're connected, even if I don't quite understand how. There's a hell of a lot I don't understand, and I don't know how much of it *you* understand, and I don't have long to talk. But this wall between us is incredibly important—Coinneach calls it a timeslip, and it's keeping the most horrible thing I've ever seen out of the wellsprings. It's your enemy, Coinneach says. And the connection between us, you and me, makes the barrier weaker. I'm not going to let that monster get to you." Sweat beaded on Terry's forehead and upper lip, as his second-hand memory of the carnage in the park forced its way to the surface. "So I'm letting Coinneach and his *darag* send me away until they can figure out a better way to keep the wellsprings secure." His voice wavered, threatened to crack. "I'll come back. I will. Don't try to come after me, it's not safe."

THIS MOMENT, HUMAN. THIS.

The wind rose.

"I'll come back— "

Chapter Twenty-Five

The silence that followed Maelduin's declaration was near-total, broken only by the wind heard only in his memory, and the remembered echo of Terry's scream.

Accept, damn you. Maelduin blinked stinging sweat out of his eyes.

A rattling sound—keys in a lock—shattered the silence. A door crashed open, followed by uneven footsteps.

Maelduin cursed under his breath, and raised his head just enough to see the intruder. A human, dark-haired and dark-eyed, handsome in a rough-hewn unshaven way. And he was looking at Tiernan as if he questioned Tiernan's sanity, or his own. "You didn't even bring your goddamned sword?"

"I don't need one."

Maelduin winced at the insult, but said nothing. He could lend the other *scian-damhsa* his oath-blade when it was time, if it came to that. A tidy solution, since it was going to kill him in any event. The human's dark eyes, though, might be enough to deal him a death blow by themselves, if his current glare was a fair indication. *This must be Kevin.* His uncle's *scair-anam*, a human male who loved an unlovable Fae.

251

A Fae who had killed for justice, and for love, and not for any curse.

Maelduin's life had had a single, constant center, from the moment he had been old enough to take up a blade. Then he had come to the human world, and instead of finding that center, he had acquired a second one. Now the first was a lie, and the second was out of sight, out of reach, and—if that terrified scream was any indication—perilously close to out of time.

Kevin shook his head. "You think you can take another blade-dancer with your *sciana-Clo'che?*"

Blades of living Stone?

One corner of Tiernan's mouth edged up. "I don't need to. I'm not going to fight him."

At last. "You accept my surrender, then?" Strange, how eager he was for his doom to be pronounced.

"No."

Maelduin's head jerked up as if pulled by a chain. "*No?*"

"What the fuck do you mean, 'no'?" This from Kevin, like the crack of a whip.

Maelduin was beginning to have doubts of his own, with respect to his uncle's mental soundness. And judging by the stares Tiernan was getting from the others in the room, Maelduin was in the majority.

Tiernan appeared not to notice. "If I accept his surrender, I have to kill him. And I'd rather not be a kinslayer twice over, at least not until I'm sure there's no other alternative."

A deep, calming breath didn't help matters nearly as much as Maelduin had hoped it might. *If my life is going to fall to pieces, is it really too much to ask that it fall apart in the way I was planning for?* "Under the terms of my oath, the 'other alternative' requires me to kill you. And I am unable to do that—I will most likely kill myself instead, as I bear an oath-blade sworn to your blood—unless I find Terry and Share with him. And even if I could fight you in my present condition, Terry needs me now. So there is actually no other alternative."

"I found one." Light glinted off a gold ring in Tiernan's arched brow. "Namely, I refuse to accept your surrender."

"Am I the only sane person in this room?" Kevin's face was red, his voice under tight and obvious control. "This Fae is sworn to kill you."

"I can take care of myself. You heard him yourself, he said he can't kill me until he Shares with Terry. Which means there's something he wants more than he wants my head right now."

Kevin opened his mouth, then closed it again, turning to regard Maelduin. The cold anger riding his gaze would have given a charging war-steed second thoughts. "Why do you have to Share with Terry?"

While Maelduin was trying to decide whether silence or speech was his best option, Josh spoke up. "He said he was crippled. Clumsy."

That got everyone's attention, especially Tiernan's. Maelduin flushed under his uncle's keen regard, but refused to look away. "I was warned the Pattern would take something from me. It stole my skill with a blade, as well as my grace in the use of it. The skill it took me a lifetime to acquire and hone."

Kevin's lips narrowed to a thin line. "And you want it back."

"The only thing I want back is the one who holds

half my soul." The words were out before Maelduin thought, but he would not call them back even if he could. His soul knew what he needed. Rescuing Terry mattered more to him than his revenge, and he valued Terry over the skills he had spent his life perfecting.

He had been wrong. His life did not have two centers; it had one. One who needed his help, yet might not want him.

Life was easier when I believed I was cursed.

Conall frowned. "Then why surrender?"

"Because a blade-dancer who would trust another *scian-damhsa*, one who is bloodsworn, is a fool." Maelduin spoke softly, distracted, trying to plumb the silence that had followed Terry's cry, to make sense of the whispers of wind in his memory. "And my uncle is no fool."

Tiernan chuckled. "You're kneeling in the middle of a room full of men, and males, who know better." He put out a hand, showing he was unarmed, and also clearly intending to help Maelduin to his feet. "And I officially don't accept your surrender."

Maelduin recognized the substance of the hand extended to him. It was living Stone, the elemental form of Earth, the Demesne they shared. He took it, and marveled at the warmth of it.

Getting up was difficult to the point of humiliation. No one spoke—though the dragonet hissed in what might have been laughter. Maelduin ignored it, choosing to look instead at the male he was sworn to kill. "Why did you feel you needed no blade to meet me?" he blurted into the awkward silence.

Tiernan said nothing, but extended his crystal hand again. Even warier of the gesture a second time,

Maelduin stared as Tiernan produced a grace-blade from the *Clo'che* of his own hand, balanced it perfectly across two fingers as the harsh light winked off its wickedly sharp edge, then flipped it into the air and reabsorbed it back into his hand.

Scian-Clo'che.

"I carry all the blades I need," Tiernan replied at last.

He could have killed me, as I stood here and gaped like an amad'n. *Like the fool I am and have always been.* "You do mean to let me live, else you would have killed me already."

"I would never come between a male and his *scair-anam.*" Tiernan looked as if he might be about to say more, but then subsided, frowning slightly at a meaningful look from his own *scair-anam.*

When Kevin turned back to Maelduin, his expression was slightly less severe. *Very* slightly. "Maybe my *scair-anam* doesn't need a mere human's protection, but he damned well has it." Perhaps Maelduin only imagined the human was less ill disposed toward him than he had been. "You want him to turn his back on you, let you go, because it's more urgent for you to somehow break through that wall and rescue Terry than it is for you to kill him, the way you've been planning to do your whole life."

"Yes."

"Why the urgency? Make me understand what's going on here."

He is truly afraid for his SoulShare. My uncle. The sudden warmth he felt toward the human startled Maelduin. "I heard Terry call for help, just now. He's in pain, or danger, or both."

Tiernan, Kevin, and Rhoann eyed Maelduin, with varying degrees of disbelief. Conall and Josh, though, were looking at one another, and nodding.

"The SoulShare bond," Conall murmured. "You could sense me, and I could sense you, when I was trapped in the mirror. And when you were trapped in the Realm."

Josh's hand slipped into Conall's. "Even before we'd finished Sharing."

Maelduin allowed himself a small sigh of relief. *They understand. Maybe more than I do.* And if they did... "If you have had this experience before... might you know why I hear only in memory?"

Now he had everyone's attention. *"Cac marh lobadh."* Conall's whisper was probably inaudible to anyone but a Fae. "Are you sure about that?"

"Yes." *And if the mage is nervous, I probably should be too.* "Each time I hear Terry's voice, it is as if he spoke some time ago, but I failed to hear him then, and only remember his words now."

A scattering of freckles stood out against the paleness of the red-haired mage's skin. "I think I know what the wall is. We're all on the far side of a timeslip. And going by what Rhoann said and what I saw under Purgatory, I think it's around all the—"

"Maelduin... if you can hear me..."

Maelduin turned away from the others and clapped his hands over his ears, the better to focus on the new memory of Terry's voice.

"I was wrong. We're connected..."

Terry didn't seem frightened. Not like he had been a few minutes before, at any rate.

"There's a hell of a lot I don't understand, and..."

Someone laid a hand on Maelduin's arm. He shook it off roughly. "Let me concentrate!"

"*… keeping the most horrible thing I've ever seen out of the wellsprings. It's your enemy, Coinneach says. And the connection between us, you and me, makes the barrier weaker. I'm not going to let that monster get to you.*"

Terry's voice was unsteady. Maelduin hated the fear he heard.

"*So I'm letting Coinneach and his* darag *send me away until they can figure out a better way to keep the wellsprings secure. I'll come back. I will. Don't try to come after me, it's not safe. I'll come back—*"

Silence, broken only by the whispering of wind.

The hand touched his arm again. It was Tiernan's, the hand warm living Stone. "What is it? What's happened?"

"He's gone. He told me not to follow, that it's not safe." Maelduin turned to study the barrier. "My *scair-anam* has a great deal to learn about Fae."

Chapter Twenty-Six

Terry landed hard, on his hands and knees. Given what it had felt like the last time Coinneach and his *darag* had messed with his reality, staying down was probably a good idea, at least until he figured out what was going on.

This is ice.

Solid ice. With blue-white fire dancing in it, sometimes flaring brightly, sometimes almost invisible. It looked like the same kind of pattern he'd seen on the floor. He thought he could see water through it in places, too.

And holy Christ, it was cold. It seemed like some warmth was coming up through the floor—arriving the same way he had, maybe—but it didn't stand a chance against the biting air. Most of the warm air turned to mist, ghosting off in little eddies and arabesques.

This, um, may not be much of a long-term solution. Was Coinneach even going to be able to hear him? Shit, they probably should have worked that out before whisking him away to wherever-this-was.

What is the problem?

Whew. *I'm not sure where I am, but it's made of ice. And it's hella cold.* His fingers white and numb already, Terry sat back on his heels and started trying to rub some warmth back into his hands.

Almost immediately, warmer air started rising out of the floor. Which meant more mist—a lot more, enough to make the air feel heavy—but mist was better than air cold enough to take his breath and freeze the inside of his nose.

Is that better?

It'll do. I'm still not dressed for this, though. That was an understatement. His light khaki jacket had been fine for November in D.C., but it might as well have been a paper bag against the chill radiating up and out from the floor and the walls.

My darag *will continue to send warmer air through the wellspring. And we will hurry. My* darag *is already consulting with the other* daragin.

Thanks.

Terry's gaze traveled up the icy blue walls surrounding him, up to where a layer of swirling magick, identical to the walls and ceiling of the prison he'd just left, capped the pit of ice. His kinetic sense, finely honed by years of dancing, told him the floor was rocking under him, ever so slightly.

Where the hell am I?

* * *

The monster woke up too quickly for Janek to have any chance of putting up a fight. One second he was staring past his toes at the faintly glowing circle in the ice, his stomach trying to turn over the way it always did when his human eyeball looked too long at magick—and the next, he was looking down at the bitch's red flowing gown, and couldn't feel a fucking thing.

Shit.

"That was… unpleasant." The female's voice might as well have been a toad's. A dried-up roadkill toad's.

I thought you got off on that kind of thing. The male was as much of a wiseass as ever, though he wasn't as quick with his comeback as he usually was. *The more unpleasant, the better*.

"Your wit is misplaced." The female's heels slipped and scraped against the ice as she tried to push herself up. "And this is ridiculous."

Save your strength. We're going to need it to Fade.

Fuck no. *Fading's not going to do you any more good than trying to suck down that magick did.*

Oh, good, the expert.

Janek wasn't sure who rolled their shared eyes. He didn't give a shit. *If you try to Fade us, my human body isn't going to be able to take it. And that body is all the meat you have.*

The female finally staggered to her feet. Where she had been lying—where Janek had been lying, before the rest of them woke up—there was a brown smear of what passed for Janek's blood, and a few smallish chunks of skin, still frozen to the ice.

Doesn't look like you're in such great shape now, Meat. Janek could feel the male smiling, the kind of smile that would make babies scream. *Besides, you were dead for a while after we broke through the kill-ward the mage put up around Purgatory. We did just fine pushing the meat wagon around without you.*

I wasn't dead, asshole. But you just go on thinking that a little longer.

"Squabbling is useless." The bitch took a couple of steps toward the lid covering the hole, then stopped. "There is nothing there for us. There is nothing here for us. If you die, you die." She shrugged. "We must go. Now."

Yes.

NOW.

Janek was never going to forget the way his guts wrenched, and caught fire, when the monster started to Fade. Not as long as he lived. Which was only going to be a couple of seconds. Not even time for any last words. Well, fuck that.

The female shrieked as Janek tipped their body toward the magick, as her feet skidded on the ice. And in her panic, she let go control over their body.

Janek could have had some last words after all. But as he fell forward into the magick, burning alive from the inside, all he could do was laugh.

Fate was almost as big a bitch as the one he'd been carrying around inside his head.

* * *

Conall was the first to react as Maelduin headed for the barrier; he gestured as if to channel magic, cursed, and let his hand fall, shaking it as if something had burned or bitten him. "Wait…"

"Why?" Maelduin decided not to glance back over his shoulder at the red-haired mage; he had managed to reach the barrier without tripping over anything, and wanted his good fortune to continue.

261

"Would you wait, if it were your *scair-anam* on the other side?"

"Of course not. But—"

Maelduin did not listen—had no intention of listening, really. He rested his hand open-palmed, on the barrier. It was a strange sensation, or lack thereof; there was no solid surface under his hand, no warmth or coolness or smoothness or hardness. Only a place where his hand would not go.

But it would, because he wished it to. Because Terry was on the other side.

Our connection makes the barrier weaker? Good. Maelduin closed his eyes and pushed.

The nothingness resisted. Maelduin leaned against it with both hands, straining.

The nothingness vanished. Maelduin fell forward, stumbled, and landed on his face in the sparking, hissing net of the wellspring, in front of a pair of dark-skinned bare feet.

Fool! roared a lightning-lashed gale in his mind. *Why did you not listen to your human?*

* * *

Maybe it's safe to stand up. Terry eyed the ice beneath him suspiciously, hoping the hints of moving water he thought he could see through it meant that there was a lot of very clear ice under him, and not a couple of inches of dirty murky ice.

Something popped, soundlessly, like eardrums on an airplane.

Terry couldn't see through the floor anymore; the ice, and the fire inside it, were covered with the same magick that had formed the walls of his old prison and the lid of his new one.

He was hit with a blast of ice-laden air so cold it made him gasp and arch back.

And when he looked up, it was into the laughing face of hell itself, as the monster from his vision, half its head made of glowing red crystal and muscles visible under flapping rags of dead inked flesh, fell spread-eagled toward him, with nothing between him and it but the frigid air.

Terry screamed.

The monster's laughter changed to a ragged shriek.

The monster... vanished.

Terry stared at where it had been, shaking uncontrollably, the air burning in his lungs. "Holy shit, *Santa madre de Dio*, sweet fucking bleeding Christ..."

Where had it gone? He didn't care, as long as it wasn't falling on him. It was gone. It was *definitely* gone. Which meant the timeslip wasn't needed any more, and the *darag* could bring him back to warmth and safety. And—maybe—Maelduin.

Coinneach!

No answer. Not even an echo.

Oh, Jesus. The language of the *Gille Dubh* couldn't penetrate the timeslip barrier. And neither could their magick.

All of a sudden, the roaring wind sounded a lot like the monster's laughter. Only colder.

Chapter Twenty-Seven

The apparent source of the wind and the fury, a handsome naked dark-skinned man, stood over Maelduin, hands balled into fists... and his toes turning into roots, which sank into the floor and made the wood groan. No man, then. And not friendly.

And not Terry.

"Where is my *scair-anam*?" Maelduin scrambled to his feet, hand on his sword-hilt. His awareness of his surroundings, preternatural even for a Fae, had not deserted him along with his coordination; Terry was nowhere to be seen, heard, or scented, which meant he had been gone for some time. Longer, surely, than the few moments that had passed for Maelduin since hearing his farewell.

He is where we sent him to keep him, and the timeslip, safe from what you have just done. The male's voice was strange, formed from a wind heard but not felt and the play of moonlight on leaves— though 'play' was the wrong word for the anger glinting off every word. *You have broken the timeslip; it takes all our strength to hold one small piece of it now against the creature you call the* Marfach.

Maelduin knew he should care about the barrier

against the *Marfach*. The very name somehow managed to stir up ancient racial nightmares, a faceless, formless being, madness, twisted darkness. But the timeslip was the problem of those who understood it and controlled it. "Send me to him. Send me where you sent him."

Impossible.

"Maelduin!" Conall was all but jumping up and down, trying to get his attention. "Can you understand what Coinneach is saying?"

It had not occurred to Maelduin to wonder at his understanding of the language of wind and light. "Yes. Can you?"

"No such luck. I'm Demesne of Air, and a commoner—I can understand every language carried by the air, but the *Gille Dubh* and the *daragin* speak mind to mind, and use light besides. What is he—"

"He is saying that he cannot send me where Terry has gone." Maelduin glared at the *Gille Dubh*. "Perhaps he forgets I do not need his help."

"If you're thinking of Fading, stop thinking." The mage's voice was sharp. "Using living magick wasn't safe around any of the wellsprings even before tonight, much less so now—especially this close to the great nexus."

Something about Conall's expression cut off Maelduin's intended retort before it reached his lips. Amazing, how one so youthful in appearance could look so severe.

I cannot use the wellsprings to send you to your human because the last piece of the timeslip is in the way. It lies between the Marfach *and the wellspring closest to it. Once that piece comes down, the* daragin *tell me there is no replacing it, and no way to keep the* Marfach *from the wellsprings.*

Daragin, and *Gille Dubh.* Conall had mentioned them before, as had Terry. Maelduin had overlooked those words, in the barrage of others. He had no time to spare now for old legends or old disdains, and besides, the male standing before him looked nothing like a dumb half-wooden animal.

But there was something else, hidden in what the *Gille Dubh,* Coinneach, had told him.

A blade-dancer must know the ground like his own body.

The ground.

Maelduin shivered once, sharply. "The last piece of the barrier also lies between me and Terry."

Yes. That is why we cannot send you to him. If the expressions of the *Gille Dubh* were like those of Fae, or humans, Coinneach regretted his words.

Then Terry is with the Marfach. Maelduin refused to speak the words aloud, to give them even that small measure of reality—yet in his mind, the words became the wind and moonlight of the *Gille Dubh*'s language.

And Coinneach heard. *Yes... and no. We cannot see through the barrier, so we know very little for certain. However, if the monster were actually touching the barrier, we would know. Its magick is... not compatible with that of Mother Sun.*

He is safe, then.

For the moment.

Your comfort is a cold thing. Maelduin turned to Conall, who was stepping into the circle of Josh's arms. "Terry is in danger. Tell me how I can go to him safely."

"You can't do it from here. You have to get away from the wellspring—"

Josh shook his head. "Conall, *d'orant,* no. He can't help."

Maelduin's eyes narrowed. "I thought you understood the SoulShare bond."

"I do." Josh appeared less than impressed by the most cutting look Maelduin could muster. "I've also seen you in action. If Terry's in any kind of danger, and you try to rescue him, no offense, but you're likely to get both of you killed."

"Fuck." Maelduin had heard the word often enough by now to be reasonably confident in his use of it. And it was appropriate. His grip tightened reflexively around the hilt of his sword—his accursed blood-bound sword. It would kill him—gladly, if truesilver took satisfaction in the fulfillment of its purpose—if he had to raise it against the *Marfach* before he killed his uncle with it. Or if, as was far more likely, he cut himself drawing it. Any blood other than Tiernan's would be the ink on the warrant for his execution.

And, more to the point, he would be of no use to Terry if he were dead.

Maelduin was presented with an impossible situation. Which, to a *scian-damhsa,* meant only that the rules wanted changing. "What if we were to complete our Sharing?"

No one, not even the *Gille Dubh,* greeted this suggestion with anything that might be mistaken for approval, and Rhoann was the only one willing to look him in the eyes. "If Terry is in danger, circumstances are unlikely to allow *dhábh-archann.*"

Maelduin grimaced. No doubt the Water Fae was correct—

though Maelduin couldn't remember the last time he had heard any Fae use the archaic term *two-become-one* to refer to sex. "What other chance do I have?"

Conall chewed thoughtfully on his lower lip. "I wonder if there's some way I could channel a Finding and go after him myself."

"It's a little late in the year for fireworks, this side of the Atlantic," Tiernan drawled. "If Fading's a bad idea around a wellspring, one of your channelings would be several orders of magnitude worse than bad."

"You're never more purely irritating than when you're right."

"I'd invite you to bite me, but I don't need the distraction right now." Tiernan's crystal hand wrapped around the length of his hair and twisted, in what looked like a habitual gesture. One Maelduin recognized as his own. "No living magick because of the wellspring, no wellspring because of the timeslip, and the only Fae who can find Terry can't do anything to help him until he Shares with him and kills me."

Kevin growled. "I hope you don't think you're funny, *lanan*, because you aren't."

Tiernan's words stung. And Maelduin had no need of the extra lash. *This must end.* "Enough of this—Terry needs me *now*, not when you all finish debating what can be done without me."

The room went silent; even the dragonet and the *savac-dui* stared at Maelduin. Maelduin was beyond caring who stared. "Clumsy I may be, but the blades are danced in the mind as well as the body, and I am neither dull nor incompetent." *Though I nearly forgot that.* Love and worry were apparently near-cousins.

All the Fae in the room looked as if they had

something to say; one by one, though, each subsided, under the intensity of Maelduin's regard.

"Good." Maelduin turned back to Coinneach, startling the *Gille Dubh* out of what he guessed was some inner communion with his *darag*. "Has there been any change with Terry? Is the *Marfach* any nearer?"

There has been no change.

Conall went as pale as a white doe's milk. "The *Marfach*?"

Did I not say—no, I suppose I didn't. Or I said it only to Coinneach. "Yes, the last piece of the timeslip is keeping the monster out of the wellsprings. But the *darag* can tell if the creature touches its magick, and so far it has not."

"Somehow I'm not terribly reassured. And that's only one of your problems. Or one of Terry's, more like." The grim, purposeful Conall was back, displacing the fresh-faced youth. "If Terry's been sent to the same place I sent the *Marfach*, your *scair-anam* is in Antarctica."

Maelduin's gift of language showed him what Conall meant, with appalling clarity. An unprotected Fae could survive in such a place, for a while at least. But a human? *His* human?

And then there was the *Marfach*…

"I have to go to him. I have no choice. He will freeze, he will die."

Yes. I see, I understand, through you. We would not have sent him there had we known. The wind that was Coinneach's voice faded to the barest whisper. *And you are free to go as you will.* Coinneach stared at the floor, but this time there was no air of communication about him, no sense that he spoke with his *darag. You are likewise free to return. But if the* Marfach *is still there, we dare not release the last of the timeslip to bring your human home.*

Taking a deep breath, Maelduin released his white-knuckled grip on his sword. Such a grip made a blade useless as anything but a cudgel. "If the *Marfach* is still there, I will kill it."

Conall cleared his throat. "We've given that some thought ourselves, a time or two. Legend says it can't be done, and so far legend's been a pretty reliable source of information."

Maelduin shrugged. "Has anyone tried a bloodsworn sword forged with truesilver?"

"No." His uncle's voice had an edge to it. "And neither can you. Even assuming you don't kill yourself just drawing the damned thing, it'll kill you if you use it on the *Marfach* before you…" Tiernan glanced at his human, who was doing a fair impression of a thundercloud, and subsided.

"If it does, see that someone brings Terry home."

That really is all that matters. Even if I don't understand why.

Carefully, Maelduin stepped down from the raised piece of flooring—caught himself in time to keep from flinching as Tiernan stepped forward and took his arm. There was none of the mockery Maelduin expected in Tiernan's blue-topaz gaze, and only a hint of the eternal calculation of the *scian-damhsa*. What was his uncle thinking?

"Where should I go to Fade safely?"

Conall pointed toward an unfinished doorway, down what might at some point become a corridor. "Go all the way to the back of the studio—get as far away from the wellspring as you can—and you'll minimize the damage you do to the wellspring."

Maelduin hadn't gone more than a few paces when a sudden insistent warmth clasped his finger. A heavy gold ring, the air around it shimmering with something like heat—a signet ring, carved or cast with the image of a flame. Or was it?

Conall craned his neck to look at the ring Maelduin held up. "The *Croí na Dóthan*," he breathed.

Heart of Flame. "What is it?" Maelduin stopped short just before running into a bare metal wall support.

"It's the Royal signet of our Prince in exile, Rian Aodán. It's truegold."

Heat flared from the ring, as if the metal knew it was being discussed. Which it might; truegold, like the truesilver in Maelduin's sword, knew its own purpose. It differed from truesilver, though, in that it made up its own mind as to what that purpose was.

Maelduin recognized the name of the Prince, of course. The tale of the Lost Prince had been a scandal when he had been stolen, and again when he had returned—not that Maelduin had paid much attention. He had had other things with which to concern himself. Even now, the story mattered chiefly because Prince Royal Rian Aodán had been—was—a Fire Royal, a Fire elemental.

Hope for Terry encircled Maelduin's finger.

* * *

Why can't I move?

Actually, he could move. A little. The only things that were frozen to the surface under him were his

271

jeans and one arm of his light jacket. Terry blamed the heavy mist — it had soaked his clothes, and now it was freezing them.

Maybe the wind was doing that, though. It sure as hell wasn't helping.

It had been a while since he'd been able to open his eyes — they were frozen shut, too — so he didn't bother trying. There wasn't anything to see, anyway. Just ice, and magick. And the wind had been like knives against his eyeballs anyway, so nope, no point in trying to get another look around.

Magick.

Maelduin.

He was an idiot for hoping the gorgeous Fae would come after him. Certifiable.

But, then, he'd been an idiot all along. It was just a shame he wasn't going to get a chance to be the right kind of idiot.

… sorry…

* * *

"I'd channel all the blankets you could carry—I'd channel you a bonfire, if you could carry it." Conall glanced back over his shoulder, to where the sparking, flaring pattern in the floor, and the dark figure guarding it, were still visible through the partly-finished walls. "But drawing on living magick right now would just make the wellspring worse."

Maelduin wished the mage would shut up. He needed to relax, and he needed to concentrate, and neither was possible at the moment. Still, he might need the information Conall was giving him. *Know the ground before engaging.* "Will it even be safe to bring Terry back through the wellspring?"

"I wish I could give you a guarantee. But it's the only way, for a human. Fading requires magick, and even a fully Shared human doesn't have enough of it to Fade."

Kevin cleared his throat. "That's not quite true. Tiernan Faded me once, accidentally. I lived through it." His hand sought and found Tiernan's. "But we don't know what kind of shape Terry's in, and we do know that letting the *daragin* handle the transportation doesn't damage the wellsprings as much as using living magick around them does."

Maelduin was glad his uncle's mate seemed somewhat less likely to want to murder him out of hand than he had previously. Assuming Maelduin survived to return from Terry's prison, Tiernan was not likely to need help.

Unless he and Terry somehow Shared.

…why can't I move?

Not a memory, this time—a whisper, barely a breath, wind and moonlight, cut into his thoughts.

"Maelduin, how are you going to—"

Maelduin waved Conall to silence and focused on the whisper.

… Maelduin…

Maelduin's heart kicked painfully in his chest. "I have to go. Now." He closed his eyes, his magickal sense questing outward, and inward. Seeking the other half of his soul, and the human he would have sought even without it, on the other side of a strange world.

… sorry…

Maelduin Faded.

Chapter Twenty-Eight

The cold and the wind combined to take Maelduin's breath away almost before he was solid enough to have any. Even the rapidly spreading warmth from the Royal signet on his finger did little to make it easier to breathe. He was surrounded on all sides by rough walls of ice in every shade of blue, rising perhaps four times his height to a circle of bright cloud-covered sky.

The *scian-damhsa* in him saw all this, assessed dangers, prepared defenses. Maelduin saw only the still, ice-limned body lying huddled on a floor of swirling *darag* magick.

How did this happen so quickly? He dropped to his knees beside Terry, brushing ice crystals from his face, shivering with the intensity of his relief as mist from one wisp of breath and then another curled from between Terry's lips to be caught and whirled away by the wind. And the ice melted where his fingers traced; gently he stroked Terry's eyelids, his mouth.

Eyelids fluttered, then closed. "Too cold." Only a Fae could have heard Terry's whisper. "Le' me sleep."

"No." Maelduin lay down alongside Terry, wrapping an arm and a leg around him, hoping the warmth of his hands extended to the rest of him. "I will *not* let you sleep." The Realm had its cold places, generally visited only by the foolhardy; a Fae died only from mortal wounds or extreme old age, but he could freeze, and wait indefinitely for some other Fae to find him. A few had told their stories… so Maelduin knew that letting Terry fall asleep under present circumstances was a very bad idea.

"Sleeping."

"*No.*" Maelduin pressed his lips to Terry's forehead and tightened his grip.

A few minutes passed, during which Maelduin went from staring intently at Terry's closed eyes to squinting up into the bright cloud cover, eyes slitted against the icy wind, wondering when the image out of his race's nightmares would appear. And then Terry began to shake, deep shuddering waves. Maelduin wished he knew whether this was an improvement. He suspected it wasn't.

What can I do?

Even newly lost in an unfamiliar world, betrayed by his own body, Maelduin had never felt this helpless. He'd never actually *been* this helpless, because he'd had Terry with him.

It was more than a matter of getting back what he had lost; Terry gave him more than the missing piece of himself. The warmth, the sweetness of the human's touch… his own desire to say, to do anything that might make Terry smile… his longing for another's soaring beauty… none of this had been a part of him in the Realm, when his soul was whole.

Terry was… more. More than the other half of his own soul.

And Terry was freezing, despite Maelduin's embrace.

I have to do something. Something else.

Once more, he brushed the ice from Terry's cheeks, stroked his eyelids. Once again, dark lashes fluttered, stilled.

"*Lán'ghrásta—*" Maelduin's voice broke; he laced his fingers with Terry's cold ones and held on tightly, willing heat and life back into his human. Willing in vain, as the wind forced its way between their bodies.

What use was a lifetime of skill, of hard-won grace, against this preternatural cold? Only magick could ransom Terry's life, magick no Earth Fae possessed.

Truegold gleamed between the linked fingers of Fae and human.

Maelduin's hands shook as he removed the *Croí na Dóthan* and slipped it onto Terry's icy finger. Instantly the lash of the wind bit deeper; Maelduin felt as if the air were being drawn from his lungs, and his every gasp for breath left him empty, colder within than without.

A Fae could ignore the chill, for a while. Maelduin held his shivering human close, and waited.

* * *

What do you mean, it's gone? Gone as in you left it in the shower? Or gone as if it's gone off gallivanting?

Rian rolled on top of Cuinn, tangling both their legs in the bedsheets, and held his hand up in front of Cuinn's face—the hand with a dent around the base of the fourth finger. *The* Croí na Dóthan *goes where it fecking wants to.* A fair enough characterization, given that it had followed the infant Prince Royal Rian Aodán from the Realm and had managed not to get itself lost in the twenty-one years it had taken said Prince Royal to realize who he was. *And no, it's not in the shower, I saw it go off just now. Gallivanting, if you like.*

Well, hell. Cuinn grimaced; his bondmate was still growing into the Royalty of which the ring was symbol and token, true, but the signet was a part of Rian's own personal history as well as his connection with a life he didn't remember. *Can you sense where it's gone?*

Give me a moment, and I might. Rian closed his eyes, reaching for Cuinn's hand as he did so.

Cuinn curled his fingers around Rian's, lending his bondmate his strength without stopping to think about it, while holding back just enough to avoid distracting him in his search. Being in constant mind-to-mind contact with his almost-human Fae prince was starting to grow on him—although it would have been nice not to have been left with no way to communicate with anyone else unless Rian translated his thoughts into speech.

Not that he blamed the *daragin* for what they'd done to him—

Feckitall. Almost had it. Rian growled, in a way Cuinn found incredibly fetching. *I think it went to D.C. But if it did, it's gone again.*

Care to go track it down?

Cuinn purely loved Rian's grin. *Think we should put on some clothes first? It was somewhere near Raging Art-On and Big Boy, and we don't want to go about making promises to the humans we've no intention of keeping.*

I'd say you're no fun, but I'd be lying. Cuinn slid out of bed and reached for the jeans he'd tossed over the bedside chair. Or had his bondmate done that? Seemed more likely.

By the time he had matters settled to his liking, Rian was already tucked into his skin-tight leather trousers and was shrugging into a vest of the same. Cuinn stifled a groan—at least he could still show his appreciation for his *scair-anam*'s literally scorching sensuality, the *daragin* had left him that much. *Remind me to spank the* Croí *when you get it back—there are some things a Fae doesn't appreciate being dragged away from.*

One thing, in your case at least. Rian's laughter didn't help Cuinn's condition any. *The sooner we're off, the sooner we're home.* Back to their tiny Greenwich Village apartment, all the Royal chambers the two of them needed. *Shall we aim for Raging Art-On? The* Croí *was somewhere near there, at least for a moment or two.*

Cuinn shook his head. *It's early enough that Josh or Terry might still have customers. How about the dance studio? That'll be empty.*

Good thought. With a wink, Rian Faded.

Cuinn followed, third and fourth fingers hooked in a surreptitious luck-sign. He knew where they were heading, of course, but his own Fades tended to gravitate toward the strongest source of magick near his destination. Hopefully that was going to be Rian, this time, and not the restless great nexus next door to the studio.

278

He hadn't quite finished taking form when he was swarmed by angry silver-blue sparks like hornets, stinging against his chest and arms. *What the particular fuck?* He raised a hand to channel a ward—

—but then he saw where he was, and lowered his hand with another hasty, silent curse. Channeling Loremaster-level magick in an angry wellspring was as far from a good idea as he could imagine, and his imagination was excellent. Especially when the magick-well was probably pissed precisely because he'd landed in the middle of it.

Slaidar-mhor.

The leaf-whisper language of the *daragin* and the *Gille Dubh* calling him the "Great Thief" was not what Cuinn wanted to hear at the moment, and under the circumstances Coinneach's frowning face wasn't high on his list of favorite sights, either. Several sarcastic responses came to mind, but he resolutely ignored all of them. One never knew what the *Gille Dubh* might hold against the Fae race as a whole, and he personally was running out of faculties he could spare in the event Coinneach took offense at a stray—or not so stray—thought.

Slowly the flock of silver-blue shards settled back into the web of the new wellspring, flaring when they touched—Cuinn was almost willing to swear he heard them sizzle. Untethered living magick—they'd seen it at the wellspring next to the nexus, but not at the other ones. *Fuck.* He drew a deep, unsteady breath as the last of the magick disappeared back into the lines of the wellspring, unable to escape the feeling he'd just dodged a bullet.

Now all he had to do was dodge a lightning strike, a lightning strike named Coinneach—

We need to speak with you, Loremaster.

So much for dodging. Yet Coinneach didn't seem angry, just pensive. Looking from the floor to Cuinn to someplace off in the distance, as if listening to a wind only he could hear. Which he probably was.

Trying to sneak off was probably a bad idea. But so was interrupting the *Gille Dubh*'s communion with his *darag*. Of course, so was not having any clue how a wellspring had turned up in the middle of a half-built dance studio, and not knowing where Rian had landed. And so was ignoring a summons to conversation with the entities who had taken his voice.

Cuinn cleared his throat—which was purely unnecessary to mental conversation, but some habits were hard to break. *Can it wait? I seem to be missing my* scair-anam, *and I think he needs to see what's going on here.*

He is near. But we must speak first.

For the first time, Cuinn noticed that darkness had fallen around the wellspring. Some magick of the tree folk, probably, since the wellspring wasn't throwing a fit. And he himself couldn't do a fucking thing in response, not without risking blowing up the wellspring under his feet.

Although he knew someone who could, and probably would. *I hope whatever you want to talk about is worth having a pissed-off fire elemental waiting on the other side when you drop this channeling, with the instincts of an arsonist and all the patience characteristic of his kind.*

Coinneach laughed—a genuine, thoughtful chuckle, not a mocking dance of moonlight on leaves. *I think it is. Perhaps even your* scair-anam *might find it so.*

I'm willing to listen. Especially being as short on other options as he was. *But you might want to tell me what's on your mind before it starts getting hot in here.*

Our minds. The *Gille Dubh's* smile faded, but didn't go away entirely. *We were wrong about you. I was wrong about you.*

Cuinn blinked. *Me personally?*

Yes. All the slaid—*all the Fae of Purgatory. But you in particular.*

There was a chance, a nonzero chance, that the world might be ending. Prudently, Cuinn kept that thought to himself. *Seriously?*

I saw what you sought to save us from in the Sundering.

Íosa, Muire agus Íosaef. The gods were Rian's, as was the exclamation, but the exclamation, at least, was catching. He'd tried in vain, millennia ago, to explain the *Marfach* to the tree folk, and his failure to do so had all but killed two races. *How did you—why did you—*

My darag *had thought to shield me from seeing, but when he showed Terry, I also saw.*

When it—wait, Terry? Cuinn held up a hand. *Terry as in the gorgeous dancer who's so bad at relationships he could almost be a Fae? That Terry?*

I believe so, yes. Unless there is another Terry.

You were showing Terry the Marfach*? Why?*

There will be time for that tale later, if Maelduin is able to bring him back.

Maelduin? Someone had apparently let a razorwing loose in Cuinn's gut. The feeling was unpleasant in the extreme. Almost as unpleasant as the thought of Tiernan's vengeful nephew having found his way to the next world over, and being mixed up with Josh and Bryce's ex. *Back from where?*

Others will answer your questions soon. No one else, though, can say what I must. Coinneach squared his shoulders, showing off—inadvertently, Cuinn guessed—a hard-muscled physique that would undoubtedly prove a sore distraction to any Fae not *scair'ain'e. You did what you could to save us—not just the* Gille Dubh *and the* daragin, *but all the folk of two worlds. And the Fae... I have seen, you are not as you once were.*

The intensity of Cuinn's relief had more or less the same salutary effect on his balance as a judiciously-applied two-by-four. *Are you saying we're back in your good graces? You're willing to trust us? To trust me?*

There was always a certain innocence to the strange gaze of the *Gille Dubh.* Sometimes, though, a Fae had to look very, very hard to find it. *If you are willing to trust me.*

Faen had a great many words for 'irony.' At the moment, Cuinn couldn't bring a single one to mind; he was too busy living into the concept. *I'm guessing a simple 'yes' isn't going to be enough.*

Coinneach shook his head. *Hold still. Completely still.*

Before Cuinn could react, the *Gille Dubh*'s hand was around his throat. Not tightly, but firmly.

I—

No. Fuck, those eyes were hypnotic. Dark brown, almost black, like the rich earth of the Realm, shot through with darts of a brilliant apple-green. *What I need to do is not supposed to be possible. I would appreciate minimal distractions.*

For perhaps the first time in his long life, Cuinn an Dearmad did as he was told.

Starting at Coinneach's shoulder, his arm shifted, twisted, became wood. The hardness, the grain, worked its way down his arm to his elbow, his forearm. At that point, Cuinn couldn't see it anymore, but he thought he had a good idea of what to expect next, and braced himself for the moment when the hand around his throat solidified. He could feel power in it, the same strange magick that powered travel through the wellsprings and had stolen his voice.

Then he gasped, as his own neck stiffened, from under his jaw nearly to his collarbone. He could still breathe, though his breath felt and sounded strange, like wind through a wooden flute.

He's turning me into a tree. He's turning me into a fucking tree.

Revenge, after he'd given Coinneach and all his kind more than two millennia of oblivion?

Now *there* was logic a Fae could understand.

Rian, dhó-súil, *I'm sorry. Don't burn them...*

Coinneach's hand fell away; the *Gille Dubh* staggered, caught himself. Cuinn's throat relaxed, the skin and muscle softened, and everything between his head and his shoulders was his own again—though that didn't stop him from checking with a hand, just to be sure everything was what it was supposed to be.

And the darkness fell away, revealing a semi-circle of Fae and humans. Tiernan, Kevin, Rhoann, Josh—with *Scathacrú* and *Árean* orbiting him like a couple of crazed moonlets—Conall, transforming

283

before his eyes from ginger twink to thunder-browed mage... and Rian, Cuinn's beloved, blue eyes ablaze through a curtain of blond hair and heat crazing the air around his hands.

Heat, and the first curls of flame.

"Twinklebritches, can you channel a fire extinguisher?" Cuinn croaked.

* * *

"Terry. *Lán 'ghrásta*, please. Wake up."

He hadn't fallen asleep. That would have been idiotic. Anyone knew better than to fall asleep in the cold, even a New Jersey kid who had never personally been colder than when making a deli run during a blizzard because his selfish-ass boyfriend had had a craving for licorice ice cream...

"Terry. *Please*."

If Maelduin was as upset as he sounded, maybe Terry *had* fallen asleep. Shit.

But... he wasn't cold. He was perfectly comfortable. Other than his clothes feeling damp, anyway.

"Terry..."

I'm an ass. Terry opened his eyes... and dear God, there was Maelduin. Beautiful blue eyes staring right back at him. "You came," he croaked—his voice, at least, seemed to think he'd been frozen.

Maelduin's smile made Terry feel even warmer, and the hesitant kiss that followed it stole Terry's breath. "Of course I came." Chill fingers brushed hair from Terry's forehead. "Did you think I wouldn't?"

"I told you not to—oh, *shit*." Terry tried to sit up,

but the best he could manage was pushing himself up to prop himself on an elbow. "The timeslip—the *Marfach*—what's happened?"

"You're lying on the last of the barrier." Maelduin urged him to lie back down; what had been ice and a glittering web under him was now the same translucence that had surrounded him back in the studio. "I broke it trying to come after you. And the *Marfach*…"

The Fae craned his neck to study the circle where ice met sky; when he turned back to Terry, his eyes were oddly bright, ice crystals lingering on impossibly long lashes. "I'm here to get you out of here, whatever it takes. The *Marfach* matters less to me than you do."

You can't mean that, Terry nearly blurted. Sure, he'd hoped, when Coinneach sent him away. But all that meant was that he'd managed to forget, yet again, that hope was just another four-letter word.

Wait. Something in Maelduin's eyes, and in the sudden tightness of his grip on Terry's hand, brought Terry up short. He'd forgotten their bond, the force strong enough to break the desperate magick of the *daragin.*

Maybe Maelduin did mean exactly what he'd said. What Terry had secretly longed to hear someday, despite years of trying to convince himself words like those were strictly for other men.

Maybe all Terry had to do was believe him.

Something dug into Terry's fingers as Maelduin squeezed his hand. A ring, a massive gold ring with a figure carved into the flat oval surface. Heat radiated from the metal, warping the air around it and somehow burrowing straight into Terry's bones.

Maelduin saw him looking, and turned the ring slightly, letting the carving catch the light. "It's called the *Croí na Dóthan*—the Heart of Flame."

"It's beautiful." An understatement—it was breathtaking. And it was probably what was keeping him alive at the moment. Strangely, though, Terry was much more interested in looking at the face of the Fae who had followed him into hell to rescue him from the devil itself. He was pretty sure he was being warmed as much by blue eyes, a hesitant smile, a barely visible scruff of blond beard and the memory of chafing his own lips tender against it, as by the gorgeous golden trinket.

Maybe… I finally chose right?

He wriggled his fingers, just enough to feel Maelduin's touch and make the light dance on the patterned gold. "I don't suppose this is a proposal?"

Terry felt his face go red even before he'd finished blurting the nonsensical words. *Dear God. I'm lying at the bottom of a pit of ice, a monster straight out of Satan's worst nightmares probably breathing down the back of my neck, and I start playing Bachelor - The Gay Edition?*

Maelduin frowned. Even his frown was gorgeous, although the ice in his eyebrows was worrisome. "I… am not sure I understand."

Damn. Damn, damn, damn. Merde. Dannazione. *Damn.*

Maelduin's hand closed around his. "It's my heart. Is that the same thing as a 'proposal'?"

Oh dear God. Terry stared, for what felt like forever, his brain doing a decent imitation of Bambi on the ice. "I — uh… maybe. Yes."

Maelduin's smile transformed his face. His eyes brightened, and for the first time Terry noticed the brilliant blue was faceted, clear, like perfect gemstones. His skin, pale from the bitter cold, flushed and warmed, turning pellets of ice to tiny trickles of water. And his mouth, God, that smile was the most kissable thing he'd ever seen in his life.

And all of it was because he'd just proposed. *To me. He's that happy because of me.*

I finally chose right.

* * *

The wonder writ plain on Terry's face snatched away what little of Maelduin's breath the wind had left him. *Fae have been fools, as long as there have been Fae, to think that magick and intrigue are better than what I see here.*

Terry's fingers brushed Maelduin's cheek, and he shivered in a way that had nothing to do with the cold. *Or have we feared this? Have we fled, as a race, from something we could not control... and which might control us?*

Maelduin captured Terry's hand in his, letting the warmth of it penetrate his chilled fingers. "If I understand the word, a 'proposal' is a thing that wants answering. Yes?"

Terry flushed, and even over the howl of the wind Maelduin could hear his heart racing. "You're right. And... yes. Whatever you mean by it. Yes."

'Miracle' was another word Maelduin had heard from the trapped spirits in the box. Another word he had not fully understood; it had something to do with

287

impossibility, and more to do with the kind of wonder he saw in Terry's eyes and heard in his breathless laughter. Now, though, he understood it fully, as magick welled up in him and spilled out, and drew him down to kiss the human male who was his *scair-anam* — and his willing mate.

Terry gasped beneath him, and shivered, and arched. And nothing in Maelduin's life had ever felt as wonderful as Terry's arms going around him, Terry accepting him. Not even the sex and the magick that had left him dazed and breathless.

"Is this SoulSharing?" Terry whispered.

Maelduin could feel his human's lips moving against his own, and breathed in the heat of his breath. The elemental Fire of the *Croí na Dóthan* was superficial compared to this warmth; Maelduin could even ignore the rising shriek of the wind. For now.

"I think so." 'This' was certainly a most unFae sensation—love, without trickery, without artifice, without proof asked or proof given.

"I should have believed you, then." The unsteadiness of Terry's voice surprised Maelduin. "All this happened because I didn't believe you."

"No." Maelduin laid a finger over Terry's lips. "You should not have believed me, because I was not worthy of belief. Not then." The magick of their Sharing still danced on Terry's skin, beautiful and distracting. "And I look forward to persuading you that I am no longer a complete *amad'n*. But first I need to get both of us out of this... incredibly inhospitable place."

"I don't think Coinneach can hear me from here. I tried the mind-speech, for a long time, until I—I think I fell asleep." Terry shivered, with the memory of cold or with the actuality; the wind seemed to know a chance of rescue had arrived, and was determined to claim its prize.

Perhaps even the Fire in the *Croí* was insufficient to beat back this cold for long. And Fae were naturally resistant to temperature extremes, more so than humans—but even Fae had their limits. "The barrier is the problem. The *Gille Dubh* and *daragin* dare not drop it until they're certain the *Marfach* is nowhere nearby."

Terry glanced upward, almost involuntarily, and shuddered. "I saw it, I think. Just for a second. But then it disappeared."

"Disappeared? How?" Maelduin ducked his head to bury his face in the warm hollow between Terry's neck and shoulder, grateful for the respite from the wind.

"I'm not sure. I thought it just vanished. But I might have looked away, I'm not sure. It's... hard to look at."

"I was not aware it was possible to look at it at all. I have only ancient stories of it, but those stories say that the *Marfach* is formless, and a Fae who looks at it will go mad."

"Your stories may be out of date. Or maybe not. It's... beyond hideous." Somehow, Maelduin could tell the spasm running through Terry was a shudder, and not a shiver.

Maelduin was doing enough shivering for both of them. "I can bear hideousness. Let me be certain the monster is gone."

And then what? He thought he might be able to locate the other Fae with his magickal sense, but

Fading back to tell Coinneach it was safe to bring Terry home would require a level of calm and concentration impossible to achieve in the freezing gale.

Perhaps I should have thought of this sooner.

One step at a time.

"What are you going to do?"

Maelduin eyed the rough face of the ice, stretching up all around them toward the gray, cloud-scudding sky, three times the height of a tall Fae. "Climb. Look. And if the *Marfach* is waiting, kill it."

He was not expecting Terry's quickly-muffled snort of laughter. "Did I make a joke?"

"Sorry. No." Terry bit his lip. "But you can't walk across my living room without being attacked by the furniture, and maybe the floor. I can't let you try to climb that wall, you'll fall and break a leg and I missed the Boy Scout meeting where they demonstrated how to improvise a splint out of rolled-up towels."

New words and new meanings flowed over Maelduin, leaving little or no trace. All that remained with him was the laughter in the words and the love behind them. Enough, and more than enough—an embarrassment of riches. He opened his hand and cupped the warmth of Terry's cheek in his palm. "We are Shared, *lán'ghrásta*. Furniture and floor have lost their power over me." *I hope.*

Terry's smile was as warm as his kiss. "Be careful, then. This wind is almost as dangerous as my carpet." The smile lingered on Terry's lips, but worry welled up in his eyes. "And if that thing is up there, don't stick around."

"No longer than necessary. I promise."

Before Terry's eyes could break his resolve, Maelduin rose, bracing himself against the gale, working his fingers to bring warmth and feeling back into them. The ice rising up around him was far from smooth; he had climbed rock faces more sheer, and that with his *comhrac-scátha* seeking to pull him down.

If my skills are truly my own again...

He closed his eyes, and remembered Terry's warmth. His acceptance.

They are ours.

Maelduin leaped, working his fingers into cracks in the ice almost halfway up the wall, seeking purchase with the soft toes of his boots. His fingers were so cold, he scarcely felt the chill of the ice, and there was no time to cling to the frozen face; he boosted himself up, squinting into the wind and finding places for his hands by sight rather than by touch.

Just below the surface he finally paused, pressed close against the wall so as not to be torn away by the wind. For all he could tell by listening, a horde of *Marfaicha* waited over his head—the wind surely sounded like some sort of monster. And for the first time he wondered how he was to kill a creature legend said could not die. Oh, every mythical evil had its weak point, probably equally mythical—supposedly the *Marfach* could not abide water, and could be made to die if it forgot its own nature. But the only water within reach was frozen solid, and if there was a channeling to give evil incarnate amnesia, Maelduin had no notion what it might be.

And then there was his sword to contend with—if his uncle's blood was not the first it tasted, it would turn in his hand and kill him.

Maelduin would have shrugged, but keeping his numb grip on the ice was more important than a gesture. If the *Marfach*'s blood was the first to stain his sword, it would buy Terry a chance to live.

A moment's lull in the wind ended the chase of thought after thought; Maelduin braced the sole of his right boot against a near-vertical wedge of ice, dug the fingers of his left hand into a crevice, and vaulted to the surface. His sword cleared its scabbard as he leaped; he landed in a crouch, turning slowly, his breath hissing through clenched teeth as the wind, apparently angry at having missed an opportunity to kill him, sliced into every inch of his skin as if he were naked.

He was alone. Alone in the most desolate land- and sea-scape he had ever seen. Crumpled ice surrounded him, shades of gray, dirty white, and a dull blue under a leaden sky. Water stretched to the horizon in one direction, studded with floating islands of ice; in the other direction, a field of jagged broken ice extended for an unguessable distance, until it met with what might have been a landmass. Or maybe it was simply more ice.

What hell is this? And where was the *Marfach*? Maelduin turned on his heel, squinting into the wind, studying the outcroppings of ice, the shadows they cast, looking for anything that moved or any shadow other than what a chunk of ice would lead one to expect.

Nothing.

Maelduin's gaze caught on something not white or gray or blue, something stuck to the ice. Rough patches of brownish red, and something paler; he knelt beside one of the blotches and brushed away pellets of ice.

The brownish red was blood, from the way it had dripped and splashed. And the other might have been flesh, though grayer than any Maelduin had ever seen, left by a creature frozen to the surface and uncaring of what it might leave behind in its attempt to escape.

But it had escaped. It was gone.

Maelduin turned; three strides brought him to the edge of the icy pit, and a leap took him over the brink. And the wind took him.

This might have been a bad idea—

He landed several body-lengths from a wide-eyed Terry, his chilled muscles reverberating with the shock of his landing.

"Looks like my furniture won't be a threat anymore," Terry murmured, barely audible over the wind.

Maelduin ran back to Terry and fell to his knees. "It's gone. There's no sign of it." He cupped both of his hands around one of Terry's, heat coming off the *Croí* as if it were a live ember.

"Thank God." Terry flexed his fingers, tickling the inside of Maelduin's palm. Deliberately, or not, Maelduin wasn't sure—but either way, he could scarcely feel it. "Now what do we do?"

Damn. The proverbial Vile King's third question. "Somehow, we have to let the *daragin* know the barrier is no longer needed."

"But they can't hear us through it."

"Tally one. And tally two, the *folabod'ne* wind keeps me from concentrating long enough to Fade

293

back to your studio to gain help that way." As if it heard its name being called, a blast of wind whirled down into the pit; Maelduin ducked his head and narrowed his eyes to slits, but the blade of the wind bit deep just the same.

"How do you stand it?" Terry's voice was soft, unsteady. "I would have frozen to death if you hadn't come for me."

Maelduin brushed his cheek against Terry's, numb lips curving into a smile at the faint sensation of beard against beard. "We're a hardier race than we look."

"No one's hardy enough to deal with this for long."

There was no answer Maelduin could think of, so me made none.

Terry turned his hand in Maelduin's, just enough to set the diffuse light gleaming along the curves of the *Croí na Dóthan.* "How long do you think its warmth will last?" He looked up, into Maelduin's eyes, and brushed away a strand of hoar-frosted hair. "Maybe if we trade it back and forth, we can both—"

The ring vanished from Terry's finger.

"*Merde,*" Terry whispered.

Maelduin's gift didn't translate. It didn't need to.

The wind howled again, like a *bean sidhe* scenting death.

"Fuck you, and the night-mare you rode in on," Maelduin murmured—no need to shout, when the wind was as close as his own skin. He wrapped his arms more tightly around Terry, drawing the human's head down to rest against his shoulder, and closed his eyes. "Hold tight, *lán'ghrásta.*"

Neither of them saw the scattered silver-blue light of the wellspring flare up as the barrier melted away. And no one—not even the wind—saw them disappear.

Chapter Twenty-Nine

"Shit! Get him away from the wellspring!"

The glare Lasair shot Conall would probably have set fire to anyone who wasn't a master mage. However, no one argued with Conall when he used that tone; Kevin, and everyone else except Coinneach, stepped back to let Lasair maneuver Bryce's unconscious form past the sprung-flooring sample roiling with sharp-looking flecks of silver-blue light, toward a pool of blessedly ordinary light created by one of the lights clipped to the studs marking where the walls of the studio were eventually going to go.

The reason for the tone was obvious to anyone who could see magick—Lasair was carrying Bryce the same way he'd once held the *Marfach* clear of the ground, with a channeling he'd once used on obstreperous adult Fade-hounds in the Realm. And whatever was going on with the wellsprings was triggered by magick. Not so much by elemental magick, and Lasair's channeling had a bit of Fire bound up in it, but the wellspring was all riled up just the same.

Lasair hauled Bryce to the back of the framed-in studio space and settled him carefully on the floor.

"There isn't even supposed to be a wellspring in here," the Fae muttered, kneeling beside Bryce. "Whose good idea was that?"

Cuinn cleared his throat. "That would have been the good idea of Tiernan's vengeance-minded nephew, newly arrived from the Realm."

If the circumstances had been even slightly less dire, Kevin probably would have laughed out loud at the look on Lasair's face. They'd all worn their own versions of that look a few minutes ago, when they'd heard Cuinn's voice for the first time in months.

Lasair, though, recovered quickly from the shock, apparently having other things on his mind. "When the dragon knocks down the gate, the wolves rush in behind it. Bryce collapsed in our hotel room when something happened to the *Marfach*; we decided to come over here and let you know what had happened in person, but he screamed and passed out cold in the taxi."

And you held it together long enough to get him here. Fae love—even a Fae's love for quite possibly the most thoroughly unlovable human on the Eastern seaboard—had been enough to enable Lasair to overcome the bred-in-the-bone Fae terror of enclosed moving conveyances.

Conall knelt beside Bryce, motioning sharply for Rhoann to join him. Bryce had already refused Rhoann's brand of magickal healing once, and Lasair looked ready to enforce his *scair-anam*'s wishes, but changed circumstances—

"What the feck?"

Rian was holding his hand out in front of himself, staring at the *Croí na Dóthan*, encircling his finger as if it had never left.

Cuinn took Rian's hand in his own, studying the ring. "You said it went off with Maelduin?" he asked no one in particular.

Josh nodded. "To keep him warm, most likely. Him or Terry."

"Well, I could see it stepping away to let the nexus guardian's would-be murderer freeze to death." Cuinn didn't look displeased at the prospect, and Kevin caught himself nodding in agreement.

"But not Terry." Josh spoke quietly, firmly.

"No. Not Terry." Cuinn looked back over his shoulder, to where Coinneach stood silent guard over the wellspring. And the air was filled with shadow and moonlight, a sharp gust of wind rattling the leaves of unseen trees.

Coinneach nodded and closed his eyes. The wind rose, then died.

And a cloud of wicked-edged magick rose in the circle of the wellspring, with two men lying in the middle of it.

No. One man, and one Fae. Both rimed with frost, huddled around each other.

"Off the wellspring!" Conall's voice snapped like a whip.

Maelduin scrambled to his feet and helped Terry up. No, he didn't scramble—he flowed, graceful as water.

Shit. They must have Shared. Kevin's teeth ground together as Maelduin and Terry stepped down from the low platform. Maelduin's arm was around Terry's waist, and Terry's hand sought Maelduin's; ice broke and fell from their clothing and hair, melting to leave puddles on the concrete floor.

Conall eyed the disturbed magick suspiciously; only when he was convinced it was subsiding did he turn to Maelduin and Terry. "Is the *Marfach* dead? Or gone?"

"Gone, as far as I could tell." Maelduin shook his head, sending ice and water flying. "We were in a pit of ice. I climbed out of it, and there was so little to be seen, I'm certain I would have seen it if it had been there. And there were bits of its flesh and blood frozen to the ice."

"It Faded."

The slurred sound of Bryce's voice and his feeble attempt to sit up were possibly the only things that could have taken everyone's collective attention off the newly returned pair. Everyone's attention but Kevin's, anyhow; he was all ears, but there was no way he was taking his eyes off his husband's sworn killer.

"I don't think so." Conall sounded dubious at best. "Its substance is human, and humans can't Fade—and I've already force-Faded the whole monster a couple of times, so even if it had a tolerance for it, it wouldn't risk a voluntary Fade."

Groggy as he was, Bryce still managed a weak snort. "Your theory is impeccable. But I don't think the *Marfach* gives a fuck about your theory. It Faded. Trust me. And unless I'm sorely mistaken, it survived the experience."

Several groans greeted Bryce's announcement. "It could be feckin' anywhere." Rian's Belfast cadence was grim. "We're at war, and we've no notion where the enemy is."

"It'll be a long time recovering from this. Just a

299

gut feeling." Bryce ignored the groans, and what sounded like his *scair-anam* smacking him. "Sorry-not-sorry. If I don't laugh, I try to hand myself my stomach. I prefer laughing."

"We're safe for a little longer, then." Tiernan didn't sound particularly alarmed. The way he was studying his nephew, though, left Kevin feeling more than merely alarmed. "Hopefully we can spare at least a few minutes to clear a few things up."

"Are you out of your fucking mind?" Kevin hissed.

Tiernan rested his crystal hand on Kevin's shoulder, in a way that took him back to that first night in Purgatory, the first step in a short intense dance of seduction. This time, there was no gentle brush of lips against his ear, but the voice he loved was just as soft. "He's a Fae, *lanan*. He's not just going to forget about an oath."

Kevin's throat felt tight. "I know. But couldn't we pretend for a few minutes?"

* * *

Terry didn't like the way Tiernan was looking at Maelduin. Not hostile, not exactly, unless you thought a butcher looking at a choice side of beef was hostile.

"Maelduin, what's going on?" he whispered.

It took him a second to realize Maelduin was giving Tiernan exactly the same look.

"It's… complicated, *lán'ghrásta*." Terry could almost feel the effort it took for Maelduin to tear his gaze away from the other Fae.

The other Fae. *Merde*. How many of the people he knew weren't human?

"I wouldn't mind the short-form explanation."

Maelduin chuckled absently. "Since you ask... I have devoted my life to finding and killing my father's murderer, who is also my father's brother. Since coming to your world, though, I have learned that my father violated my mother, and was also her brother. And Tiernan..."

"Is the Fae you've been looking for," Tiernan finished, seeming to ignore Terry's open-mouthed shock. "Which means we have some unfinished business."

No one seemed happy with this announcement—not Tiernan, not Maelduin, and most definitely not Kevin, whose beard-shadowed face bore a distinct resemblance to a storm cloud.

Instinctively, Terry stepped between Maelduin and the others. He took both of Maelduin's hands in his, holding them so tightly his own hands shook and looking up into his Fae's blue eyes—faceted eyes, he'd seen that for the first time after they'd Shared.

"*Lan-ghrásta—*"

"No. Not yet. Let me talk." Maelduin's face, so like Tiernan's, had reassurance written all over it, and Terry wasn't ready to be reassured.

"As you wish." Maelduin's lips brushed Terry's forehead.

Terry took a deep breath. "You've asked me to accept a hell of a lot in the last few days. Or, well, maybe you haven't exactly asked me, but I've had to accept things just the same. That there's a whole world next door to mine that I've never had any reason even to imagine existed before. That a man who seemed to appear in my studio like magic really *did* appear

301

magickally. That the most incredible man I've ever met is really a Fae who wants to marry me. That there's a monster out there somewhere so vile and so dangerous I ended up getting sent to hell—"

"Antarctica, actually. Or so the others say."

"Same difference. Sent to Antarctica because the alternative was risking letting ultimate evil loose on the world."

"I agree, *m'fein*. My own. It *is* too much."

"No. No, it wasn't. It isn't. I've seen it, felt it, it may sound crazy but it's all real. But… this?" He gripped Maelduin's hands tighter, until his own knuckles went white. "Now I have to believe that you're here because you're sworn to commit a murder. You're going to murder my landlord. Because he murdered your father."

"He damned well isn't," Kevin growled.

Maelduin's gaze never left Terry, but one blond eyebrow went up. "I was just going to say that, actually."

Terry didn't dare look away from Maelduin to discover the sources of the gasps behind him. As far as he was concerned, as long as Maelduin was looking into his eyes, Maelduin would forget all about being a murderer, or maybe being murdered himself, since Tiernan didn't seem to be the type to take an attempted execution lying down.

"I'm curious." Tiernan's voice came from somewhere over Terry's right shoulder. "I've never seen a Fae go back on a blood oath before. What changed your mind?"

"An oath sworn for the sake of a lie is no true oath." Maelduin gathered Terry close, cupping his head in one hand, caressing his cheekbone with his thumb. "And I prefer living for a truth to killing for a lie."

Living for a truth. He means me. Us. Terry held his breath, listening to Maelduin's heart beating under his ear. *Us.*

Maelduin cursed, flinched, stepped back. Terry smelled smoke.

"*Elirei!*" Conall snapped, and from the way Rian reacted, Terry guessed the word referred to him. "Can you do something?"

The smoke was coming from the scabbard of the sword Maelduin wore at his waist; Rian strode forward and reached toward it, then snatched his hand back as though he'd just touched a live wire. "Not a thing. That's no Fire magick."

"It's setting my scabbard on fire well enough," Maelduin offered mildly, trying to ease his leg away from the dangling leather and firmly moving Terry to his other side.

"Maybe I can—"

An arc of energy, a nearly invisible warping of the air, fountained from the hilt of the sword, and even Terry stepped back—urged by Maelduin, an instant before the arc found his hand. Maelduin cursed, his arm trembling with some great effort.

And then he went silent—everyone did—as Maelduin's sword hissed from what was left of its scabbard and flew, literally flew, into his hand.

Tiernan was the first to find his voice; a voice eerily like Maelduin's. "I'm going to venture a guess that it won't allow you to put it down."

Maelduin opened his hand and flexed his wrist. The sword stayed put.

Tiernan sighed. And Terry realized that for the first time, he was seeing his Fae landlord without gloves, as a crystal long-knife seemingly grew out of a left hand formed of the same crystal. Crystal that moved, and gripped the blade as if it were still part of the hand.

This is not good.

Conall cleared his throat. "Bryce, do you think you can make it upstairs to our apartment if the rest of us help?"

"Why should I—"

Tiernan didn't look at the ruffled investment banker; his attention was all focused on Maelduin, with an intensity Terry had never seen before. "This dance wants space."

And then he did look away, his eyes pleading with Kevin. "Go with them, *lanan.*"

"Like hell I will." Sweat beaded on Kevin's brow, and for a second Terry wondered if the lawyer was going to be sick.

Come to think of it, he wasn't feeling too well, himself.

Maelduin took Terry's hand, stroking the back with his thumb, as the other Fae, and the humans other than Kevin, made their way to the door and Coinneach simply vanished in a breath of wind. "You should go, too."

A glib remark lurked just behind Terry's lips, eager to get out. *I wish you'd told me you were this crazy before I agreed to marry you.* But he couldn't speak. He just looked up into Maelduin's bright blue eyes and shook his head.

I'm not going to leave you. Now, or ever.

That one wouldn't come out either. Damn.

* * *

This isn't happening.

As usual, reality wasn't listening to Kevin; he slumped back against what he hoped was a solid section of drywall, as Terry lowered himself to sit on a spool of heavy electrical cable near the opposite wall. And Tiernan, his *scair-anam*, his husband, his Fae, his heart, tested the heft of a blade of living Stone and calmly eyed the *scian-damhsa* who had spent his whole life becoming a weapon with a single purpose.

Kevin didn't want to watch, but didn't dare look away. And closing his eyes was out of the question; every time he was stupid enough to do *that*, his premonition swept back over him, inescapable and smothering.

Don't leave me. Don't you dare. Don't you fucking dare.

"You don't want to do this." Tiernan spoke calmly, with a touch of ironic humor.

"I do not." Maelduin lifted his sword in what might have been a salute, or might have been one last futile attempt to let go of the thing. "But I seem to be left no choice in the matter."

"Then *scian'a'schian* let it be, until blades no longer thirst."

Kevin wanted to make it stop—he could feel himself move, feel his body lunging forward, stepping between the two blades before they could meet, forcing them to acknowledge the idiot human who refused to let his husband and his husband's nephew kill one another. But he didn't lunge. He couldn't move. He watched, instead, as two beautiful predators touched blades, silver ringing against crystal, and then stepped back to take one another's measure.

The two circled, marking out the boundaries of the irregular space with their feet. Learning the bounds of the arena. Once they'd made one circuit, Kevin was sure either one of them could have made another blindfolded.

Tiernan crouched slightly, waiting. Kevin thought he understood—a long knife wasn't an offensive weapon, not against a sword. *Why didn't you bring your damned sword?*

He'd only seen one sword in his vision. His premonition. Whatever the hell it had been.

Maelduin feinted, drawing Tiernan out—leaped, landing soundlessly behind him, like a cat, sword raised. Tiernan pivoted, catching Maelduin's blade on the hilt of his knife, changing the shape of the knife to let the sword pass harmlessly down the hand-guard and away.

You weren't expecting that, were you? Kevin smiled grimly at Maelduin's startlement. But the other Fae wasn't startled nearly long enough; he stepped back and circled, his gaze locked with Tiernan's, the harsh illumination of the clip-on lights glinting off his sword.

This can't be happening. Wait, I already know that.

Maelduin bore down on Tiernan with a flurry of cuts and slashes, each barely but perfectly blocked, turned aside. Kevin drew back as the two males passed him, trying not to make eye contact with Tiernan, not wanting to distract him. But Tiernan saw, just the same. And he smiled.

Don't leave me. Don't you dare.

Kevin stopped breathing. He was pretty sure his heart stopped beating, as the combatants closed with one another. Steel and truesilver rang against crystal; bodies strained together, parted, clashed. Every time Maelduin stepped back, Kevin tensed—a knife fighter had the advantage in close. A sword was a distance weapon by comparison. And Maelduin had fucking long arms, and knew how to use them to advantage.

Maelduin's jaw clenched; with no more warning than that, he moved in, one viciously efficient cut after another after another. Tiernan caught each one on the indestructible Stone blade and hilt of his knife, slowly giving ground. Maelduin followed, inexorable.

Across the room, a pale and shaken Terry looked ready to dive into the fray himself. *Maybe if we both do it… it would distract them, at least—oh, shit!*

Maelduin had backed Tiernan up nearly to the edge of the wellspring; Tiernan stopped, knowing he'd fall if he took another step back, and Maelduin raised his sword high. Before Kevin could react, Tiernan dove toward the other Fae, tucked, and rolled, twisting impossibly as he rolled to come to his feet facing Maelduin's unprotected back.

Jesus, Ianan, *end this—*

Maelduin spun and dropped into a crouch.

You don't want to end this.

The dance began again, escalating quickly as Kevin struggled to slow his breathing. He could see why the Fae called it blade-dancing—it really was a dance, a gorgeous lethal dance that made anything in *Crouching Tiger, Hidden Dragon* look like a child's first steps. Blow after blow, relentless motion blurring

307

parry into riposte into moves Kevin had no names for and would have sworn were impossible.

Yet... no blood. Sweat, yes, there was plenty of that. Gasping for breath, grunting as breath was jarred from bodies, gritting of dust and sand underfoot... but no blood.

Kevin made himself watch more closely. He was no expert in swordplay, but he'd learned a thing or two from watching Tiernan practice, and from front-row seats at several pitched battles with the *Marfach*. He had a fairly good idea what a battle to the death between expert swordsmen—swordsFae—was supposed to look like. And it wasn't supposed to look like this.

Tiernan's not trying to win. No—he's trying not to win. Slight missteps, and overcorrections; catching the truesilver blade against his blade of living Stone at just the wrong angle, and straining too hard to push it back from his arm or his throat. His *scair-anam* was making everything about this fight to the death harder than it had to be, and more dangerous.

He doesn't want to kill his nephew.

Which would make no sense to a Fae... or at least, it would make no sense to the kind of Fae Tiernan had always claimed to be, cursed and devoid of even the essential Fae capacity for kin-love.

He's wrong. He's always been wrong.

And being wrong was going to get Tiernan killed.

* * *

Losing the instincts, the inner balance he had acquired over a lifetime of training had been as close to the ancient legends of humans' Hell Maelduin had ever come. And right now, he would have given almost anything to be rid of that particular set of skills again. Honed through decades of dances with his *comhrac-scátha*, his instincts guided his body and sword through every turn and slash and block, watching eagerly for a single opening. That opening would come, surely—Tiernan was the greatest *scian-damhsa* Maelduin had ever faced, but he made mistakes. Maelduin did not. His instincts refused to let him.

He stalked forward, purposeful and tired of the histrionics of the *haricín*-form. If Tiernan wanted to close with him, take an advantage for himself, let him. Maelduin and his bloodsworn blade would deal with it.

"This blade has one purpose only, and that purpose my own: to sate itself on the blood of the male who killed my father." The mage had traced the ancient words of the oath, and Maelduin's personal geas, on the blade with the tip of a cockatrice's feather dipped in salt and oil as Maelduin spoke them. *"And if it should be used first for any other purpose, may it turn in my hand and slay me where I stand."*

Beautiful, powerful words. However, the words of channelings were themselves blades of a sort; at least, they had the same capacity to turn on one. In fact, the sword was impatient beyond the scope of the oath binding it—in theory, Maelduin should have been able to throw the sword in the ocean, assuming he could find one, or even hide it under the cushions of Terry's sofa, and all would have been well. But the sword, it seemed, wanted to fulfill his oath, one way or another.

His sword slashed down, catching the tip of

Tiernan's crystal knife an instant before it would have opened up his wrist. Tiernan swept past, turning only when he had gained a narrow space, probably an unfinished hallway, easier to defend with a short blade.

If he fights only to defend, he fights to lose.

Maelduin did not want his uncle to lose. It was as simple, and as strange, as that. His oath had been a lie since it was spoken, and only Tiernan had cared enough to tell him so. He had no desire to kill the only Fae who had ever been truthful with him, for the sake of a lie.

Yet oath and sword had both twisted in his hand. Truesilver was metal which understood its own purpose, and this blade understood too well. If he failed to kill Tiernan, he himself would never be safe—the sword could turn on him at any moment.

Maybe I should take that chance. Maelduin advanced on Tiernan, as slowly as he could without making the invitation to run too obvious to ignore.

Movement off to his right caught his eye. Terry, his face pale and tear-streaked, pressed a fist against his mouth, trying to smother soft sounds of distress still perfectly audible to Fae hearing.

Terry. If Maelduin abandoned his oath, and the sword took him, what would happen to Terry? What happened to a SoulShare when the other half of his soul died?

Something blurred past Maelduin, something that gleamed. Startled, he turned; Tiernan had shifted his long knife to his right hand, and a small, wicked crystal dart appeared in his left hand. *From* his left hand, from the living Stone of it.

This dart Tiernan threw straight for Maelduin's eyes. A sword made a terrible shield, but his *comhrac-scátha* had tried such a thing with ordinary knives, often enough that the counter was instinctive.

Maelduin never saw the third dart, but he felt it tear through his shirt and glance off his ribs. Blood bloomed around the wound; Terry gasped; Kevin took a step forward, halted.

Twice the height of a Fae away, Tiernan stood motionless, expressionless, his gaze locked with Maelduin's. Maelduin nodded slowly, once. The message of the dart was clear. A *scian-damhsa* always hit precisely what he aimed at. Maelduin's heart had been bared, his life forfeit. And his uncle had not taken it.

Tiernan went down on one knee, reached behind himself to clear his hair away from his neck.

"What the hell do you think you're doing, *lanan?*" Kevin's voice was low, tightly controlled, but perilously close to breaking for all that.

Tiernan paused and looked up at his *scair-anam;* Maelduin was unable to read the look that passed between them, but if Tiernan's intent had been to calm his male, his husband, he had done a terrible job of it; Maelduin was fairly sure Kevin wouldn't charge him in the next minute or so, but after that what happened would be a cast of the rods.

Then Tiernan's regard turned to Maelduin, and what Maelduin saw in the blue topaz eyes so like his own in the moment before his uncle ducked his head was nothing like resignation.

"I know the oath you took as well as you do." Tiernan took a deep breath, let it out slowly. "Do what it takes to sate your blade."

311

Why was Tiernan drawing his attention to the words of his oath?

"... *this blade has one purpose only, and that purpose my own...*"

... and my purpose is not to kill.

Maelduin strode forward, his boot heels loud against the concrete floor in the silence. Tiernan slowly turned his head to watch him approach, the hint of a smile touching his lips.

"Give me your hand."

Tiernan shifted his long knife back into his left hand, reabsorbing the Stone of it into his hand, and held out his empty right hand, palm up, steady.

Maelduin whipped his blade down and across, cutting Tiernan's palm just deeply enough to draw blood. He held up the sword, searching for and finding the thin red line along its edge, shining in the harsh light.

A *scian-damhsa* always hit precisely what he aimed at.

"My blade has had its fill of your blood, *dre'thair dtuismiorí.*"

Quickly he cut his own right palm, using the same spot on the blade. If he was wrong, if his oath demanded Tiernan's life after all, he would know now.

A line of bright red beads welled up along his palm. Nothing more.

He reached down and clasped bleeding hands with his uncle, raising him to his feet.

An extremely awkward moment passed as the two regarded each other; then, moved by the same impulse, they embraced. "*Geal'le'mac.*" Tiernan's voice was muffled in Maelduin's shoulder and hair. *Almost-son.*

Kevin cleared his throat. "Don't get comfortable, *lanan*, I'm still kind of seriously considering killing you myself."

Yes, this human was a good mate for a Guaire. And perhaps an uncle of a sort to Maelduin, as well.

All three looked around at the sound of Terry slumping against the wall, then sliding to the floor.

Chapter Thirty

"Terry? *Lán'ghrásta?*"

"You smell nice," Terry mumbled. It was true, Maelduin smelled amazing. At the moment, though, Terry was mostly fishing for something to talk about other than his tendency to pass out at the sight of blood.

Lips brushed his forehead, and he opened his eyes to find himself looking into Maelduin's clear blue eyes and relieved smile. Tiernan and Kevin were both crouched behind Maelduin, craning their necks to look over his shoulder.

"You okay?" Kevin rested a hand on Tiernan's shoulder for balance.

"I'm fine." Terry blushed. "I... don't do blood very well. Unless I'm piercing someone, or inking them. Ask Josh, he'll tell you."

Tiernan chuckled. "I might do that. He and the others are probably giving birth to mixed litters of puppies and kittens upstairs, wondering what's happened to us."

Kevin arched a brow. "And you think their experiments in animal husbandry are more important than..." His gesture took in all four of them, the room, the wellspring.

Tiernan could raise an eyebrow with the best of them, and his had a gold ring in it for accent. Looking from his landlord to his lover, Terry felt like several different kinds of idiot for not having recognized the family resemblance sooner. Although if he'd been asked to guess, he would have assumed Tiernan was the younger of the two by several years. *Probably a Fae thing.*

"I think our newest *scair-anaim* would probably appreciate a little alone time."

Terry didn't have much attention to spare for the ensuing conversation between Tiernan and Kevin. He was way too preoccupied with the Fae holding his hands, looking into his eyes, shifting his weight to sit down on the floor beside him instead of crouching.

So he was more than a little bemused to find himself in the passenger seat of Kevin's Mercedes, easing out of a narrow parking space behind the Purgatory construction site, while Tiernan joined everyone else in Conall and Josh's apartment and Maelduin Faded home ahead of him.

"You really didn't have to do this."

Kevin finished fixing his phone in a bracket on the dashboard—the Merc was a lovely beast, but it clearly dated back to well before anyone had thought to build Internet access into a car—and shook his head, chuckling softly. "Oh, but I did. If you'd insisted on the Metro, Maelduin would have insisted on going with you, to make sure you didn't pass out again on the way home. And I think you've seen about how well that would work. Fae and subways aren't a happy combination."

"True. Are…" Terry cleared his throat, abruptly and inexplicably shy. "Are all Fae like that?"

"Most of them." Kevin eased the car to a stop at a light. "Cuinn and Lochlann have had more time than the rest to get over it—they're both somewhere around 2,500 years old, give or take, and Lochlann in particular had a stretch of maybe five or six centuries when he couldn't use magick at all, including for Fading. But I don't think any Fae has ever willingly gotten into a moving enclosed conveyance, if he had any other option."

Two thousand five hundred years old. "Every time I learn something about Fae, I end up learning there are about a million more things I don't know." Garish colors played through the interior of the car, neon lights from storefronts, stoplights, a movie marquee.

"Welcome to the club." Kevin smiled, but it seemed to Terry that his heart wasn't in it. "I don't think that ever stops."

They made the next few lights in sequence, Terry watching Kevin and trying not to look like he was watching. He didn't know the lawyer all that well—mostly through encounters at Purgatory, one of which had been memorable due to Kevin's talents as an amateur stripper and his husband's delight in persuading him to put those talents on display. It was obvious that Kevin adored his husband—*his SoulShare*, Terry reminded himself—and would do anything for him.

"That must have been hell for you to watch," Terry blurted. "Back in the studio."

"I'm starting to lose track of the number of times I've seen hell in the last few years." Kevin's profile wasn't so much grim as distant. Sad, even. "But yeah, it was. I haven't been able to shake a bad feeling

316

lately, when it comes to Tiernan and swords." He shrugged, a barely perceptible motion. "A Fae's gotta do what a Fae's gotta do, though. And that goes for your Fae as much as it does for mine."

My Fae. A glance in the car's side mirror confirmed Terry's suspicion that he was grinning like an idiot. Not that he cared.

"Is this your building?"

"No—next block, third on the left. You can pull into the alley just past it to turn around, if you want."

Terry looked up as Kevin waited for the cross traffic to clear. There was a light in his window, and a figure standing there, a shadow against the curtain. By the time the Mercedes was pulled in next to the dumpster, Terry's heart was pounding. *He's in there. He's waiting for me.*

Kevin laughed softly and released the lock on the passenger door. "If I'd had any doubts you two somehow managed to Share in Antarctica, the look on your face would clear them right up."

Terry blushed so hard his scalp felt tight. "I... well, we…"

"Get out, already." The lawyer grinned, then sobered. "And if you think of it, thank Maelduin for not killing my husband when he had the chance."

"I will."

Terry let himself into the building, cursing the key for sticking in the lock the way it always did. Not wanting to waste any more time, he took the stairs to the third floor two and three at a time instead of waiting for the elevator — and when was the last time he had done that?

When had he *ever* done that?

317

Two nights ago—two nights!—he'd walked Maelduin slowly and carefully up these stairs, afraid to even try putting him on the elevator after what had just happened on the subway. Last night, he'd schlepped Thai take-out food up the stairs, the climb having been a small price to pay to avoid an elevator full of someone's sodden birthday party making a pit stop between one club and the next.

Now…

Now everything had changed.

Before he could get his keys out of his pocket, the door to his apartment swung open. Maelduin, his Fae, his beloved, his SoulShare, sex-appeal incarnate, blond hair tumbling down around his face and framing blue eyes and a scorching smile, was wrapped in Terry's bathrobe, an orange velour abomination Terry had bought years ago because it made him laugh.

It had lost none of its magic over the years. Terry clamped his mouth firmly shut against a giggle, but all that did was ensure the sound came out as a snort.

Maelduin was still smiling, but he was also looking more confused by the second. "What is it?"

"Oh, God…" Terry gave up trying to hold in his laughter. "That robe doesn't even fit me properly… and you're at least six inches taller than I am!"

The Fae's puzzled glance down at his knees stole what little remained of Terry's composure—and then everything became delight as Maelduin's arms closed around him and drew him into the apartment, as he heard the door click closed behind them.

"I'm sorry." Terry's voice was muffled against Maelduin's chest.

"You do not sound sorry." Terry couldn't see the

Fae, but he could hear the laughter in his voice. "Laugh. Please. I like it."

"You said that before." Terry turned his head to rest his cheek against Maelduin's chest. "Is that why you put my bathrobe on?"

"No." Kisses stirred Terry's hair. "You don't like blood. I have healed—I was only scratched—but my clothes are bloody."

"Oh." The reminder was enough to sober Terry, at least a little. "We can do laundry later. If you want. You're going to need new clothes, though—"

"You have had enough worries for any human for one day." A finger under Terry's chin tilted his face up. "I am not going to add to those worries."

As cold as he'd been, not even an hour ago, Terry thought he might melt under Maelduin's kiss. Only an idiot would spoil a perfect moment like this by trying to talk.

Enter idiot, stage right. "You're the one who's had worries. Not me."

Maelduin's sigh against Terry's lips was warm, and sweet, and maybe just a tiny bit exasperated. "Do I have to take you to bed?"

"I'd say yes."

Terry felt Maelduin's smile against his lips before he saw it. "As you wish."

Terry squawked—there really wasn't any other word that adequately captured his total loss of dignity—as Maelduin picked him up and headed for the bedroom. "Careful!"

Maelduin laughed, and the sound sent abrupt shivers arrowing down Terry's spine. Light, musical, almost innocent yet completely erotic... he'd never heard any sound like it. *And now I get to hear it for the rest of my life…*

Maelduin settled Terry on the bed, and covered his body with his own, shrugging out of the bathrobe. Terry tangled his legs with Maelduin's and wrapped his arms around the Fae's hard torso, as if he still needed the heat of his lover's body to drive away the remembered chill of the Antarctic wind.

"Yes," Maelduin whispered, gently taking Terry's earlobe between his teeth.

"Yes what?"

"Hold me. Please." Maelduin kissed and nibbled along Terry's jaw, down his throat. "When I woke, this morning, in your arms… I had never felt anything like it before. I want more."

Something in Maelduin's voice brought a lump to Terry's throat. He shifted his weight to hold Maelduin closer, wishing he'd had a chance to shuck his clothes before finding himself covered with naked Fae. "Nobody's ever just held you?"

"No one that I remember." Maelduin placed a lingering kiss in the hollow at the base of Terry's throat, then raised his head. "Fae are artists of pleasure, giving and receiving it. But holding someone, like this, is a very different thing." Maelduin's smile left Terry short of breath. "Although the choice is difficult—you have already showed me how adept you are at the *rinc-daonna*."

"What's that?"

Maelduin's cheeks went pink. He looked adorable. "The 'human dance,' I suppose you would say. It was one of the names Fae had for sex with humans, when our two worlds were one."

"You don't have to choose between them. Between being held and... dancing. If you really want to stay, I mean."

Terry wanted the words back even before they were all out of his mouth. *Yes, I really just reminded him that he doesn't have to stay.* Merde. *Maybe I am still jinxed. Or just amazingly inept.*

"Why would I want anything else?" Maelduin traced over Terry's lips with a fingertip. "Your world is my home, you have my soul, and you love me as no other ever has. You opened your home and shared your bed with a clumsy *amad'n* who could have tripped over his own shadow."

"I think maybe you did, once or twice." Terry couldn't help smiling. "As if that would have been a reason not to love you."

"You had some reason, though, that seemed good to you at the time." Maelduin's gaze dropped briefly.

Terry winced. "I have... kind of a history of bad choices. It got to the point where I assumed any choice I made would be bad. So if I wanted you—and I did, believe me—it had to have been a terrible idea."

Strangely, Maelduin looked up at this, and smiled. "And I believed Fae could not love, and I was cursed above all other Fae. So whatever I felt for you could not be love." He kissed the tip of Terry's nose. "We are two shoes cast by the same horse, you and I."

Believing it's better to be right than happy. "I think you're right."

Maelduin raised himself up just enough to let him start unbuttoning Terry's shirt. "May I suggest, *lán'ghrásta*, that we stop giving each other reasons not to love, and start loving?"

321

* * *

The row of tiny buttons proved more difficult to manage than Maelduin had expected. Not that he was still clumsy—but the utterly delicious way Terry was wriggling underneath him, trying to help him, was a distraction almost beyond bearing.

"Is something wrong?"

Terry's clear-eyed innocence made Maelduin suspect the effect might not be accidental. "Not yet," he growled, quietly delighted at the way the sound of his voice made Terry's eyes go wide. "But soon, if you continue to make it impossible for me to concentrate…"

No, that was not an innocent smile. "You think you've got problems? I may be the first man ever circumcised by the zipper of his own jeans."

The flood of images touched off by Terry's unfamiliar words took Maelduin several seconds to process; the processing left him no less confused than he had been, and slightly appalled. Terry's laughter—at his expression, no doubt—recalled his attention to what he was supposed to be doing, and also begged for a kiss, which he was happy to provide.

"I suspect we're not going to get me out of anything with you still lying on me," Terry ventured, once Maelduin let him speak again.

"You have a point." Maelduin rolled off Terry and stretched out on his back to watch his human disrobe—and, since tormenting was a game most profitably played by two, he gave his erection a few lazy strokes as he enjoyed the sight.

"Oh, fuck me." Terry ignored the last few

buttons, whether accidentally or on purpose, Maelduin had no idea, ripping the shirt off and sending tiny projectiles flying.

"I thought that was the idea."

"What happened to my solemn, formal Fae? And I just hope I'm not out of lube."

Maelduin reached for the button of Terry's jeans, turning aside briefly to hide a grin. "Your solemn, formal Fae wants you too much to stand on ceremony, and even at the best of times is only patient when waiting for an opening to present itself in combat. Which this is not, not exactly."

"Point to you." Terry grinned and leaned back on his elbows, letting Maelduin undo the button and slipping a hand into his jeans to shield his evident erection as Maelduin slid the zipper down.

Kneeling astride Terry's knees, Maelduin started working his jeans down, but quickly encountered two unexpected obstacles: Terry's formidable thigh muscles and the dampness of the heavy fabric, no doubt the product of Antarctic ice-melt. A few frustrated tugs were all he had patience for; moving Terry's hand aside, he took his cock into his mouth, nearly to the root, and groaned with delight as Terry gasped and arched upward.

"*Merde*," Terry whispered, gripping the sheets in his fists.

Maelduin pulled back, enough to give himself room to slide his tongue around the rim of Terry's head and tease the nerve bundle underneath. He was instantly rewarded with the taste he remembered, musk and the tang of salt, bead after bead.

And he straightened, eyes wide with startled

arousal. Ripples of sweetest pressure massaged his own erect cock, and a trickle of fluid like liquid glass ran down the side and gleamed in the short curly nest of hair at the base.

"Jesus." Terry's head was pillowed on one arm, and he was staring, rapt. "I want... oh, fuck, I want..."

"What?" Curious, Maelduin gripped himself, milking more of the crystal fluid that was an Earth Fae's seed from his aching cock, and watching Terry's. Terry's cock jerked, darkened, compressed, and wept one pearl after another.

"What's happening?" Terry could barely whisper; sweat trickled from his forehead, down his temples.

Maelduin swallowed hard. "I feel what you feel. You feel what I feel. *M'anam-sciar.* And what is it you want?"

"Being able to stay conscious for the next few minutes would be great." Terry's voice had mostly deserted him, but his smile had not. "This is going to be fucking incredible."

"Few minutes?" Maelduin leaned forward, covering Terry's body with his own, holding himself up with one arm just enough to let him reach between the two of them with his other hand and encircle both of their cocks. "You underestimate a Fae, *lán'ghrásta.*"

"Oh, dear God." Terry's fingers sank into Maelduin's ass; he wrapped his legs around Maelduin's, letting Maelduin feel the strength of the thighs that had let Terry soar in the beautiful pictures Maelduin had admired. "I hope the smile on my face makes the coroner jealous as hell."

"You..." Maelduin gave up trying to understand

his human. Testing the boundaries of this new bond they shared was definitely more interesting than either coroners or—*fiánn sachant!*—circumcision. "Less talk, please. More…"

"Pleasure?" Terry nipped Maelduin's throat, licked delicately.

Pleasure?

Time hung suspended, as two worlds rearranged themselves, Maelduin and his *scair-anam* at their hearts. Two males, one soul, discovering in the other what one had thought lost, and the other had been sure never existed.

"Love," Maelduin replied, kissing Terry deeply, tasting his faint unsteady cry. "*And* pleasure," he added, as their bodies started to move together—because he was, after all, Fae.

Love, and pleasure… and magick. Maelduin could feel it, could see it, swirling across his skin, spilling onto Terry, caressing him. It was rejected no more.

No more am I.

Maelduin hadn't expected the abrupt intensity of their shared sensations, the swift crest of desire. Fae took pride in drawing out every joining, driving a partner or partners to fever pitch, only to draw back from the sweet abyss and approach it again. And again, and preferably again. But the increasing heat and pressure in his sac, the delicious soft friction of cock against cock and the brush of short wiry hair, and Terry's undulating body and increasingly frantic moans — all experienced twice over—made it evident that release was going to come far too soon.

"Sorry." His voice was tight, hoarse.

325

"Sorry?" Terry's fist tangled in Maelduin's hair, pulling him down into a kiss that turned into a moan that turned into a curse. "We're going to be—*merde, merde*, merde—" Terry's body tensed, trembling, his thighs locked around Maelduin's hips.

We're going to be fucking perfect—

They came together, perfectly, so perfectly Maelduin forgot to breathe. His body strained against Terry's, his cock pulsed alongside Terry's. And living magick poured from him into his human, heightening and prolonging pleasure past anything he had ever experienced. Both of them were quickly slick, the scent of Fae and human musk heavy in the air, luscious wet sounds accompanying their gradually slowing thrusts.

"We're going to be doing this for the rest of our lives." Terry's arms curved up and around Maelduin, as if they were infinitely heavy. Slowly, his legs relaxed, dropped to the bed.

"This, and other things." He traced the curve of Terry's ear with his tongue, loving the way Terry shivered.

"S-such as?"

Maelduin slid his forearms under Terry's neck and looked down at him, a curtain of his own hair shutting out the room around them. He didn't need to see, though, to remember the beautiful pictures, the joyful soaring that had found its way into a Fae's heart.

"Teach me to fly…"

Chapter Thirty-One

Cuinn would have laughed at the way Conall was trying to wedge himself into a corner of the nexus chamber, if hadn't been close to doing the same thing himself. "So bring me up to speed, Twinklebritches. Why does the wellspring look like a school of miniature magical piranhas and feel like it wants to take me apart atom by atom?"

"Piranhas?" Conall squinted into the foam of silver-blue light. "I was thinking more along the lines of nightmare nest-floss."

"Poetic of you. What's happened?"

Conall sat back on his heels with a sigh. "Hard to be sure, without any word from the Realm. And no, there hasn't been any—about the only reason I dare come down here anymore is to check and see whether anyone's left a message."

"Give me your best guess, then, *draoi ríoga*."

The ginger mage grimaced. "You asked for it." He squared his shoulders, and in the simple movement went from a fidgeting twink to a master mage taking up a weight no one else, Cuinn most emphatically included, was up to bearing. "Having a single entry point into the Realm for all of this world's ley energy,

327

going through the nexus and the Pattern, isn't sustainable. The pressure's too great, and what we're seeing here is magick flowing back in our direction, with so much force that it's coming untethered from the wellsprings."

"Fuck us all in sequence." Cuinn stared at the wayward living magick—and past it, to the Great Nexus linking the human world and the Realm. A link that was too fucking dangerous to use any more. "What happens if everyone's favorite nemesis of all that's good and light encounters one of these new and improved wellsprings before we can find it and cap it off?"

"First, I'm not even sure they can be capped any more. Using as much magick around them as a *Marfach*-proof ward would take could just as easily set them off, and I don't think any god in the human pantheon would venture a guess as to what would happen next."

"'First' implies a 'second.'"

"Cheery, aren't you? Second, the *Marfach* can feed off any magick it finds, tethered or un-. And frankly, I don't know if it would dive into a wellspring and try to swim back to the Realm, or treat it as a refueling stop and come straight for the source." He nodded toward the whirlpool of the nexus. "Needless to say, either option is untenable."

"You mages and your big words. Remember, I'm just a simple Royal consort, in the employ of our Highness' pleasure."

"I'm starting to wonder why Coinneach gave you your voice back." Conall rolled his eyes, peridot-green gleaming in the wellspring-light.

"You missed me, admit it." The urge to tease the mage faded as Cuinn gazed into the shifting magickal light. "What the hell do we do?"

Conall ground the heels of his hands into his eyes, then let his head fall back. "I can only think of one answer, and if you can come up with a better one I'm all ears. But I think…" He drew a deep, shuddering breath. "In order to take the pressure off, the nexus has to stop being the only source of ley energy for the Realm. Which means the Pattern, the conduit on the Realm side, has to come down. The worlds have to come back together, the way they were before the Sundering."

"But what about the…"

"The *Marfach* has to die."

* * *

Where the fuck are we?

Janek would have snarled, if he'd had the energy. He'd hoped he was finally dead. Bad enough to be proved wrong—having the proof be the male's hoarse voice was a whole extra level of suckage.

His eyes opened. Two eyes. *What the fuck?* He could see they were all occupying the bitch's body, but even when the four of them weren't using Janek's physical body, whatever was left of him only saw things through the one eye Guaire had left him.

The female gasped and started crab-walking backward. Janek was stuck with seeing only what she wanted to look at, and she didn't want to look at whatever was freaking her out, but he managed to catch a glimpse of ocean, waves and spray. And rocks.

329

Not ice. *Thank fuck.* Rocks covered with green slimy weeds. The female was trying to back their body away from the water, slipping and catching herself; Janek couldn't feel the rocks under her, but he was used to that too.

At least we aren't stuck to the ice any more. The male thought that was funny. Janek thought the male could shove a broken baseball bat up his ass. **Not that Meat's going to miss a pound or two of flesh. Am I right, Meat?**

Apparently they were all forgetting about if-you-die-you-die. One big bitchy family again. *I can think of a couple of pounds you'd be better off without, but then you wouldn't have anything to do with your fucking hands.* Janek waited, bracing himself for the mental bitchslap that was coming.

Meat?

Right here, asscrumb.

Silence. Janek thought he could hear the crash of waves.

Meat?

He could feel the female smiling. "We are not breathing." She put a hand to her chest, then to her neck. "We have no heartbeat."

Like fuck we don't.

The male was smiling, too. **Don't look now, but I think we got lucky.**

"Yes. Our poor meat wagon is finally dead."

AND YET WE LIVE.

They shuddered at the abomination's grating voice. All of them, the late unlamented Janek O'Halloran included.

IT IS TIME FOR US TO GO HOME.

330

An Excerpt from
Back Door into Purgatory
Book Nine of the SoulShares Series

Chapter One

November 15, 2013 (human reckoning)
The Realm

The soft chiming of Aine's water-clock, three hours before dawn, found her in the empty, echoing space between sleep and wakefulness. No sleeping-draught, and no channeling, would have let her sleep soundly tonight, not when she knew what was happening not five minutes' walk from her bower. She was no longer part of the Loremasters' conclaves, but something within her still moved to their rhythm.

Yawning, she sat up and reached for the sheer robe draped across the end of her sleeping-couch; as she settled the robe over her shoulders, she ran a quick channeling through her thick red hair. Nothing elaborate, just enough so as not to arrive at the Pattern-tower looking as if she'd turned and tossed the entire night.

Her fellow Loremasters would know, though. They always did.

Picking up parchment and quill and inkstone, she stepped down from her bower. The grass was cool against her bare feet, the breeze gentle and scented with night-blooming flowers. The light of floating Fire-flies was enough to light her path, but a sliver of the full moon was already showing itself above the distant hills to the east.

Aine shuddered at the reminders of what was to come.

Once, I could have walked between the worlds, as easily as I cross this greensward. Centuries ago, before the Fae and human worlds were sundered, before the Pattern blocked every road from world to world, a Fae who knew the way could step from one world into the next—easily, in the places where the walls between worlds were thin. But a Loremaster could walk where she would, in those days.

Light shone through the window-slits of the tower, clear white light, beckoning her. She was the only one of the tower's denizens who needed such, of course: a courtesy to her altered state.

When she Faded into the tower, Dúlánc's *tabhse* was waiting for her, kneeling in a meditative pose near the center of the web of the Pattern. 'Ghost' was, of course, not what the eldest Loremaster's image was at all—what Aine saw was a projection of the embodiment of his soul, both body and soul caught in the silver-blue lines of the Pattern beneath her feet. Calling him his own *tabhse* was simply a concession to his sense of humor.

She knelt facing the elderly Fae, setting aside her writing implements and arranging the skirts of her robe and night-dress as carefully as if they were the finest gown and she were his guest at a wine-tasting. Only when every last fold was settled to her liking did she meet his gaze. "Is it done?"

His eyes were his answer; his nod merely confirmed it. "The Foreseeing is complete."

"And?" Aine wished she could be as calm as Dúlánc seemed to be, but she had never been much good at that. She was more like Cuinn, the youngest of them—though Cuinn was, of course, a law unto himself—and could not quite keep the edge of her fear from her voice.

"The endgame has begun." The Loremaster sighed deeply, soundlessly. "There are many paths forward for those who must fight; all but one end in chaos, and blood, and two worlds begging in vain to have the twisted evil of the *Marfach's* tainted magick removed from them."

"All but one?" Aine arched a brow. "And where does that one path end?"

"Darkness. The darkness of our own unknowing." Dúlánc shrugged, a tight little gesture. "One path would not reveal its end to us, no matter how we pressed."

"Then that is the path our Fae in the human world must take."

Again the Loremaster nodded. "If the monster had not forced our hand at the time of the Sundering, if we had not had to act before we were ready, our shaping of events would have led them surely to the right course of action. As it was, the corrections we attempted from time to time worked—"

"Mostly." Aine's eyes narrowed. "Our interference caused a great deal of pain to those whose goodwill we needed." Most Fae—and certainly most Loremasters—would have no objection to using humans as bait for exiled Fae. But Aine, more than any of them, had come to know the Fae and humans of the expatriate Demesne of Purgatory.

"Those Fae and their humans repaid us by rejecting our plan and using brute magickal force on the Pattern." There was no anger in Dúlánc's voice, not anymore; this was an old argument, and a fruitless one. "Their interference turned us onto an unknowable path."

"And here we find ourselves." Aine glanced up at the sole round window in the row of slits; the moon was not yet visible, but the glow in the night sky heralded its coming. *Her* coming, if Cuinn's tale was to be believed. "Am I to send them a message?"

"Yes." Dúlánc turned his head to follow the direction of her gaze. "And then we must prepare to hold the portal with all our strength. That much we know."

Aine reached for her writing implements; spreading the parchment on the clear stone in front of her, and channeling a few drops of water onto the inkstone, she touched quill to stone, then looked up. "What am I to tell them?"

Dúlánc was silent for the space of a few breaths, his *tabhse* looking around at the brilliant strands of silver-blue wire embedded in the stone of the floor, the strands holding the souls and the bodies of over a thousand Loremasters, who had given up everything else they were in order to form the last line of defense against the ancient enemy of their race. "We dare not direct them, even to the slight extent that we know what they will do. If we tell them what to do, they will fall from the narrow way, and we—and they—will lose everything."

"It has ever been thus." Actually, the reply that came first to Aine's mind came in Cuinn's remembered voice. *No shit, Sherlock, what was your first clue?* It had never been clear to Aine whether the injunction against giving directions to the Fae of Purgatory had its roots in the innate nature of the magickal construct designed to bring two worlds and the monster seeking to destroy them into alignment at the perfect time, or in the essence of Fae stubbornness. Probably both. "Then what shall I write?"

"They do not need to be reminded of what they must do—they need to be reminded of who they are. Or, in some cases, who they have become, since they left us."

Impossible to keep Cuinn's words from her lips any longer. "Could you possibly be any more cryptic? I do have all night, after all."

Dúlánc laughed. "We miss having you among us, *chara*. Very well; listen closely."

Taking her lower lip between her teeth, Aine wrote, in flowing *d'aos'Faein* script:

Osclór, Nartú
Tobar, Soladán
Nidantór, Breathea
Glanadorh, Coromór, Farthor
Scian-omprór, Nachangalte
Crangaol, Síofra
Gastiór, Laoc, Caomhnór
Fánadh, Ngarradh

"Make haste, sister." Dúlánc's voice was even

softer than it had been, as she finished writing and blew gently on the parchment; he was fading from view as he spoke. The magickal lights went out, one by one, as he vanished, leaving only the light of the full moon flooding the chamber, nearly centered in the round window.

Aine wondered if her cohorts could hear the hammering of her heart, disembodied as they all were. Leaving quill and stone on the crystal floor, she stood and channeled her mageblade. The sword of pure truesilver, the price of a Demesne's worth, appeared in her hand; bound to her, and to her protection, it was about to be tested as no sword had ever been.

She bent and placed the blade flat on the floor, and stepped onto it. The metal was cold and hot at once under her bare feet, surely too slender for her purpose. But she had no choice. Writing directly through the Pattern no longer worked; this was their last chance to send a message to the exile Demesne, and the only way to be sure their missive survived the hammer-winds and passed through the Pattern was for a Loremaster to channel an equal force to drive it through.

Without being driven through it herself.

The moon cleared the window-rim, burning white surrounded by the blackness of the night. Aine wondered that the full moon had ever seemed benign to her. *Does she hate us, for her captivity?*

A breeze caught at the hem of her robe, playful, teasing. A gust darted up under her gown, then tugged. Tugged harder. Wind circled her, no longer teasing, wrapping robe and nightgown around her legs.

I would have done better naked. Aine clutched

the parchment and stared at the floor, waiting. Waiting for the crystal to fall away, for the floor to be full of stars.

A blast of wind rocked her, forcing her to step off the sword-blade. She snatched her foot back and planted it firmly on the hilt of the sword, before she was even aware of the chill of the stone.

Crystal vanished. All that was beneath her now was the Pattern, wire-blades as thin as a thought, capable of slicing soul from soul. And all that was between her and such a fate was the sword on which she balanced, barefoot and buffeted by a captive hurricane.

She had to act now, swiftly, while the way was open, and before she could fall again. She braced herself against winds pushing her this way and that, whirling, their voice a low ragged howl shaking the walls of the confined space, and held the parchment out in front of her. The gale caught it like a sail, tried to wrest it from her.

I have a tempest of my own.

Closing her eyes, she channeled Air. Living magick and elemental answered her summons, welled up from within her and flowed through her and trembled in her outstretched hands. The wind rocked her, battered her—but she was finding its rhythm now, balancing on the sword as if it were an unbroken riding-eagle.

And when the wind blasted upward, she was ready; she spread her hands atop the parchment, palms down, and released her own whirlwind.

The winds fought briefly over the precious sheet, but Aine poured magick into her captive gale, and the

337

Loremasters' message vanished through the deadly lacework.

The wind roared, like a living thing. Perhaps it was. It had been conjured to hunt, and it had been cheated; nothing in the tower looked or smelled or tasted like prey, save the red-haired Loremaster in her lilac robes, balanced precariously on her mageblade.

It was easier with her eyes closed; her body knew what to do, when to push back, when to lean away. She wished she could close her ears, to distance herself from the insane howling of the gale, but she could not spare the concentration for the channeling.

Surely it's nearly over—

The wind blasted Aine from behind, a stooping gryphon complete with a paralyzing roar. Caught off guard, she fell forward.

And landed on her knees, on cold crystal, in a chamber gone silent and still.

She huddled on the stone, gasping for breath, exultant. She had done her part; the Loremasters' message had gone to the human world. It was sealed away now, on the far side of the portal.

Perhaps forever.

Glossary

The following is a glossary of the *Faen* words and phrases found in *Hard as Stone, Gale Force, Deep Plunge, Firestorm, Blowing Smoke, Mantled in Mist, Undertow,* and *Stone Cold*. The reader should be advised that, as in the Celtic languages descended from it, spelling in *Faen* is as highly eccentric as the one doing the spelling.

(A few quick pronunciation rules — bearing in mind that most Fae detest rules—single vowels are generally 'pure', as in ah, ey, ee, oh, oo for a, e, i, o, u. An accent over a vowel means that vowel is held a little longer than its unaccented cousins. "ao" is generally "ee", but otherwise diphthongs are pretty much what you'd expect. Consonants are a pain. "ch" is hard, as in the modern Scottish "loch". "S", if preceded by "i" or "a", is usually "sh". "F" is usually silent, unless it's the first letter in a word, and if the word starts with "fh", then the "f" and the "h" are *both* silent. "Th" is likewise usually silent, as is "dh", although if "dh" is at the beginning of a word, it tries to choke on itself and ends up sounding something like a "strangled" French "r". Oh, and "mh" is "v", "bh" is "w", "c" is always hard, and don't forget to roll your "r"s!)

a'bhei'lár　　　　lit. "to be the center"; an extremely charismatic person

ach   but

adhmacomh   wood-bodied. An insult.

adhmam   admit, confess

a'gár'doltas   vendetta (lit. "smiling-murder")

agean   ocean

agla   fear(n.)

állacht   beautiful. Can be used to describe persons of any gender.

    m'állacht   my beauty. Fiachra's pillow-name for Peri.

amad'n   fool, idiot

anam   soul

    m'anam   my soul. Fae endearment.

    n'anamacha   their souls

aon-arc   unicorn

asiomú   'reversal-vengeance'. The act of making oneself crave whatever is being done to one as a punishment, thereby turning one's punisher into one's procurer.

asling   dream

át   spot

   át mil   (pl. *átenna milis*) sweet spot

atráth   postponement. As close as *Faen* gets to a word for 'truce.'

batagar   arrow

beag   little, slight

blas   taste (v. imp.)

bod   penis (vulgar)

   bod-snadhm   dick-knot. An unpleasant situation.

bodlag   limp dick (much greater insult than a human might suppose)

bragan   toy (see phrase)

briste   broken

buchal alann   beautiful boy

cac   excrement

ca'fuil?   Where?

callte   hidden

carn	pile
ceangal	(1) chains
ceangal	(2) Royal soul-bonding ceremony in the Realm (common alt. spelling *ceangail*)
cein fa?	Why?
céle	general way of referring to two people
le céle	together (alt. form *le chéle*)
a céle	one another, each other
chara	friend
cho'halan	so beautiful
chort-gruag	"bark-hair". Derogatory way of referring to a dark-haired Fae
Clo'che	living Stone
cnasaigh	heal (v. imp.)
coladh	sleep
comart'	symbol

comhrac-scátha	mirror-foe; a magickal duplicate of the bearer whose only purpose is to fight to death or dismissal
cónai	live
co'salach	lit. "dirty feet". Implies feet growing in the dirt, like tree roots.
crann	tree
a'chrann	a tree
craobód	twig-dick. Insult, occasionally lethal.
crocnath	completion
m'crocnath	my completion. One of Cuinn's pillow-names for Rian
croí	heart
Croí na Dóthan	*Heart of Flame*, the signet of the Royal house of the Demesne of Fire
Cruan'ba	The Drowner. Name given to the *Marfach* by the Fae of the Demesne of Water.
Cu droc!	Bad dog!
cugat	to you

cúna	aid, assistance
dalle	blindness; verbal component of an Air mage's blinding channeling
danamhris	Lit. "to be done unto." One of the darkest words *as'Faein* for torture.
daoir	1. beloved; 2. expensive
d'aos'Faen	Old Faen, the old form of the Fae language. Currently survives only in written form.
dara-láiv	lit. "second-hand". Euphemism for masturbation.
dar'cion	brilliantly colored. Conall's pillow-name for Josh.
dearmad	forgotten
deich	ten
deich meloi	ten thousand
derea	end
desúcan	fix, repair
dhábh-archann	lit. "two-become-one". Rare Fae euphemism for sex.

dhó-súil	fire-eyes. One of Cuinn's pillow-names for Rian.
dóchais	hope (n.) (alt. spelling dócas)
dolmain	hollow hill, a place of refuge
domhnacht	depths
Domhnacht Rúnda	the Secret Depths, Rhoann's refuge in the Realm
doran	stranger, exile
d'orant	impossible. Josh's pillow-name for Conall.
draoctagh	magick
m'dhraoctagh	my magick. Rhoann's pillow name for Mac.
Spiraod n'Draoctagh	Spirit of Magick. Ancient Fae oath. Or expletive. Sometimes both.
draoi	teacher
dre'fiur	beloved sister
dre'thair	beloved brother

dre'thair dtuismiorí	beloved brother of my parents (beloved to the speaker, in this instance, not necessarily to the parents)
dubh	black, dark
dúrt me	I said
dúsi	Wake up (imp.)
ecáil	will see
a'ecáil	I will see
eiscréid	shit
Elirei	Prince Royal
fada	long (can reference time or distance)
Faen	the Fae language.
Laurm Faen	I speak Fae.
as'Faein	in the Fae language. *Laur lom as'Faein*—I speak in the Fae language.
Fai'mhal	feral Fae, also called Wyld-Fae. Legendary Fae who supposedly survived the Sundering without being sheltered and changed by the Loremasters.

fan   wait (imp.)

fiáin   wild

fiánn   living magick

   fiánn sachant! magick forbid (it)!

fíor   true

fiur-mhac   nephew (lit. "sister's son"; see *thair-mhac*)

flua   wet

fola   wounded, injured

folabodan   Fae sex toy. Derived from *fola*, injured, and *bod*, penis

   fola'magairl   bloody testicles. A common epithet.

folath   bleed

folathóin   bloody asses

fonn   keen, sharp

fracun   whore, Comes from an ancient Fae word meaning "use-value"—in other words, a person whose value is measured solely by what others can get from him or her.

ful-claov	blood-sword; a magickal weapon usually formed from the channeler's own blood
gallaim	I promise
galtanas	promise (n., archaic)
gan	general negative—no, not, without, less
gan derea	without end, eternal
gaoirn	wolves
g'demin	true, real
g'deo	forever
geal	bright, brilliant
cho'geal	as bright
geal'le'mac	almost-son, as dear as a son
g'féalaidh	may you (pl.) live (see phrases)
g'fua	hate (v.)
g'mall	slowly
grafain	wild love, wild one. Lochlann's pillow name for Garrett.

gran	sun
an'ghran	the sun
halan	beautiful
haricín	hurricane; a form, or style, of Fae swordplay
iasc	fish (n.)
iasc'in	little fish. Rhoann's mother's pet name for him.
impi	I beg
inní-cnotálte	lit. "knitted-guts." An intestinal disturbance brought on by nerves.
laba	bed
as a'laba!	(Get) off the bed!
lae	day
laghda	debasement, groveling
lámagh	hot (v., p.t.)
lán'ghrásta	graceful, implying flight.
lanan	lover. Tiernan's pillow name for Kevin, and vice versa

lanh   son

   laród-scatha   mirror-trap. Essentially a magickal ball with no exterior, only a mirrored interior. And the sweet revenge of all of us who failed solid geometry in high school.

lasihoir   healer

Lath-Ríoga   Half-Royal. A name for Rhoann.

laurha   spoken (see phrases)

   related words   *laurm*, I speak; *laur lom*, I am speaking, I speak (in) a language

lobadh   decayed, rotten

lofa   rotten

mac   son, son of

   mac'fracun   son of a whore

macánta   honesty

machtar   desperation; root word of *macánta*

madra   dog

magarl   testicles (alt. spelling *magairl)*

ma'nach	mine
Marfach, the	the Slow Death. Deadliest foe of the Fae race.
marh	dead
martola	beef
marú	kill
Mastragna	Master of Wisdom. Ancient Fae title for the Loremasters.
milat	feel, sense
minn	oath
mo mhinn	my oath
misnach	courage
nach	general negative; not, never
né	not, is not
n-oí	night
'nois	now
ollúnta	solemn
onfatath	infected

orm	at me
pian	pain
pracháin	crows
prasach'te	hot mess. Means almost exactly the same thing to a Fae as it does to a human.
rachtanai	addicted (specifically, to sexual teasing)
réaltaí	star (pl. *réaltaí*)
Ridiabhal	lit. "king of the devils", Satan. A borrowed word, as Fae have neither gods nor devils.
rílacha	(it) rules
rinc	dance
rin'gcatha gríobhan	"labyrinthine dance". A euphemism for Fae sexuality
rinc-daonna	"human dance", a game of teasing and sexually overloading humans
Rinc'faring	the Great Dance, an annual gathering of hundreds of Fae light-dancers
rinc'lú	little dance

rochar   harm (n.)

rúnda   secret

sallacht   extremely stubborn

saor   free

sasann   we stand

savac-dui   black-headed hawk, Conall's House-guardian

scair'anam   SoulShare (pl. *scair-anaim*)

    m'anam-sciar   my SoulShare

    scair'aine'e   the act of SoulSharing

    scair'ainm'en   SoulShared (adj.)

scian   knife

scian'a'schian blade to blade; a duel

    scian-damsai   knife-dances. An extremely lethal type of formalized combat.

    sciana-Clo'che   knives of living Stone

scílim   I think, I believe

scol-agna	lit. "school of wisdom", school for children with high magickal potential
selbh	possession
sibh	you (pl.)
slántai	health, tranquillity

   slántai a'váil   "Peace go with you". A mournful farewell.

snadhm	knot
s'náthe	strand, necklace
s'ocan	peace, be at peace
sol'fiáin	(v.) complete, make complete
spára	spare
spára'se	spare him
spiraod	spirit
suait	turbulent
súil	eyes
sule-d'ainmi	lit. "animal-eyes", dark brown eyes

sumiúl	fascinating, beguiling. Lasair's pillow-name for Bryce
sus	up
s'vra lom	I love (lit. "I have love on me")
taobhan	diversion, plaything. Term for a non-Royal Fae who occupies the bed of a Royal before the Royal is pair-bonded
ta'sair	I'm free (exclam.)
tátha	bound; verbal component of an Air mage's binding channeling
thair-mhac	nephew (lit. "brother's son"; see *fiur-mhac*)
thar	come (imp.)
Thar lom.	Come with me.
thogarm'sta	answer (imp.)
toghairm	summoned, called
Tirr Brai	Folk of Life, or Folk of Power. Living beings with magickal essence.

t'mé   I'm

tón   ass (not the long-eared animal)

tón-grabrog   ass-crumb (of the clinging variety)

torq   boar

tráll   slave

tragód'mhan   Fae dramatic form, relating in often lurid detail the consequences of lust unfortuitously expressed.

tre   three

Tre... dó... h'on... Three.... two... one...

tréan-cú   strong hound. Lasair's nickname for Setanta, his blind runt Fade-hound puppy

tróhi   fight (imp.)

trora   the vee of muscle over the hips of a Fae or human male. A noted aphrodisiac.

trych   an unspecified eyeless creature

tseo   this, this is (see phrases)

turran'agne	mind-shock, the effect on a Fae of magickal overload
uisca	water
uiscebai	strong liquor found in the Realm, similar to whiskey
veissin	knockout drug found in the Realm, causes headaches
viant	desired one. A Fae endearment.

Useful phrases:

...tseo mo mhinn ollúnta.   This is my solemn oath.

G'féalaidh sibh i do cónai fada le céle, gan a marú a céle.
"May you live long together, and not kill one another." A Fae blessing, sometimes bestowed upon those Fae foolhardy enough to undertake some form of exclusive relationship. Definite "uh huh, good luck with that" overtones.

bragan a lae   "toy of the day." The plaything of a highly distractible Fae.

Fai dara tú pian beag. Ach tú a sabail dom ó pian I bhad nís mo.   You cause a slight pain. But you are the healing of more.

Cein fa buil tu ag'eachan' orm ar-seo?   Why do you look at me this way?

Dóchais laurha, dóchais briste.   Hope spoken is hope broken.

Bod lofa dubh.   Lit. "Black rotted dick." Not a polite phrase.

Scílim g'fua lom tú.   I think I hate you.

S'vra lom tú.   I love you.

Sus do thón.   Up your ass.

D'súil do na pracháin, d'croí do na gaoirn, d'anam do n-oí gan derea.   "Your eyes for the crows, your heart for the wolves, your soul for the eternal night." There is only one stronger vow of enmity in the Fae language, and trust me, you don't want to hear that one.

Lámagh tú an batagar; 'se seo torq a'gur fola d'fach.   "You shot the arrow; this wounded boar is yours." The equivalent *as'Faein* of "You broke it; you buy it." Often used in its shortened form, *"Lámagh tú an batagar."* (or *"Lámagh sádh an batagar"* for "they shot." It's probably only a matter of time before some Fae in the human world, taking his cue from "NMP" for "not my problem", comes up with "LTB".

Tá dócas le scian inas fonn, nach milat g'matann an garta dí g'meidh tú folath.
Fae proverb: Hope is a knife so keen, you don't feel the cut until you bleed.

G'ra ma agadh. Thank you.

Tam g'fuil aon-arc desúcan an lanhuil damast I d'asal. G'mall. "May a unicorn repair your hemorrhoids. Slowly." One can only imagine….

Magairl a'Ridiabhal. Satan's balls.

Se an'agean flua, a'deir n'abhann. The ocean is wet, says the river. The pot calling the kettle black.

galtanas deich meloi "promise of ten thousand." A promise given by a Fae, to give ten thousand of something to another, usually something that can only be given over time. Considered an extravagant, even irrational showing of devotion.

Támid faoi ceangal ag a'slabra ceant. We are bound by the same chains.

Né seo a'manach. This isn't for me.

mo phan s'darr lear sa masa   my favorite pain in the ass

Dúrt me lath mars'n   I told you so

Bual g'mai, aris.   Well met, again.

An'Faei a ngaill, ta'Fhaei an tráll.   The Fae who needs(, that Fae) is a slave.

lasr, s'oc as fola   Flame, frost and blood. A Fae oath, a little milder than the ones involving hearts and eyes and wolves and suchlike.

Do dalat-serbhisach.   "Your saddle-servant." The equivalent of "at your service." Usually sarcastic.

Fan lel'om. Bh'uil tú ag'eistac lom?   Stay with me. Do you hear me?

An-bfuil tuillt aige a'hartáil? Nó an-bfuil sé a'fracuin?   Is he worth saving? Or does he only have use-worth?

Sé ar'chann de dúnn.   He is one of us.

Ca' atá tú a'rá?   What are you saying?

Ní fed'r lom an'uscin lat.   I can't understand you.

Tá cúna saor in asc is'daoir.   Free aid is the dearest.

A'buil gnas le lom ar-gúl.   Fuck me backwards.

A'buil gnas le leat a's a'madra dúsigh tu suas leis.
Fuck you and the dog you woke up with.

Blas mo thón.   Taste my ass.

Sasann muid le chéle.   We stand together. Unofficial motto of the Demesne of Purgatory.

Tá'siad marh.   They're dead.

draoi ríoga   royal wizard (actually Irish, rather than *Faen*, Rian's title for his court mage)

Bei mé tú a'ecáil g'deo.   I will see you forever.

Tá thú toghairm.   Thou art summoned. (very formal)

Cac'iasc i'uisca suait.   Fish-shit in turbulent water. An expression of frustration.

Tá tú cho'geal an ghran a crocta's'náthe de réaltaí.
As brilliant as the sun on a strand (necklace) of stars. Heavily sarcastic.

Bain trall ascomath chu'garradh a'chrann.   As well try to un-cut a tree.

361

Cnasaigh croí le m'anam-scair.　　Heal (the one who is) the heart of my SoulShare.

Cadagh dom a tacht ar'shúl ó anseo le...　　Allow me to come away with...

Ta'bhar mé fhéin le... Take me with....

in loco scintillans braccis　　Latin. "In place of [the one with] twinkling trousers."

Magairl snáthith ar'srang!　　Testicles threaded on a wire!

mac'fracun fola'the　　Bloody-assed son of a whore. And yes, Conall did kiss his mother with that mouth.

Gafa id'r cú-cémne a's tine.　　Caught between (the) Fade-hound and (the) fire. An unenviable position.

About the Author

Rory Ni Coilean majored in creative writing, back when Respectable Colleges didn't offer such a major. She had to design it herself, at a university which boasted one professor willing to teach creative writing: a British surrealist who went nuts over students writing dancing bananas in the snow, but did not take well to high fantasy. Graduating Phi Beta Kappa at the age of 19, she sent off her first short story to an anthology that was being assembled by an author she idolized, and received one of those rejection letters that puts therapists' kids through college.

For the next 30 years or so she found other things to do, such as going to law school, ballet dancing (at more or less the same time), volunteering as a lawyer with Gay Men's Health Crisis, and nightclub singing, until her stories started whispering to her. Currently, she's a lawyer and a legal editor; the proud mother of a budding filmmaker; and is busily wedding her love of myth and legend to her passion for m/m romance. She is a four-time Rainbow Award finalist.

Books in this Series by Rory Ni Coileain:

Hard as Stone: Book One of the SoulShares Series

Gale Force: Book Two of the SoulShares Series

Deep Plunge: Book Three of the SoulShares Series

Firestorm: Book Four of the SoulShares Series

Blowing Smoke: Book Five of the SoulShares Series

Mantled in Mist: Book Six of the SoulShares Series

Undertow: Book Seven of the SoulShares Series

Other Riverdale Avenue Books You Might Like

The Siren and the Sword: Book One of the Magic University Series
By Cecilia Tan

The Tower and the Tears: Book Two of the Magic University Series
By Cecilia Tan

The Incubus and the Angel: Book Three of the Magic University Series
By Cecilia Tan

The Prophecy and the Poet: Book Four of the Magic University Series
By Cecilia Tan

Spellbinding: Tales From Magic University
Edited by Cecilia Tan

Mordred and the King
By John Michael Curlovich

Collaring the Saber-Tooth: Book One of the Masters of Cats Series
By Trinity Blacio

Dee's Hard Limits: Book Two of the Masters of Cats Series
By Trinity Blacio

Caging the Bengal Tiger: Book Three of the Masters of Cats Series
By Trinity Blacio

17744747R00203